A TEXT BOOK OF

CLOUD COMPUTING

FOR
SEMESTER – I
FINAL YEAR (B.E.) DEGREE COURSE IN
INFORMATION TECHNOLOGY

As Per the New Revised Syllabus

(2012 Pattern)

TANMAY A. DESHPANDE
CCDH, CCAH, Cloudera University
Research Engineer,
Deptt. of Cloud Computing,
Infosys Ltd. Pune.
Contributor – Cloud Book
(International Cloud Magazine).

NITIN N. SAKHARE
M. E. (Comp. Networks)
Assistant Professor,
Computer Engineering, Deptt.,
Vishwakarma Insti. of Inform. Technology
Kondhwa (Bk), Pune.

GANESH R. KADAM
M.E. (Soft. Engg.)
Software Engineer,
Symantec software India Pvt. Ltd.
Pune.

PALLAVI S. BANGARE
M. E. (Information Technology)
Assistant Professor,
Deptt. of Information Technology,
Sinhgad Academy of Engineering,
Kondhwa (Bk), Pune 48.

NIRALI PRAKASHAN
ADVANCEMENT OF KNOWLEDGE

N3714

CLOUD COMPUTING (BE. IT.)

ISBN 978-93-5164-712-6

Second Edition	:	June 2017
©	:	Authors

Published By :   Polyplate

NIRALI PRAKASHAN

Abhyudaya Pragati, 1312, Shivaji Nagar,
Off J.M. Road, PUNE – 411005
Tel - (020) 25512336/37/39, Fax - (020) 25511379
Email : niralipune@pragationline.com

☞ **DISTRIBUTION BRANCHES**

PUNE

Nirali Prakashan : 119, Budhwar Peth, Jogeshwari Mandir Lane, Pune 411002, Maharashtra
Tel : (020) 2445 2044, 66022708, Fax : (020) 2445 1538
Email : bookorder@pragationline.com, niralilocal@pragationline.com

Nirali Prakashan : S. No. 28/27, Dhyari, Near Pari Company, Pune 411041
Tel : (020) 24690204 Fax : (020) 24690316
Email : dhyari@pragationline.com, bookorder@pragationline.com

MUMBAI

Nirali Prakashan : 385, S.V.P. Road, Rasdhara Co-op. Hsg. Society Ltd.,
Girgaum, Mumbai 400004, Maharashtra
Tel : (022) 2385 6339 / 2386 9976, Fax : (022) 2386 9976
Email : niralimumbai@pragationline.com

☞ **DISTRIBUTION BRANCHES**

JALGAON

Nirali Prakashan : 34, V. V. Golani Market, Navi Peth, Jalgaon 425001,
Maharashtra, Tel : (0257) 222 0395, Mob : 94234 91860

KOLHAPUR

Nirali Prakashan : New Mahadvar Road, Kedar Plaza, 1st Floor Opp. IDBI Bank
Kolhapur 416 012, Maharashtra. Mob : 9850046155

NAGPUR

Pratibha Book Distributors : Above Maratha Mandir, Shop No. 3, First Floor,
Rani Jhanshi Square, Sitabuldi, Nagpur 440012, Maharashtra
Tel : (0712) 254 7129

DELHI

Nirali Prakashan : 4593/21, Basement, Aggarwal Lane 15, Ansari Road, Daryaganj
Near Times of India Building, New Delhi 110002
Mob : 08505972553

BENGALURU

Pragati Book House : House No. 1, Sanjeevappa Lane, Avenue Road Cross,
Opp. Rice Church, Bengaluru – 560002.
Tel : (080) 64513344, 64513355,Mob : 9880582331, 9845021552
Email:bharatsavla@yahoo.com

CHENNAI

Pragati Books : 9/1, Montieth Road, Behind Taas Mahal, Egmore,
Chennai 600008 Tamil Nadu, Tel : (044) 6518 3535,
Mob : 94440 01782 / 98450 21552 / 98805 82331,
Email : bharatsavla@yahoo.com

niralipune@pragationline.com | www.pragationline.com

Also find us on [f] www.facebook.com/niralibooks

Dedicated to...
Lord Venketeshwara, Shri. Swami Samarth, Nirmal Baba,
My Mom & Dad

- Tanmay A. Deshpande

Dedicated to...
My Mom, Dad & Family Members

- Ganesh R. Kadam

Dedicated to...
My Father & Mother for their full support.

- Nitin N. Sakhare

Dedicated to...
My daughter Survi for her infinite patience & inspiration.

- Pallavi Bangare

PREFACE TO THE SECOND EDITION

We are glad and excited to announce that the First Edition of this book received an overwhelming response from the engineering student community, compelling us to release its **Second Edition** within a very short period of time.

This thoroughly revised **Second Edition** has been updated with additional matter, including all University Examination Papers for practice.

Special care has been taken to maintain high degree of accuracy in the theory and numericals throughout the book.

We take this opportunity to express our sincere thanks to Dineshbhai Furia of Nirali Prakashan, a reputed pioneer in the publication field. Our special thanks to Jignesh Furia and Mrs. Nirali Verma for their effective cooperation and great care in bringing out this revised edition. We also appreciate the efforts of M. P. Munde and the entire staff of Engineering Books Deptt. of Nirali Prakashan namely Mrs. Deepali Lachake (Co-ordinator) and Mrs. Shilpa Kale for bringing this book to the students in a timely manner.

We sincerely hope that this **"Second Edition"** will also be warmly received by all concerned as in the past.

Valuable suggestions from our esteemed readers to improve the book are most welcome and highly appreciated.

Pune –   **Authors**

PREFACE TO THE FIRST EDITION

It gives us great pleasure in presenting the book on **"Cloud Computing"**, which is written as per New reviesed syllabus (2012 pattern) of Savitribai Phule Pune University, Pune and in most concised form.

Cloud Computing is an essential ingredient of modern computing systems. Computing concepts, technology, and architectures have been developed and consolidated in the last few decades; many aspects are subject to technological evolution and revolution. Thus, writing a text book on this classical and yet continuously evolving field is a great challenge.

Looking at the way Cloud Computing is evolving, IT giants have already started to shift their core business on Cloud. According to Gartner report, 99% IT companies will adopt Cloud as their primary business by 2014. So looking at the market scenario, knowledge of cloud computing is essential for every IT professional, if he needs to survive in the industry.

The book is as per New Revised Examination Scheme which has been implemented from this academic year. According to this, In-Semester assessment carries 30 Marks over first three units and End-Semester Examination carries 70 Marks over entire syllabus of which the first three units will carry 20 Marks and units 4, 5 and 6 will carry 50 Marks.

We have provided **Sample Question Papers of In-Semester University Exam. 30 Marks and End-Semester Theory University Exam 70 Marks are given to students for practice.**

We gratefully acknowledge this co-operation from **Shri. Dineshbhai Furia, Shri. Jignesh Furia Mrs. Nirali Verma, Shri. M.P. Munde**, Mrs. Deepali Lachake (Co-ordinator) Mrs. Shilpa Kale, Mrs. Roshan Khan, Miss. Rajashri Jadhav of Nirali Prakashan. Our special thanks to our family members, students, and all those who directly or indirectly supported us in this project.

Any suggestions and feedback for the improvement will be appreciated and acknowledged.

Pune   **Authors**

August 2015

SYLLABUS

Unit I : Introduction to Cloud Computing   6 Hours

Defining Cloud computing, Essential characteristics of Cloud computing, Cloud deployment model, Cloud service models, Multitenancy, Cloud cube model, Cloud economics and benefits, Cloud types and service scalability over the cloud, challenges in cloud NIST guidelines.

Unit II : Virtualization, Server, Storage and Networking   6 Hours

Virtualization concepts, types, Server virtualization, Storage virtualization, Storage services, Network virtualization, Service virtualization, Virtualization management, Virtualization technologies and architectures, Internals of virtual machine, Measurement andprofiling of virtualized applications. Hypervisors: KVM, Xen, HyperV, Different hypervisors and features.

Unit III : Monitoring and Management   6 Hours

An architecture for federated cloud computing, SLA management in cloud computing: Service provider's perspective, Performance prediction for HPC on Clouds, Monitoring Tools.

Unit IV : Security   6 Hours

Cloud Security risks, Security, Privacy, Trust, Operating system security, Security of virtualization, Security risks posed by shared images, Security risk posed by a management OS, Trusted virtual machine monitor.

Unit V : Cloud Implementation and Applications   6 Hours

Cloud Platforms: Amazon EC2 and S3, Cloudstack, Intercloud, Google App Engine, Open Source cloud Eucalyptus, Open stack, Open Nebulla etc., Applications.

Unit VI : Ubiquitous Computing   6 Hours

Basics and Vision, Applications and Requirements, Smart Devices and Services, Human Computer Interaction, Tagging, Sensing and controlling, Context-Aware Systems, Ubiquitous Communication, Management of Smart Devices, Ubiquitous System Challenge and outlook.

CONTENTS

INTRODUCTION TO CLOUD COMPUTING

1.1 INTRODUCTION TO CLOUD COMPUTING

1.1.1 What is Cloud Computing?

- Cloud computing is nothing but a specific style of computing where everything from computing power to infrastructure, business apps are provided "as a service". It's a computing service rather than a product.

- In cloud, shared resources, softwares and information is provided as a metered service over the network. When the end user accesses some service is cloud, he is not aware of where that service is coming from or what is platform being used or where it is being stored.

- Cloud computing is not a new technology, its just a way of using old services effectively. Now lets have look on history of cloud computing.

In 1960's '**John McCarthy**' stated that

"*computation may someday be organized as a **Public Utility**".

This is the actual concept we use in cloud computing today.

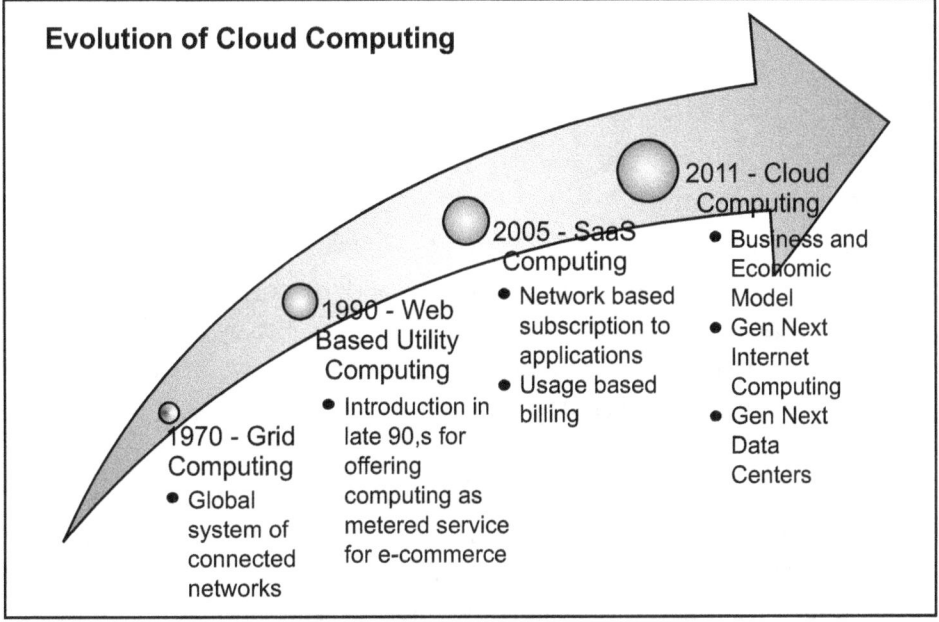

Fig. 1.1 : Evolution of Cloud Computing

In 1990's Telecommunication companies commercialized large networks by offering **VPN(Virtualized Private Network)** service for communications using the advancement of the internet calling them '**Telecom Cloud**'.

From there we got the term"**Cloud**".

Grid Computing

A form of distributed and parallel computing, whereby a 'super and virtual computer' is composed of a cluster of networked, loosely coupled computers acting in concern to perform very large tasks.

Utility Computing

The "packaging of computing resources, such as computation and storage, as a metered service similar to a traditional public utility, such as electricity.

1.1.2 Definition

According to NIST's Definition of Cloud Computing

Cloud computing is a model for enabling convenient, on-demand network access to a shared pool of configurable computing recourses (e.g. networks, servers, storage , applications and services) that can be rapidly provisioned and released with minimal management effort or service provider interaction.

1.1.3 Characteristics   (Nov. 16, May 17)

- On-Demand
- Mulitenancy
- Availability
- Scalability
- Security
- Cost effective
- Green source of energy

- **On Demand**

In cloud computing, resources are available on demand, meansif you require a service like data storage, it can be made available in couple of minutes just by approaching the vendor like Amazon Web Services. Or if you need asurvey conducting tool, you just have to approach SaaS (Software as a service) provider.

- **Multitenancy**

Multi-tenant literally means multiple users using a shared pool of resources. Multitenancy refers to a principle in software architecture where a single instance of the software runs on a server, serving multiple client organizations (tenants). With a multitenant architecture, a software application is designed to virtually partition its data and configuration, and each client organization works with a customized virtual application instance.

- **Availability**

Cloud apps are hosted on virtualized servers, where multiple instances of severs are available as a back up.Mean even if one server goes down, there ca be other server which can take place to serve the purpose. Amazon web services gives 99.999999% availability which is not possible to achieve by traditional servers.

- **Scalability**

In clouds, recourses can be provisioned dynamically, we can scale up our application storage, computation horizontally without a second's down time. Scalability is an important characteristic, specially when it comes to keep your application running at peak time. So if your application is running by traditional way of storage then its not possible to handle extreme traffic suddenly. But on the other hand, if you are using cloud recourses then that can be achieved in seconds. In western countries, Christmas time is a peak time for online shops, now a days they are using cloud resources to handle the traffic. Same way, in the month of March and Feb, Income Tax web sites need to handle huge traffic, in such situation cloud computing will be a great solution for this.

- **Security**

Cloud resources are as secure as normal computing resources. Centralization of data, gives more chance for improvement of the security, but concerns can persist about loss of control over certain sensitive data e.g. In case of IaaS(Infrastructure as a service) data is not present on-premise, it is present with the vendor like Amazon. Security is often as good as or better than other traditional systems, in part because providers are able to devote resources to solving security issues that many customers cannot afford.However, the complexity of security is greatly increased when data is distributed over a wider area or greater number of devices and in multi-tenant systems that are being shared by unrelated users. In addition, user access to security audit logs may be difficult or impossible. Private cloud installations are in part motivated by users' desire to retain control over the infrastructure and avoid losing control of information security.

- **Cost Effective**

Its been observed that on an average only 30-40 % of server capacity is used in case of traditional resources. Means if we have to run10 application on 10 different servers, we have bear the cost of all ten servers, its electricity cost, maintenance cost, administration cost. On the other hand,you can run same 10 apps on max 3-4 servers depending upon the usability.Means you are saving the cost for rest of 5-6 servers.All we don't have to actually buy the servers nor a real space to build them. This thing makes the cloud computing cost effective.

- **Green Computing**

As we have seen in the above paragraph, in cloud computing, resources are used efficiently, we are actually reducing our carbon foot print by reducing the use of electricity, which was being wasted in traditional computing.

1.2 CLOUD PROVIDER

A service provider that offers customers storage or software services available via a private (private cloud) or public network (cloud). Cloud provider is a company which hosts the servers on its premises and make the services available on-demand. Some examples of cloud providers are Google, Amazon, Rackspace, Microsoft etc.

1.3 CLOUD SERVICE MODELS   (Nov. 16, May 17)

In cloud, everything from storage to computation is provided as a service. Depending in the nature of service, it is divided into following services:

* Software as a service (SaaS)
* Platform as a Service (PaaS)
* Infrastructure as a Service (IaaS)

1.3.1 Software as a Service (SaaS)

Software as service is cloud deployment model in which a software is built centrally by provider and is given for use to the end users on-demand via a thin client like web browser. Here instead of buying a software, user pays per use.

SaaS is model,

* of Software Deployment where an application is hosted as serviceprovided to customers across internet.
* where Applications (word processor, CRM etc) or Application Services (mail, schedule, calendar) execute in the **cloud** using the interconnectivity of the internet to propagate data.SaaS has become a common delivery model for most business applications, includingaccounting, collaboration, customer relationship management (CRM), enterprise resource planning (ERP), invoicing, human resource management (HRM), content management (CM) and service desk management. SaaS has been incorporated into the strategy of all leading enterprise software companies.

Benefits of SaaS

* **Faster Time to Market of Business Apps**
* Means the time, application is ready for use, can be made available to end user. Suppose, a SaaS provider develops an application, he does not have to market it, no need to the licensing, what all he has to do is just make that available on centralized server.

* **Any Time any Where Access**

  Means if I purchase a software service, I can use it anywhere and on any device as I don't have to actually install it on my PC, I just have to access the service through a web browser. So a software service purchased can be accessible on my desktop, laptop or any other media device.

* **Elimination of Licensing Risk**

  As we have all seen, piracy is a big issue at the moment in software industry, but if make all softwares as service, piracy can be controlled on larger extent. Also, to the licensing of software is a big overhead, that can be avoided by the use of SaaS.

- **Elimination of Version Compatibility**

  Here, we are maintaining the software centrally. So any changes or updates to the software can be made available to all users in just one commit to the central server. So, compatibility and version controlling is a very easy task for the software provider.

- **Reduced Hardware Foot Print**

- As we can access any software services on just a click of a web browser, there is no need to buy the expensive hardware to install the software. Any commodity hardware can be used to access the services.

- **Lower Operating and Maintenance Cost**

  Software is service is developed and maintained on centralized server, so there is an efficient use of space and energy, which ultimately results in low cost of operating. Also, if there is any need of upgradation, can be achieved through minimum resources, which reduces the maintenance cost whencompared to traditional computing

- **Consumption Based Expenditure**

  As it's a pay per use model, we can access the services only when required and pay for only that usage, which makes it costand energy effective.

Challenges of SaaS

- **Extension of the On-premises Security Model to the SaaS Provider (data privacy and ownership)**

  Here, from computation to storage, we don't have direct control on data. So, our data will always be with SaaS provider and we have to be dependent on its availability.

- **Governance and Billing Management**

  Pay per use model has to be customized depending on the end user's preference. Some common pay per use models are as follows

- Per user per month
- Per transaction
- Per GB of storage per month

Sometimes its difficult to keep governance on such usage, for that there is need of good metering devices.

- **Synchronization of Client and Vendor Migration**

  Sometimes if there is a need to change the software service provider, migration from one such provider to other is a difficult thing as every software provider uses its own way of storage and computation. So migration of already existing data from one provider is not possible as of now, as there is no standardization followed in SaaS industry.

- **Need of Good Connectivity**

  As all service are available on clouds, and nothing is present on local machine, we have to be dependant on internet connectivity. Performance of that service is greatly affected by speed and availability of the network. But we live in the edge of 3G and 4G network services, so connectivity is not a big issue at the moment.

Some important SaaS providers are as follows:

- Salesforce.com

1.3.2 Platform as a Service   (Aug. 16)

Platform as a service is a cloud model, in which a computation platform is provided as a service to end user. PaaS is mainly used by developers to deploy their code on public cloud. Once the code is deployed, from computation to storage everything happens in cloud, at provider's end.PaaS offerings facilitate the deployment of applications without the cost and complexity of buying and managing the underlying hardware and software and provisioning hosting capabilities, providing all of the facilities required to support the complete life cycle of building and delivering web applications and services entirely available from the Internet.

In PaaS,

- Applications are built on the 'Cloud platform, using variety of technologies. Like Java, Python, .NET, Ruby etc.
- PaaS offers development environments that can be used to develop'cloud-ready' applications.
- Has got inherent dynamic scalling capabilities
- Development environment + runtime = Provides everything a developer needs to build an application
- Developer only needs to deploy his code on platform and rest will be taken care by PaaS provider.

Benefits of PaaS

- **Enables Developer to Focus on the Application Code and the Business Logic**

  In PaaS, we only have to deploy the code, irrespective of what is the run time platform, its capacity, database storage. So it makes developer to focus on code building rather than wasting time in buying the server space, buying the hardware, buying the database etc.

- **Natural fit for Development, Testing and Production Environments**

  In development environment, it is expected to make the environments available quick and ready to use, so PaaS becomes a natural fit for development. Also, if someone wants to try some web application's success, then he can first try launching that application on PaaS and if successful, can be developed on larger scale

- **Instant Provisioning – Takes Few Minutes**

  Its quick, in most popular PaaS providers like Google App Engine and Cloud Foundry, it takes seconds to get the environment development ready.

- **Inherent Dynamic Scalability**

  As its in Clouds, applications can scale to any extent without any delay or discontinuity in application presence.

- **Eliminates the Complexities of Hardware and Software Dependencies**

  In PaaS, developer is only need to deploy the code in cloud, so that can be achieved through simple desktop with commodity hardware. As the code will be running on provider platform, this eliminates the complexities of hardware and software dependencies.

Challenges of PaaS

- **Risk of Vendor Lock-in**

  Vendor lock-in poses a big challenge when the application needs to be migrated to a different PaaS provider/platform, since platform is proprietary of to the vendor and not standardized.

- **Interoperabilty and Connectivity with Existing On-premises Applications**

  Computation platform changes from vendor to vendor. So its difficult to have an integrate Pass and an application which is running on traditional computation logic as the PaaS application will be running at provider's premise and normal application will be in-premise

- **Has to rely on 3rd party performance and scalability SLAs**

  When we deploy an application on PaaS provider's platform, we loose control on it and we have to be dependent on their system's performance. Consider a scenario where there is PaaS provider, developer company and service consuming company, here the Service Level Agreement just cannot be between Service consuming company and developer company, we have consider the PaaS provider for its SLAs.

- **Potential Security Risk and Loss of Control Over the Data since it's Located Out of Premises**

  As we are deploying code on Public Cloud, sometimes it can be a threat to the sensitive data. Also, complete data, though produced by user, is owned by PaaS provider and the end user won't be having any control over it.

- **Currently Supported to few Programming Languages like java, python, .NET, ruby etc.**

Some PaaS Providers

  - Google App Engine
  - Cloud Foundry
  - Hereko
  - Rails Engine

1.3.3 Infrastructure as a Service(IaaS)

Infrastructure as a service is to take the servers on rent instead of buying them directly and pay for the use.

IaaS is,

- The Computer Infrastructure comprising of Servers, Storage and Network is delivered as a service
- Rather than buying and owning the infrastructure, clients can buy this as a fully outsourced service

- Clients pay only for the resources they consume on a **Utility Computing**basis. Similar to public utility services such as Electricity, Public Transport etc.
- IaaS has the ability to provide single server up to entire data centers
- With IaaS the processing, storage, network capacity and other fundamental computing resources are rented out on need basis.

Benefits of IaaS

- **Effective Infrastructure Utilization**

  Its been found that, on an average a server just uses 30%-40% of its capacity in a year when it comes to computation and storage. In Iaas, resources are used on shared basis as in 2-3 applications are deployed on a single server. By using shared pool of resources we are actually saving the energy and other expenses. If a sudden demand comes, cloud applications can be scaled up in no time.

- **Highly Automated Resulting in Faster Provisioning of Resources**

  To get a server for development is just a matter of few clicks. Most of IaaS providers gives template for servers required. Also, to use the server space, neitheryou actually need to buy the floor space for server nor you have to buy the expensive hardware.

- **Cab Quickly and Easily Meet the Changing Dynamic Demand for Consumption**

  There is one device called Load balancer so when a Load balancer comes to know that server has met the threshold capacity (70% or more) it triggers an event to add a new server to the service. So when needed service is available.

- **Reduced cost due to**
  - Less hardware resources
  - Less real estate space for on-premise
  - Less power consumption
  - Less manual work and hence lesser administration

Challenges in IaaS

- **Integration outside the enterprise firewall across the cloud boundry for consuming resources from the public cloud IaaS.**

  Use of Public cloud to store the sensitive data is threat. In public cloud, as control over data is lost, we have to be dependent on IaaS provider's availability. Its difficult to make a gateway when we are trying to integrate in-premise, firewall protected application with application hosted on public cloud.

- **Migration of applications in terms of assessing the fitment from dimensions such as Technology, Security etc.**

  As we have seen in case of PaaS and SaaS, its difficult to migrate an application, hosted on traditional devices to an IaaS cloud as there is no stardardized process followed.

- **Vendor reliability and potential security risk when the service are consumed from public cloud IaaS providers.**

As there is no control over data, we have to be dependent on vendor for the availability of the application.

- **Need of good connectivity in termsof network bandwidth and internet availability IaaS Providers**
  - Amazon Web services
  - Rackspace Cloud Hosting

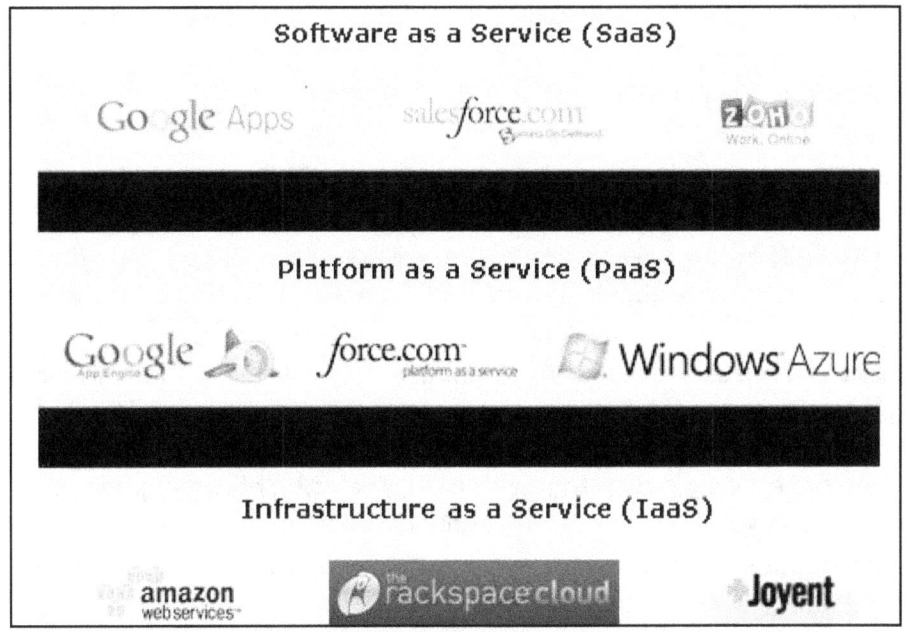

Fig. 1.2 : Software as a Service (SaaS)

1.4 ADMINISTERING AND MAINTAINING THE CLOUD SERVICES

Administration of Cloud services are similar to traditional way of administrating the servers and data centers, only difference here is cloud administrating requires less manpower than as compared to traditional data center administration.

1.5 BENEFITS AND LIMITATIONS   (Nov. 16, Aug. 16)

Traditional Vs. Cloud Computing

Parameter	Traditional Computing	Cloud Computing
Resource Provisioning	Weeks	Minutes
Scalability	Add resources manually	On-Demand scalability
Delivery Model	Buy Assets	Buy Service
Flexibility	Traditional procurement	Self Service
Cost	Additional Yearly CAPEX	Pay Per Use

Benefits of Cloud Computing

- **Reduced Cost**

  Cloud technology is paid incrementally, saving organizations money.

- **Increased Storage**

  Organizations can store more data than on private computer systems.

- **Highly Automated**

  No longer do IT personnel need to worry about keeping software up to date.

- **Flexibility**

  Cloud computing offers much more flexibility than past computing methods.

- **More Mobility**

  Employees can access information wherever they are, rather than having to remain at their desks.

- **Allows IT to Shift Focus**

  No longer having to worry about constant server updates and other computing issues, government organizations will be free to concentrate on innovation.

- **Scalability :** You can scale your business' storage needs seamlessly rather than having to go out and purchase expensive programs or hardware. A not-for-profit ran a cookbook project and was able to pay for all the cloud apps they needed to create, implement and market their project on a month to month basis. They didn't have to purchase a piece of hardware, buy software licenses or worry about overloading their servers.

- **Automatic Updates :** There is no need for IT to worry about paying for your future updates in terms of software and hardware.

- **Remote Access :** Employees, partners and clients can access, and update information wherever they are, rather than having to run back the office.

- **Disaster Relief :** With your company's data safely stored on secure data centers instead of your server room (previously known as your storage closet), losing power due to hurricanes, earthquakes or a construction worker cutting the power lines, you are back at work as long as you have an internet connection.

- **Ease of Implementation :** Your IT team may not like this, but implementing cloud services is as easy as, well, setting up a LinkedIn page.

- **Skilled Vendors :** Who would you rather manage and protect your data? A company such as InfoStreet (with over 16 years experience serving enterprise clients), IBM or Amazon or your IT staff.

- **Response Time :** Cloud computing accomplishes a better response time in most cases than your standard server and hardware.

- **Even playing field for small firms :** This allows small companies to complete more effectively with some of the larger businesses, balancing the playing field. Your small business can utilize the same tools that Fortune 100 companies use and can do this because with cloud computing, your business will only pay for what you need.

Limitations of Cloud Computing

- **Network Connection**

  The concept assumes that the client has reliable network connection. If there are problems of network connectivity, accessing the cloud also becomes a problem. Performance of the cloud applications also depend on the performance of network at client's side. Upload and download speeds are slower as compared to that of a local server.

- **Security and Privacy**

  The biggest concerns about cloud computing are security and privacy. Users might not be comfortable handing over their data to a third party. This is an even greater concern when it comes to companies that wish to keep their sensitive information on cloud servers. While most service vendors would ensure that their servers are kept free from viral infection and malware, it is still a concern considering the fact that a number of users from around the world are accessing the server. Privacy is another issue with cloud servers. Ensuring that a client's data is not accessed by any unauthorized users is of great importance for any cloud service. To make their servers more secure, cloud service vendors have developed password protected accounts, security servers through which all data being transferred must pass and data encryption techniques. After all, the success of a cloud service depends on its reputation, and any sign of a security breach would result in a loss of clients and business.

- **Dependency (loss of control)**

  - Quality problems with CSP (Cloud Service Providers). No influence on maintenance levels and fix frequency when using cloud services from a CSP.
  - No or little insight in CSP contingency procedures. Especially backup, restore and disaster recovery.
  - No easy migration to an other CSP.
  - Measurement of resource usage and end user activities lies in the hands of the CSP.
  - Tied to the financial health of another Company.

- **Cost**

  Higher costs : While in the long run, cloud hosting is a lot cheaper than traditional technologies, the fact that it's currently new and has to be researched and improved actually makes it more expensive. Data centers have to buy or develop the software that will run the cloud, rewire the machines and fix unforeseen problems (which are always there). This makes their initial cloud offers more expensive. Like in all other industries, the first customers pay a higher price and have to deal with more issues than those who switch later (although it would be very hard to create and improve new technologies without these initial adopters).

- **Decreased flexibility**

  This is only a temporary problem (as the others on this list), but current technologies are still in the testing stages, so they don't really offer the flexibility they promise. Of course, that will change in the future, but some of the current users might have to deal with the facts that their cloud server is difficult or impossible to upgrade without losing some data, for example.

- **Knowledge and Integration**

  Knowledge : More and deeper knowledge is required for implementing and managing SLA contracts with CSP's. Since all knowledge about the working of the cloud (e.g. hardware, software, virtualization, deployment) is concentrated at the CSP, it is hard to get grip on the CSP.

  Integration : Integration with equipment hosted in other data centers is difficult to achieve. Peripherals integration. Printers (Bulk) and local security IT equipment (e.g. access systems) is difficult to integrate. But also (personal) USB devices or smart phones or groupware and email systems are difficult to integrate.

1.6 DEPLOY APPLICATION OVER CLOUD

- Before deploying an application over cloud, we have to first do the analysis of our requirements, we have to see :
  - What is the purpose of this application?
  - What are the target users?
  - Is this a new marketing product?
  - What is the duration of use?
  - What kind of content is expected?
  - What is the time to market?
  - Any specific programming language requirements?
  - What is the budget?

- After we get this requirement, we have to finalize on what cloud model we are going to work on, means if the application contains sensitive information of an organization then Private Cloud can be a good option, if not so, then can opt for cheap cloud i.e. Public Cloud.

- Once we decide on this, we have to finalize on what services we have to buy means SaaS, PaaS or IaaS. In case of generalized applications like Survey Tools or CRM tools.

- SaaS is a best option to go with. If we have any specific requirement and have developers to work on application then PaaS can be a good option. If we have some requirement which is out of scope of PaaS we should be going with IaaS.

- Once we decide on Cloud Deployment model and Cloud Service Offering, we have choose a best in class vendor, which gives facilities to in our budget and then we have sign the SLAs.

- Once the requirements and structural designing is done, actual development can be done and at the end of it, we have our cloud application ready for deployment.

1.7 COMPARISON OF SAAS, PAAS AND IAAS

Parameter	SaaS	PaaS	IaaS
Definition	Software as Service	Platform as a Service	Infrastructure as a Service
Deployment Model	Public Cloud	Public Cloud	Public/Private/Hybrid Cloud
Time to Market	Very Less	More than SaaS	More than SaaS
Flexibility in Specifications	Very Less	Good	Most Flexible
End User	Common People	Developers	Administrators
Cost	Cheaper	Free of cost upto certain threshold	Expensive
Data Control	Very Less	Better than SaaS	More controlled
Maintenance	Maintained by Provider	Maintained Partially by Developer and Partially by Provider	Completely maintained by developing organization or individual
Suitable For	Common Business apps like mails, CRMs etc.	Any application	Any application, mostly application with huge data.

1.8 CLOUD DEPLOYMENT

A. Public Cloud

- The public cloud, offer applications, storage and other services to the general public by a service provider. This is based on "pay-as-you-go" model. A public cloud is constructed with a view to offer unlimited storage space and increased bandwidth via Internet to all businesses.
- Public clouds are owned, hosted and operated by third-party service providers. A public cloud caters to all kind of requirements from small, medium or big businesses.
- A public cloud is the most simplest to setup as it liberates that subscriber from woes of hardware, application and bandwidth expenses. Enterprises pay for only those condiments which they are utilizing.

- Users have to pay a monthly bill for public cloud services. Public cloud functions on the prime principle of storage demand scalability, which means it requires no hardware device.
- Popular examples of public clouds include Amazon Elastic Cloud Compute, Google App Engine, Blue Cloud by IBM and Azure services Platform by Windows.

Public cloud caters to four basic characteristics that are as follows:

- **Flexible and Elastic Environment :** Public clouds like Google App engine or Amazon elastic cloud compute offers its users highly flexible cloud environment. They enable users to share and store data as per their personal capacities. They can decide what to share and what not to share with their clients.
- **Freedom of Self-Service :** Public clouds encourage users to create a cloud on their own without taking anyone's help. These are pre-configured clouds existing on Internet. The only thing businesses that wish to opt for public cloud need to do is to visit public cloud portals and get started with it. You don't have to depend upon on any third party help to create or run this type of cloud. It will be managed and handled by you as you will be the prime proprietor of it.
- **Pay for what You Use :** This particular characteristic enables cloud technology more accessible for businesses to work in a synchronized fashion. The more you use cloud services, better will be the future business prospects. However, payment is charged on the basis of cloud services used by users.
- **Availability and Reliability :** Yet another feature of public cloud is that, it is available to all and believes inagility. You can catch up with your work any time you wish and from any corner of the globe. Not only users become more independent in running important business tasks but also more efficient in strengthening customer relations across the globe.

B. Private Cloud

- Private cloud is a cloud infrastructure build exclusively for a single organization, deployed within certain boundaries like fire wall settings whether managed internally or by a third-party and hosted internally or externally.
- Users are charged on the basis of per Gigabyte usage along with bandwidth transfer fees.
- Data stored in the private cloud can only be shared amongst users of an organization and third party sharing depends upon trust they build with them.
- Popular examples of private cloud include Amazon Virtual Private Cloud (Amazon VPC), Eucalyptus Cloud Platform, IBM Smart Cloud Foundation and Microsoft Private Cloud There are two variations of private clouds :
- **On-Premise Private Cloud :** This format, also known as an "internal cloud," is hosted within an organization's own data centre. It provides a more standardized process and protection, but is often limited in size and scalability. Also, a firm's IT department would incur the capital and operational costs for the physical resources with this model. On-premise private clouds are best used for applications that require complete control and configurability of the infrastructure and security.

- **Externally-Hosted Private Cloud :** This private cloud model is hosted by an external cloud computing provider. The service provider facilitates an exclusive cloud environment with full guarantee of privacy. This format is recommended for organizations that prefer not to use a public cloud infrastructure due to the risks associated with the sharing of physical resources :

Some of the characteristics of private cloud are :

- **Enhanced Security Measures :** Security has become one of the primary concerns for many organizations especially for financial institutions. Let's take a bank or a mortgage company, the confidentiality and security of their critical data is the utmost concern. Virtual private cloud computing comes equipped with a customizable and thorough firewall and a plethora of security tools which ensure maximum protection against unauthorized use, hacking and other such malicious attempts.
- **Dedicated Resources :** The essence of private cloud is "no compromise". As a subscriber to private cloud computing an enterprise has its own dedicated resources such as processor time and data buses which ensure optimum performance.
- **Greater Customization :** Private cloud services are acquiescent and customizable so they can be molded to suit the exact requirements of an enterprise. This in turns bestows the enterprise with more control over their data.

C. Hybrid Cloud

- Hybrid clouds combine the advantages of private and public clouds, offer flexibility, control and security of multiple deployment models as shown in the Fig. 1.3. IT organizations use hybrid clouds to employ cloud bursting for scaling across clouds.
- Cloud bursting is an application deployment model in which an application runs in a private cloud or data centre and "bursts" to a public cloud when the demand for computing capacity increases.
- A primary advantage of cloud bursting and a hybrid cloud model is that an organization only pays for extra compute resources when they are needed. Hybrid cloud architecture requires both on-premises resources and off-site (remote) server-based cloud infrastructure.

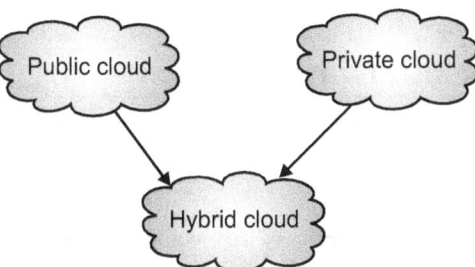

Fig. 1.3 : Hybrid Cloud as a Combination of Public Cloud and Private Cloud

Some of the characteristics of hybrid clouds are:

- **Optimal Utilization :** The available server resources in typical data centres are actually used from 5-20%. This is because of peak loads which are ten times higher than that of the average load. Hence, servers are mostly idle, generating unnecessary costs. Hybrid clouds can increase server utilization by scaling out to public resources to handle crowds.

- **Data Centre Consolidation :** Instead of providing the capacity to cope for worst-case scenarios, a private cloud only needs resources in average cases. The option to burst out allows server consolidation and hence resulting in reduction of operating costs. In particular, this includes the costs for hardware, power, cooling, maintenance, and administration.

- **Risk Transfer :** The companies themselves are responsible for keeping up and running their data centre and private cloud. The public cloud provider has to ensure a high uptime for their service. Using a hybrid cloud model, "the risk of misestimating work load is shifted to the cloud vendor from the service operator". Most of the cloud providers have service level agreements which ensure an uptime of more than 99.9% per year, i.e., a downtime of maximum of 9 hours per year.

- **Availability :** The high availability in the corporate data centre is difficult and expensive, because it requires redundancy, backups, and geographic dissemination. Especially in companies where IT is not the core business, the expertise in this area is rather limited. In a hybrid cloud environment, the public cloud can scale up or take over operations completely if the company's data centre is unavailable due to failures or Distributed Denial of Service (DDoS) attacks.

D. Community Cloud

- The cloud infrastructure is shared between the organizations with similar interests and requirements whether managed internally or by a third-party and hosted internally or externally.

- The costs are spread over fewer users than a public cloud (but more than a private cloud), so only some of the cost savings potential of cloud computing are realized.

- This may help limit the capital expenditure costs for its establishment as the costs are shared among the organizations.

- For example, all the government agencies in a city can share the same cloud but not the non government agencies.

1.8.1 Public Cloud versus Private Cloud   (Nov. 16)

Public Cloud and Private Cloud have their own distinct characteristics. We compare the Public Cloud and Private Cloud as shown in the Fig. 1.4, to get a clearer understanding of using one over the other.

- **Accessibility :** A private cloud, functions independently for an organization and that too behind firewall settings does prove to be accessible. By stating this, we mean that a private cloud cannot be accessed from anywhere and at any point of time. It is completely managed by the users working for an organization. Public Cloud architecture is built with the view to create an accessible business environment that can be shared and accessed from any part of the globe and at any time of the hour using internet.

- **Scalability :** Private cloud gives scalable business environment, public cloud infrastructures is that they are typically larger in scale than a private cloud, which provides clients with seamless, on-demand scalability.

- **Data Security Risks :** Security of data is utmost priority of cloud providers so that they offer customers a reliable and flexible cloud environment. Data security risks of private cloud are less as compared to the one stored in public cloud.

- **Initial Cost :** Private cloud initial cost is expensive, but gets minimal at later stages of using it as a service. In a public cloud, initial cost is minimal, but if data is stored for a long period of time, it proves to be expensive.

- **Availability and Reliability :** These are the two factors that make public cloud computing service more popular. The reason being, it is available to users via web installed at a given server off-premises.

- **Data Storage :** Larger amounts of data can be stored in the private cloud for a lower cost. Many different types of data can be stored in the public cloud however large amounts stored for long periods tend to get pricey.

- **Public Clouds have Better Utilization Rates :** With private cloud, your organization still has to build and maintain all kinds of servers to meet spikes in demand across various divisions or functions. Public cloud offers the same spare demand on a pay-as-you-need-it basis.

- **Public Clouds Offer Greater Elasticity :** An organization will never consume all the capacity of a public cloud, but organizations private cloud is another matter entirely. Public cloud offers greater elasticity compared to private cloud

- **Private Clouds Tend to Use Older Technology than Public Clouds :** You may have spent hundreds of thousands of dollars on new hardware and software for a private cloud, but try getting your organization to agree to that every year. Hence private clouds tend to use older technology compared to a public cloud.

- **Public Clouds get Enterprises out of the "Datacenter Business" :** establishing private cloud probably gets you in deeper into the DC business than with traditional on-premises servers. For instance, the public cloud is like an apartment building filled with multiple tenants while a private cloud is like an apartment building you have to yourself.

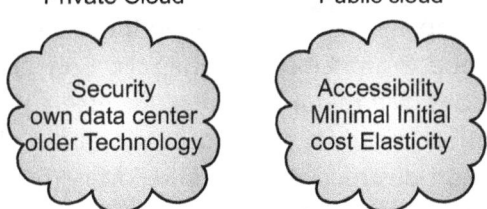

Fig. 1.4 : Comparison between Public Cloud and Private Cloud

1.8.2 Which Deployment Model to Choose Among Public, Private and Hybrid Cloud

A public cloud is the obvious choice when

- Public Cloud Computing is the easiest of cloud solutions to setup and maintain and is the preferred choice of most small scale and start-up enterprises, that don't require high data security measures. These companies often don't have much capital and have less risk in losing information due to theft or security breaches.
- Your standardized workload for applications is used by lots of people, such as e-mail.
- You need to test and develop application code.
- You have SaaS (Software as a Service) applications from a vendor who has a well-implemented security strategy.
- You need incremental capacity (the ability to add computer capacity for peak times).
- You are doing collaboration projects.
- You are doing an ad-hoc software development project using a Platform as a Service (PaaS) offering cloud.

A private cloud is the obvious choice when

- Private cloud has been adopted by industries when security is something of primary concern such as finance and health care which have some of the most rigorous compliance requirements. Your business is your data and your applications. Therefore, control and security are paramount.
- Your business is part of an industry that must conform to strict security and data privacy issues.
- Your company is large enough to run a next generation cloud data center efficiently and effectively on its own.

A hybrid environment is best choice when.

- Your company wants to use a SaaS application but is concerned about security. Your SaaS vendor can create a private cloud just for your company inside their firewall. They provide you with a virtual private network (VPN) for additional security.
- Your company offers services that are tailored for different vertical markets. You can use a public cloud to interact with the clients but keep their data secured within a private cloud.
- The management requirements of cloud computing become much more complex when you need to manage private, public, and traditional data centers all together. You will need to add capabilities for federating these environments.
- Using the private cloud for mission-critical applications and using public clouds for non-critical applications. A firm, for example, may use a private cloud for production deployment and a public cloud for test and development of lower-tier applications.
- Another example is non-destructive Disaster Recovery (DR) testing. Organizations can test if their production environment is DR-ready by tapping the public clouds without any disruption.

1.9 CLOUD MULTI-TENANCY

- The term Multi-tenancy has gotten significant attention after the rise of cloud computing in the global market. Most of the time, the term is misused when describing cloud computing. I imagine it is as confusing as the term cloud computing was a year back!
- A few of us may relate multi-tenancy with a database or application architecture, while others think it has something to do with virtualization. Both views are correct, depending on the context.
- Currently, I am leading a team of developers about to start working on an educational institute management application for a group of institutes.
- Should we proceed with the tried and tested path of single-tenant application, or use the unknown, and less travelled but more challenging, multi-tenant SaaS? The development team was more enthusiastic to get the application architected as a multi-tenant SaaS.
- But how could we design the application (and the database) so that a single instance of it (and the database) could be shared by all the member institutes? This led us to brainstorm the idea of multi-tenancy.
- And I must confess designing a multi-tenant application is definitely not child's play, especially if you are designing it on a traditional platform (ASP.NET, SQL Server etc). It may be a bit easier to architect a multi-tenant SaaS on a cloud PaaS.

What is Multi-tenancy?

Think of *tenants* as customers (clients) of a service. Before we discuss more about tenants let us understand the following :

SaaS can have two broad categories.

1. Line-of-Business (LOB) services like CRM and Project management solutions are meant for enterprise customers. A few examples are :

- SalesForce CRM
- Google Apps for business
- DeskAway
- Impel CRM
- Freshdesk

2. Consumer-oriented services are meant for the general public and may be offered free of cost. Examples are :

- Dropbox (Now they are also offering *Dropbox for teams* : enterprise version)
- Microsoft Skydrive
- Gmail, Google Apps (Free), Google Analytics.

Multitenancy is fundamental technology that clouds use to share IT resources cost-efficiently and securely. Just like in an apartment building, where many tenants cost-efficiently share the common infrastructure of the building but have walls and doors that give them privacy from other tenants, a cloud uses multitenancy technology to share IT resources securely among multiple applications and tenants (businesses, organizations, etc.) that use the cloud. Some clouds use virtualization-based architectures to isolate tenants, others use custom software architectures to get the job done.

1.9.1 Multi-tenancy Implementation Based on Service Models

1. **Infrastructure as a Service (IaaS) :**
- Tenants on a multi-tenant application share infrastructure resources like servers and storage devices. Here multi-tenancy is achieved using Virtual Machines (VMs).

What are Virtual Machines (VMs)?
- In simple words, your application will be executed on a virtual computer (also known as an instance). You have your choice of virtual computer, meaning that you can select a configuration of CPU, memory and storage that is optimal for your application.
- The following diagram depicts a simplified illustration of multi-tenant implementation in IaaS. The image shows a cloud provider that has a number of virtual machines (VMs) available that it can allocate to clients; block A shows vm_4, vm_5, ... , vm_n. Block A shows 2 clients – A and B.
- Client A can access and use vm_1 and vm_2. Client B can access vm_3. Block B shows entry of a new client C who has access to vm_4, vm_5 and vm_6.

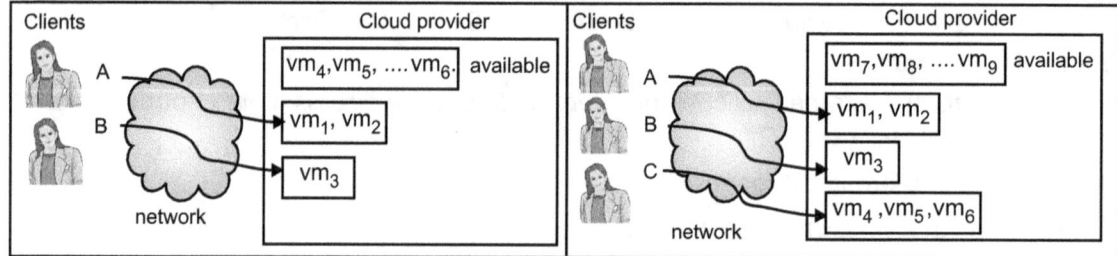

Fig. 1.5 : Cloud Providers and Virtual Machines

2. **Platform as a Service (PaaS) :**
- Here different processes may share an operating system and networking services.
- PaaS multi-tenancy means that, like a Heroku or a Cloud Bees, the platform can isolate code from different apps/vendors on the same OS instance (usually by commingling processes and databases on OS instances).
- This removes the need to allocate a whole VM per application stack component, improving efficiency.
- The following diagram is a simplified illustration of a multi-tenant PaaS. The PaaS provider has an inventory of applications, namely A, B, C, D.
- Here a tenant can be a developer, or a customer (C_1 in the Fig. 1.6). As shown in the following Fig. 1.6 : the developer is creating applications and the customer is consuming them B → exr_1 and B → exr_2. In brief, multiple developers and customers are sharing the resources provided by PaaS. PaaS can also use the services of an IaaS.

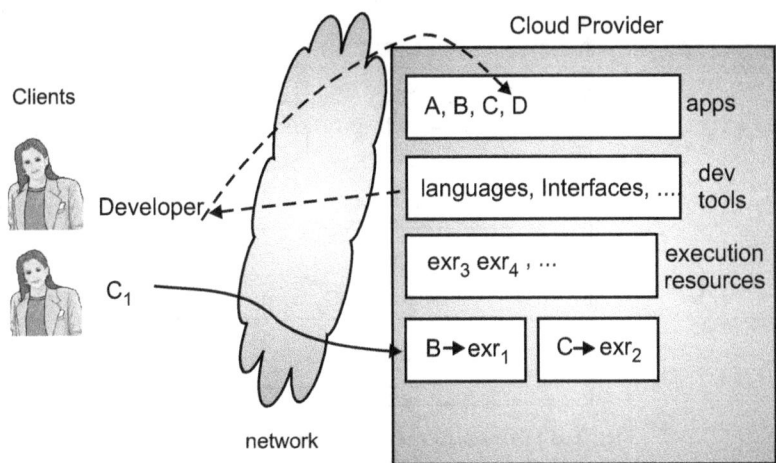

Fig. 1.6 : Interaction : Cloud Provider and Developer

3. Software as a Service (SaaS) :

- Here multi-tenancy is marked by a single application instance (i.e. code base) and single database instance for supporting multiple customers.

- Customers are sharing the same code base and the data is stored on the same set of tables distinguished by Tenant ID. Stated simply: The separation of data is logical and not physical. In a database table records can be saved in the following format

TenantID	CustName	Address		
4	TenantID	ProductID	ProductName	
1	4	TenantID	Shipment	Data
6	1	4711	324965	2006-02-21
4	6	132	115468	2006-04-08
	4	680	654109	2006-03-27
		4711	324956	2006-02-23

Fig. 1.7 : Sample Database Table

A unique TenantID will distinguish between the records of different customers. In reality it's not as simple as we are assuming here, because, if it's a line-of-business (i.e. enterprise) application we again need to distinguish between the records of multiple users of the same customer.

- Also, the presentation layer (User Interface) needs to be provided with settings/configuration options which can offer unique user experience to each customer.

- The following simplified illustration depicts how three customers C_1, C_2 and C_3 are sharing a single application on a single database.

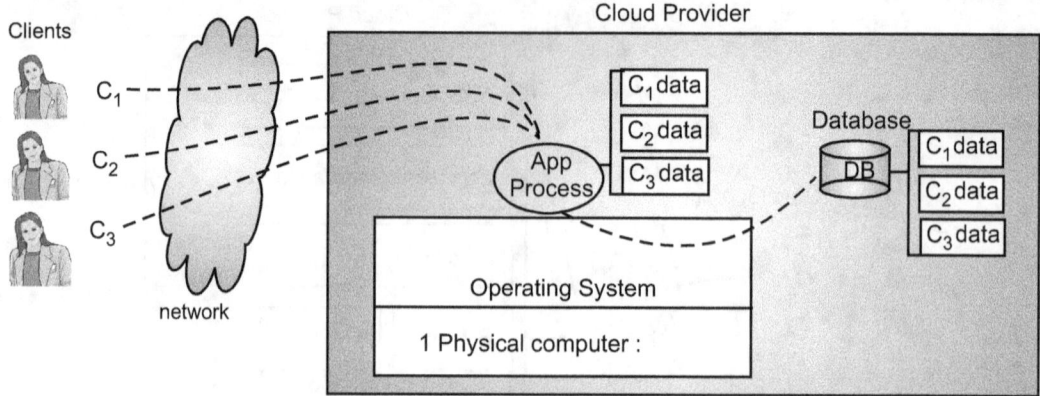

Fig. 1.8 : Client Accessing App Over Cloud

- A Microsoft document on multi-tenant SaaS architecture proposes SaaS architecture which is more mature than the model described above, also known as *SaaS at maturity level iv*. Check the following Fig. 1.9.

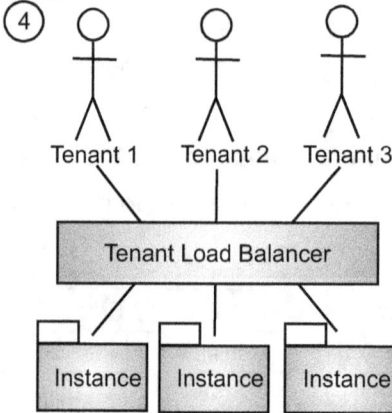

Fig. 1.9 : Saas at Maturity Level

- The above Fig. 1.9 shows the most matured multi-tenant SaaS model. This is somewhat similar to the hybrid of Fig. 1.5 and Fig. 1.8. In simple words, a multi-tenant SaaS architecture making use of virtualization based multi-tenant IaaS.

- The cloud provider hosts multiple clients on a load-balanced farm of*identical instances*, with each customer's data kept separate.

1.9.2 Multi-tenancy Risk

- In a multi-tenant SaaS architecture a single application and database instance is shared with multiple customers.

- This simply means that the same database and same set of tables can be used to store the records of multiple customers. It is very rare but it may happen that a flaw in the software while querying the data can lead your adversary (who may be a customer of the same service) to access your record.

- At the IaaS level Virtual Machines (VMs) can be attacked by other VMs residing on the same physical host.
- Although these risks are minimized using robust **access policies** and strong **encryption,** you must educate yourself about the security measures in place for a multi-tenant SaaS.

As a Customer do you really need to care if the SaaS is really multi-tenant?

- Yes. Though multi-tenancy is cloud vendor's responsibility you must care to know a little about how it is implemented in the service you are going to use. Everything's fine until the number of customers your provider is supporting increases.
- Once the number grows, it becomes very difficult to manage upgrades on a per customer basis. Later, it may increase the price of the service because the provider may need to engage more resources to maintain multiple versions of code and database per customer.

1.10 CLOUD ECONOMIC AND BENEFITS

1.10.1 Economic Context

- Like energy, computing has become an essential component of any economy. Historically, the size of an economy was directly related to the energy it consumed.
- Likewise, a person's professional growth, the growth of an organization, or the growth of a country as a whole can directly be related to the computing power they use.
- Rising energy costs, combined with a growing global awareness of the potential impact of climate change due to carbon emissions puts a renewed focus on energy usage and its associated carbon footprint.
- The challenge today is to increase computing power consumption with lower energy consumption. Every enterprise in the world is facing a global economic recession that has profoundly affected all developed countries as well as those developing countries that produce products sold in those markets.
- Uncertain times also bring opportunities, but taking advantage of strategic opportunities typically must now be done quickly without additional capital funds or additional corporate resources.
- For information technology (IT) managers, energy cost management is not a small issue. In addition, the maintenance of legacy enterprise data centers absorb the majority of IT budgets and IT managers are looking for ways to create increased capacity and flexibility within their current computing facility and hardware footprint thereby lowering costs and increasing their Return On Assets (ROA).
- Because capacity planning for traditional enterprise data centers must accommodate the company's peak load periods, there is typically very low server utilization during non-peak periods which, depending on the industry, may be most of the year. The last few years have seen a trend in data center management towards server virtualization which

allows faster deployment of specialized server configurations and towards higher server density without increasing the size of the data center or its staff overhead or even higher energy consumption.

- However, these alternatives still require significant investments and long-term technology commitments and there has been increasing attention paid to alternatives that provide the pay-as-you-go options, unlimited scalability, quick deployment, and the minimal maintenance requirements. Cloud computing is a computing paradigm that promises to meet all these requirements.

1.10.2 Economic Benefits

- Occasionally used to refer to the economics of cloud computing, the term "Cloudonomics" was coined by Joe Weinman.
- He examined the strategic advantages provided by public utility cloud services over private clouds and traditional data centers.
- He posits that public utility clouds are fundamentally different than traditional data center environments and private clouds.
- For individual enterprises, cloud services provide benefits that broadly fall into the categories of lowering overall costs for equivalent services (you pay only for what you use), increased strategic flexibility to meet market opportunities without having to forecast and maintain on-site capacity, and access to the advantages of cloud provider's massive capacity: instant scalability, parallel processing capability which reduces task processing time and response latency, system redundancy which improves reliability, and better capability to repel botnet attacks.
- Further, public cloud vendors can achieve unparalleled efficiencies compared to data centers and private clouds because they are able to scale their capacity to address the aggregated demand of many enterprises, each having different peak demand periods.
- This allows for much higher server utilization rates, lower unit costs, and easier capacity planning netting a much higher return on assets than is possible for individual enterprises.
- Finally, because the location of the public cloud vendor's facilities are not tied to the parochial interests of the individual clients, they are able to locate, scale, and manage their operations to take optimum advantage of reduced energy costs, skilled labor pools, bandwidth, or inexpensive real estate.
- These are not the only benefits that have been identified. Matzke suggests that the levels of required skills or specialized expertise along with the required economies of scale drive the optimum choice for resourcing IT initiatives.
- For him, the availability of scalable skills combined with other economies of scale are among the compelling benefits of cloud computing. This is especially true for enterprises that are located in labor markets that have very few or only very expensive IT staff resources available with the requisite skills.

1.10.3 Economic Costs

- The costs associated with cloud computing facing early adopters include the potential costs of service disruptions; data security concerns; potential regulatory compliance issues arising out of sensitive data being transferred, processed or stored beyond defined borders.
- Limitations in the variety and capabilities of the development and deployment platforms currently available; difficulties in moving proprietary data and software from one cloud services provider to another; integration of cloud services with legacy systems.
- Cost and availability of programming skills needed to modify legacy application to function in the cloud environment; legacy software CPU-based licensing costs increasing when moved to a cloud platform, etc.

1.10.4 Company Size and the Economic Costs and Benefits of Cloud Computing

- The economic costs or benefits of implementing cloud services vary depending upon the size of the enterprise and its existing IT resources/overheads including legacy data center infrastructure, computer hardware, legacy software, maturity of internal processes, IT staffing and technical skill base.
- These determine the strategic costs and benefits that accrue to individuals and corporations depending upon their relative size.
- In the past, large corporations have had an advantage over small corporations in their access to capital and their ability to leverage their existing human, software, and hardware resources to support new marketing and strategic initiatives.
- However, since the advent of cloud computing, the barriers to entry for a particular market or market segment for a startup company have been dramatically reduced and cloud computing may have tipped the balance of strategic advantage away from the large established corporations towards much more nimble small or startup companies.
- A small, dedicated, and talented team of individuals can now pool their individual talents to address a perceived market need without an immediate need for a venture capital funds to provide the necessary IT infrastructure.
- There are a number of cloud providers who provide software development environments that include the requisite software development tools, code repositories, test environments, and access to a highly scalable production environment on pay-as-you-go basis.
- Also contributing to this trend is the open-source movement. While licensing issues, support, and feature considerations may dissuade larger enterprises from using open source software in the development and deployment of their proprietary products, the

availability of open source software in nearly every software category has been a boon to SMEs, the self-employed, and start-ups.

- As these small companies grow into midsize and large companies they face changing cost equations that modify the relative costs and benefits of cloud computing.
- For instance, at certain data traffic volumes the marginal costs of operating on a cloud provider's infrastructure may become more expensive than providing the necessary IT infrastructure in-house.
- At that point, there may be advantages of a mixed-use strategy in which some of the applications and services are brought in-house and others continue to be hosted in the cloud. The following tables will identify the differences that SMEs and large enterprises face in both the benefits and costs of cloud services.

1.10.5 The Economics of Green Clouds

- The development of green data centers and green clouds is shaped by two important factors. The first is a global awareness of the devastating potential of climate change due to human activity primarily through carbon emissions.
- The second is the rising costs of energy. These two factors have focused IT infrastructure planning and decision-making on energy cost reduction, dynamic resource allocation strategies and have moved green issues from the category of nice-to-do to strategically important for all midsize and large corporations.
- Public cloud providers locate their data centers where bandwidth, cheap energy, abundant water for cooling, and proximity to markets are optimal.
- Google and other cloud providers have focused on creative approaches to efficient resource usage including not only electricity usage but also water recycling and equipment recycling upon disposal.
- Through purchasing servers and other equipment designed to minimize energy usage and in the modular design and management of their data centers, these cloud providers minimize the non-computing energy overhead and maximize their utilization rates through the dynamic allocation of computing resources.
- This combination of lower energy overhead amortized over a much higher server utilization rate allows cloud suppliers to provide computing services far more efficiently with a much smaller energy and carbon footprint.
- Because of the scale of operations of large cloud providers, they are able to achieve efficiency rates and server utilization rates that are unachievable in even large corporate data center operations.
- Thus, cloud computing holds the promise of not only providing attractive cost savings at the enterprise level but also may contribute to the larger societal objectives of energy efficiency and environmental protection and sustainable development.

1.11 TYPES OF CLOUD COMPUTING: PRIVATE, PUBLIC AND HYBRID CLOUDS

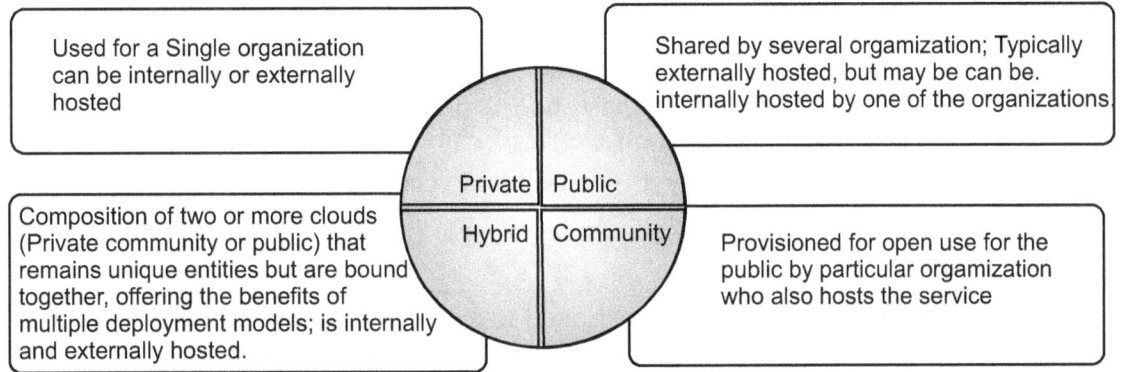

Fig. 1.10 : Types of Clouds

- A recent study conducted by KPMG found that 81% of businesses were either evaluating cloud services, planned a cloud implementation or had already implemented a cloud strategy. Fewer than one in 10 said they had no immediate plans to start using the cloud. No matter how businesses decide to move to the cloud, one thing's clear: they are moving to the cloud.

- With cloud computing technology, large pools of resources can be connected through private or public networks. This technology simplifies infrastructure planning and provides dynamically scalable infrastructure for cloud based applications, data, and file storage. Businesses can choose to deploy applications on Public, Private, Hybrid clouds or the newer Community Cloud.

- What are the differences between these types of cloud computing, and how can you determine the right cloud path for your organization? Here are some fundamentals of each to help with the decision-making process.

1.11.1 Public

- Public clouds are made available to the general public by a service provider who hosts the cloud infrastructure. Generally, public cloud providers like Amazon AWS, Microsoft and Google own and operate the infrastructure and offer access over the Internet. With this model, customers have no visibility or control over where the infrastructure is located. It is important to note that all customers on public clouds share the same infrastructure pool with limited configuration, security protections and availability variances.

- Public Cloud customers benefit from economies of scale, because infrastructure costs are spread across all users, allowing each individual client to operate on a low-cost, "pay-as-you-go" model.

- Another advantage of public cloud infrastructures is that they are typically larger in scale than an in-house enterprise cloud, which provides clients with seamless, on-demand scalability.
- These clouds offer the greatest level of efficiency in shared resources; however, they are also more vulnerable than private clouds.

A public cloud is the obvious choice when :
- Your standardized workload for applications is used by lots of people, such as e-mail.
- You need to test and develop application code.
- You need incremental capacity (the ability to add compute resources for peak times).
- You are doing collaboration projects.

1.11.2 Private

- Private cloud is cloud infrastructure dedicated to a particular organization. Private clouds allow businesses to host applications in the cloud, while addressing concerns regarding data security and control, which is often lacking in a public cloud environment.
- It is not shared with other organizations, whether managed internally or by a third-party, and it can be hosted internally or externally.

There are two variations of private clouds :
- **On-Premise Private Cloud :** This type of cloud is hosted within an organization's own facility. A businesses IT department would incur the capital and operational costs for the physical resources with this model. On-Premise Private Clouds are best used for applications that require complete control and configurability of the infrastructure and security.
- **Externally Hosted Private Cloud :** Externally hosted private clouds are also exclusively used by one organization, but are hosted by a third party specializing in cloud infrastructure. The service provider facilitates an exclusive cloud environment with full guarantee of privacy. This format is recommended for organizations that prefer not to use a public cloud infrastructure due to the risks associated with the sharing of physical resources.
- Undertaking a private cloud project requires a significant level and degree of engagement to virtualize the business environment, and it will require the organization to reevaluate decisions about existing resources.
- Private clouds are more expensive but also more secure when compared to public clouds. An Info-Tech survey shows that 76% of IT decision-makers will focus exclusively on the private cloud, as these clouds offer the greatest level of security and control.

When is a Private Cloud for you?
- You need data sovereignty but want cloud efficiencies.
- You want consistency across services.
- You have more server capacity than your organization can use.
- Your data center must become more efficient.
- You want to provide private cloud services.

1.11.3 Hybrid

- Hybrid Clouds are a composition of two or more clouds (private, community or public) that remain unique entities but are bound together offering the advantages of multiple deployment models. In a hybrid cloud, you can leverage third party cloud providers in either a full or partial manner; increasing the flexibility of computing. Augmenting a traditional private cloud with the resources of a public cloud can be used to manage any unexpected surges in workload.
- Hybrid cloud architecture requires both on-premise resources and off-site server based cloud infrastructure. By spreading things out over a hybrid cloud, you keep each aspect of your business in the most efficient environment possible. The downside is that you have to keep track of multiple cloud security platforms and ensure that all aspects of your business can communicate with each other.

Here are a couple of situations where a hybrid environment is best :

- Your company wants to use a SaaS application but is concerned about security.
- Your company offers services that are tailored for different vertical markets. You can use a public cloud to interact with the clients but keep their data secured within a private cloud.
- You can provide public cloud to your customers while using a private cloud for internal IT.

1.11.4 Community

- A community cloud is a is a multi-tenant cloud service model that is shared among several or organizations and that is governed, managed and secured commonly by all the participating organizations or a third party managed service provider.
- Community clouds are a hybrid form of private clouds built and operated specifically for a targeted group. These communities have similar cloud requirements and their ultimate goal is to work together to achieve their business objectives.
- The goal of community clouds is to have participating organizations realize the benefits of a public cloud with the added level of privacy, security, and policy compliance usually associated with a private cloud. Community clouds can be either on-premise or off-premise.

Here are a couple of situations where a community cloud environment is best :

- Government organizations within a state that need to share resources.
- A private HIPAA compliant cloud for a group of hospitals or clinics.
- Telco community cloud for telco DR to meet specific FCC regulations.

Cloud computing is about shared IT infrastructure or the outsourcing of a company's technology. It is essential to examine your current IT infrastructure, usage and needs to determine which type of cloud computing can help you best achieve your goals. Simply, the cloud is not one concrete term, but rather a metaphor for a global network and how to best utilize its advantages depends on your individual cloud focus.

1.12 SERVICE SCALABILITY OVER THE CLOUD

1.12.1 Understanding Performance, Scale and Throughput

Because the terms *performance*, *scale*, and *throughput* are used in a variety of ways when discussing computing, it is useful to examine their typical meanings in the context of cloud computing infrastructures.

- **Performance :** Performance is generally tied to an application's capabilities within the cloud infrastructure itself. Limited bandwidth, disk space, memory, CPU cycles, and network connections can all cause poor performance. Often, a combination of lack of resources causes poor application performance. Sometimes poor performance is the result of an application architecture that does not properly distribute its processes across available cloud resources.

- **Throughput :** The effective rate at which data is transferred from point A to point B on the cloud is throughput. In other words, throughput is a measurement of raw speed. While speed of moving or processing data can certainly improve system performance, the system is only as fast as its slowest element. A system that deploys ten gigabit Ethernet yet its server storage can access data at only one gigabit effectively has a one gigabit system.

- **Scalability :** The search for continually improving system performance through hardware and software throughput gains is defeated when a system is swamped by multiple, simultaneous demands. That 10 gigabit pipe slows considerably when it serves hundreds of requests rather than a dozen. The only way to restore higher effective throughput (and performance) in such a "swamped resources" scenario is to scale, add more of the resource that is over loaded.

For this reason, the ability of a system to easily scale when under stress in a cloud environment is vastly more useful than the overall throughput or aggregate performance of individual components. In cloud environments, this scalability is usually handled through either horizontal or vertical scaling.

1.12.2 Horizontal and Vertical Scalability

- When increasing resources on the cloud to restore or improve application performance, administrators can scale either horizontally (out) or vertically (up), depending on the nature of the resource constraint.

- Vertical scaling (up) entails adding more resources to the same computing pool, for example, adding more RAM, disk, or virtual CPU to handle an increased application load.

- Horizontal scaling (out) requires the addition of more machines or devices to the computing platform to handle the increased demand. This is represented in the transition from Fig. 1.11 to Fig. 1.12 below.

Fig. 1.11 : Basic, Single Silo, n-tier architecture

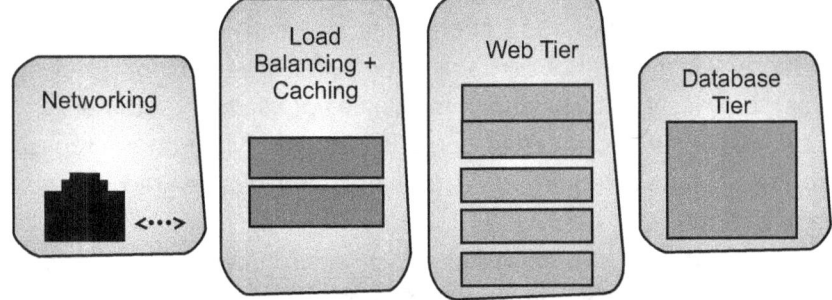

Fig. 1.12 : Horizontally scaled load balancing and web-tier. Vertically scaled database tier

- Vertical scaling can handle most sudden, temporary peaks in application demand on cloud infrastructures since they are not typically CPU-intensive tasks.
- Sustained increases in demand, however, require horizontal scaling and load balancing to restore and maintain peak performance. Horizontal scaling is also manually intensive and time consuming, requiring a technician to add machinery to the customer's cloud configuration.
- Manually scaling to meet a sudden peak in traffic may not be productive, traffic may settle to its pre-peak levels before new provisioning can come on line.

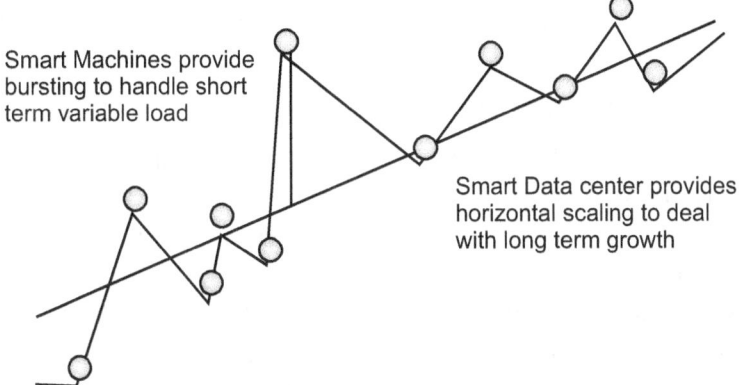

Fig. 1.13 : Horizontal Scaling

- Businesses may also find themselves experiencing more gradual increases in traffic. Here, provisioning extra resources provides only temporary relief as resource demands continue to rise and exceed the newly provisioned resources.

1.12.3 Administrative and Geographical Scalability

- While adding computing components or virtual resources is a logical means to scale and improve performance, few companies realize that the increase in resources may also necessitate an increase in administration, particularly when deploying horizontal scaling.
- In essence, a scaled increase in hard or virtual resources often requires a corresponding increase in administrative time and expenses.
- This administrative increase may not be a one-time configuration demand as more resources require continual monitoring, backup, and maintenance.
- Companies with critical cloud applications may also consider geographical scaling as a means to more widely distribute application load demands or as a way to move application access closer to dispersed communities of users or customers.
- Geographical scaling of resources in conjunction with synchronous replication of data pools is another means of adding fault tolerance and disaster recovery to cloud-based data and applications.
- Geographical scaling may also be necessary in environments where it is impractical to host all data or applications in one central location.

1.12.4 Practical and Theoretical Limits of Scale

While scalability is the most effective strategy for solving performance issues in cloud infrastructures, practical and theoretical limits prevent it from ever becoming an exponential, infinite solution.

- Practically speaking, most companies cannot commit an infinite amount of money, people, or time to improving performance.
- Cloud vendors also may have a limited amount of experience, personnel, or bandwidth to address customer application performance.
- Every computing infrastructure is bound by a certain level of complexity and scale, not the least of which is power, administration, and bandwidth, necessitating geographical dispersal.

1.12.5 Addressing Application Scalability

- For a cloud computing platform to effectively host business data and applications, however, it must accommodate a wide range of performance characteristics and network demands. Storage, CPU, memory, and network bandwidth all come into play at various times during typical application use.
- Application switching, for example, places demands on the CPU as one application is closed, flushed from the registers, and another application is loaded. If these applications are large and complex, they put a greater demand on the CPU.
- Serving files from the cloud to connected users stresses a number of resources, including disk drives, drive controllers, and network connections when transferring the data from the cloud to the user.

- File storage itself consumes resources not only in the form of physical disk space, but also disk directories and metafile systems that consume RAM and CPU cycles when users either access or upload files into the storage system.
- As these examples illustrate, applications can benefit from both horizontal and vertical scaling of resources on demand, yet truly dynamic scaling is not possible on most cloud computing infrastructures. Therefore, one of the most common and costly responses to scaling issues by vendors is to over-provision customer installations to accommodate a wide range of performance issues.

1.12.6 Application Development to Improve Scalability

- One practical means for addressing application scalability and to reduce performance bottlenecks is to segment applications into separate silos. Web-based applications are theoretically stateless, and therefore theoretically easy to scale, all that is needed is more memory, CPU, storage, and bandwidth to accommodate them, as was depicted in Fig. 1.14. However, in practice Web-based applications are not stateless.
- They are accessed through a network connection(s) that requires an IP address(es) that is fixed and therefore stateful, and they connect to data storage (either disk or database) which maintains logical state as well as requiring hardware resources to execute.
- Balancing the interaction between stateless and stateful elements of a Web application requires careful architectural consideration and the use of tiers and silos to allow some form of horizontal resource scaling.
- To leverage the most from resources, application developers can break applications into discrete tiers, state or stateless processes, that are executed in various resource silos. Fig. 1.15 depicts breaking an application into two silos identified by their DNS name.

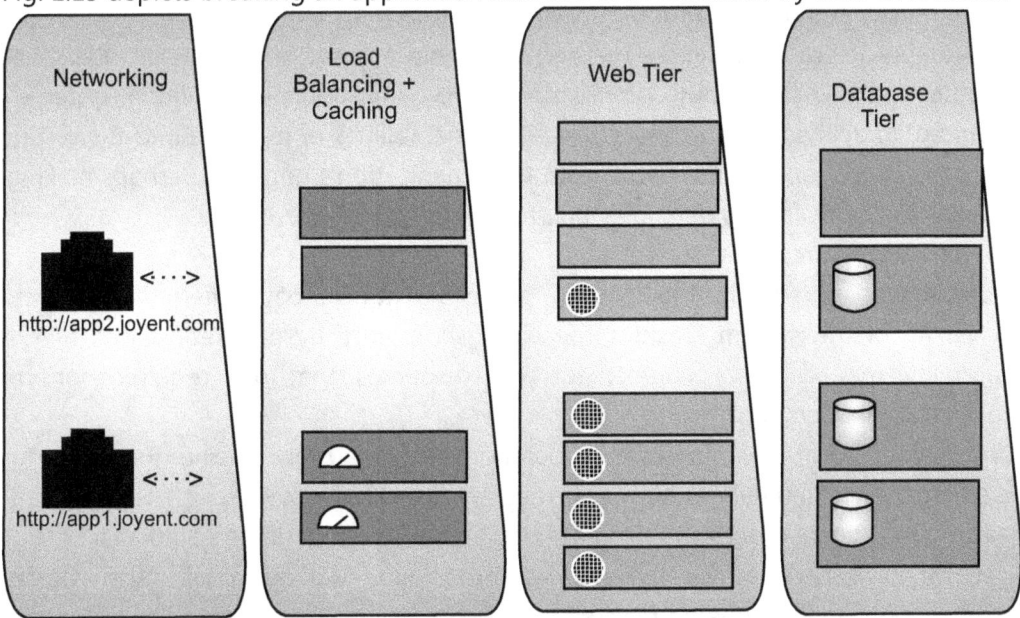

Fig. 1.14 : Scalability Improvement

- By segregating state and stateless operations and provisioning accordingly, applications and systems can run more efficiently and with higher resource utilization than under a more common scenario.

1.13 CHALLENGES IN CLOUD NIST GUIDELINES   (May 17)

- The terms of traditional information technology outsourcing contracts, particularly those involving sensitive data, can serve as guidelines for cloud computing initiatives.
- Three main security and privacy issues in service contracts have been identified previously and are relevant to outsourcing public cloud computing services:

Inadequate Policies and Practices : The security policies and practices of the cloud provider might not be adequate or compatible with those of the organization. The same issue applies to privacy as well. This can result in complications such as the following :

- Undetected intrusions or violations due to insufficient auditing and monitoring policies by the cloud provider.
- Lack of sufficient data and configuration integrity due to a mismatch between the organization's and the cloud provider's policies for separation of duty (i.e., clear assignment of roles and responsibilities) or redundancy (i.e., having sufficient checks and balances to ensure an operation is done consistently and correctly).
- Loss of privacy due to the cloud provider handling sensitive information less rigorously than the organization's policy dictates.

Weak Confidentiality and Integrity Sureties :

- Insufficient security controls in the cloud provider's platform could affect negatively the confidentiality and privacy, or integrity of the system.
- For example, use of an insecure method of remote access could allow intruders to gain unauthorized access, modify, or destroy the organization's information systems and resources; to deliberately introduce security vulnerabilities or malware into the system; or to launch attacks on other systems from the organization's network, perhaps making the organization liable for the damages incurred.

Weak Availability Sureties :

- Insufficient safeguards in the cloud provider's platform could negatively affect the availability of the system. Besides the applications directly affected, a loss of system availability may cause a conflict for key resources that are required for critical organizational operations.
- For example, if disruptive processing operations (e.g., load rebalancing due to site failure or emergency maintenance) are performed by the cloud provider at the same time as peak organizational processing occurs, a denial of service condition could arise.
- A denial of service attack targeted at the cloud provider could also affect the organization's applications and systems operating in the cloud or at the organization's data center.

- Assurances furnished to the organization by the cloud provider to support security claims, or by a certification and compliance review entity paid by the cloud provider, should be verified whenever possible through independent assessment by the organization.

- Moreover, a third-party certification or other assurances from the cloud provider do not necessarily grant a tenant application or system that same level of certification or compliance; those elements would likely require a separate certification assessment for that specific cloud environment. Other noteworthy concerns, which are indirectly related to security and privacy, also exist with outsourcing to public clouds.

- One of the most prevalent and challenging concerns is called the principal-agent problem. Another is the attenuation of an organization's technical expertise.

Principal-Agent Problem :

- The principal-agent problem occurs when the incentives of the agent (i.e., the cloud provider) are not aligned with the interests of the principal (i.e., the organization). Because it can be difficult to determine the level of effort a cloud provider is exerting towards security and privacy administration and remediation, the concern is that the organization might not recognize if the service level is dropping or has dropped below the extent required.

- One confounding issue is that increased security efforts are not guaranteed to result in noticeable improvements (e.g., fewer incidents), in part because of the growing amounts of malware and new types of attacks.

Attenuation of Expertise :

- Outsourced computing services can, over time, diminish the level of technical knowledge and expertise of the organization, since management and staff no longer need to deal regularly with technical issues at a detailed level.

- As new advancements and improvements are made to the cloud computing environment, the knowledge and expertise gained directly benefit the cloud provider, not the organization.

- Unless precautions are taken, an organization can lose its ability to keep up to date with technology advances and related security and privacy considerations, which in turn can affect its ability to plan and oversee new information technology projects effectively and to maintain accountability over existing cloud-based systems.

QUESTIONS

1. Define cloud computing and explain the characteristics of cloud computing.
2. Explain cloud service models in short.
3. How applications are deployed over cloud?
4. Explain the following
    (a) Public cloud
    (b) Private cloud
    (c) Hybrid cloud
5. Explain the term cloud multi-tenancy in detail.
6. Write short note on multi-tenancy implementation based on service models.
7. Explain the benefits of cloud computing.
8. Write short note on service scalability over the cloud.

VIRTUALIZATION, SERVER, STORAGE AND NETWORKING

2.1 INTRODUCTION

- The IT industrys focus on virtualization technology has increased considerably in the past few years.
- The concept of virtualization has its origins in the mainframe days in the late 1960s and early 1970s, when IBM invested a lot of time and effort in developing robust time-sharing solutions.
- At that time main intention behind virtualization was to allow large expensive mainframes to be easily shared among different application environments.
- Time-sharing refers to the shared usage of computer resources among a large group of users, aiming to increase the efficiency of both the users and the expensive computer resources they share.
- This model represented a major breakthrough in computer technology : The cost of providing computing capability dropped considerably and it became possible for organizations, and even individuals, to use a computer without actually owning one.
- IT industry is constantly searching for a way to utilize the resources in most efficient way.
- The best way to improve resource utilization, and at the same time simplify data center management, is through virtualization.
- Data centers today use virtualization techniques to make abstraction of the physical hardware, create large pools of logical resources consisting of CPUs, memory, disks, file storage, applications, networking, and offer those resources to users or customers in the form of agile, scalable, consolidated virtual machines.
- The core meaning of virtualization is to enable a computing environment to run multiple independent systems at the same time.
- Virtualization is an industry-changing movement that will touch all aspects of IT infrastructure and drive new levels of flexibility and dynamism in IT.

2.2 OVERVIEW OF VIRTUALIZATION   (Nov. 16, Aug. 16, May 17)

- Virtualization is a technique for hiding the physical characteristics of computing resources from the way other systems, applications or end users interact with them.
- Virtualization is a framework or methodology of dividing the resources of a computer into multiple execution environments, by applying one or more concepts or technologies such as hardware and software partitioning, time-sharing, partial or complete machine simulation, emulation, quality of service, and many others.

- We all are aware of the simple mechanism that one physical machine runs one operating system at any given time.
- By virtualizing the machine, we are able to run several operating systems (and all of their applications) at the same time.
- Virtualization provides the following two functionalities :
    1. Making multiple physical resources appear to function as a single logical resource. Refer Fig. 2.1.

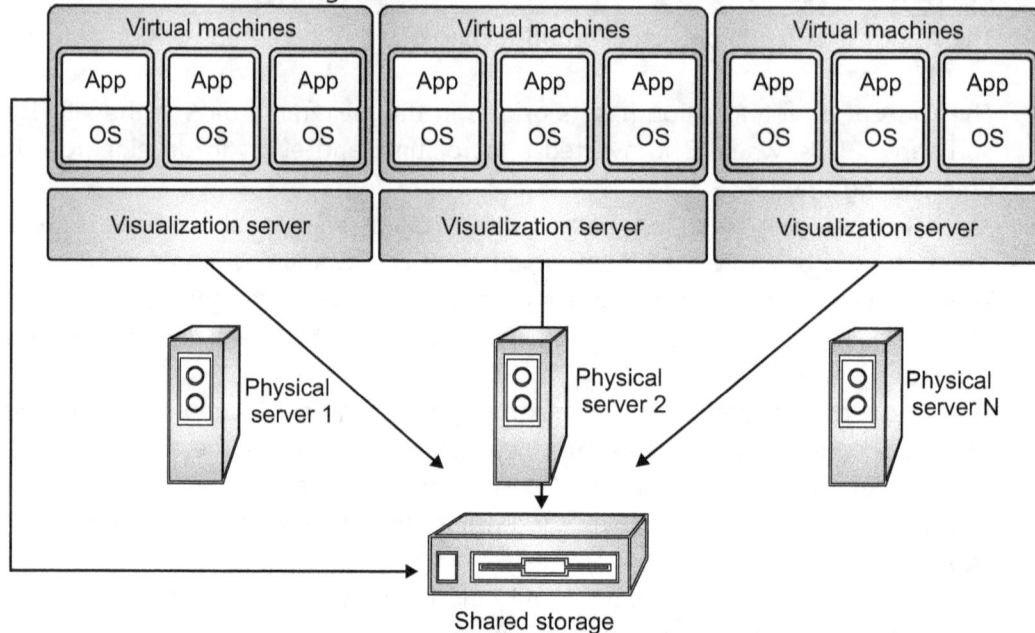

Fig. 2.1 : Multiple Physical Resources as a Single Logical Resource

    1. Making a single physical resource appear to function as multiple logical resources. Refer Fig. 2.2.

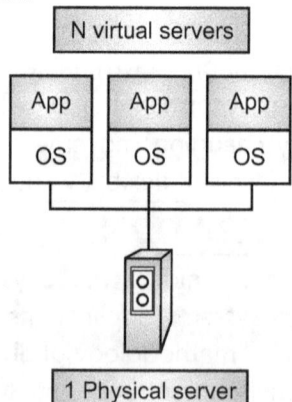

Fig. 2.2 : Single Physical Resource as a Multiple Logical Resources

- Now let's understand the difference between multitasking, multithreading and virtualization.

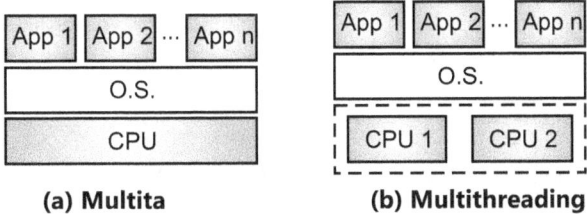

(a) Multita　　　　　　**(b) Multithreading**

Fig. 2.3

- In case of multitasking, there is only one Central Processing Unit (CPU) and one operating system which can be used for running several applications. Refer Fig. 2.3 (a)
- Whereas in case of multithreading there can be two or more physical as well as logical instances of CPU, called as threads which can be used for running several applications. Refer Fig. 2.3 (b).
- Parallel processing is made possible by letting the number of applications to run on multiple cores.
- Virtualization describes a process which enables the sharing of resources of one or more computers, namely its CPU, memory or hard disk, through the creation of virtual hardware platforms, operating systems, storage devices or network resources.
- This improves the performance existing system, allowing users to run more software and applications without the need to install new hardware or appliances. Refer Fig. 2.4.
- With the virtualization it is possible to create several instances of CPUs, called as virtual CPU and operating systems.
- Each instance (CPU + Operating System) is treated as separate entity and it is responsible for running number of applications.

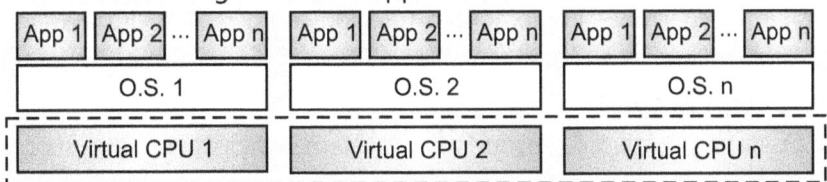

Fig. 2.4 : Virtualization

- Till now we have seen the virtualization and what can be done using virtualization. Now let's turn towards the basic entities which are used for creating virtual environment.

1. Virtual Machines

- Virtual machines are presentation of a real machine using software that provides an operating environment which can run or host a guest operating system. Virtual machines are created and managed by virtual machine monitors.

- Virtual machines are simply implementation of a machine that executes programs as if it is a real machine.
- These virtual machines are basically categorized into two types :
  (a) Process virtual machines.
  (b) System virtual machines.

(a) Process Virtual Machines

- Process virtual machines run as a normal application inside an operating system to abstract away the details of the underlying hardware.
- These are designed to provide a platform-independent environment to a single process (i.e., program).
- The environment is created when its associated process is started and destroyed when that process exits.
- Process virtual machines allow program to execute in the same way regardless of the physical platform it is running on.
- They are implemented using an interpreter.
- The programmer's code is not compiled, but the interpreter requires compilation before providing the processing environment.

(b) System Virtual Machine

- System virtual machines allow multiplexing (time sharing) of the underlying hardware between different operating systems.
- These are designed to provide a complete platform which can support the execution on multiple, and different, operating systems.
- They allow time-sharing of underlying hardware between virtual machines.
- In system virtual operating systems remain isolated from one another.
- The Instruction Set Architecture (ISA) provided by the virtual machine can be different from that of the real machine.
- System virtual machines implemented through the use of a Virtual Machine Monitor (VMM) also-known-as a Hypervisor.

2. Guest Operating System

- Guest operating system is an operating system which is running inside the created virtual machine.

3. Hypervisor

- Hypervisor is a thin layer of software that generally provides virtual partitioning capabilities, which runs directly on hardware, but below the higher-level virtualization services.
- Hypervisors are classified into two categories.

(a) Native Hypervisor (Hardware-Level)

- Native hypervisor is a software which runs directly on top of a given hardware platform as a control program for operating systems. Refer Fig. 2.5.

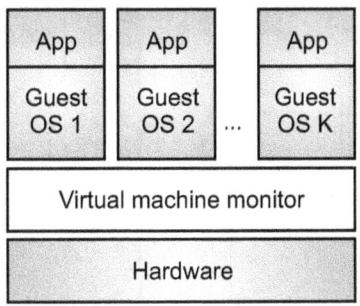

Fig. 2.5 : Native Hypervisor

- It is where actual virtualization begins.

(b) Hosted Hypervisor (OS-Level)

- Hosted hypervisor is software which runs within an operating system environment as a control program for other operating systems.
- Virtual Machine Monitor layer is moved one level higher as compared to Native VMs.
- Hosted hypervisor runs within a Host operating system environment.
- An operating system is installed first; as usual, on top of Hardware.
- A Virtual Machine Monitor is then installed within the Host OS.
- Guest operating systems can be installed on top of the VMM layer.
- Host OS sees the VMM as a process.
- VMM controls the allocation of time between Guest operating systems.
- Guest operating system is segregated from the rest of the environment. Refer Fig. 2.6.

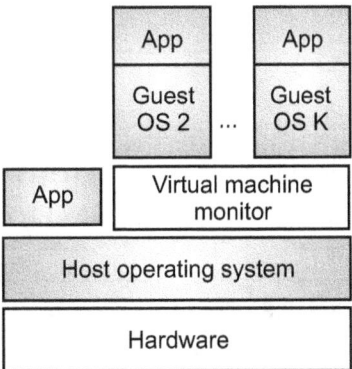

Fig. 2.6 : Hosted Hypervisor

4. Virtual Machine Monitor

- Above entities use the terms like hypervisor and virtual machine monitor, but they are conceptually different.
- Virtual Machine Monitor (VMM) is a software that runs in a layer between host operating system and one or more virtual machines that provides the virtual machine abstraction to the guest operating systems. Refer Fig. 2.7.

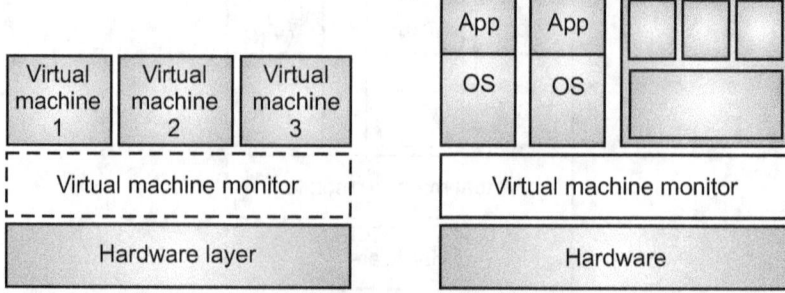

Fig. 2.7 : Role of Virtual Machine Monitor in Virtualization

- With full virtualization, the virtual machine monitor exports a virtual machine abstraction identical to a physical machine, so that standard operating systems can run just as they would on physical hardware.

2.3 THE VIRTUAL SERVER

- Before directly moving to the virtual server concept, first we must understand the traditional server concept.

- Servers can be considered as a whole unit that includes the hardware, the OS, the storage, and the applications.

- Servers are often referred to by their function i.e. the Web server, the SQL server, the file server, etc. Refer Fig. 2.8.

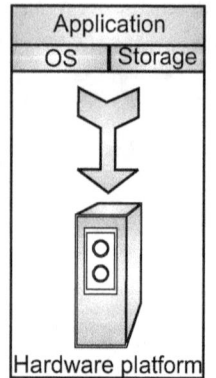 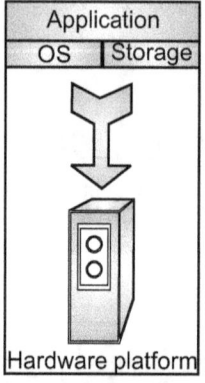 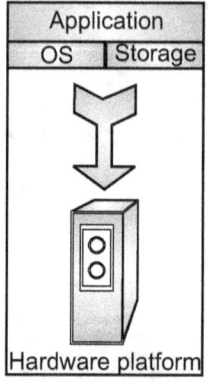 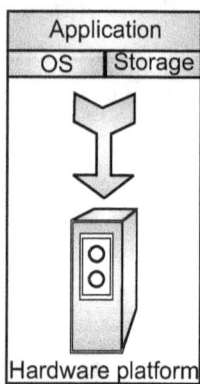

Fig. 2.8 : Traditional Servers

- If the any of the server is overloaded or that server fills up then the system administrators must add in a new server.

- If there are no multiple servers and if a service experiences a hardware failure, then the service is down completely. Refer Fig. 2.9.

- It is also possible to implement clusters of servers to make them more fault tolerant. However, even clusters have limits on their scalability, and not all applications work in a clustered environment.

- Although traditional servers mentioned above provide many advantages such as easy deployment, easy to backup, less complexity we must not ignore disadvantages such as expenses to maintain hardware, limited scaling, difficulty in replication, difficulty in maintaining redundancy, under utilization of processor etc.

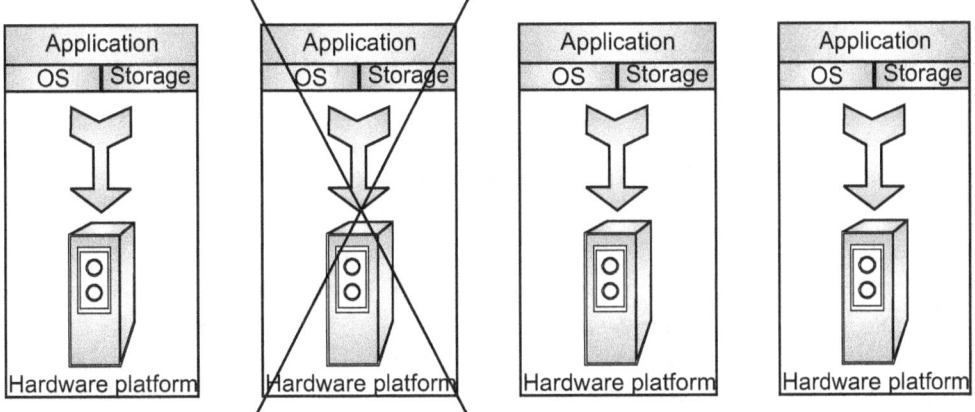

Fig. 2.9 : Service is Completely Down if Server Fails

- Virtual servers are implemented using virtualization to overcome the disadvantages of traditional servers mentioned above.

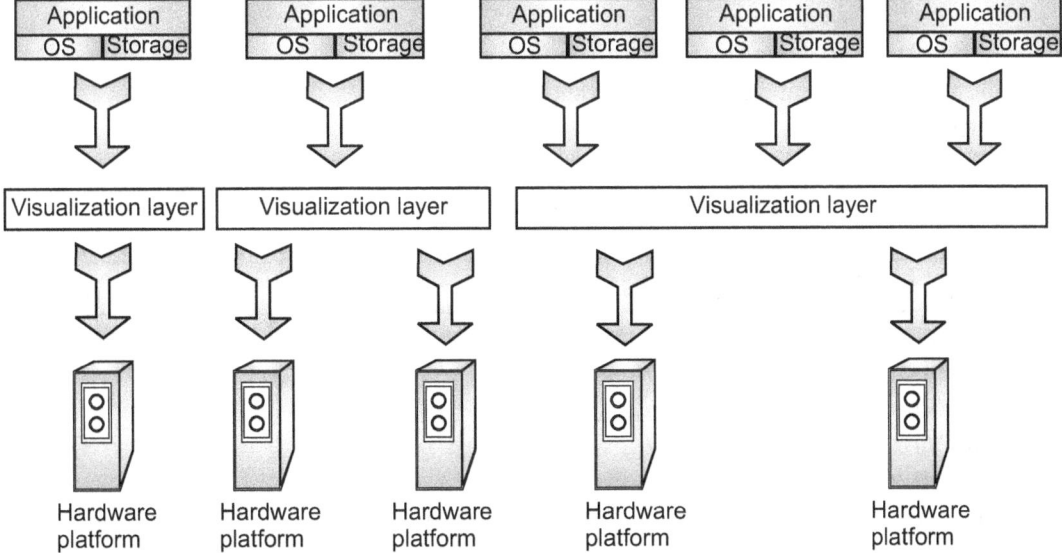

Fig. 2.10 : Virtual Server

- Virtual servers seek to encapsulate the server software away from the hardware.
- This includes the OS, the applications, and the storage for that server.
- Servers end up as mere files stored on a physical box, or in enterprise storage.

- A virtual server can be serviced by one or more hosts, and one host may contain more than one virtual server. Refer Fig. 2.10.
- Virtual servers can still be referred to by their function i.e. email server, database server, etc.
- If the environment is built correctly, virtual servers will not be affected by the loss of a host.
- Hosts may be removed or added at any time and as per requirement to fulfill the requirements.
- Virtual servers can be scaled out easily.
- If the administrators find that the resources supporting a virtual server are being taxed too much, they can adjust the amount of resources allocated to that virtual server.
- Server templates can be created in a virtual environment to be used to create multiple, identical virtual servers.
- Virtual servers themselves can be migrated from host to host almost at will.

Advantages of Virtual Servers
- Resource pooling.
- Highly redundant.
- Highly available.
- Rapidly deploy new servers.
- Easy to deploy.
- Reconfigurable while services are running.
- Optimizes physical resources by doing more with less.

Disadvantages of Virtual Servers
- Slightly harder to conceptualize.
- Slightly more costly (must buy hardware, OS, Apps and now the abstraction layer).

2.4 TYPES OF VIRTUALIZATION (Aug. 16)

- Virtualization approaches are classified into the following five types :
1. Emulation
2. Full Virtualization
3. Para Virtualization
4. Operating System Level Virtualization
5. Application Level Virtualization

2.4.1 Emulation

- In this approach, virtual machine simulates the entire hardware set needed to run unmodified guests for completely different hardware architectures.
- It is used to create new operating systems for the hardware which is in design phase and not in physical form.

- Virtual Machine provides a "guest" operating system the (simulated) hardware environment it expects.
- Software is unaware that it is really talking to a virtualized device. Refer Fig. 2.11.

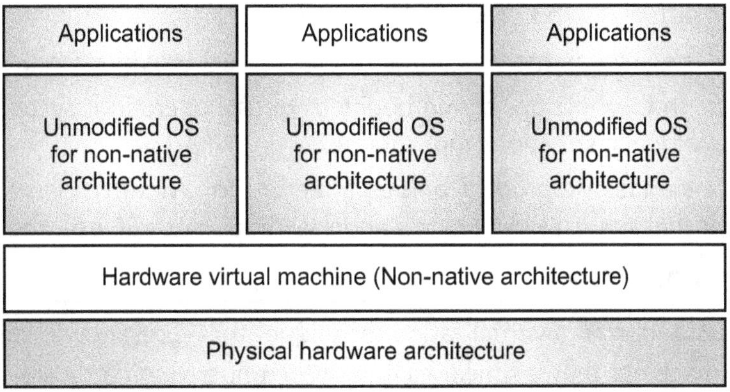

Applications
Applications
Applications
Unmodified OS for non-native architecture
Unmodified OS for non-native architecture
Unmodified OS for non-native architecture
Hardware virtual machine (Non-native architecture)
Physical hardware architecture

Fig. 2.11 : Emulation

- Each interaction between Guest device driver with the emulated device hardware requires transaction with VMM.
- The real hardware does its job as usual, but the VMM must now translate the result for the guest.
- **Advantage :** Guest Software need not be modified
- **Disadvantage :** Must pay Performance Penalty.

2.4.2 Full Virtualization

- Full virtualization is a native kind of virtualization in which hypervisor runs directly on top of a given hardware platform as a control program for operating systems.
- It is similar to emulation except it is designed to simulate the underlying hardware which is physically available.

Applications
Applications
Unmodified OS for non-native architecture
Unmodified OS for non-native architecture
Unmodified OS for non-native architecture
Hypervisor (VMM)
Physical hardware architecture

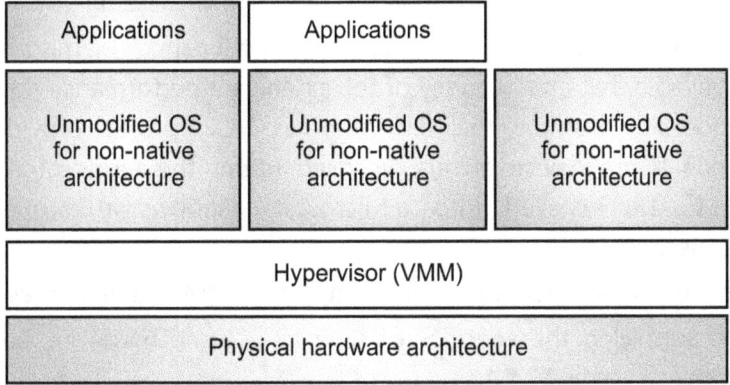

Fig. 2.12 : Full Virtualization

- It runs unmodified guests on a physical machine.

- It gives the flexibility to move entire virtual machines from one host to another host very easily, but for the cost of performance due to the overhead added by the emulator Layer. Refer Fig. 2.12.
- Examples : Virtual PC and VMware Workstation.
- VMware is the first commercial virtualization product provider for x86 architecture.
- It enables the execution of unmodified guest operating systems through the translation of x86 instructions that cannot be virtualized.
- Hyper-V, a standalone product and as a feature for Windows Server 2008, windows edition translates guest kernel mode and real mode into x86 user mode.

2.4.3 Para Virtualization

- Para virtualization is a virtualization technique that presents a software interface to virtual machines that is similar to that of the underlying hardware.
- Application Programming Interface (API) is provided to the Guest OS by the VMM so the guest may utilize the hardware.
- The hypervisor exports a modified version of the underlying physical hardware.
- The intent of the modified interface is to reduce the portion of the guest's execution time spent performing operations which are substantially more difficult to run in a virtual environment compared to a non-virtualized environment.
- A successful para virtualized platform may allow the Virtual Machine Monitor (VMM) to be simpler (by relocating execution of critical tasks from the virtual domain to the host domain), and/or reduce the overall performance degradation of machine-execution inside the virtual-guest.
- Para virtualization requires the guest operating system to be explicitly ported for the para-API. This is because a conventional OS distribution that is not para virtualization-aware cannot be run on top of a para virtualizing VMM.
- However, even in cases where the operating system cannot be modified, components may be available that enable many of the significant performance advantages of para virtualization. For example, the Xen Windows GPLPV project provides a kit of para virtualization-aware device drivers, licensed under the terms of the GPL, that are intended to be installed into a Microsoft Windows virtual-guest running on the Xen hypervisor.
- Thus with para virtualization guest interacts with VMM at a higher level of abstraction
- Instead of supplying the specifics of how to use the hardware, software provides general requests to the VMM.
- Para virtualization decreases the number of interactions between Guest and VMM for a specific operation. Refer Fig. 2.13.

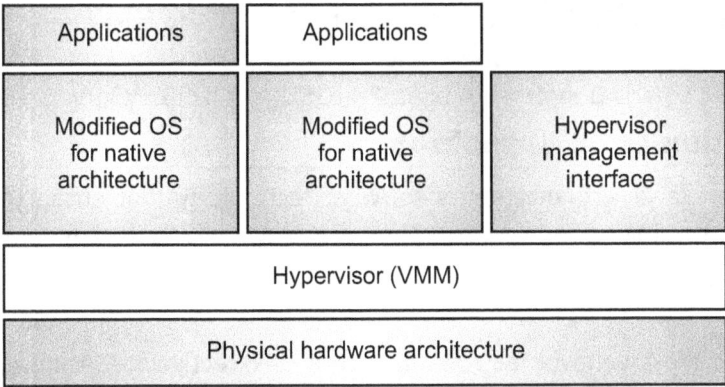

Fig. 2.13 : Para Virtualization

- **Advantage :** Better Performance.
- **Disadvantage :** Guest OS must be modified to use API.

2.4.4 Operating System Level Virtualization

- With operating system level virtualization virtual machine monitor software is not required.
- With this technique of virtualization single OS image handles all the guest images in different isolated containers.
- There is host OS that handles all other guest OS images present in respective containers.
- OS level virtualization does not support running different operating systems (Specifically, different kernel) at a time.
- With OS level virtualization instead of virtualizing the hardware, it is possible to run multiple virtual instances of same OS on single hardware.
- Thus with OS level virtualization only single kernel runs at a time.
- Single kernel means very low overhead (1 to 3%) compared to standalone server.
- Containers are the entities which provide isolation between processes.
- Each process appears as separate OS. Refer Fig. 2.14.

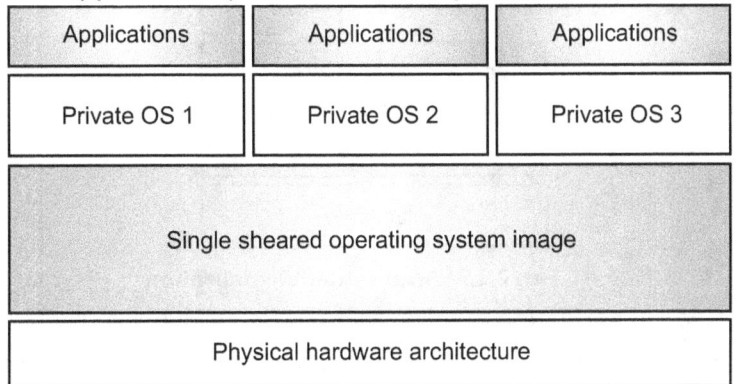

Fig. 2.14 : OS Level Virtualization

- **Advantage :** Best Performance / Scalability, Ease of Administration.
- **Disadvantage :** Only virtualizes copies of same OS.
- **Examples :** Solaris Containers/Zones, FreeBSD Jails, Linux VServers and OpenVZ.

2.4.5 Application Level Virtualization   (Aug. 16)

- Application level virtualization is software technology that encapsulates application software from the underlying operating system on which it is executed.
- A fully virtualized application is not installed in the traditional sense, although it is still executed.
- The application behaves at runtime like it is directly interfacing with the original operating system and all the resources managed by it, but can be isolated or sandboxed to varying degrees.
- In this context, the term "virtualization" refers to the object being encapsulated (application), which is quite different from its meaning in hardware virtualization, where it refers to the object being abstracted (physical hardware).
- Application level virtualization is also known as process virtualization.
- Application virtualization is the approach of running applications inside a virtual execution environment.
- The virtual execution environment provides a standard API for cross platform execution and manages the consumption of application's local resources such as threading model, environment variables, user interface libraries and objects.
- Modern operating systems such as Windows and Linux can include limited application virtualization.
- For example, Windows 7 provides Windows XP Mode that enables older Windows XP application to run unmodified on Windows 7.

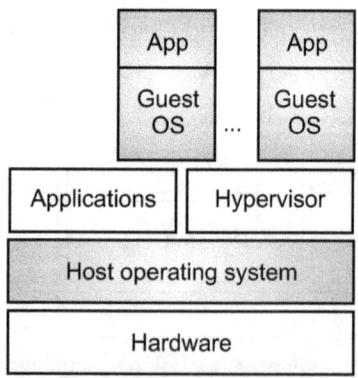

Fig. 2.15 : Application Virtualization

- Full application virtualization requires a virtualization layer.
- Application virtualization layers replace part of the runtime environment normally provided by the operating system.

- The layer intercepts all disk operations of virtualized applications and transparently redirects them to a virtualized location, often a single file.
- The application remains unaware that it accesses a virtual resource instead of a physical one.
- Since the application is now working with one file instead of many files spread throughout the system, it becomes easy to run the application on a different computer and previously incompatible applications can be run side-by-side.

2.5 NEED AND ADVANTAGES OF VIRTUALIZATION   (Aug. 16)

2.5.1 Need of Virtualization

- We have already learnt about virtualization concepts, virtual machine and types of virtualization.
- Still we are not really sure of why there is need of virtualization.
- Most of the businesses often use a combination of a number of application servers, web servers, image servers, audio-video servers, document servers and database servers.
- Above mentioned hardware infrastructure is not being used well almost all the time.
- If the 75% of the hardware appears as being used at any point of time on the basis of average number of server requests recorded, the servers are still largely under-utilized.
- The servers typically take only about 1-10 ms to service each request. However it should be much faster.
- Given this extremely short amount of time taken to service the request, the amount of time the server machine is kept up and running relative to the actual time spent by it servicing the requests, is much higher.
- This clearly indicates that a significant amount of energy is wasted per server in the process of keeping the servers up and ever-ready to service requests upon their arrival.
- Cumulative energy wasted is actually high considering the fact that we use not one server for each purpose, but a number of them for different purposes.
- Maximizing the server utilization is limited by the number of incoming server requests.
- Even if we have done our best to ensure that server spends a good fraction of time servicing requests, this equivalent to the number of requests the server receives at any point of time.
- Virtualization is the technique for eliminating this wastage and maximizing the profit.
- We already know that virtualization essentially means to create multiple, logical instances of software or hardware on a single physical hardware resource.

- This technique simulates the available hardware and gives every application running top of it, the feeling that it is the unique holder of the resource.
- The details of the virtual, simulated environment are kept transparent from the application.
- Organizations use this technique to perform the tasks away from many of their physical servers and map these functions onto one robust, evergreen physical server.
- This is beneficial in terms of cost of maintenance and reduced energy wastage.
- Since we have fewer physical servers, we need only their maintenance and therefore maintenance becomes much easier and cheaper.
- Also the amount of energy wasted is a function of the number of physical servers which is clearly much lower in virtualized environment.

2.5.2 Advantages of Virtualization

- Allows applications to run in environments that do not suit the native application :
  1. Wine allows some Microsoft Windows applications to run on Linux.
  2. CDE, a lightweight application virtualization, allows Linux applications to run on another platform.
- May protect the operating system and other applications from poorly written or buggy code and in some cases provide memory protection and IDE style debugging features.
- Uses fewer resources than a separate virtual machine.
- Run applications that are not written correctly, for example applications that try to store user data in a read-only system-owned location.
- Run incompatible applications side-by-side, at the same time and with minimal regression testing against one another.
- Reduce system integration and administration costs by maintaining a common software baseline across multiple diverse computers in an organization.
- Implement the security principle of least privilege by removing the requirement for end-users to have Administrator privileges in order to run poorly written applications.
- Simplified operating system migrations.
- Improved security, by isolating applications from the operating system.
- Allows applications to be copied to portable media and then imported to client computers without need of installing them, so called Portable software.

2.5.3 Limitations of Virtualization

- Not all software can be virtualized. Some examples include applications that require a device driver and 16 bit applications that need to run in shared memory space.
- Some types of software such as anti-virus packages and applications that require heavy OS integration are difficult to virtualize.
- Only file and registry-level compatibility issues between legacy applications and newer operating systems can be addressed by application virtualization.

- For example, applications that don't manage the heap correctly will not execute on Windows Vista as they still allocate memory in the same way, regardless of whether they are virtualized or not.
- For this reason, specialist application compatibility fixes (shims) may still be needed, even if the application is virtualized.
- Moreover, in software licensing, application virtualization bears great licensing pitfalls mainly because both the application virtualization software and the virtualized applications must be correctly licensed.

2.6 XEN OVERVIEW　　　　　　　　　　　　　　(Nov. 16, May 17)

2.6.1 Introduction to XEN

- Virtualization of operating systems is used in many different computing areas. It finds its applications in server consolidation, energy saving efforts, or the ability to run older software on new hardware.
- Number of systems have been designed which use virtualization to subdivide the many resources of a modern computer.
- Some require specialized hardware, or cannot support commodity operating systems.
- Some target 100% binary compatibility at the expense of performance. Others sacrifice security or functionality for speed.
- Few offer resource isolation or performance guarantees; most provide only best effort provisioning, risking denial of service.
- Xen, an x86 virtual machine monitor which allows multiple commodity operating systems to share conventional hardware in a safe and resource managed fashion, but without sacrificing either performance or functionality.
- Xen is a virtualization system supporting both para-virtualization (PV)and hardware assistant full virtualization (HVM).
- The name XEN has evolved from neXt gENeration virtualization.
- This is achieved by providing an idealized virtual machine abstraction to which operating systems such as Linux, BSD and Windows, can be ported with minimal effort.

2.6.2 Basic Components of XEN Environment

- A Xen virtual environment consist of several items that work together to deliver the virtualization environment.
- The basic components of a Xen-based virtualization environment are the Xen hypervisor, the Domain0, any number of other VM Guests, and the tools, commands, and configuration files that let you manage virtualization.
- Collectively, the physical computer running all these components is referred to as a virtual machine host because together these components form a platform for hosting virtual machines.

- Xen virtualization environment consists of following components :
1. Xen Hypervisor.
2. Domain 0 Guest.
3. Domain Management and Control (Xen DM&C).
4. Domain U Guest (Dom U).
5. PV Guest.
6. HVM Guest.

The diagram below shows the basic organization of these components.

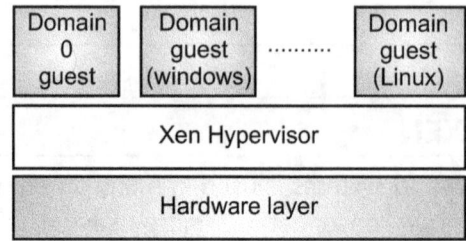

Fig. 2.16 : Block diagram of Xen virtualization Environment

1. The Xen Hypervisor

- The Xen hypervisor sometimes referred to generically as a virtual machine monitor, is an open-source software program that coordinates the low-level interaction between virtual machines and physical hardware.
- The Xen hypervisor is the basic abstraction layer of software that sits directly on the hardware below any operating systems. It is responsible for CPU scheduling and memory partitioning of the various virtual machines running on the hardware device.
- The hypervisor not only abstracts the hardware for the virtual machines but also controls the execution of virtual machines as they share the common processing environment.
- It has no knowledge of networking, external storage devices, video, or any other common I/O functions found on a computing system.

2. The Domain 0

- The virtual machine host environment, also referred to as domain0 or controlling Domain.
- The term "Domain 0" refers to a special domain that provides the management environment. This may be run either in graphical or in command line mode.
- Domain 0, a modified Linux kernel, is a unique virtual machine running on the Xen hypervisor that has special rights to access physical I/O resources as well as interact with the other virtual machines (Domain U : PV and HVM Guests) running on the system.
- All Xen virtualization environments require Domain 0 to be running before any other virtual machines can be started.

- Two drivers are included in Domain 0 to support network and local disk requests from Domain U PV and HVM Guests; the Network Backend Driver and the Block Backend Driver. Refer Fig. 2.17.

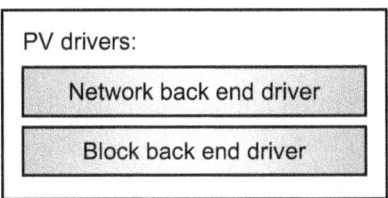

Fig. 2.17 : Drivers of Domain 0

- The Network Backend Driver communicates directly with the local networking hardware to process all virtual machines requests coming from the Domain U guests.
- The Block Backend Driver communicates with the local storage disk to read and write data from the drive based upon Domain U requests.

3. **Domain U**

- Domain U guests have no direct access to physical hardware on the machine as a Domain 0 Guest does and is often referred to as unprivileged.
- All para-virtualized virtual machines running on a Xen hypervisor are referred to as Domain U PV Guests and are modified Linux operating systems, Solaris, FreeBSD, and other UNIX operating systems.
- All fully virtualized machines running on a Xen hypervisor are referred to as Domain U **HVM Guests** and run standard Windows or any other unchanged operating system.

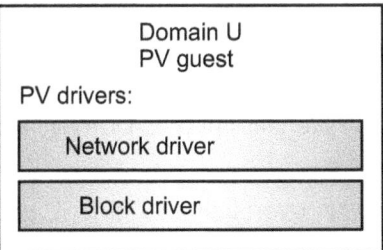

Fig. 2.18 : Divers of Domain U

- The Domain U PV Guest virtual machine is aware that it does not have direct access to the hardware and recognizes that other virtual machines are running on the same machine.
- The Domain U HVM Guest virtual machine is not aware that it is sharing processing time on the hardware and that other virtual machines are present.
- A Domain U PV Guest contains two drivers for network and disk access, PV Network Driver and PV Block Driver. Refer Fig. 2.18.

- A Domain U HVM Guest does not have the PV drivers located within the virtual machine; instead a special daemon is started for each HVM Guest in Domain 0.

4. Qemu-DM

- Qemu-DM supports the Domain U HVM Guest for networking and disk access requests.
- The Domain U HVM Guest must initialize as it would on a typical machine so software is added to the Domain U HVM Guest, Xen virtual firmware, to simulate the BIOS an operating system would expect on startup.
- Every HVM Guest running on a Xen environment requires its own Qemu daemon.
- This tool handles all networking and disk requests from the Domain U HVM Guest to allow for a fully virtualized machine in the Xen environment.
- Qemu-DM must exist outside the Xen hypervisor due to its need for access to networking and I/O and is therefore found in Domain 0. Refer Fig. 2.19.
- A new tool, Stub-dm, is in development for future versions of Xen that will remove the need for a Qemu-DM running for every Domain U HVM Guest and will instead provide a set of services available to every Domain U HVM Guest.

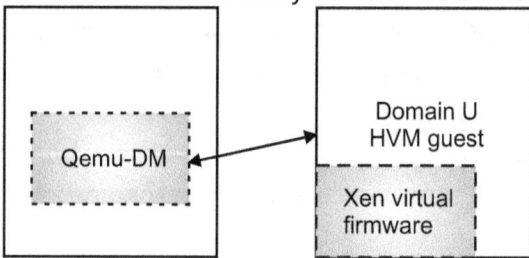

Fig. 2.19 : Qemu-DM

5. Domain Management and Control

- A series of Linux daemons are classified as Domain Management and Control by the open source community.
- These services support the overall management and control of the virtualization environment and exist within the Domain 0 virtual machine.

6. Xend

- The Xend daemon is a python application that is considered the system manager for the Xen environment.
- It leverages the libXenctrl library to make requests of the Xen hypervisor.
- All requests processed by the Xend are delivered to it via an XML RPC interface by the Xm tool. Refer Fig. 2.20.
- The Xend daemon (Xend) stores configuration information about each virtual machine and controls how virtual machines are created and managed.

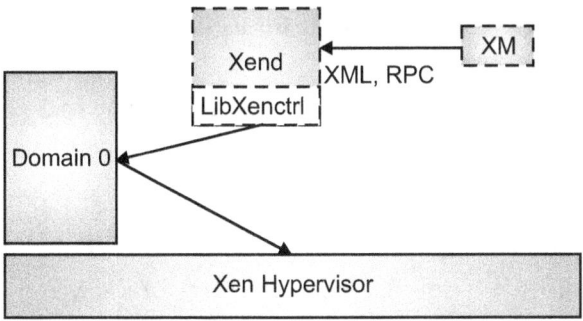

Fig. 2.20 : Xend Daemon

7. **Xm**

- Xm is the command line tool that takes user input and passes to Xend via XML RPC.

8. **Xenstored**

- The Xenstored daemon maintains a registry of information including memory and event channel links between Domain 0 and all other Domain U Guests.
- The Domain 0 virtual machine leverages this registry to setup device channels with other virtual machines on the system.

9. **LibXenctrl**

- LibXenctrl is a C library that provides Xend the ability to talk with the Xen hypervisor via Domain 0.
- A special driver within Domain 0, privcmd delivers the request to the hypervisor. Refer Fig. 2.21.

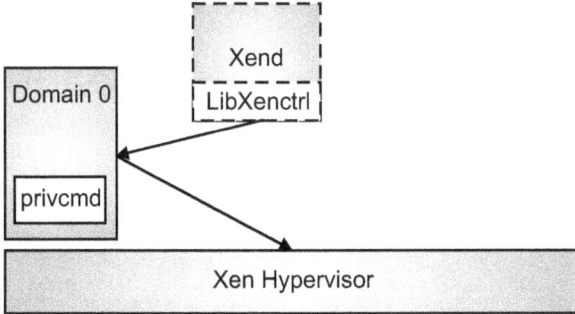

Fig. 2.21 : LibXenctrl

10. **Xen Virtual Firmware**

- The Xen Virtual Firmware is a virtual BIOS that is inserted into every Domain U HVM Guest to ensure that the operating system receives all the standard start-up instructions it expects during normal boot-up providing a standard PC-compatible software environment.

11. **Xen PCI Passthru**

- A new feature in Xen designed to improve overall performance and reduce the load on the Domain 0 Guest is PCI Passthru which allows the Domain U Guest to have direct access to local hardware without using the Domain 0 for hardware access.

- The Domain U Guest is given rights to talk directly to a specific hardware device instead of the previous method of using Fronted and Backend drivers.

2.6.3 Xen Operation

- This subsection demonstrates how a para-virtualized Domain U is able to communicate with external networks or storage via the Xen hypervisor and Domain 0.

2.6.3.1 Domain 0 to Domain U Communication

- As stated earlier, the Xen hypervisor is not written to support network or disk requests thus a Domain U PV Guest must communicate via the Xen hypervisor with the Domain 0 to accomplish a network or disk request.
- The example shown below shows a Domain U PV Guest writing data to the local hard disk.
- The Domain U PV Guest PV block driver receives a request to write to the local disk and writes the data via the Xen hypervisor to the appropriate local memory which is shared with Domain 0.
- An event channel exists between Domain 0 and the Domain U PV Guest that allows them to communicate via asynchronous inter-domain interrupts in the Xen hypervisor.
- Domain 0 will receive an interrupt from the Xen hypervisor causing the PV Block Backend Driver to access the local system memory reading the appropriate blocks from the Domain U PV Guest shared memory.
- The data from shared memory is then written to the local hard disk at a specific location.

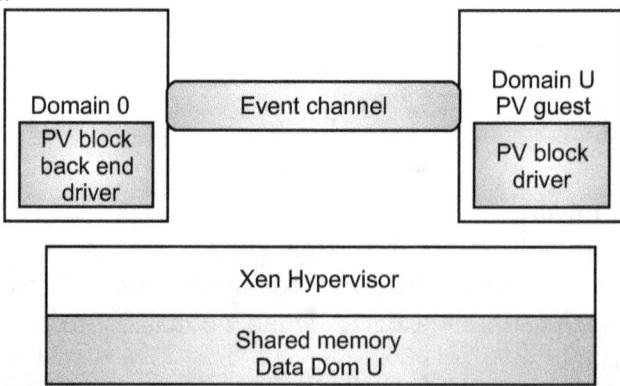

Fig. 2.22 : Domain 0 to Domain U Communication

- The event channel is shown in Fig. 2.22 as a direct link between Domain 0 and Domain U PV Guest which is a simplified view of the way the system works.

- In fact, the event channel runs through the Xen hypervisor with specific interrupts registered in Xenstored allowing both the Domain 0 and Domain U PV Guest to quickly share information across local memory.

2.6.4 Understanding Virtualization Modes

- Guest operating systems are hosted on virtual machines in either full virtualization mode or para-virtual mode.(Refer 2.4)
- There are several ways to implement virtualization.
- Two leading approaches are full virtualization and para-virtualization. Each virtualization mode has advantages and disadvantages.
- Full virtualization is designed to provide total abstraction of the underlying physical system and creates a complete virtual system in which the guest operating systems can execute.
- No modification is required in the guest OS or application; the guest OS or application is not aware of the virtualized environment so they have the capability to execute on the VM just as they would on a physical system.
- This approach can be advantageous because it enables complete decoupling of the software from the hardware.
- As a result, full virtualization can streamline the migration of applications and workloads between different physical systems.
- Full virtualization also helps provide complete isolation of different applications, which helps make this approach highly secure.
- However, full virtualization may incur a performance penalty. The VM monitor must provide the VM with an image of an entire system, including virtual BIOS, virtual memory space, and virtual devices.
- The VM monitor also must create and maintain data structures for the virtual components, such as a shadow memory page table.
- These data structures must be updated for every corresponding access by the VMs.
- In contrast, para-virtualization presents each VM with an abstraction of the hardware that is similar but not identical to the underlying physical hardware.
- Para-virtualization techniques require modifications to the guest operating systems that are running on the VMs.
- As a result, the guest operating systems are aware that they are executing on a VM allowing for near-native performance.
- Para-virtualization methods are still being developed and thus have limitations; including several insecurities such as the guest OS cache data, unauthenticated connections, and so forth.

2.6.5 The Virtual Machine Interface

- Table 2.1 presents an overview of the para-virtualized x86 interface, classified into three broad aspects of the system : memory management, the CPU, and device I/O.

Table 2.1 : Virtual Machine Interfaces

Memory Management	
Segmentation	Cannot install fully-privileged segment descriptors and cannot overlap with the top end of the linear address space.
Paging	Guest OS has direct read access to hardware page tables, but updates are batched and validated by the hypervisor. A domain may be allocated discontinuous machine pages.
CPU	
Protection	Guest OS must run at a lower privilege level than Xen.
Exceptions	Guest OS must register a descriptor table for exception handlers with Xen. A side from page faults, the handlers remain the same.
System Calls	Guest OS may install a 'fast' handler for system calls, allowing direct calls from an application into its guest OS and avoiding in directing through Xen on every call.
Interrupts	Hardware interrupts are replaced with a lightweight event system.
Time	Each guest OS has a timer interface and is aware of both `real' and `virtual' time.
Device I/O	
Network, Disk, etc.	Virtual devices are elegant and simple to access. Data is transferred using asynchronous I/O rings. An event mechanism replaces hardware interrupts for notifications.

2.6.5.1 Memory Management

- Virtualizing memory is the most difficult part of para-virtualizing an architecture in terms of the mechanisms required in the hypervisor and modifications required to port each guest OS.

- The task is easier if the architecture provides a software managed TLB as these can be efficiently virtualized in a simple manner.

- Associating an address-space identifier tag with each TLB entry allows the hypervisor and each guest OS to efficiently coexist in separate address spaces because there is no need to flush the entire TLB when transferring execution.

- Unfortunately, x86 does not have a software managed TLB; instead TLB misses are serviced automatically by the processor by walking the page table structure in hardware.

- Thus to achieve the best possible performance, all valid page translations for the current address space should be present in the hardware-accessible page table.
- Moreover, because the TLB is not tagged, address space switches typically require a complete TLB flush.
- Given these limitations, two decisions are made :
  - (a) Guest OSs are responsible for allocating and managing the hardware page tables, with minimal involvement from Xen to ensure safety and isolation; and
  - (b) Xen exists in a 64MB section at the top of every address space, thus avoiding a TLB flush when entering and leaving the hypervisor.
- Each time a guest OS requires a new page table, for example a new process is being created, it allocates and initializes a page from its own memory reservation and registers it with Xen.
- At this point the OS must give up direct write privileges to the page-table memory : All subsequent updates must be validated by Xen.
- This restricts updates in a number of ways, including only allowing an OS to map pages that it owns, and disallowing writable mappings of page tables.
- Guest OSes may batch update requests to pay back the overhead of entering the hypervisor.
- The top 64MB region of each address space, which is reserved for Xen, is not accessible or remappable by guest OSs.
- This address region is not used by any of the common x86 architectures.
- So this restriction does not break application compatibility.
- Segmentation is virtualized in a similar way, by validating updates to hardware segment descriptor tables. The only restrictions on x86 segment descriptors are :
  - (a)   They must have lower privilege than Xen.
  - (b)   They may not allow any access to the Xen reserved portion of the address space.

2.6.5.2 CPU

- Virtualizing the CPU has several implications for guest OSs.
- Principally, the insertion of a hypervisor below the operating system violates the usual assumption that the OS is the most privileged entity in the system.
- In order to protect the hypervisor from OS misbehavior (and domains from one another) guest OSs must be modified to run at a lower privilege level.
- Many processor architectures only provide two privilege levels.
- In these cases the guest OS would share the lower privilege level with applications.
- The guest OS would then protect itself by running in a separate address space from its applications, and indirectly pass control to and from applications via the hypervisor to set the virtual privilege level and change the current address space.
- Again, if the processor's TLB supports address-space tags then expensive TLB flushes can be avoided.

- Efficient virtualizing of privilege levels is possible on x86 because it supports four distinct privilege levels in hardware.
- The x86 privilege levels are generally described as rings, and are numbered from zero (most privileged) to three (least privileged). Refer Fig. 2.23.

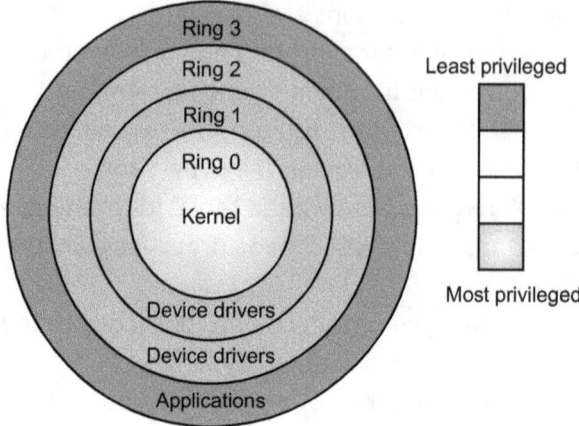

Fig. 2.23 : x86 Privilege Rings

- OS code typically executes in ring 0 because no other ring can execute privileged instructions, while ring 3 is generally used for application code. To our knowledge, rings 1 and 2 have not been used by any well-known x86 OS.
- Any OS which follows this common arrangement can be ported to Xen by modifying it to execute in ring 1. This prevents the guest OS from directly executing privileged instructions, yet it remains safely isolated from applications running in ring 3.
- Privileged instructions are para-virtualized by requiring them to be validated and executed within Xen. This applies to operations such as installing a new page table, or yielding the processor when idle.
- Any guest OS attempt to directly execute a privileged instruction is failed by the processor, either silently or by taking a fault, since only Xen executes at a sufficiently privileged level.
- Exceptions, including memory faults and software traps, are virtualized on x86 very straightforwardly.
- A table describing the handler for each type of exception is registered with Xen for validation.
- The handlers specified in this table are generally identical to those of real x86 hardware. This is possible because the exception stack frames are unmodified in our para-virtualized architecture. The sole modification is to the page fault handler, which would normally read the faulting address from a privileged processor register (CR2); since this is not possible, we write it into an extended stack frame2.
- When an exception occurs while executing outside ring 0, Xen's handler creates a copy of the exception stack frame on the guest OS stack and returns control to the appropriate registered handler.

- Typically only two types of exception occur frequently enough to affect system performance : System calls (which are usually implemented via a software exception), and page faults.

- Performance of system calls can be improved by allowing each guest OS to register a 'fast' exception handler which is accessed directly by the processor without indirecting via ring 0; this handler is validated before installing it in the hardware exception table.

- Unfortunately it is not possible to apply the same technique to the page fault handler because only code executing in ring 0 can read the faulting address from register CR2; page faults must therefore always be delivered via Xen so that this register value can be saved for access in ring 1.

- Safety is ensured by validating exception handlers when they are presented to Xen. The only required check is that the handler's code segment does not specify execution in ring 0.

- Since no guest OS can create such a segment, it suffices to compare the specified segment selector to a small number of static values which are reserved by Xen.

2.6.5.3 Device I/O

- Rather than emulating existing hardware devices, as is typically done in fully-virtualized environments, Xen exposes a set of clean and simple device abstractions.

- This allows us to design an interface that is both efficient and satisfies requirements for protection and isolation. To this end, I/O data is transferred to and from each domain via Xen, using shared-memory, asynchronous buffer descriptor rings.

- These provide a high-performance communication mechanism for passing buffer information vertically through the system, while allowing Xen to efficiently perform validation checks (for example, checking that buffers are contained within a domain's memory reservation).

- Similar to hardware interrupts, Xen supports a lightweight event delivery mechanism which is used for sending asynchronous notifications to a domain. These notifications are made by updating a bitmap of pending event types and, optionally, by calling an event handler specified by the guest OS.

2.6.6 Xen Architecture

- Xen is open source virtualization software based on para-virtualization technology. This subsection provides an overview of the Xen architecture.

- Fig. 2.24 shows the architecture of Xen hosting four VMs (Domain 0, VM 1, VM 2, and VM 3). This architecture includes the Xen Virtual Machine Monitor (VMM), which abstracts the underlying physical hardware and provides hardware access for the different virtual machines.

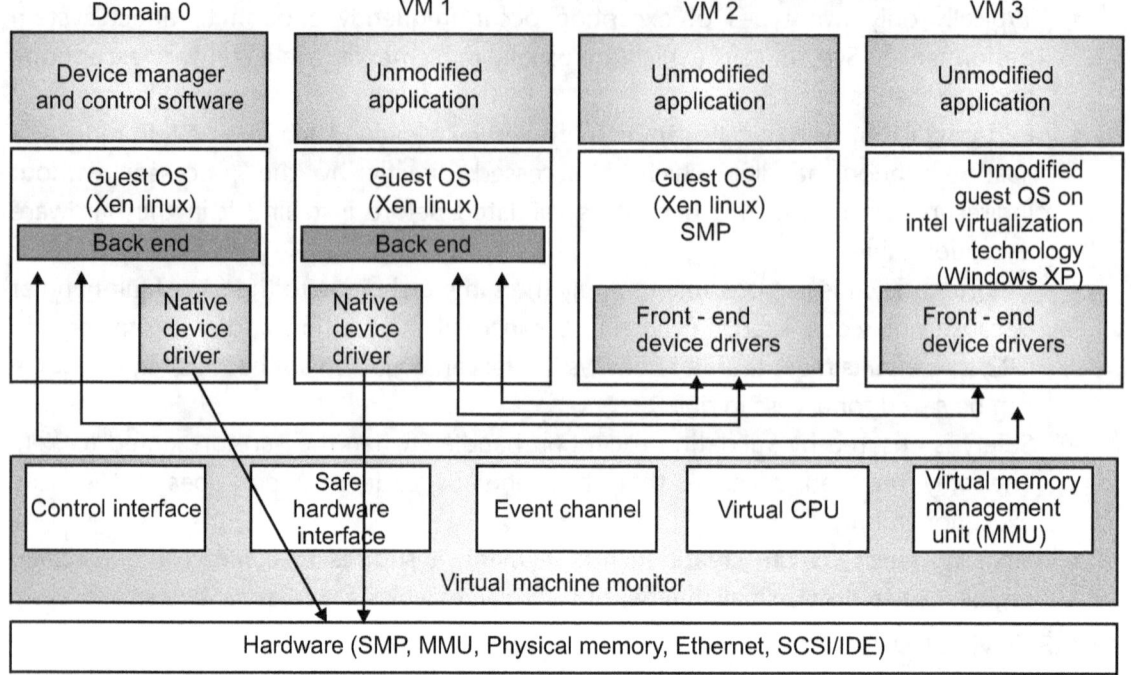

Fig. 2.24 : Xen Architecture

- Fig. 2.24 also shows the special role of the VM called Domain 0. Only Domain 0 can access the control interface of the VMM, through which other VMs can be created, destroyed, and managed.

- Management and control software runs in Domain 0.

- Administrators can create virtual machines with special privileges such as VM 1 that can directly access the hardware through secure interfaces provided by Xen.

- Administrators can create other virtual machines that can access the physical resources provided by Domain 0's control and management interface in Xen.

2.6.6.1 CPU Operations

- The Intel x86 architecture provides four levels of privilege modes. These modes, or rings, are numbered 0 to 3, with 0 being the most privileged.

- In a non-virtualized system, the OS executes at ring 0 and the applications at ring 3. Rings 1 and 2 are typically not used.

- In Xen para-virtualization, the VMM executes at ring 0, the guest OS at ring 1, and the applications at ring 3. This approach helps to ensure that the VMM processes the highest privilege, while the guest OS executes in a higher privileged mode than the applications and is isolated from the applications.

- Privileged instructions issued by the guest OS are verified and executed by the VMM.

2.6.6.2 Memory Operations

- In a non-virtualized environment, the OS expects contiguous memory.

- Guest operating systems in Xen para-virtualization are modified to access memory in a non-contigious manner.
- Guest operating systems are responsible for allocating and managing page tables. However, direct writes are intercepted and validated by the Xen VMM.

2.6.6.3 I/O Operations

- In a fully virtualized environment, hardware devices are emulated.
- Xen para-virtualization exposes a set of clean and simple device abstractions. For example, I/O data to and from guest operating systems is transferred using shared memory ring architecture (memory is shared between Domain 0 and the guest domain) through which incoming and outgoing messages are sent.
- Modifying the guest OS is not feasible for non–open source platforms Windows operating systems.
- As a result, such operating systems are not supported in a para-virtualization environment.

2.7 X86 VIRTUALIZATION

2.7.1 Introduction to x86 Virtualization

- x86 virtualization refers to hardware virtualization for the x86 architecture.
- It allows multiple operating systems to simultaneously share x86 processor resources in a safe and efficient manner.
- In the early days of x86 virtualization, all CPUs were implemented essentially the same 32-bit architecture and the virtual machine monitor (VMM) always used software techniques to run guest operating systems.
- Later uniformity no longer exists. CPUs today come in 32 and 64 bit variants. Some CPUs have hardware support for virtualization; others do not. Moreover, this hardware support comes in multiple forms for virtualizing different aspects of the x86 architecture.
- This subsection provides description of x86 architecture from virtualization point of view along with the understanding of :
  (a) Which CPU features are required.
  (b) Which CPU features can be utilized (but are not required).
  (c) Which CPU features can be virtualized that is, made available to software running in the virtual machine.
- With a better understanding of how CPU features are required, used, and virtualized we can more precisely talk about what can be virtualized, what performance levels may result for a given combination of CPU, guest operating system, and how workloads may respond to adjusting configuration parameters both for software running in the virtual machine and at the underlying hardware level.

2.7.2 x86 Architecture- History

- The x86 architecture has roots that link back to 8 bit processors built by Intel in the late 1970s.
- As manufacturing capabilities improved and software demands increased, Intel extended the 8-bit architecture to 16 bits with the 8086 processor.
- With the arrival of the 80386 CPU in 1985, Intel extended the architecture to 32 bits known as IA-32, but the vendor use the generalized term as x86 .
- From the last two decades, the basic 32-bit architecture remained the same, although successive generations of CPUs added many new features such as chip floating point unit, support for large physical memories and vector instructions.
- In 2003, AMD introduced a 64-bit extension to the x86 architecture, after that Intel announced its own 64-bit architectural extension of IA-32 known as IA-32e. The AMD and Intel 64-bit extensions are extremely similar, with some minor differences which is crucial for virtualization.

2.7.3 VMware ESX

- VMware released the first version of VMware Workstation in 1999. It ran on, and virtualized, 32 bit x86 CPUs.
- Later VMware switched to the ESX Server product. This ESX server used a custom built kernel instead of workstation which relies on either Linux or Windows.
- The custom built kernel also known as VMkernel is designed to be scalable and efficiently run a workload that consists primarily of virtual machines while providing strong information and performance isolation among the virtual machines.
- The VMkernel row in Table 2.2 shows the architectural requirements for running the VMkernel itself in different versions of ESX.

Table 2.2 : Physical and Virtual CPU Options

	ESX 1.0-2.5	ESX 3.0	ESX 3.5	ESX 4.0
VMkernel	32 bit	32 bit	32 bit	64 bit
Virtual CPU	32 bit	32-64 bit	32-64 bit	32-64 bit

- All versions of ESX before 4.0 can run on the 32-bit x86 architecture. They also can run on x64 CPUs but do not take advantage of the 64-bit architectural extensions.
- With VMware ESX 4.0, a 64-bit CPU is required to run the VMkernel. However this requirement causes a slight loss of hardware compatibility.
- After 2009 the majority of server CPUs implements the x64 architecture, making it desirable to use the large 64 bit address space and other architectural advances to improve performance and scalability.

2.7.4 Virtualizing 32- and 64-bit CPUs

- The VMkernel does not run virtual machines directly. Instead, it runs a VMM that in turn is responsible for execution of the virtual machine.
- Each VMM is dedicated to one virtual machine. To run multiple virtual machines, the VMkernel starts multiple VMM instances.
- Because the VMM decouples the virtual machine from the VMkernel, it is possible to run 64 bit guest operating systems on a 32 bit VMkernel (and vice versa) as long as the underlying physical CPUs have all the required features.
- VMM can also be designed which can take advantage of a 64-bit physical CPU to run a 64-bit guest operating system efficiently, even if the underlying VMkernel runs in 32-bit mode.
- The Virtual CPU row in Table 2.2 shows which versions of ESX can run just 32-bit virtual machines and which can run both 32- and 64-bit virtual machines.

2.7.5 Execution Modes

- The VMM implements the virtual hardware on which the virtual machine runs. This hardware includes a virtual CPU, virtual I/O devices, timers, and other devices.
- The virtual CPU has three important features :
  a. The virtual instruction set.
  b. The virtual memory management unit (MMU).
  c. The virtual interrupt controller (PIC or APIC).
- The VMM can implement each of these aspects using either software techniques or hardware techniques. The combination of techniques used to virtualize the instruction set and memory determines an execution mode.

2.7.5.1 Instruction Set Virtualization

- In order to run one or more virtual machines safely on a single host, ESX must isolate the virtual machines so that they can not interfere with each other or with the VMkernel.
- In particular, it must prevent the virtual machines from directly executing privileged instructions that could affect the state of the physical machine as a whole. Instead, it must intercept such instructions and emulate them so their effect is applied to the virtual machine's hardware, not the physical machine's hardware. For example, issuing the reboot command in a virtual machine should reboot just that virtual machine, not the entire host.
- Now we will see some software and hardware techniques for x86 virtualization.

Software Technique : Binary Translation

- The original approach to virtualizing the 32 bit x86 instruction set is just-in-time binary translation (BT).

- This approach is implemented in all versions of VMware ESX, and it is the only approach used in VMware ESX 1.x and 2.x. This approach is actually called as BT32 as this technique virtualizes the 32-bit architecture.
- When running a virtual machine's instruction stream using binary translation, the virtual machine instructions must be translated before they can be executed. Refer Fig. 2.25.
- When a virtual machine is about to execute a block of code for the first time, ESX sends this code through a just-in-time binary translator, much like a Java virtual machine (JVM) which translates Java byte code on the fly into native instructions.

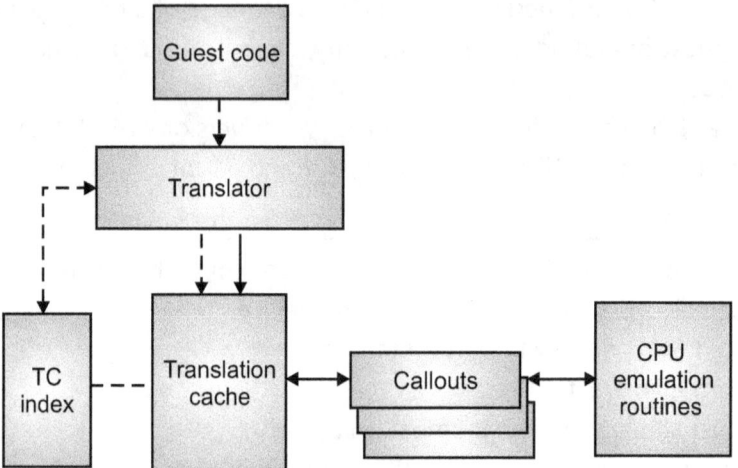

Fig. 2.25 : Binary Translation

- The translator in the VMM does not perform a mapping from one architecture to another, but instead translates from the full unrestricted x86 instruction set to a subset that is safe to execute. In particular, the binary translator replaces privileged instructions with sequences of instructions that perform the privileged operations in the virtual machine rather than on the physical machine.
- This translation enforces encapsulation of the virtual machine while preserving the x86 semantics as seen from the perspective of the virtual machine.
- To keep translation overheads low, the VMM translates virtual machine instructions the first time they are about to execute, placing the resulting translated code in a translation cache.
- If the same virtual machine code executes again in the future, the VMM can reuse the translated code from the translation cache, thereby amortizing the translation costs over all future executions.
- To reduce translation cost further and to minimize memory usage by the translation cache, the VMM combines binary translation of kernel code running in the virtual machine with direct execution of user mode code running in the virtual machine. This is safe because user mode code cannot execute privileged instructions.

- A Binary Translation-based VMM must enforce a strict boundary between the part of the address space that is used by the virtual machine and the part that is used by the VMM. The VMware VMM enforces this boundary using segmentation.
- Segmentation is a hardware feature of the x86 CPU that links back to its 16 bit ancestors. A segment is a consecutive range of memory, identified by a base (the starting address) and a limit (the length of the segment).
- Whenever an x86 instruction accesses memory, it does so with respect to a particular segment.
- The segmentation hardware checks the memory address against the segment limit. If it is within the limit, the base address is added and the access is permitted to proceed. If the address exceeds the limit, the memory access is aborted and the processor raises a protection fault.
- Since most of the modern operating systems, including Windows, Linux make limited use of segmentation, it is possible for the VMM to use segmentation to enforce the boundary between virtual machine and VMM.
- In rare cases when the uses of segmentation by the virtual machine and the VMM conflict, the VMM can perform software segmentation checks again, causing a slight loss of performance.
- In 2003, when AMD extended the x86 architecture from 32 to 64 bits, it eliminated segment limit checks for 64-bit code although 32 bit code still retained segment limit checks for backwards compatibility. This change meant that a BT-based VMM could not use segmentation to protect the VMM from a 64-bit virtual machine. In other words, BT32 could virtualize the 32-bit x86 architecture efficiently, but BT64 could not virtualize the 64-bit architecture efficiently.
- To overcome this AMD added segment limits back into 64-bit code. Thus, all 64-bit AMD CPUs can run virtual machines with BT64.
- The Intel 64-bit extensions to the x86 architecture also omitted support for segment limit checks for 64-bit code. Unlike AMD, however, Intel has not added support for segment limit checks in subsequent processors. This limitation makes it inefficient to run 64-bit virtual machines using BT64 on Intel CPUs.

Table 2.3 : Support for Binary Translation (BT)

	ESX 1.0-2.5	ESX 3.0	ESX 3.5	ESX 4.0
AMD	BT32	BT32 , BT64	BT32, BT64	BT32, BT64
Intel	BT32	BT32	BT32	BT32

Hardware Technique : VT-x and AMD-V

- During the transition from 32-bit to 64-bit hardware, both Intel and AMD recognized the importance of virtualization. Both companies began designing hardware that made it easier for a VMM to run virtual machines.

- The first hardware designs by both of them focused on how to virtualize the 32- and 64-bit x86 instruction set.
- The Intel design, called VT-x got the importance because it provided a way to virtualize 64-bit virtual machines efficiently. (BT64 is not efficient because of the lack of segment limit checks in 64 bit mode on Intel CPUs.)
- AMD subsequently introduced AMD-V to provide hardware support for instruction set virtualization (virtualization of 64 bit virtual machines using BT64 was possible already for AMD CPUs).
- VT-x and AMD-V are similar in aim. Both designs allow a VMM to do away with binary translation while still being able to fully control the execution of a virtual machine by restricting which kinds of (privileged) instructions the virtual machine can execute without intervention by the VMM.
- VT-x and AMD-V both allow a VMM to give the CPU to a virtual machine for direct execution (an action called a VM entry) up until the point when the virtual machine tries to execute a privileged instruction.
- At that point, the virtual machine execution is suspended and the CPU is given back to the VMM (an action called a VM exit). The VMM then follows the inspection of the virtual machine instruction that caused the exit as well as other information provided by the hardware in response to the exit.
- With the relevant information collected, the VMM emulates the virtual machine instruction against the virtual machine state and then resumes execution of the virtual machine with another VM entry.

Table 2.4 : Support for Hardware Instruction Set Virtualization

	ESX 1.0-2.5	ESX 3.0	ESX 3.5	ESX 4.0
AMD	-	AMD-V32, AMD-V64	AMD-V32, AMD-V64	AMD-V32, AMD-V64
Intel	-	VT-x64	VT-x64	VT-x64

2.7.5.2 Memory and MMU Virtualization

- All modern x86 CPUs implement virtual memory, which is a technique for flexibly mapping multiple virtual address spaces (typically one per process) into a possibly smaller amount of physical memory.
- However, for the x86 architecture, the mapping is specified using a set of memory-resident hierarchical 4KB page tables. A tree of such page tables, identified by a root page table, specifies the entire mapping of a virtual address space into physical memory.
- The x86 MMU contains two main structures : a page table walker and a content-addressable memory called a translation lookaside buffer (TLB) to accelerate address translation lookups.

- When an instruction accesses a virtual address, segmentation hardware converts the virtual address to a linear address by adding the segment base. Then the page table walker receives the logical address and traverses the page table tree to produce the corresponding physical address. Refer Fig. 2.26.

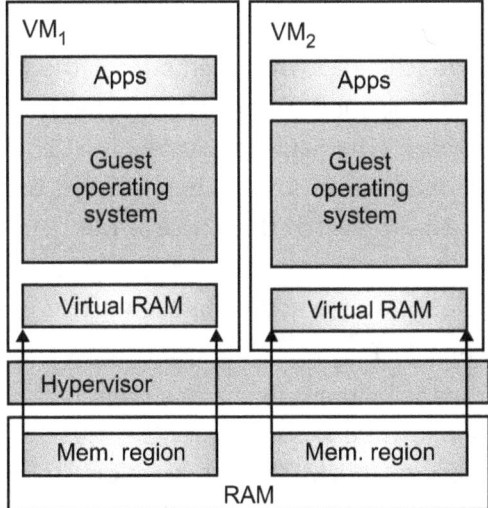

Fig. 2.26 : Memory Virtualization

- When the page table walk completes, the pair is inserted into the TLB to accelerate future accesses to the same address.
- Accordingly, the task of the VMM is not only to virtualize memory but to virtualize virtual memory so that the guest operating system can use virtual memory.
- To accomplish this task, the VMM must virtualize the x86 MMU. It does so by having the VMM remap addresses a second time, below the virtual machine, from physical address to machine address, to confine the virtual machine to the machine memory that the VMM and VMkernel have allowed it to use.

Software Technique : Shadow Page Tables

- To virtualize memory without special hardware support, the VMM creates a shadow page table for each primary page table that the virtual machine is using.
- The VMM populates the shadow page table with the composition of two mappings :
  a. The Logical address : Physical Address mapping specified by the guest operating system, obtained from the primary page tables.
  b. The Physical address : Logical Address mapping defined by the VMM and VMkernel.
- By building shadow page tables that capture this composite mapping, the VMM can point the hardware MMU directly at the shadows, allowing the virtual machine's memory accesses to run at native speed while being assured that the virtual machine cannot access machine memory that does not belong to it.

- However, shadow page tables incur overheads in following situations.
  a. When the virtual machine updates a primary page table, the VMM must trap the update and propagate the change into the corresponding shadow page table or tables. This slows down memory mapping operations as well as creation of new processes in virtual machines.
  b. When the virtual machine touches memory for the first time, the shadow page table entry mapping this memory must be created on demand, slowing down the first access to memory. (The native equivalent is a TLB miss.)
  c. When the virtual machine switches context from one process to another, the VMM must intervene to switch the physical MMU to the new process' shadow page table root.
  d. Shadow page tables consume additional memory.

Hardware Technique : RVI and EPT

- To address the overheads inherent in shadow page tables, both AMD and Intel now build special purpose hardware to support MMU virtualization.
- AMD introduced support for MMU virtualization, called RVI, in the quad-core Opteron CPU. Intel introduced similar functionality, called EPT, in its "Nehalem" generation of CPUs.
- Just as AMD-V and VT-x are similar in their aim, so are RVI and EPT. Both designs permit the two levels of address mapping to be performed in hardware by pointing the physical MMU at two distinct sets of page tables.
- The first is defined by the virtual machine and the second, invisible to the virtual machine, is controlled by the VMM.
- Given these two mappings, the physical CPU's page walker can walk the two sets of page tables to produce pairs that are cached in the TLB.
- This arrangement does away with shadow page tables at the cost of a single set of nested or extended page tables that map from physical address to machine address.
- Because the nested or extended page tables are largely static and need no update whenever the virtual machine creates or modifies page tables, the VMM need not interfere when virtual machine page tables are updated. Moreover, the VMM does not need to be involved in virtual machine context switches. The virtual machine can change the page table root on its own.
- Although RVI and EPT have compelling advantages, there is one potential downside : A TLB miss is now more expensive because it must be serviced by a two-level page walker.
- For most workloads, RVI or EPT provides an overall performance win over shadow page tables.
- For workloads that suffer frequent TLB misses or perform few context switches or page table updates RVI or EPT does not perform well.

Table 2.5 : Support RVI and EPT

	ESX 1.0-2.5	ESX 3.0	ESX 3.5	ESX 4.0
AMD	-	-	yes	yes
Intel	-	-	-	yes

2.7.5.3 Monitor Modes

- This subsection describes a two way choice between software and hardware techniques for instruction set virtualization (BT on one hand and AMD-V or VT-x on the other hand) and for memory virtualization (shadow page tables on one hand and RVI or EPT on the other hand).

- However the two forms of hardware support are not orthogonal. RVI is inseparable from AMD-V and EPT is inseparable from VT-x. This leaves only three valid combinations :

  a. BT(software) and MMU - binary translation and shadow page tables.

  b. HV(software) MMU –AMD-V or VT-x and shadow page tables.

  c. HV(hardware) MMU –AMD-V with RVI or VT-x with EPT.

  (HV stands for hardware support for instruction virtualization)

- Above three options are called as monitor modes because they describe the way the VMM runs a particular virtual machine on a given physical CPU.

Choice of Monitor Mode

- When a virtual machine is powering on, the VMM inspects the physical CPUs features and the guest operating system type to determine the set of possible execution modes.

- On ESX 3.0 and earlier only one monitor mode can be executed. Refer tables 2.2, 2.3, 2.4, 2.5.

- However from ESX 3.5, and especially with ESX 4.0, there are cases in which more than one execution mode is possible.

- In such a case VMM first finds the set of modes allowed. Then it restricts the allowed modes by configuration file settings. Finally, among the remaining sets, it chooses the "preferred" mode. The following examples illustrate the process :

  a. ESX 3.5 on an AMD CPU and a 64 bit virtual machine - The allowed modes are BT-(software) + MMU and HV-(hardware) + MMU (AMD-V with RVI). The preferred option for a 64 bit virtual machine is HV(hardware) + MMU, so the VMM chooses this mode at power on time.

  b. ESX 3.5 on an Intel Nehalem CPU and a 64 bit virtual machine - Run with HV(software) + MMU (because ESX 3.5 does not support EPT).

  c. ESX 4.0 on an AMD CPU and a 64-bit virtual machine - The choice is among BT-(software) + MMU, HV-(software) + MMU, and HV-(hardware) MMU. HV-(hardware) + MMU wins.

    d. ESX 4.0 on an older Opteron CPU and a 64-bit virtual machine - Only one option is available : BT-(software) + MMU (because ESX cannot use AMD-V on this CPU).

    e. ESX 4.0 on an Intel Nehalem CPU and a 64-bit virtual machine - The allowed modes are HV-(software) + MMU and HV-(hardware) + MMU (BT is not allowed for 64-bit virtual machines on Intel CPUs because segment limit checks are missing). The VMM chooses HV-(hardware) + MMU.

- Certain features may restrict the available modes. For example, VMware Fault Tolerance cannot use RVI or EPT because of their lack of determinism, and it avoids BT, thus only choice left is HV-(software) + MMU.

- When multiple choices remain, a prioritization algorithm runs to choose the best mode :

    a. For ESX 3.5, the only case in which there is a choice is on AMD CPUs on which BT-(software) + MMU and HV-(hardware) + MMU might both be available. The default choice for 32-bit virtual machines is BT-(software) + MMU. For 64-bit virtual machines, it is HW-(hardware) + MMU.

    b. For ESX 4.0, many more situations can result in multiple allowable execution modes.

    c. The general priority for CPUs that have hardware support for APIC virtualization is : HV-(hardware) + MMU, followed by HV- (software) + MMU, followed by BT-(software) + MMU.

    d. For CPUs without hardware support for APIC virtualization, the order for 32-bit Windows guest operating systems is : HV- (hardware) + MMU, followed by BT-(software) + MMU, followed by HV-(software) + MMU.

Specifying the Preferred Monitor Mode

- In some cases, an explicit specification of monitor mode preference may be needed.

- Although this situation is rare, the complexity of workloads and virtual machine configurations makes a manual approach more desirable in cases in which the default choice leads to less than optimal performance.

- In virtual machine configuration files, we can restrict the set of modes by setting one or both of the following options :

    monitor.virtual_mmu = software | hardware | automatic

    monitor.virtual_exec = software | hardware | automatic

- Choose from software, hardware, or automatic can be made for each variable. Both ESX 3.5 and ESX 4.0 recognize the monitor.virtual_mmu setting. Only ESX 4.0 recognizes monitor.virtual_exec.

- We can express all possible ESX 3.5 mode choices with the monitor.virtual_mmu option alone.

- If a setting is not specified, the effect is the same as automatic. If it is set to hardware, it forces the use of the given form of hardware support if the feature is available and supported. Likewise, if the setting is software, the VMM attempts to run the virtual machine without the given form of hardware support, if allowed.
- Although the configuration file settings are flexible enough to express all of the 2×2 possible combinations, only three of the four combinations are valid. Valid combinations are used to select one of the three execution modes.
- If the CPU does not support the requested execution mode, the settings are ignored. In addition, the settings are ignored if the CPU implements the execution mode but the version of ESX does not support it.

2.8 INSTALLATION AND CONFIGURATION

- Xen is an open-source para-virtualizing virtual machine monitor (VMM), or "hypervisor", for a variety of processor architectures including x86. Xen can securely execute multiple virtual machines on a single physical system with near native performance.
- Xen can be used for
a. **Server Consolidation**
   Move multiple servers onto a single physical host with performance and fault isolation provided at the virtual machine boundaries.
b. **Hardware Independence**
   Allow legacy applications and operating systems to exploit new hardware.
c. **Multiple OS Configurations**
   Run multiple operating systems simultaneously, for development or testing purposes.
d. **Cluster Computing**
e. Management at VM granularity provides more flexibility than separately managing each physical host, but better control and isolation than single-system image solutions, particularly by using live migration for load balancing.
f. **Hardware Support for Custom OSes.**
   Allow development of new OSes while benefiting from the wide-ranging hardware support of existing OSes such as Linux.

2.8.1 Installation

- The Xen distribution includes three main components : Xen itself, ports of Linux and NetBSD to run on Xen, and the user-space tools required to manage a Xen-based system.
- The following is a full list of basic items. Items marked '†' are required by the xend control tools, and hence required if you want to run more than one virtual machine; items marked '*' are only required if you wish to build from source.

1. A working Linux distribution using the GRUB boot loader and running on a P6- class or newer CPU.

2. The iproute2 package.

3. The Linux bridge-utils1 (e.g., /sbin/brctl).

4. The Linux hotplug system2 (e.g., /sbin/hotplug and related scripts). On newer distributions, this is included alongside the Linux udev system3.

- All above mentioned tools are required by the xend control tools.

1. Build tools (gcc v3.2.x or v3.3.x, binutils, GNU make).

2. Development installation of zlib (e.g., zlib-dev).

3. Development installation of Python v2.2 or later (e.g., python-dev).

4. LaTex and transFig. are required to build the documentation.

- Above mentioned tools are required only if user wish to build virtual machine from source.

- Once these prerequisites are satisfied, it is possible to install either a binary or source distribution of Xen.

2.8.2 Installing from Binary Tarball

- Pre-built tarballs are available for download from the XenSource downloads page :
  http://www.xensource.com/downloads/

- Once user has downloaded the tarball, simply unpack and install :

  # tar zxvf xen-3.0-install.tgz

  # cd xen-3.0-install

  # sh ./install.sh

- Once the binaries are installed user need to configure your system.

2.8.3 Installing from RPMs

- Pre-built RPMs are available for download from the XenSource downloads page :
  http://www.xensource.com/downloads/

- Once user has downloaded the RPMs, he typically install them via the RPM commands :

  rpm -iv rpmname

2.8.4 Installing from Source

This part describes how to obtain, build and install Xen from source.

2.8.4.1 Obtaining the Source

- The Xen source tree is available as either a compressed source tarball or as a clone of master Mercurial repository.

- **Obtaining the Source Tarball**

  Stable versions and daily snapshots of the Xen source tree are available from the Xen download page :

  http://www.xensource.com/downloads/

- **Obtaining the Source via Mercurial**

  The source tree may also be obtained via the public Mercurial repository at : http://xenbits.xensource.com

2.8.4.2 Building from Source

The top-level Xen Makefile includes a target "world" that will perform following functionalities :

- Build Xen.
- Build the control tools, including xend.
- Download (if necessary) and unpack the Linux 2.6 source code, and patch it for use with Xen.
- Build a Linux kernel to use in domain 0 and a smaller unprivileged kernel, which can be used for unprivileged virtual machines.
- After the build has completed top-level directory is created called dist/ in which all resulting targets will be placed. Two XenLinux kernel images are very important one with a "-xen0" extension which contains hardware device drivers and drivers for Xen's virtual devices, and one with a "-xenU" extension that just contains the virtual ones.
- These are found in dist/install/boot/ along with the image for Xen itself and the configuration files used during the build.
- To customize the set of kernels built user needs to edit the top-level Makefile.

  KERNELS ?= linux-2.6-xen0 linux-2.6-xenU. This can be changed to include any set of operating system kernels which have configurations in the top-level buildconFig.s/ directory.

2.8.4.3 Custom Kernels

- If you wish to build a customized XenLinux kernel (e.g. to support additional devices or enable distribution-required features), you can use the standard Linux configuration mechanisms, specifying that the architecture being built for is xen, e.g :

```
# cd linux-2.6.12-xen0
# make ARCH=xen xconFig.
# cd..
# make
```

- It is also possible to copy an existing Linux configuration (.conFig.) into e.g. linux-2.6.12-xen0 and execute :

```
# make ARCH=xen oldconFig.
```

- Only difference between the two types of Linux kernels that are built is the configuration file used for each. The "U" suffixed (unprivileged) versions don't contain any of the physical hardware device drivers, leading to a 30% reduction in size; hence you may prefer these for your non-privileged domains. The "0" suffixed privileged versions can be used to boot the system, as well as in driver domains and unprivileged domains.

2.8.4.4 Installing Generated Binaries

- The files produced by the build process are stored under the dist/install/ directory.
- To install them in their default locations, use the coomand :

  # make install

- Alternatively, users with special installation requirements may wish to install them manually by copying the files to their appropriate destinations.
- The dist/install/boot directory will also contain the conFig. files used for building the XenLinux kernels, and also versions of Xen and XenLinux kernels that contain debug symbols such as (xen-syms-3.0.0 and vmlinux-syms-2.6.12.6-xen0) which are essential for interpreting crash dumps.

2.8.5 Configuration

- Once you have built and installed the Xen distribution, it is simple to prepare the machine for booting and running Xen.

2.8.5.1 GRUB Configuration

- An entry should be added to grub.conf (often found under /boot/ or /boot/grub/) to allow Xen / XenLinux to boot. This file is sometimes called menu.lst, depending on your distribution. The entry should look something like the following :

  title Xen 3.0 / XenLinux 2.6

  kernel /boot/xen-3.0.gz dom0_mem=262144

  module /boot/vmlinuz-2.6-xen0 root=/dev/sda4 ro console=tty0

- The kernel line tells GRUB where to find Xen itself and what boot parameters should be passed to it (setting the domain 0 memory allocation in kilobytes and the settings for the serial port).
- The module line of the configuration describes the location of the XenLinux kernel that Xen should start and the parameters that should be passed to it. These are standard Linux parameters, identifying the root device and specifying it be initially mounted read only and instructing that console output be sent to the screen.
- When installing a new kernel, it is recommended that you do not delete existing menu options from menu.lst, as you may wish to boot your old Linux kernel in future, particularly if you have problems.

2.8.5.2 Serial Console

- Serial console access allows you to manage, monitor, and interact with your system.
- This can allow access from another nearby system via a null modem ("LapLink") cable or remotely via a serial concentrator.

- System's BIOS, bootloader (GRUB), Xen, Linux, and login access must each be individually conFig.ured for serial console access. It is not strictly necessary to have each component fully functional, but it can be quite useful.

a. Serial Console BIOS Configuration

- Enabling system serial console output neither enables nor disables serial capabilities in GRUB, Xen, or Linux, but may make remote management of your system more convenient by displaying POST and other boot messages over serial port and allowing remote BIOS configuration.
- It is advised to refer your hardware vendor's documentation for capabilities and procedures to enable BIOS serial redirection.

b. Serial Console GRUB Configuration

- Enabling GRUB serial console output neither enables nor disables Xen or Linux serial capabilities, but may made remote management of your system more convenient by displaying GRUB prompts, menus, and actions over serial port and allowing remote GRUB management.
- Adding the following two lines to your GRUB configuration file, typically either /boot/grub/menu.lst or /boot/grub/grub.conf will enable GRUB serial output.

  serial --unit=0 --speed=115200 --word=8 --parity=no --stop=1

  terminal --timeout=10 serial console

- Note that when both the serial port and the local monitor and keyboard are enabled, the text "Press any key to continue" will appear at both. Pressing a key on one device will cause GRUB to display to that device. The other device will see no output. If no key is pressed before the timeout period expires, the system will boot to the default GRUB boot entry.

2.8.5.3 Serial Console Xen Configuration

- Enabling Xen serial console output neither enables nor disables Linux kernel output or logging in to Linux over serial port. It does however allow you to monitor and log the Xen boot process via serial console and can be very useful in debugging.
- In order to conFig.ure Xen serial console output, it is necessary to add a boot option to your GRUB conFig.; e.g. kernel / boot / xen.gz dom0_mem = 131072 com1 = 115200, 8n1 console=com1,vga This conFig.ures Xen to output on COM1 at 115,200 baud, 8 data bits, no parity and 1 stop bit.
- It is also possible to conFig.ure XenLinux to share the serial console; to achieve this append "console=ttyS0" to your module line.

2.8.5.4 Serial Console Linux Configuration

- Enabling Linux serial console output at boot neither enables nor disables logging in to Linux over serial port. It does however allow you to monitor and log the Linux boot process via serial console and can be very useful in debugging.

- To enable Linux output at boot time, add the parameter console=ttyS0 (or ttyS1, ttyS2, etc.) to your kernel GRUB line. Under Xen, this might be :

  module /vmlinuz-2.6-xen0 ro root=/dev/VolGroup00/LogVol00 \

  console=ttyS0, 115200to enable output over ttyS0 at 115200 baud.

2.8.5.5 Serial Console Login Configuration

- Logging in to Linux via serial console, under Xen or otherwise, requires specifying a login prompt be started on the serial port. To permit root logins over serial console, the serial port must be added to /etc/securetty.
- To automatically start a login prompt over the serial port, add the line :

  c:2345:respawn:/sbin/mingetty ttyS0 to /etc/inittab. Run init q to force a reload of your inttab and start getty.

- To enable root logins, add ttyS0 to /etc/securetty if not already present.

2.8.5.6 TLS Libraries

- Users of the XenLinux kernel should disable Thread Local Storage (TLS) (e.g. by doing a mv /lib/tls /lib/tls.disabled) before attempting to boot a Xen- Linux kernel4.
- It is always possible to run TLS by restoring the directory to its original location (i.e. mv /lib/tls.disabled /lib/tls). The reason for this is that the current TLS implementation uses segmentation in a way that is not permissible under Xen. If TLS is not disabled, an emulation mode is used within Xen which reduces performance substantially. To ensure full performance you should install a 'Xen-friendly' (nosegneg) version of the library.

2.8.6 Booting Xen

- It should now be possible to restart the system and use Xen. Reboot and choose the new Xen option when the Grub screen appears.
- It should look much like a conventional Linux boot. The first portion of the output comes from Xen itself, supplying low level information about itself and the underlying hardware. The last portion of the output comes from XenLinux.
- You may see some error messages during the XenLinux boot. These are not necessarily anything to worry about—they may result from kernel configuration differences between your XenLinux kernel and the one you usually use.
- When the boot completes, you should be able to log into your system as usual. If you are unable to log in, you should still be able to reboot with your normal Linux kernel by selecting it at the GRUB prompt.
- Booting the system into Xen will bring you up into the privileged management domain, Domain0. At that point you are ready to create guest domains and "boot" them using the xm create command.
- The first step in creating a new domain is to prepare a root filevsystem for it to boot. Typically, this might be stored in a normal partition, an LVM or other volume manager partition, a disk file or on an NFS server.

- A simple way to do this is simply to boot from your standard OS install CD and install the distribution into another partition on your hard drive.
- To start the xend control daemon, type

  # xend start

- Once the daemon is running, you can use the xm tool to monitor and maintain the domains running on your system.

2.8.7 Booting Guest Domains

2.8.7.1 Creating a Domain Configuration File

- Before you can start an additional domain, you must create a configuration file.
- Two example files are provided here which you can use as a starting point :

  /etc/xen/xmexample1 is a simple template configuration file for describing a single VM.

  /etc/xen/xmexample2 file is a template description that is intended to be reused for multiple virtual machines.

  Setting the value of the vmid variable on the xm command line fills in parts of this template.

- Copy one of these files and edit it as appropriate. Typical values you may wish to edit include :

  kernel

  Set this to the path of the kernel you compiled for use with Xen

  (e.g. kernel ="/boot/vmlinuz-2.6-xenU").

  memory

  Set this to the size of the domain's memory in megabytes (e.g. memory = 64).

  disk

  Set the first entry in this list to calculate the offset of the domain's root partition, based on the domain ID. Set the second to the location of /usr if you are sharing it between domains (e.g. disk = ['phy:your hard drive%d,sda1,w' % (base partition number + vmid), 'phy:your usr partition,sda6,r'].

  dhcp

  Uncomment the dhcp variable, so that the domain will receive its IP address from a DHCP server (e.g. dhcp="dhcp").

- You may also want to edit the **vif** variable in order to choose the MAC address of the virtual ethernet interface yourself. For example: vif = ['mac=00:16:3E:F6:BB:B3'] If you do not set this variable, xend will automatically generate a random MAC address from the range 00:16:3E:xx:xx:xx, assigned by IEEE to XenSource as an OUI (organizationally unique identifier). XenSource Inc. gives permission for anyone to use addresses randomly allocated from this range for use by their Xen domains.

2.8.7.2 Booting the Guest Domain

- The xm tool provides a variety of commands for managing domains. Use the create command to start new domains. Assuming you've created a configuration file myvmconf based around /etc/xen/xmexample2, to start a domain with virtual machine ID 1 you should type :

  # xm create -c myvmconf vmid=1

- The -c switch causes xm to turn into the domain's console after creation. The vmid=1 sets the vmid variable used in the myvmconf file.

- Now you should be able to see the console boot messages from the new domain appearing in the terminal in which you typed the command, culminating in a login prompt.

2.8.7.3 Starting / Stopping Domains Automatically

- It is possible to have certain domains start automatically at boot time and to have dom0 wait for all running domains to shutdown before it shuts down the system.

- To specify a domain is to start at boot-time, place its configuration file under /etc/xen/auto/.

- You can then enable it in the appropriate way for your distribution.

- For instance, on Red Hat :

  # chkconFig. --add xendomains

- By default, this will start the boot-time domains in runlevels 3, 4 and 5. You can also use the service command to run this script manually,

  e.g : # service xendomains start- Starts all the domains with conFig. files under / etc / xen / auto/.

- # service xendomains stop - Shuts down all running Xen domains.

2.8.8 Domain Management Tools

2.8.8.1 Xend

- The Xend node control daemon performs system management functions related to virtual machines. It forms a central point of control of virtualized resources, and must be running in order to start and manage virtual machines.

- Xend must be run as root because it needs access to privileged system management functions. An initialization script named /etc/init.d/xend is provided to start Xend at boot time.

- Use the tool appropriate (i.e. chkconFig.) for your Linux distribution to specify the run levels at which this script should be executed, or manually create symbolic links in the correct run level directories.

- Xend can be started on the command line as well, and supports the following set of parameters :

  # xend start start xend, if not already running

  # xend stop stop xend if already running

  # xend restart restart xend if running, otherwise start it

  # xend status indicates xend status by its return code

  A SysV init script called xend is provided to start xend at boot time make install installs this script in /etc/init.d. To enable it, you have to make symbolic links in the appropriate run level directories or use the chkconFig. tool, where available. Refer Fig. 2.27.

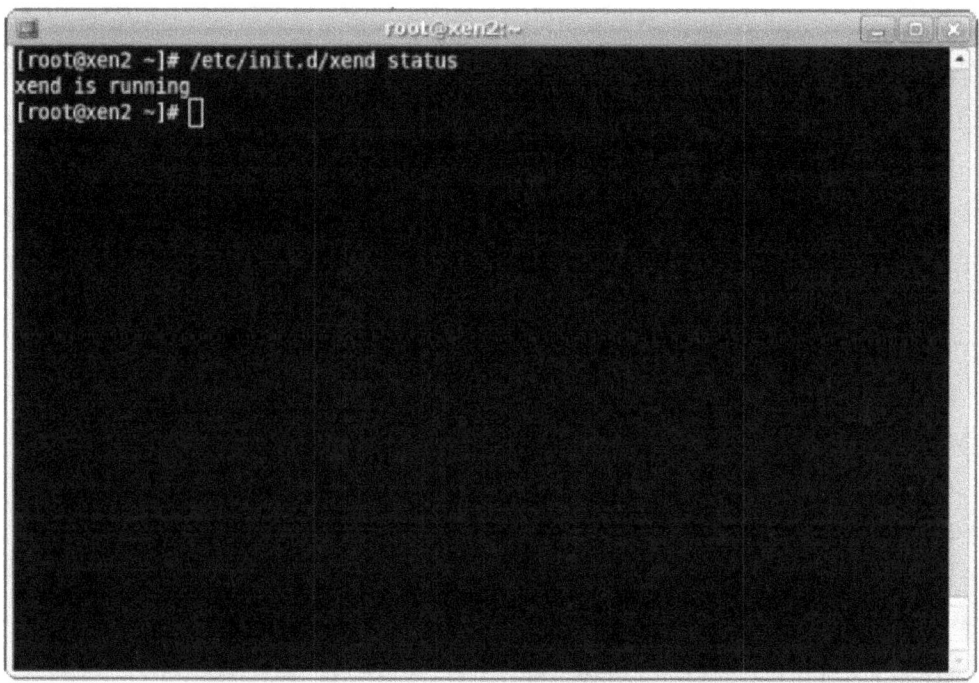

Fig. 2.27 : Status Message Showing Xend is Running

- Once xend is running, administration can be done using the xm tool.
- As xend runs, events will be logged to /var/log/xen/xend.log and (less frequently) to /var/log/xen/xend-debug.log. These, along with the standard syslog files, are useful when troubleshooting problems.

2.8.8.2 ConFig.uring Xend

- Xend is written in Python. At startup, it reads its configuration information from the file /etc/xen/xend-conFig.sxp.
- The Xen installation places an example xend-conFig.sxp file in the /etc/xen subdirectory which should work for most installations.
- Some of the most important parameters are discussed below.

- An HTTP interface and a Unix domain socket API are available to communicate with Xend. This allows remote users to pass commands to the daemon. By default, Xend does not start an HTTP server. It does start a Unix domain socket management server, as the low level utility xm requires it.

- For support of cross-machine migration, Xend can start a relocation server. This support is not enabled by default for security reasons.

- Here important point to note that xend configuration file modifies the defaults and starts up Xend as an HTTP server as well as a relocation server.

- From the file :

  #(xend-http-server no)

  (xend-http-server yes)

  #(xend-unix-server yes)

  #(xend-relocation-server no)

  (xend-relocation-server yes)

  Comment or uncomment lines in that file to disable or enable features that you require.

  Connections from remote hosts are disabled by default :

  # Address xend should listen on for HTTP connections.

  # Specifying 'localhost' prevents remote connections.

  # Specifying the empty string " (the default) allows all connections.

  #(xend-address ")

  (xend-address localhost)

- It is recommended that if migration support is not needed, the xend-relocation-server parameter value be changed to "no".

2.8.8.3 Xm

- The xm tool is the primary tool for managing Xen from the console. The general format of an xm command line is :

  # xm command [switches] [arguments] [variables]

- The available switches and arguments are dependent on the command chosen. The variables may be set using declarations of the form variable=value and command line declarations override any of the values in the configuration file being used, including the standard variables described above and any custom variables (for instance, the xmdefconFig. file uses a vmid variable).

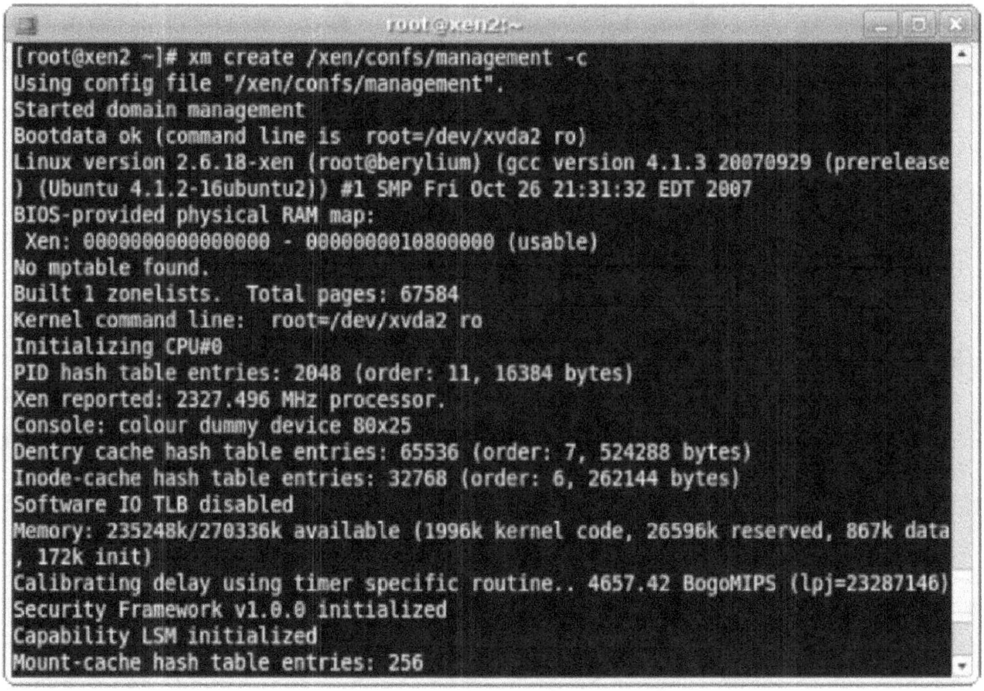

Fig. 2.28 : Xm Create Command

2.8.8.4 Basic Management Commands

- One useful command is # xm list which lists all domains running in rows of the following format :

  name domid memory vcpus state cputime

- The meaning of each field is as follows :

  name - The descriptive name of the virtual machine.

  domid - The number of the domain ID this virtual machine is running in.

  memory - Memory size in megabytes.

  vcpus - The number of virtual CPUs this domain has.

  state - Domain state consists of 5 fields :

  r - running

  b - blocked

  p - paused

  s - shutdown

  c - crashed

  cputime - How much CPU time (in seconds) the domain has used so far. Refer Fig. 2.29.

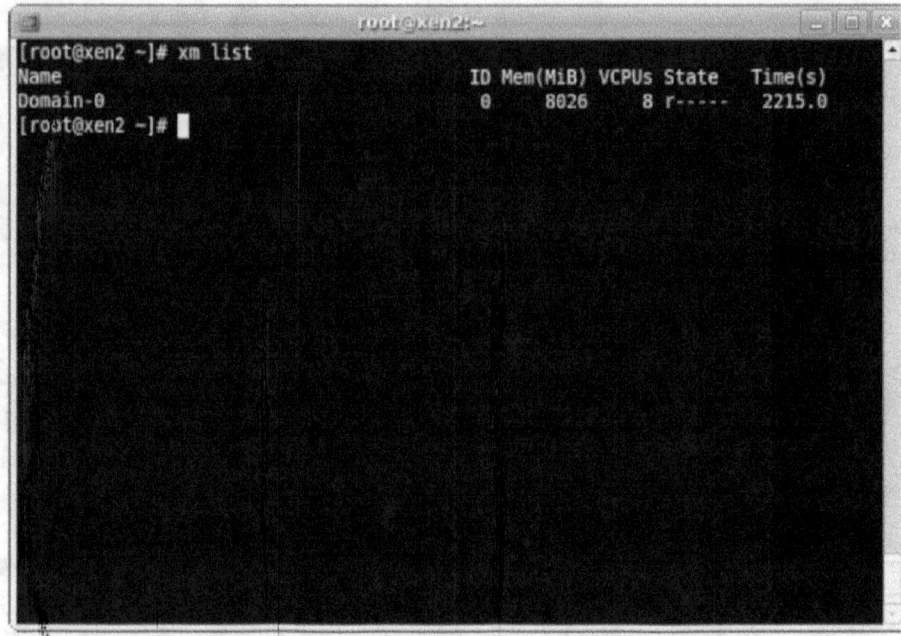

Fig. 2.29 : Xm List On A Machine With No Guest Running

- The xm list command also supports a long output format when the - 1 switch is used. This outputs the full details of the running domains in xend's SXP configuration format. Refer Fig. 2.30.

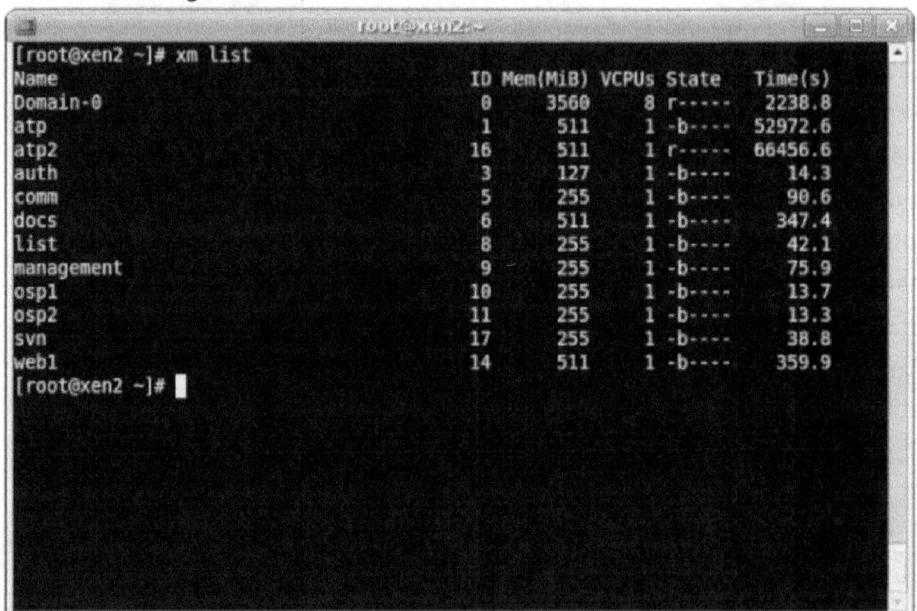

Fig. 2.30 : Xm List Showing Several Vms Running

- If you want to know how long your domains have been running for, then you can use the # xm uptime command.
- You can get access to the console of a particular domain using the # xm console command (e.g. # xm console myVM).

2.8.8.5 Domain Scheduling Management Commands

- The credit CPU scheduler automatically load balances guest VCPUs across all available physical CPUs on an SMP host. The user need not manually pin VCPUs to load balance the system. However, user can restrict which CPUs a particular VCPU may run on using the xm vcpu-pin command.
- Each guest domain is assigned a weight and a cap. A domain with a weight of 512 will get twice as much CPU as a domain with a weight of 256 on a contended host. Legal weights range from 1 to 65535 and the default is 256.
- The cap optionally fixes the maximum amount of CPU a guest will be able to consume, even if the host system has idle CPU cycles. The cap is expressed in percentage of one physical CPU : 100 is 1 physical CPU, 50 is half a CPU, 400 is 4 CPUs and so on. The default, 0, means there is no upper cap.
- When you are running with the credit scheduler, you can check and modify your domain's weights and caps using the xm sched-credit command :
  xm sched-credit -d <domain> lists weight and cap.
  xm sched-credit -d <domain> -w <weight> sets the weight.
  xm sched-credit -d <domain> -c <cap> sets the cap.

2.9 VIRTUAL MACHINE BOOTING AND CONFIGURATION

- Virtual machine configuration is the arrangement of resources assigned to a virtual machine. The resources allocated to a virtual machine (VM) typically include allocated processors, memory, disks, network adapters and the user interface.
- Before you can use virtualization, the virtualization packages must be installed on your computer. Virtualization packages can be installed either during the host installation sequence or after host installation using Subscription Manager.
- Many users install Virtualization Workstation on a dual-boot or multiple-boot computer so they can run one or more of the existing operating systems in a virtual machine. Sometimes you may want to use the existing installation of an operating system rather than reinstall it in a virtual machine.
- To support such installation virtual machine booting makes it possible for you to use a physical IDE disk or partition, also known as a raw disk, inside a virtual machine.
- You may sometimes want to run an operating system inside a virtual machine and at other times want to run that same installation of the operating system by booting the

host computer directly into that operating system. If you want to use this approach, you must be aware of some special considerations.

- The issues arise because the virtual hardware that the operating system sees when it is running in a virtual machine is different from the physical hardware it sees when it is running directly on the host computer. It is as if you were removing the boot drive from one physical computer and running the operating system installed there in a second computer with a different motherboard, video card and other peripherals - then moving it back and forth between the two systems.

- The general approach for resolving these issues is to set up platforms for each of the two operating environments - the virtual machine and the physical computer. You can then choose the appropriate platform when you start the operating system. On some hardware, however, booting a previously installed operating system within a virtual machine may not work.

- Virtual machine uses description files to control access to each raw IDE device on the system. These description files contain access privilege information that controls a virtual machine's access to certain partitions on the disks. This mechanism prevents users from accidentally running the host operating system again as a guest or running a guest operating system that the virtual machine was not conFig.ured to use. The description file also prevents accidental corruption of raw disk partitions by badly behaved operating systems or applications.

- If a boot manager is installed on the computer system, the boot manager runs inside the virtual machine and presents you with the choice of guest operating systems to run. You must manually choose the guest operating system that this configuration was intended to run.

- If an operating system is installed directly into a virtual machine, the operating system properly detects all the virtual devices by scanning the hardware. However, if an operating system is already installed on the physical computer (for example, in a dual-boot configuration), the operating system already is conFig.ured to use the physical hardware devices. In order to boot such a preinstalled operating system in a virtual machine, you need to create separate hardware profiles in order to simplify the boot process.

2.9.1 Creating Up Hardware Profiles in Virtual Machines

- Certain operating systems use hardware profiles to load the appropriate drivers for a given set of hardware devices. If you have a dual-boot system and want to use a virtual machine to boot a previously installed operating system from an existing partition, you must set up "physical" and "virtual" hardware profiles.

- Each virtual machine provides a platform that consists of the following set of virtual devices :

- Virtual DVD/CD-ROM

- Virtual hard disk drives

- Standard PCI graphics adapter

- Standard floppy disk drive

- PCI Bus Master IDE controller

  (includes primary and secondary IDE controllers)

- BusLogic BT-958 compatible SCSI host adapter

- Standard 101/102-key keyboard

- Mouse

- Ethernet adapter

- Serial ports (COM1-COM4)

- Parallel ports (LPT1-LPT2)

- Two-port USB hub

- Sound card compatible with the Sound Blaster AudioPCI

- This set of virtual devices is different from the set of physical hardware devices on the host computer and is independent of the underlying hardware with a few exceptions (the processor itself is such an exception).

- This feature provides a stable platform and allows operating system images installed within a virtual machine to be migrated to other physical machines, regardless of the configuration of the physical machine.

QUESTIONS

1. Explain functionalities provided by Virtualization.

2. Explain difference between multitasking, multithreading and virtualization.

3. Explain XEN Architecture with suitable diagram.

4. Write short note on :

   (a) Virtual machines

   (b) Hypervisor

   (c) Virtual machine monitor

5. Why virtual servers are used ? State its advantages and disadvantages ?

6. State types of virtualization and explain any three of them.

7. Explain Need, Advantages and Limitations of virtualization.

8. What is XEN ? What are the components of XEN Environment ?

9. Explain software and hardware techniques for X86 virtualization.

MONITORING AND MANAGEMENT

3.1 AN ARCHITECTURE FOR FEDERATED CLOUD COMPUTING

(Aug. 16)

- Utility computing, a concept envisioned back in the 1960s, is finally becoming a reality. Just as we can power a variety of devices, ranging from a simple light bulb to complex machinery, by plugging them into the wall, today we can satisfy, by connecting to the Internet, many of our computing needs, ranging from full pledge productivity applications to raw compute power in the form of virtual machines.
- Cloud computing, in all its different forms, is rapidly gaining momentum as an alternative to traditional IT, and the reasons for this are clear: In principle, it allows individuals and companies to fulfil all their IT needs with minimal investment and controlled expenses (both capital and operational).
- Cloud computing enables companies and individuals to lease resources on-demand from a virtually unlimited pool. The "pay as you go" billing model applies charges for the actually used resources per unit time.
- This way, a business can optimize its IT investment and improve availability and scalability.
- While cloud computing holds a lot of promise for enterprise computing, there are a number of inherent deficiencies in current offerings such as:

Inherently Limited Scalability of Single-Provider Clouds

- Although most infrastructure cloud providers today claim infinite scalability, in reality it is reasonable to assume that even the largest players may start facing scalability problems as cloud computing usage rate increases.
- In the long term, scalability problems may be expected to worsen as cloud providers serve an increasing number of on-line services, each accessed by massive amounts of global users at all times.

Lack of Interoperability Among Cloud Providers

- Contemporary cloud technologies have not been designed with interoperability in mind. This results in an inability to scale through business partnerships across clouds providers.
- In addition, it prevents small and medium cloud infrastructure providers from entering the cloud provisioning market. Overall, this stifles competition and locks consumers to a single vendor.

No Built-In Business Service Management Support

- Business Service Management (BSM) is a management strategy that allows businesses to align their IT management with their high-level business goals.

- The key aspect of BSM is service-level agreement (SLA) management.
- Current cloud computing solutions are not designed to support the BSM practices that are well established in the daily management of the enterprise IT departments. As a result, enterprises looking at transforming their IT operations to cloud-based technologies face a non-incremental and potentially disruptive step.

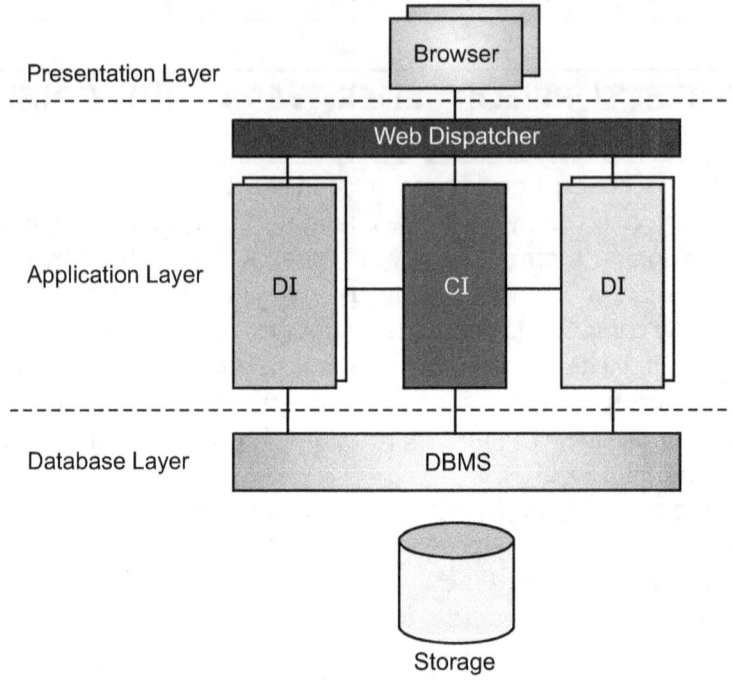

Fig. 3.1 : An Architecture for Federated Cloud Computing

The components can be arranged in a variety of configurations, from a minimal configuration where all components run on a single machine, to larger ones where there are several DIs, each running on a separate machine, and a separate machine with the CI and the DBMS.

3.1.1 Federation   (Nov. 16, May 17)

- All cloud computing providers, regardless of how big they are, have a finite capacity. To grow beyond this capacity, cloud computing providers should be able to form federations of providers such that they can collaborate and share their resources.
- The need for federation-capable cloud computing offerings is also derived from the industry trend of adopting the cloud computing paradigm internally within companies to create private clouds and then being able to extend these clouds with resources leased on-demand from public clouds.
- Any federation of cloud computing providers should allow virtual application to be deployed across federated sites. Furthermore, virtual applications need to be completely location free and allowed to migrate in part or as a whole between sites.
- At the same time, the security privacy and independence of the federation members must be maintained to allow competing providers to federate.

3.1.2 Independence   (Nov. 16, May 17)

- Just as in other utilities, where we get service without knowing the internals of the utility provider and with standard equipment not specific to any provider (e.g., telephones), for cloud computing services to really fulfil the computing as a utility vision, we need to offer cloud computing users full independence.

- Users should be able to use the services of the cloud without relying on any provider-specific tool, and cloud computing providers should be able to manage their infrastructure without exposing internal details to their customers or partners.

- As a consequence of the independence principle, all cloud services need to be encapsulated and generalized such that users will be able to acquire equivalent virtual resources at different providers.

3.1.3 Isolation

- Cloud computing services are, by definition, hosted by a provider that will simultaneously host applications from many different users. For these users to move their computing into the cloud, they need warranties from the cloud computing provider that their stuff is completely isolated from others.

- Users must be ensured that their resources cannot be accessed by others sharing the same cloud and that adequate performance isolation is in place to ensure that no other user may possess the power to directly affect the service granted to their application.

3.1.4 Elasticity   (Nov. 16, May 17)

- One of the main advantages of cloud computing is the capability to provide, or release, resources on-demand. These "elasticity" capabilities should be enacted automatically by cloud computing providers to meet demand variations, just as electrical companies are able (under normal operational circumstances) to automatically deal with variances in electricity consumption levels. Clearly the behaviour and limits of automatic growth and shrinking should be driven by contracts and rules agreed on between cloud computing providers and consumers.

- The ability of users to grow their applications when facing an increase of real-life demand need to be complemented by the ability to scale.

- Cloud computing services as offered by a federation of infrastructure providers is expected to offer any user application of any size the ability to quickly scale up its application by unrestricted magnitude and approach Internet scale.

- At the same time, user applications should be allowed to scale down facing decreasing demand. Such scalability although depended on the internals of the user application is prime driver for cloud computing because it help users to better match expenses with gain.

3.1.5 Trust

- Probably the most critical issue to address before cloud computing can become the preferred computing paradigm is that of establishing trust. Mechanisms to build and maintain trust between cloud computing consumers and cloud computing providers, as well as between cloud computing providers among themselves, are essential for the success of any cloud computing offering.

3.2 A MODEL FOR FEDERATED CLOUD COMPUTING   (Aug. 16)

- In our model for federated cloud computing we identify two major types of actors:
- Service Providers (SPs) are the entities that need computational resources to offer some service.
- However, SPs do not own these resources; instead, they lease them from Infrastructure Providers (IPs), which provide them with a seemingly infinite pool of computational, network, and storage resources.
- A Service Application is a set of software components that work collectively to achieve a common goal. Each component of such service applications executes in a dedicated VEE. SPs deploy service applications in the cloud by providing to an IP, known as the primary site, with a Service Manifestn that is, a document that defines the structure of the application as well as the contract and SLA between the SP and the IP.
- To create the illusion of an infinite pool of resources, IPs shared their unused capacity with each other to create a federation cloud. A Framework Agreement is document that defines the contract between two IPs that is, it states the terms and conditions under which one IP can use resources from another IP.
- Within each IP, optimal resource utilization is achieved by partitioning physical resources, through a virtualization layer, into Virtual Execution Environments (VEEs) fully isolated runtime environments that abstract away the physical characteristics of the resource and enable sharing.
- We refer to the virtualized computational resources, alongside the virtualization layer and all the management enablement components, as the Virtual Execution Environment Host (VEEH).
- With these concepts in mind, we can proceed to define a reference architecture for federated cloud computing. The design and implementation of such architecture are the main goals of the RESERVOIR European research project. The RESERVOIR architecture, shown in Fig. 3.2, identifies the major functional components needed within an IP to fully support the cloud computing paradigm. The rationale behind this particular layering is to keep a clear separation of concerns and responsibilities and to hide low-level infrastructure details and decisions from high-level management and service providers.

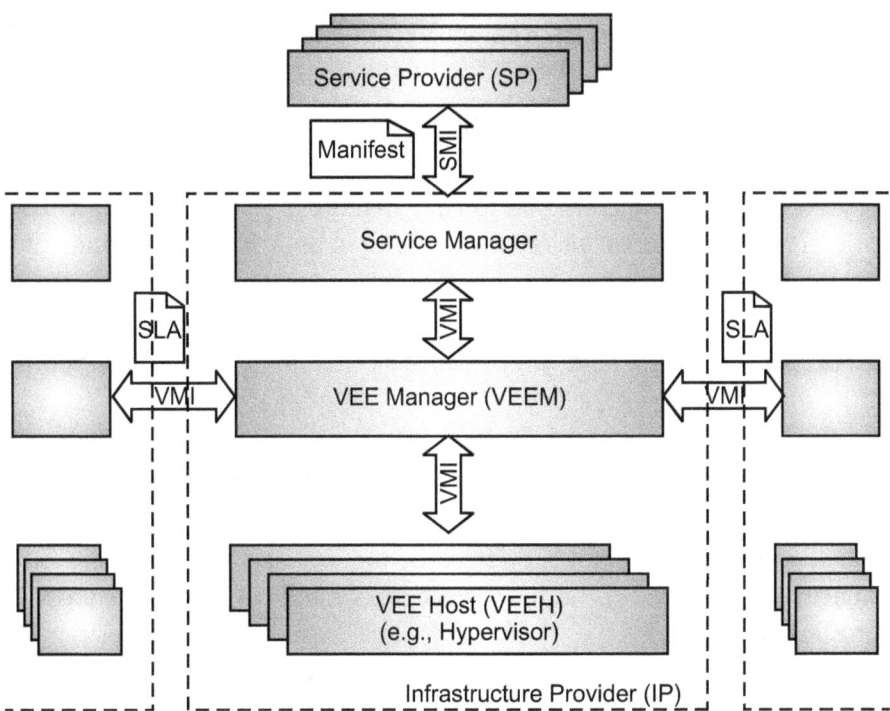

Fig. 3.2 : A model for Federated Cloud Computing

The Service Manager is the only component within an IP that interacts with SPs. It receives Service Manifests, negotiates pricing, and handles billing. Its two most complex tasks are

(1) Deploying and provisioning VEEs based on the Service Manifest and

(2) Monitoring and enforcing SLA compliance by throttling a service application's capacity.

- The Virtual Execution Environment Manager (VEEM) is responsible for the optimal placement of VEEs into VEE Hosts subject to constraints determined by the Service Manager.

- The continuous optimization process is driven by a site-specific programmable utility function.

- The VEEM is free to place and move VEEs anywhere, even on the remote sites (subject to overall cross-site agreements), as long as the placement satisfies the constraints. Thus, in addition to serving local requests (from the local Service Manager), VEEM is responsible for the federation of remote sites.

- The Virtual Execution Environment Host (VEEH) is responsible for the basic control and monitoring of VEEs and their resources (e.g., creating a VEE, allocating additional resources to a VEE, monitoring a VEE, migrating a VEE, creating a virtual network and storage pool, etc.).

- Given that VEEs belonging to the same application may be placed on multiple VEEHs and even extend beyond the boundaries of a site, VEEHs must support isolated virtual networks that span VEEHs and sites.

- Moreover, VEEHs must support transparent VEE migration to any compatible VEEH within the federated cloud, regardless of site location or network and storage configurations.

3.2.1 Features of Federation Types   (Nov. 16)

- Federations of clouds may be constructed in various ways, with disparate feature sets offered by the underlying implementation architecture. This section is devoted to present these differentiating features. Using these features as a base, a number of federation scenarios are defined, comprised of subsets of this feature set.

- The first feature to consider is the framework agreement support: Framework agreements, as defined in the previous section, may either be supported by the architecture or not.

- If framework agreements are not supported, this implies that federation may only be carried out in a more ad hoc opportunistic manner. Another feature is the opportunistic placement support.

- If framework agreements are not supported by the architecture, or if there is not enough spare capacity even including the framework agreements, a site may choose to perform opportunistic placement.

- It is a process where remote sites are queried on-demand as the need for additional resources arises, and the local site requests a certain SLA-governed capacity for a given cost from the remote sites.

- One interesting feature to take into account is the advance resource reservation support. This feature may be used both when there is an existing framework agreement and when opportunistic placement has been performed. Both types of advance reservations are only valid for a certain time, since they impact the utilization of resources at a site. Because of this impact, they should be billed as actual usage during the active time interval.

The ability to migrate machines across sites defines the federated migration support.There are two types of migration: cold and hot (or live). In cold migration, the VEE is suspended and experiences a certain amount of downtime while it is being transferred. Most modern operating systems have support for being suspended, which includes saving all RAM contents to disk and later restoring the runtime state to its prior state. Hot or live migration does not allow for system downtime, and it works by transferring the runtime state while the VEE is still running.

Focusing on networks, there can be cross-site virtual network support: VEEs belonging to a service are potentially connected to virtual networks, should this be requested by the SP. Ideally, these virtual networks will span across sites. However, this requires substantial effort and advanced features of the underlying architecture. In the same line, the federation can offer public IP addresses retention post cross-site migration.With fully virtualized networks, this may be a directly supported feature; but even if virtualized networks are not available, it may still be possible to maintain public IP addresses by manipulating routing information.

Information disclosure within the federationhas also to be taken into account. The sites in the federation may provide information to different degrees (for instance, the information exchange between sites may be larger within the same administrative domain than outside it). Information regarding deployed VEEs will be primarily via the monitoring system, whereas some information may also potentially be exposed via the VMI as response to a VEE deployment request.

The last identified feature useful to define scenario is the VMI operation support: Depending on the requirements of the federation scenario, only a subset of the VMI operations may be made available. Which operations are required may be related to the amount of information that is exposed by the remote sites; access to more information may also increase the possibility and need to manipulate the deployed VEEs.

3.3 SLA MANAGEMENT IN CLOUD COMPUTING   (Aug. 16)

- Cloud computing is essentially changing the way services are built, provided and consumed. As a paradigm building on a set of combined technologies, it enables service provision through the commoditization of IT assets and on-demand usage patterns. Now a days, cloud computing refers to a computing paradigm whose foundation is the delivery of services and ICT assets, often denoted as XaaS (Everything as a Service).

- The term refers to an increased number of cloud-based resources and services provided over the Internet, with the most common examples, following the SPI model, Software (SaaS), Platform (PaaS) and Infrastructure (IaaS) as a service.

- As the aforementioned cloud service model matures and becomes ubiquitous, it raises the possibility of improving the way services are provisioned and managed, thus allowing providers to address the (diverse) needs of consumers.

- In this context, Service Level Agreements (SLAs) emerge as a key aspect, since they serve as the foundation for the expected quality level of the service between the consumer and the provider. Nevertheless, the diversity of the proposed SLAs by providers (with marginal overlaps), has led to multiple different definitions of cloud SLAs.

- Furthermore, misconceptions exist on what is (if there is) the difference between SLAs and contract, what is the borderline, what are the terms included in each one of these documents and if and how are these linked. We provide the following definitions according to ITIL.

- A Service Level Agreement (SLA) is a formal, negotiated document that defines (or attempts to define) in quantitative (and perhaps qualitative) terms the service being offered to a Customer. Any metrics included in a SLA should be capable of being measured on a regular basis and the SLA should record by whom.

- A Contract is a legally binding agreement between two or more parties. Contracts are subject to specific legal interpretations. An alternative definition going a bit away from the pure process oriented ITIL one has been provided by the TM Forum: "A Service Level Agreement (SLA) is a formal negotiated agreement between two parties.

- It is a contract that exists between the Service Provider (SP) and the Customer.
- It is designed to create a common understanding about Quality of Service (QoS), priorities, responsibilities, etc. SLAs can cover many aspects of the relationship between the Customer and the SP, such as performance of services, customer care, billing, service provisioning, etc.
- However, although a SLA can cover such aspects, agreement on the level of service is the primary purpose of a SLA".

3.3.1 Scope and Purpose

- The purpose of this document is to serve as a starting point for the exploitation of research results stemming from European and National projects. To this end, the report identifies and delivers short descriptions of the main SLA-related contribution of each project. What is more, a set of recommendations is provided to address the requirements of different entities in the cloud ecosystem.
- The recommendations aim at facilitating wider adoption of cloud solutions and enable providers to offer a wider set of services through approaches that enable the provision of QoS guarantees (as required, for example : in future internet and mission critical applications) and facilitate efficient collaborations amongst providers. The content regarding the research outcomes has been compiled following a working group meeting that was organized and hosted by the EC in Brussels, 27 May 2013.
- As consumers move towards adopting such a Service-Oriented Architecture, the quality and reliability of the services become important aspects. However the demands of the service consumers vary significantly.
- It is not possible to fulfill all consumer expectations from the service provider perspective and hence a balance needs to be made via a negotiation process.
- At the end of the negotiation process, provider and consumer commit to an agreement. In SOA terms, this agreement is referred to as a SLA.
- This SLA serves as the foundation for the expected level of service between the consumer and the provider.
- The QoS attributes that are generally part of an SLA (such as response time and throughput) however change constantly and to enforce the agreement, these parameters need to be closely monitored.

  Due to the complex nature of consumer demands, a simple "measure and trigger" process may not work for SLA enforcement.
- Four different types of monitoring demands made by consumers are mentioned. One scenario is a consumer demands the data exposed by a service provider without further refinement such as transaction count, which is a raw metric. Second scenario is consumer requests that collected data should put into meaningful context.
- This scenario creates the requirement for a process which collects data from different sources and applies suitable algorithms for calculating meaningful results. Such metrics

include statistical measures such as average or standard deviation that need to be computed from a raw set of numbers.

- The third scenario is the consumer requests certain customized data to be collected. In the fourth scenario the consumer even specifies the way how data should be collected. Both the latter mentioned scenarios imply an advanced consumer who would have a knowledge of the inner workings of a provider and somewhat rare in practice. Other issues such as trust also need to be considered during SLA enforcement. For example : consumers may not completely trust the certain measurements provided solely by a service provider and regularly employ third party mediators.

- These mediators are responsible for measuring the critical service parameters and reporting violations of the agreement from either party.

- We believe the upcoming trend of cloud computing is an extension of the SOA paradigm and the above mentioned issue of striking a balance applies to the cloud as well. The process of managing the provider-consumer agreements in computing clouds closely resemble the generic provider-consumer agreement process we mentioned above. Hence we propose an architecture for managing cloud consumer and provider SLAs, based on the WSLA specification. We highlight two reasons to justify the importance of this research.

1. The most prominent cloud provider, Amazon EC2, puts the burden of proving SLA violations on the consumer. i.e. the consumer should take steps to enforce the SLA . Having a formalized SLA enables the setup of the enforcement process to be automated and hence relieves consumers from that burden.

2. We believe the work that significantly intersects with ours is where WSLA has been used as a base for grid service monitoring. However computing grids are very different from computing clouds in terms of
   - Business model,
   - Architecture,
   - Resource management,
   - Programming model,
   - Application model and
   - Security model.

- Hence we believe applying WSLA to the cloud context would be a significantly different effort from the previous work. Some of the important aspects we discovered are detailed. To the best of our knowledge this is the first use of WSLA in the context of cloud computing.

3.3.2 SLA Lifecycle Metamodel   (Aug. 16)

This section introduces a metamodel that captures the main phases, structures, processes and entities interactions in the SLA lifecycle. The goal of each phase, the participating actors and their role, the potential dependencies as well as the outcomes of each phase are described as follows.

- **Service Use**

Service use reflects the usage of the cloud service by a service customer. As already described the service customer may not be the end user. However, the aim of this phase is to obtain the service and thus an SLA may be signed between the customer and the service provider. The SLA includes high-level attributes related to the service / application.

- **Service Modelling**

The service modelling process aims at providing additional information with respect to the service that will be deployed in a cloud infrastructure. As the only actor having the required knowledge for the service, the developer is using a set of frameworks in order to design, model and analyse the service. Service design may be extended to include potential dependencies between service components of an application (in the case of a composite service), elasticity rules for the application or / and performance and behaviour hints that are required to guarantee the offered level of quality (e.g. increasing number of users by a factor of 1000 in a multi-tier web application requires the usage of Three times the deployed application servers and two replicas of the deployed database). The outcome of the process is captured in an artefact / document (usually in a structured XML format), which includes all the parameters affecting the service execution, usage and delivery. This artefact is named in some cases Blueprint or Manifest.

- **SLA Template Definition**

The SLA template definition process aims at generating and refining the SLA templates. All providers (i.e. service, platform and infrastructure) analyse their business objectives through a business modelling process (that may use business and pricing models simulation frameworks) in order to optimize their offerings. Furthermore, the service provider uses as a basis the blueprint / manifest of the service and refines the SLA templates (in terms of attributes values) following business modelling outcomes, while the service provider may also include additional attributes in the SLA templates reflecting for example the use of licenses. Thus, an SLA template may include the outcomes of one or more service blueprints / manifests. The outcome of this phase is an SLA template that will be published by the providers in order to be negotiated and signed by the participating entities.

- **SLA Instantiation and Management**

The goal of this phase is to instantiate an SLA (i.e. electronically signed agreement). The main process refers to the SLA negotiation, which may be extended with mechanisms for dynamic negotiation between different entities as well as with mechanisms for automatic renegotiation during runtime. Moreover, discovery is used to identify providers for specific services (based on the service parameters captured in the service blueprint / manifest). Mapping / translation refers to a process of analysing the high-level application-related attributes and mapping them to low-level resource parameters (e.g. transmission of 24 frames per second maps to network links of 13MB/s). Besides such functional parameters, nonfunctional parameters (e.g. redundancy, security, etc) may also be mapped / translated. The outcome of this phase is a signed SLA between the participating entities that includes low-level (resource-related) attributes.

- **SLA Enforcement**

The SLA enforcement phase aims at ensuring that the quality parameters (agreed in signed SLAs) are retained. All providers exploit monitoring mechanisms to obtain both infrastructure and application monitoring data, while adaptable approaches focus on adjusting the monitoring time intervals or the monitoring metrics based on the collected information during runtime. Evaluation tools are exploited to analyse the monitoring data and trigger corrective actions using SLA violation detection mechanisms, some of which enable proactive violation detection.

3.3.3 Understand Roles and Responsibilities

In order for consumers to understand specific roles and responsibilities explicitly or implicitly stated in a cloud SLA, it is important that they are aware of the various actors that can potentially participate in a cloud computing environment. The National Institute of Standards and Technology (NIST) Reference Architecture identifies five unique cloud actors:

- **Cloud Consumer :** The person or organization that maintains a business relationship with, and uses service from, cloud providers.
- **Cloud Provider :** The person, organization or entity responsible for making a service available to cloud consumers.
- **Cloud Carrier :** The intermediary that provides connectivity and transport of cloud services from cloud providers to cloud consumers.
- **Cloud Broker :** An organization that manages the use, performance and delivery of cloud services, and negotiates relationships between cloud providers and cloud consumers.
- **Cloud Auditor :** A party that can conduct independent assessments of cloud services, information system operations, performance and security of the cloud implementation.

The use of the term "broker" varies significantly and should be clarified with the various stakeholders, especially in context of a cloud SLA. An entity may provide broker services and functionality, but as a legal organizational entity not be recognized as a cloud broker, For example : an entity may perform research and negotiate on behalf of a consumer, but the actual SLA and contract terms are between the cloud consumer and cloud provider. The distinction of acting "broker like" vs. being an actual "broker" will evolve as the cloud computing industry matures and terminologies become more consistent. Due to these complexities this paper does not address all the SLA considerations for cloud brokering. Consumers need to recognize the activities and responsibilities of each cloud actor that is engaged in delivering their cloud environment, and precisely define requirements and desired service levels for each actor. This paper focuses primarily on the cloud consumer/cloud provider SLA, although other SLAs may be addressed in a particular context. In some cases, the consumer/provider relationship will indirectly include additional actors.

Fig. 3.3 illustrates an environment where a cloud provider has established a SLA with two cloud carriers to establish service levels for communication and transport. In addition to cloud provider expectations, the consumer/provider SLA in this example may also include specific carrier and transport expectations. In this case, the cloud provider is also acting as a "broker" for the other two cloud carriers.

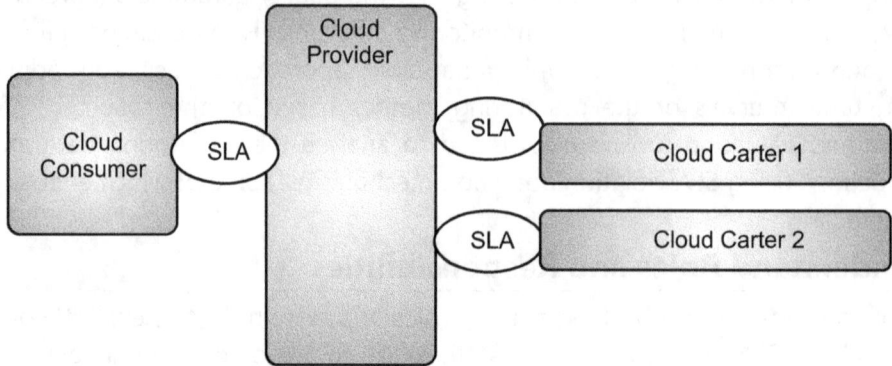

Fig. 3.3 : Indirect Relationships

Each cloud SLA will be unique based upon the consumers' requirements and the cloud ecosystem under consideration. SLAs can contain various expectations between the actors and are not limited to quantitative measures, but can include other qualitative aspects such as alignment with standards and data protection. It is strongly recommended that cloud consumers gain a solid understanding of the spectrum of SLAs that currently exist for cloud providers (and other actors as appropriate) in order to compare providers and assess trade-offs between cost and service levels.

3.4 IDENTIFY CRITICAL PERFORMANCE OBJECTIVES

- Performance goals within the context of cloud computing are directly related to efficiency and accuracy of service delivery. Performance considerations often include: availability, response time, transaction rate, processing speed, but can include many other performance and system quality perspectives.
- Consumers must decide which measures are most critical to their specific cloud environments and ensure these measures are included in their SLA.
- Performance statements that are important to the cloud consumer should be measureable and auditable, and documented in the SLA providing a comfort level to both parties.
- Performance considerations are dependent on the supported service model (IaaS, PaaS and SaaS) and the type of services provided within that model,

    For example : network, storage and computing services for IaaS.

Industry standard measures with applicable definitions should be used to improve consistency, enabling meaningful comparative and trend analysis. For instance, IEEE also has good measurement definitions and categorizations for activities such as maintenance. Other organizations and private benchmarks exist.

- The key is to always calibrate values to get an "apple to apples" comparison to an appropriate level of accuracy. To be effective, a performance metric must be clearly defined in the SLA and understood by both parties. Here are the generally accepted definitions for the two metrics of interest:

- **Availability :** Percentage of uptime for a service in a given observation period.

- **Response Time :** Elapsed time from when a service is invoked to when it is completed including delays (typically measured in milliseconds).

Cloud resources, both hardware and facilities, should also be considered when assessing critical performance objectives for cloud SLAs. Hardware includes: compute (CPU and memory), networks (routers, firewalls, switches, network links, and interfaces), storage components (hard disks), and any other physical computing infrastructure elements. Facilities include: heating, ventilation and air conditioning (HVAC), power, communications, and other aspects of the physical plant. Resources need to be clearly stated in the SLA to clarify scope, constraints and expectations for the cloud computing services of interest. To be successful, higher level business objectives and goals need to be understood such that critical resource metrics can be identified that address facility and hardware expectations. Some metrics may not be technical, but can include measures such as watts of power usage, cubic feet of network cabinets, or even revenue dollars from real estate sold. For example : one frequent objective for the IaaS service model is to reduce power usage, or perhaps reduce the footprint size of the data center.

In summary, when considering performance metrics in a cloud SLA, it is recommended that consumers:

- Understand the business level performance objectives for the cloud opportunity (for example, reduce cost and time to market per unit of software functionality).

- Identify the set of metrics that are critical to achieving and managing the business level performance objectives.

- Ensure these metrics are defined at the right level of granularity that can be monitored on a continuous basis cost effectively.

- Identify standards to provide consistency for cloud metrics in areas such as metric definitions and methods of collection.

- Analyze and leverage the metrics on an ongoing basis as a tool for influencing business decisions.

3.4.1 Evaluate Security and Privacy Requirements

- Security controls in cloud computing are, for the most part, no different than security controls in any IT environment. However, because of the cloud service models employed, the operational models, and the technologies used to enable cloud services, cloud computing may present different risks to an organization than traditional IT solutions.

- At a basic level, assets supported by the cloud fall into two general categories:

- Data

- Applications/Functions/Processes

  Information is either being moved into the cloud or applications are being executed in the cloud (from partial functions all the way up to full applications).

- A critical initial step for ensuring sufficient cloud security is establishing a classification scheme that applies throughout the enterprise, based on the criticality and sensitivity of enterprise data.

- This scheme should include details about data ownership, definition of appropriate security levels and protection controls, and a brief description of data retention and destruction requirements.

- The classification scheme should be used as the basis for applying controls such as access controls, archiving or encryption.

- When data is transferred to a cloud, the responsibility for protecting and securing the data typically remains with the collector or custodian of that data, even if in some circumstances, this responsibility may be shared with others. When it relies on a third party to host or process its data, the custodian of the data remains liable for any loss, damage, or misuse of the data. It is prudent, and may be legally required, that the data custodian and the cloud provider enter into a written (legal) agreement that clearly defines the roles, expectations of the parties, and allocates between them the many responsibilities that are attached to the data at stake.

- If privacy issues are not adequately addressed in the SLA, the cloud consumer should consider alternate means of achieving their goals including seeking a different provider, or not sending sensitive data to the cloud.

For example : If the consumer wishes to send HIPAA-covered information to the cloud, the consumer will need to find a cloud service provider that will sign a HIPAA business associate agreement or else not send that data to the cloud.

3.4.2 Identify Service Management Requirements

- The fundamental goals of any cloud computing environment are to reduce cost, improve flexibility and increase reliability of the delivery of a service. Critical to meeting these goals is a uniform, straightforward, transparent and extensible system for managing and monitoring cloud services.

- In this section we will outline some key considerations in service management when entering into a service level agreement with a cloud computing provider.

- Every computing system requires internal controls, management, automation and self-healing in order to operate in today's interconnected world, and the cloud is no different.

- Although the standards for SLA language for service management are evolving, it is of upmost importance to include provisions for the considerations outlined below in your agreements.

- **Auditing**

First and foremost in ensuring manageability of cloud services is a methodology for auditing and reviewing those services. This helps discern between providers who are fully capable of deep manageability and those who provide only a simple veneer on someone else's offerings. As stated by many an experienced manager, organizations and people do what you inspect, not what you expect.

The objective of any SLA terms in the area of auditing is multi-fold:

1. Provide you with an unbiased assessment of your ability to rely on the service provided
2. Assess the depth and effectiveness of the provider's internal systems and measures
3. Provide tools to compare quality levels with other competing providers
4. Uncover issues in your own organization's ability to interface with the provider and provide uninterrupted services.

This last objective is especially important. Many documented challenges have come not from a cloud provider's ability to service a customer, but the ability of the customer's systems to interface properly with the cloud. Therefore any audit scope should include both the provider and any internal systems exposed to the cloud to ensure a complete "envelope" of integrity.

When considering the scope of any auditing protocol, you must step beyond contract terms and conditions and ensure that you are addressing general issues of management and governance.

For example : It's insufficient to include a provision to regularly audit security and encryption keys, only to neglect addressing any internal resource allocations, scheduling, review and approval processes needed to perform the audit and address any issues stemming from the audit. Consider carefully the importance of leveraging existing methods of audit and compliance that already exist in your organization, and look to extend those to the cloud vs. creating new ones.

- **Monitoring and Reporting**

Transparency of the service level is extremely important to a successful service management protocol. While every cloud vendor offers different systems for visualizing data and its implications (web based, email based, live, reactive, portal-based), consumers should demand from any cloud SLA a minimum set of capabilities:

1. **Cloud Performance Management :** This domain focuses on the response times for systems within the cloud architecture and between the cloud and the target user systems.

2. **Load Performance :** This domain focuses on measurements and timings for when the cloud is under stress, either intentional or unintentional. As systems can perform differently when under different loads, and the interactions and dependencies of a complex cloud are often unknown in advance, it's important to visualize data both in a steady state as well as under load.

3. **Hybrid and Inter-cloud Performance :** As many clouds consist of different subsystems, often sourced from different cloud providers, it's critical to visualize data about the interactions between those hybrid cloud components.

4. **Application Performance :** This domain focuses on the applications executed from the cloud, particularly internal processing benchmarks as well as end-user experience measurement.

5. **Problem Notification :** This domain focuses on monitoring and reporting on failures and issues with the cloud system. Addressed are issues with prioritization, notification and severity level assessment.

Although the benchmarks in each of these areas are evolving, ensuring your SLA includes the ability to see, assess and react to measurements in these areas will help keep your cloud infrastructure running smoothly.

- **Metering**
- A core characteristic of many cloud services is an on-demand model, where services used are billed as they are consumed, on a time or capacity basis.
- Therefore it is important to have confidence and transparency in the metering system employed by cloud providers, as embodied in the service level agreements you build.
- At a minimum, you must ensure that metering systems employed for your cloud providers include:

1. Assurance of accurate billing, and a methodology for handing objections or challenges to any automated metered billing

2. The ability to segregate different services into different methods of billing: for example, performance testing, analytics, security scanning, backup, and virtual desktops might all be measured differently and metered separately.

3. Ability to handle taxation issues from geography to geography, and from user to user. As each country and municipality has implemented different approaches to taxation of online commerce, your provider must be able to discern between these sources of use and meter them independently.

- **Rapid Provisioning**

While auditing, monitoring, measuring and metering relate primarily to the cost savings features of the cloud, rapid provisioning is a key underlying quality of the improved flexibility that comes from the cloud. However, it's not without its own unique qualities that must translate into your service level agreements with providers:

1. Core provisioning speed. As part of a cloud SLA, there should be baseline expectations of the speed of deployment of new systems, new data, new users, new desktops or any function that's core to the service provided by the cloud vendor.

2. Customization. It's unusual that any templated method of rapid provisioning can be used "out of the box" without configuration and customization. Without careful management of the expectations and contractual levels for this function, any savings gained by

automated rapid provisioning can evaporate in the face of delays in customizations post-deployment.

3. Testing. Important to any strong SLA are provisions for testing automated deployment and scaling prior to need. This is particularly acute in areas where provisioning is employed in disaster recovery or backup situations.

4. Demand Flexibility. It does no good to have a technical solution to rapid provisioning if the system is incapable of dynamic de-provisioning to match downturns in demand.

This is not an exhaustive list of considerations, only the basic requirements of any contractual definition of rapid provisioning. Each organization will need to add their own particular additional topics, particularly for different industries or IT applications running in the cloud.

- **Resource Change**
- Change is an inevitable part of any IT system, and the cloud is no different. Fortunately, there is little that is special about the cloud in regards to considerations for change management.
- Procedures for requesting, reviewing, testing, and acceptance of changes differ little from those already in use with other IT subcontractor contracts and outsource agreements.
- The only unique issue is the sensitivity that many have to changes that have potentially radical implications, such as the cloud. In this case, extra care should be taken to manage the process carefully.

- **Upgrade to Existing Services**

A subset of change management is upgrades or improvements in existing contracted services, such as when an upgrade or patch is needed, or when a new version of an underlying management system or SaaS application is rolled out. In these cases, it's important to outline in your cloud SLA a set of basic steps for these inevitable needs.

1. Responsibility to Develop Requested Changes. There should be a clearly defined responsibility set for which party is in the lead for different types of upgrades.

For example : If the upgrade is dependent on many subsystems or people internal to an organization, not in the cloud, it might be advisable to center the responsibilities on the contracting organization vs. the cloud provider. On the other hand, if the majority of the upgrade happens with cloud-provider personnel within the cloud space, it's likely the provider would assume primary responsibility.

2. Process for Identifying a Timeline to Develop, Test and Implement the Change. There must be a clearly defined "chain of command" and project plan for all changes made to the cloud environment, properly resourced and timed to ensure reasonable contingencies and problem resolution. Here too, little is different regarding a cloud solution vs. a traditional IT solution, with the exception of the increased anxiety and scrutiny that the cloud draws today.

3. Process for Resolving Problems Resulting from Change. Since problems can often be compounded and result from multiple factors both within and outside the cloud, a SLA-based outline of upgrade procedures must include a clearly defined set of responsibilities and methods for resolving issues introduced by any upgrade.

4. Back-Out Process if the Changes Cause Major Failures. Even the best-laid plans often run aground on the rocks of reality. Cloud services providers should automatically embed rollback checkpoints throughout an upgrade plan in order to "pull the plug" and restore any upgrade to its initial state should an unexpected and unsolvable problem crop up during the upgrade procedure. Throughout the process, regular communication meetings should occur to keep both parties in sync.

3.5 MONITORING TOOLS

IT has always had monitoring and management tools. It only makes sense that these tools begin to span out into the cloud. There are some amazing solutions out there that directly answer the above questions and help you optimize you entire cloud platform. Let's take a look at a few cloud monitoring tools and management solutions which are designed to help create a more proactive cloud.

- **BMC Cloud Operations Management :** Here's your chance to create a complete cloud life-cycle management and cloud operations management solution. BMC's cloud monitoring platform enables IT organizations to really deliver the speed and service quality that users expect out of their cloud. This model helps IT organizations right-size capacity and optimize your monitoring and management processes. Furthermore, this monitoring solution integrates with OpenStack, CloudStack, and other cloud management platforms through an open API and metadata-driven user interface.

- **AppDynamics :** How about a layered approach to application intelligence? Starting with the infrastructure and moving all the way up the stack, AppDynamics is uniquely able to deliver rich performance data, learning, and analytics, combined with the flexibility to adapt to virtually any infrastructure or software environment. Some of those layers include behavioral learning and working with contextual data. Basically, you'll be able to granularly see application models, servers, services, devices, as well as information around network and machine infrastructure.

- **CA Nimsoft :** This is one of those really broad cloud monitoring options. From a services perspective, Nimsoft Monitor really offers pretty much every necessary monitoring solution. Application monitoring support includes Apache systems, Citrix, IBM, Microsoft, SAP and more. Plus, if you're working with an existing cloud infrastructure or management platform, Nimsoft integrates with Citrix CloudPlatform, FlexPod, Vblock and even your own public/private cloud model. The list of supported monitoring solutions continues to span through servers, networks, storage, virtualization and more. Basically, pick the monitoring solution you need and make sure it can integrate with your existing platform.

- **New Relic Monitor :** Already used by folks like Comcast, Citrix, GitHub and EA, New Relic offers a complete SaaS-based model for very granular cloud monitoring capabilities. This monitoring solution looks at the most critical components that make up a cloud-ready application. This includes SQL query analysis, application health statistics, transactional tracing, thread profiling, complete application mapping, and even proactive alerting. Whether the app is web, mobile, or server-based, New Relic takes into account numerous performance and optimization considerations into its monitoring algorithm.

- **Hyperic :** Did you know this is a division of VMware? Did you know Hyperic 5.0 has some pretty amazing management and monitoring solutions? Ranging from web to virtualization, this solution looks at operation intelligence and creates a powerful monitoring platform for a variety of systems. Hyperic can monitor web servers, a plethora of operating systems, applications, databases, mail servers, network environments, distributed platforms and even middleware messaging. As a component of the VMware vCenter Operations Management Suite, Hyperic collects a vast range of performance data. This includes 50,000 metrics across 80 application technologies, and it can easily extend to monitor any component in your application stack.

- **Solarwinds :** Let's pretend for a few minutes that you have a completely private cloud infrastructure. Sure, you have some minor data elements that may be spanning into a different public data center, but for the most part, it's a private cloud life. There are solutions out there that help monitor and really optimize your infrastructure. Virtualization Manager from Solarwinds offers a comprehensive monitoring solution which integrates with your VMware or Hyper-V environment. Their real-time dashboards simplify identification and troubleshooting of performance, capacity and configuration problems. Plus, you can integrate this solution with Server and Application Monitor which would provide application stack management from app to datastore.

- **Boundary :** These guys are pretty cool. Currently being run by the former Nimsoft CEO, Boundary aims to monitor and integrate with major cloud vendors to help control and manage applications as well as data. By integrating with Puppet Labs, AWS, Splunk, New Relic, AppDynamics, CA, BMC and many others, Boundary is able to enrich your monitoring solution with application topology and per-second streaming analytics. The idea is to aggregate a lot of data through Boundary and create a consolidated view. From there, you can run performance analysis, understand contextual navigation, examine application topologies, and even control architecture and APIs.

There are a lot of various solutions out there that can monitor every aspect of your cloud platform. Similarly, there are solutions which are designed to control and monitor very specific elements in your cloud like application performance, database health, and network data flow. Regardless of the type of solution you work with, there are some very good cloud monitoring, management and health maintenance considerations:

- Utilize automation and proactive remediation services wherever possible.
- Never forget to set good access control policies and always monitor security access.
- "Who watches the watchmen?" Always ensure that your monitoring system is running optimally and that configurations are kept updated.

- Not all workloads, apps, or data sets are alike   make sure to create appropriate monitoring profiles as needed
- Take the time to understand your own cloud and all its intricacies and dependencies before selecting a monitoring solution. The more you know, the better a monitoring tool can fit in.

QUESTIONS

1. Explain an architecture for federated about computing.

2. Explain the model of federated cloud computing.

3. Explain SLA management in cloud computing.

4. Explain SLA lifecycle meta model.

5. What are critical performance objectives of cloud computing?

6. Explain various monitoring tools in the contort of cloud computing.

SECURITY

4.1 CLOUD SECURITY FUNDAMENTALS

- Cloud evolution can be considered synonymous to banking system evolution. Earlier people used to keep all their money, movable assets (precious metals, stones etc.) in their personal possessions and even in underground lockers as they thought that depositing their hard earned money with bank can be disastrous.

- Banking system evolved over the period of time. Legal and security process compliances protected by Law played a big role in making banking and financial systems trustworthy.

- Now, people hardly keep any cash with them

- Most of us carry plastic money and transact digitally, cloud computing is also evolving the same way.

- Robust cloud architecture with strong security implementation at all layers in the stack powered with legal compliances and government protection is the key to cloud security.

- As Banks didn't vanish despite frauds, thefts and malpractices, cloud security is going to get evolved but as much faster rate. Digital world has zero tolerance for waiting! Evolution is natural and is bound to happen.

- So what are the steps typically a cloud service provider should follow in order to secure its cloud?

- Cloud is complex and hence security measures are not simple too. Cloud needs to be secured at all layers in its stack. Let's briefly look into major areas.

4.1.1 At Infrastructure Level

A system administrator of the cloud provider can attack the systems since he/she has got all the admin rights. With root privileges at each machine, the system administrator can install or execute all sorts of software to perform an attack. Furthermore, with physical access to the machine, a system administrator can perform more sophisticated attacks like cold boot attacks and even tamper with the hardware.

Protection Measures
- No single person should accumulate all these privileges.
- Provider should deploy stringent security devices, restricted access control policies, and surveillance mechanisms to protect the physical integrity of the hardware.

Thus, we assume that, by enforcing a security processes, the provider itself can prevent attacks that require physical access to the machines.

- The only way a sysadmin would be able to gain physical access to a node running a costumer's VM is by diverting this VM to a machine under his/her control, located outside the IaaS's security perimeter. Therefore, the cloud computing platform must be able to confine the VM execution inside the perimeter, and guarantee that at any point a sysadmin with root privileges remotely logged to a machine hosting a VM cannot access its memory.

- TCG (trusted computing group), a consortium of industry leader to identify and implement security measures at infrastructure level proposes a set of hardware and software technologies to enable the construction of trusted platforms suggests use of "remote attestation" (a mechanism to detect changes to the user's computers by authorized parties).

4.1.2 At Platform Level

Security model at this level relies more on the provider to maintain data integrity and availability. Platform must take care of following security aspects :

- Integrity.
- Confidentiality.
- Authentication.
- Defense against intrusion and DDoS attack.
- SLA.

4.1.3 At Application Level

The following key security elements should be carefully considered as an integral part of the SaaS application development and deployment process :

SaaS Deployment Model

- Data security.
- Network security.
- Regulatory compliance.
- Data segregation.
- Availability.
- Backup/Recovery Procedure.
- Identity management and sign-on process.

Most of the above are provided by PaaS and hence optimal utilization of PaaS in modeling SaaS is very important.

Some of the steps which can be taken to make SaaS secured are :

- Secure Product Engineering.
- Secure Deployment.
- Governance and Regulatory Compliance Audits.
- Third-Party SaaS Security Assessment.

4.1.4 At Data Level

- Apart from securing data from corruption and losses by implementing data protection mechanism at infrastructure level, one needs to also make sure that sensitive data is encrypted during transit and at rest.
- Apart from all the above measures, stringent security process implementation should also be part of making cloud secure. Periodic audits should happen.
- Governing security laws should be amended with advent in technologies, ethical hacking and vulnerability testing should be performed to make sure the cloud is secure across all layers.

4.2 CLOUD SECURITY RISKS   (Nov. 16, May 17)

- Cloud computing has lots of unique properties that make it very valuable. Unfortunately, many of those properties make security a singular concern.
- Many of the tools and techniques that you would use to protect your data, comply with regulations, and maintain the integrity of your systems are complicated by the fact that you are sharing your systems with others and many times outsourcing their operations as well.
- Cloud computing service providers are well aware of these concerns and have developed new technologies to address them.
- Storing data in the cloud is of particular concern.
- Data should be transferred and stored in an encrypted format. You can use proxy and brokerage services to separate clients from direct access to shared cloud storage.
- Logging, auditing, and regulatory compliance are all features that require planning in cloud computing systems. They are among the services that need to be negotiated in Service Level Agreements.

Top Security Risks

- The 2009 Cloud Risk Assessment contains a list of the top security risks related to Cloud computing. After the first review round, the top risks have turned out to be more or less unchanged from the 2009 Cloud Risk Assessment.
- The most important classes of cloud-specific risks are :
- **Loss of Governance :** In using cloud infrastructures, the client necessarily cedes control to the Cloud Provider (CP) on a number of issues that may affect security.
- At the same time, SLAs may not offer a commitment to provide such services on the part of the cloud provider, thus leaving a gap in security defences.

- This also includes compliance risks, because investment in achieving certification (e.g., industry standard or regulatory requirements) may be put at risk by migration to the cloud :
- If the CP cannot provide evidence of their own compliance with the relevant requirements
- If the CP does not permit audit by the cloud customer (CC).
- In certain cases, it also means that using a public cloud infrastructure implies that certain kinds of compliance cannot be achieved (e.g., PCI DSS).
- **Lock-in :** There still is little on offer in the way of tools, procedures or standard data formats or services interfaces that could guarantee data, application and service portability. This can make it difficult for the customer to migrate from one provider to another or migrate data and services back to an in-house IT environment. This introduces a dependency on a particular CP for service provision, especially if data portability, as the most fundamental aspect, is not enabled.
- **Isolation Failure :** Multi-tenancy and shared resources are defining characteristics of cloud computing. This risk category covers the failure of mechanisms separating storage, memory, routing and reputation between different tenants (e.g., so-called guest-hopping attacks). However it should be considered that attacks on resource isolation mechanisms (e.g. against hypervisors) are still less numerous and much more difficult for an attacker to put in practice compared to attacks on traditional OSs.

Management Interface Compromise : Customer management interfaces of a public cloud provider are accessible through the Internet and mediate access to larger sets of resources and therefore pose an increased risk, especially when combined with remote access and web browser vulnerabilities.

Data Protection : Cloud computing poses several data protection risks for cloud customers and providers. In some cases, it may be difficult for the cloud customer to effectively check the data handling practices of the cloud provider and thus to be sure that the data is handled in a lawful way. This problem is exacerbated in cases of multiple transfers of data, e.g., between federated clouds. On the other hand, some cloud providers do provide information on their data handling practices. Some also offer certification summaries on their data processing and data security activities and the data controls they have in place, e.g., SAS70 certification.

Insecure or Incomplete Data Deletion : When a request to delete a cloud resource is made, as with most operating systems, this may not result in true wiping of the data.

Adequate or timely data deletion may also be impossible (or undesirable from a customer perspective), either because extra copies of data are stored but are not available, or because the disk to be destroyed also stores data from other clients. In the case of multiple tenancies and the reuse of hardware resources, this represents a higher risk to the customer than with dedicated hardware.

Malicious Insider : While usually less likely, the damage which may be caused by malicious insiders is often far greater. Cloud architectures necessitate certain roles which are extremely high-risk. Examples include CP system administrators and managed security service providers.

Customer's Security Expectations : The perception of Security levels by Customers might differentiate from the actual security (and availability) offered by the CP, or the actual temptation of the CP to reduce costs further by sacrificing on some security aspects.

Availability Chain : Reliance on Internet Connectivity at Customer's end creates a Single point of failure in many cases.

- The risks listed above do not follow a specific order of criticality; they are just ten of the most important cloud computing specific risks identified during the assessment. In terms of criticality, loss of governance is still considered the top risk associated with moving to the Cloud.

- The risks of using Cloud computing should be compared to the risks of staying with traditional solutions, such as desktop-based models.

- To facilitate this, the 2009 Cloud Risk Assessment contains estimates of relative risks as compared with a typical traditional environment.

- These were also reconsidered during the first review round, and in many cases explanations were added. It is often possible, and in some cases advisable, for the cloud customer to transfer risk to the cloud provider.

- However not all risks can be transferred : If a risk leads to the failure of a business, serious damage to reputation or legal implications, it is hard or impossible for any other party to compensate for this damage. Ultimately, you can outsource responsibility but you can't outsource accountability.

4.2.1 Securing the Cloud   (Nov. 16, May 17)

- The Internet was designed primarily to be resilient; it was not designed to be secure. Any distributed application has a much greater attack surface than an application that is closely held on a Local Area Network.

- Cloud computing has all the vulnerabilities associated with Internet applications, and additional vulnerabilities arise from pooled, virtualized, and outsourced resources.

The following areas of cloud computing that were uniquely troublesome :

- Auditing
- Data integrity
- e-Discovery for legal compliance

- Privacy
- Recovery
- Regulatory compliance.
- Your risks in any cloud deployment are dependent upon the particular cloud service model chosen and the type of cloud on which you deploy your applications.

In order to evaluate your risks, you need to perform the following analysis :

- Determine which resources (data, services, or applications) you are planning to move to the cloud.
- Determine the sensitivity of the resource to risk. Risks that need to be evaluated are loss of privacy, unauthorized access by others, loss of data, and interruptions in availability.
- Determine the risk associated with the particular cloud type for a resource. Cloud types include public, private (both external and internal), hybrid, and shared community types. With each type, you need to consider where data and functionality will be maintained.
- Take into account the particular cloud service model that you will be using. Different models such as IaaS, SaaS, and PaaS require their customers to be responsible for security at different levels of the service stack.
- If you have selected a particular cloud service provider, you need to evaluate its system to understand how data is transferred, where it is stored, and how to move data both in and out of the cloud.
- You may want to consider building a flowchart that shows the overall mechanism of the system you are intending to use or are currently using.
- One technique for maintaining security is to have "golden" system image references that you can return to when needed. The ability to take a system image off-line and analyze the image for vulnerabilities or compromise is invaluable. The compromised image is a primary forensics tool.
- Many cloud providers offer a snapshot feature that can create a copy of the client's entire environment; this includes not only machine images, but applications and data, network interfaces, firewalls, and switch access. If you feel that a system has been compromised, you can replace that image with a known good version and contain the problem.
- Many vendors maintain a security page where they list their various resources, certifications, and credentials. One of the more developed offerings is the AWS Security Center, shown in Fig. 4.1, where you can download some backgrounders, white papers, and case studies related to the Amazon Web Service's security controls and mechanisms.

The AWS Security Center (http : //aws.amazon.com/security/) is a good place to start learning about how Amazon Web Services protects users of its IaaS service.

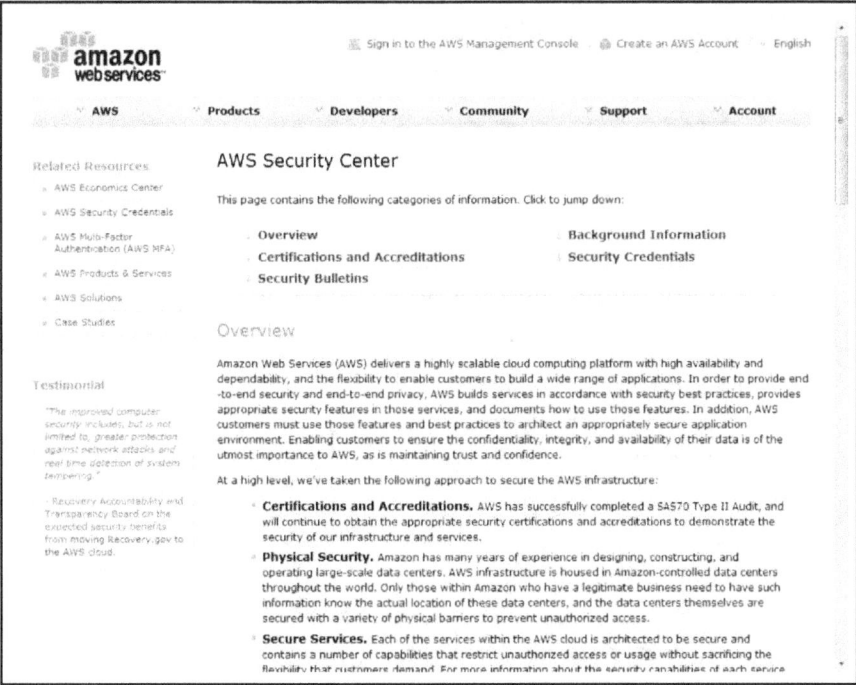

Fig. 4.1 : Amazon web serives

4.2.2 Security Service Boundary

- The CSA functional cloud computing hardware/software stack is the Cloud Reference Model. IaaS is the lowest level service, with PaaS and SaaS the next two services above. As you move upward in the stack, each service model inherits the capabilities of the model beneath it, as well as all the inherent security concerns and risk factors.

- IaaS supplies the infrastructure; PaaS adds application development frameworks, transactions, and control structures; and SaaS is an operating environment with applications, management, and the user interface. As you ascend the stack, IaaS has the least levels of integrated functionality and the lowest levels of integrated security, and SaaS has the most.

- The most important lesson from this discussion of architecture is that each different type of cloud service delivery model creates a security boundary at which the cloud service provider's responsibilities end and the customer's responsibilities begin.

- Any security mechanism below the security boundary must be built into the system, and any security mechanism above must be maintained by the customer.

- As you move up the stack, it becomes more important to make sure that the type and level of security is part of your Service Level Agreement.

The CSA Cloud Reference Model with security boundaries shown

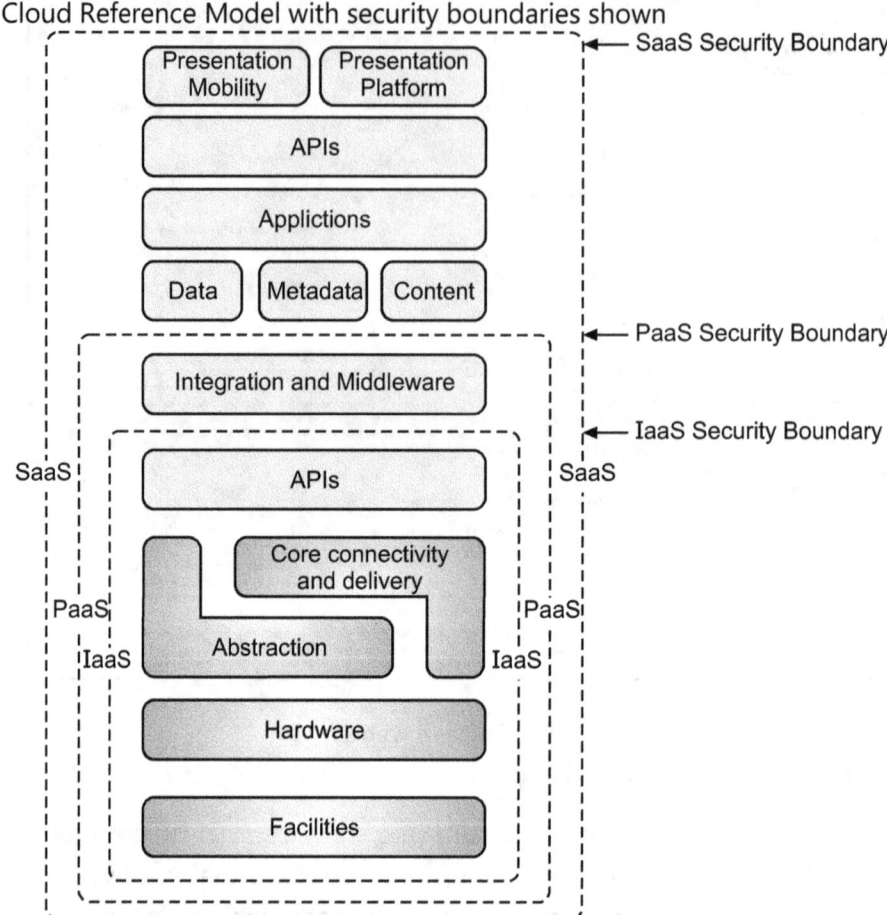

Fig. 4.2 : CSA cloud reference model

- In the SaaS model, the vendor provides security as part of the Service Level Agreement, with the compliance, governance, and liability levels stipulated under the contract for the entire stack.

- For the PaaS model, the security boundary may be defined for the vendor to include the software framework and middleware layer. In the PaaS model, the customer would be responsible for the security of the application and UI at the top of the stack.

- The model with the least built-in security is IaaS, where everything that involves software of any kind is the customer's problem.

- Numerous definitions of services tend to muddy this picture by adding or removing elements of the various functions from any particular offering, thus blurring which party has responsibility for which features, but the overall analysis is still useful.

- In thinking about the Cloud Security Reference Model in relationship to security needs, a fundamental distinction may be made between the nature of how services are provided versus where those services are located.

- A private cloud may be internal or external to an organization, and although a public cloud is most often external, there is no requirement that this mapping be made so.
- Cloud computing has a tendency to blur the location of the defined security perimeter in such a way that the previous notions of network firewalls and edge defenses often no longer apply.
- This makes the location of trust boundaries in cloud computing rather ill defined, dynamic, and subject to change depending upon a number of factors.
- Establishing trust boundaries and creating a new perimeter defense that is consistent with your cloud computing network is an important consideration. The key to understanding where to place security mechanisms is to understand where physically in the cloud resources are deployed and consumed, what those resources are, who manages the resources, and what mechanisms are used to control them.
- Those factors help you gauge where systems are located and what areas of compliance you need to build into your system.

4.2.3 Security Mapping

- The cloud service model you choose determines where in the proposed deployment the variety of security features, compliance auditing, and other requirements must be placed.
- To determine the particular security mechanisms you need, you must perform a mapping of the particular cloud service model to the particular application you are deploying.
- These mechanisms must be supported by the various controls that are provided by your service provider, your organization, or a third party. It's unlikely that you will be able to duplicate security routines that are possible on-premises, but this analysis allows you to determine what coverage you need.
- A security control model includes the security that you normally use for your applications, data, management, network, and physical hardware. You may also need to account for any compliance standards that are required for your industry.
- A compliance standard can be any government regulatory framework such as Payment Card Industry Data Security Standards (PCI-DSS), Health Insurance Portability and Accountability Act (HIPPA), Gramm–Leach–Bliley Act (GLBA), or the Sarbanes–Oxley Act (SOX) that requires you operate in a certain way and keep records.
- Essentially, you are looking to identify the missing features that would be required for an on-premises deployment and seek to find their replacements in the cloud computing model.
- As you assign accountability for different aspects of security and contract away the operational responsibility to others, you want to make sure they remain accountable for the security you need.

4.3 PRIVACY AND SECURITY IN CLOUD

Cloud computing security (sometimes referred to simply as "cloud security") is an evolving sub-domain of computer security, network security, and, more broadly, information security.

It refers to a broad set of policies, technologies, and controls deployed to protect data, applications, and the associated infrastructure of cloud computing.

4.3.1 Defining Security in the Cloud

- If we wish to enable cloud-driven growth and innovation through security, we must have a clear framing on what is meant by security.
- Security has been notoriously hard to define in the general case. The canonical goals of information security are Confidentiality, Integrity, and Availability.
- We borrow from NIST to include Accountability and Assurance, and then add a sixth category of Resilience.
- We define these terms below and map them to the cloud context, with a few examples of how they can be supported by both technical and non-technical mechanisms.
- **Confidentiality** refers to keeping data private. Privacy is of tantamount importance as data leaves the borders of the organization. Not only must internal secrets and sensitive personal data be safeguarded, but metadata and transactional data can also leak important details about firms or individuals. Confidentiality is supported by, among other things, technical tools such as encryption and access control, as well as legal protections.
- **Integrity** is a degree confidence that the data in the cloud is what is supposed to be there, and is protected against accidental or intentional alteration without authorization. It also extends to the hurdles of synchronizing multiple databases. Integrity is supported by well audited code, well-designed distributed systems, and robust access control mechanisms.
- **Availability** means being able to use the system as anticipated. Cloud technologies can increase availability through widespread internet-enabled access, but the client is dependent on the timely and robust provision of resources. Availability is supported by capacity building and good architecture by the provider, as well as well-defined contracts and terms of agreement.
- **Accountability** maps actions in the system to responsible parties. Inside the cloud, actions must be traced uniquely back to an entity, allowing for integration into organizational processes, conflict resolution and deterrence of bad behavior. Accountability is supported by robust identity, authentication and access control, as well as the ability to log transactions and then, critically, audit these logs.
- **Assurance** refers to the need for a system to behave as expected. In the cloud context, it is important that the cloud provider provides what the client has specified. This is not simply a matter of the software and hardware behaving as the client expects but that the needs of the organization are understood, and that these needs are accurately translated into information architecture requirements, which are then faithfully implemented in the cloud system. Assurance is supported by a trusted computing architecture in the cloud,

and a by careful processes mapping from business case to technical details to legal agreements.

- **Resilience** in a system allows it to cope with security threats, rather than failing critically. Cloud technology can increase resilience, with a broader base, backup data and systems, and the potential identify threats and dynamically counteract. However, by shifting critical systems and functions to an outside party, organizations can aggravate resilience by introducing a single point of failure. Resilience is supported by redundancy, diversification and real-time forensic capacity.

4.3.2 Security Issues Associated with the Cloud

- There are number of security issues/concerns associated with cloud computing but these issues fall into two broad categories : Security issues faced by cloud providers (organizations providing Software, Platform, or Infrastructure-as-a-Service via the cloud) and security issues faced by their customers.

- In most cases, the provider must ensure that their infrastructure is secure and that their clients' data and applications are protected while the customer must ensure that the provider has taken the proper security measures to protect their information.

- The extensive use of virtualization in implementing cloud infrastructure brings unique security concerns for customers or tenants of a public cloud service. Virtualization alters the relationship between the OS and underlying hardware - be it computing, storage or even networking.

- This introduces an additional layer - virtualization - that itself must be properly configured, managed and secured. Specific concerns include the potential to compromise the virtualization software, or "hypervisor". While these concerns are largely theoretical, they do exist.

4.3.3 Dimensions of Cloud Security

Correct security controls should be implemented according to asset, threat, and vulnerability risk assessment matrices. While cloud security concerns can be grouped into any number of dimensions these dimensions have been aggregated into three general areas :

- Security and Privacy.
- Compliance.
- Legal or Contractual Issues.

4.3.3.1 Security and Privacy

In order to ensure that data is secure (that it cannot be accessed by unauthorized users or simply lost) and that data privacy is maintained, cloud providers attend to the following areas :

- **Data Protection**

  To be considered protected, data from one customer must be properly segregated from that of another; it must be stored securely when "at rest" and it must be able to move securely from one location to another. Cloud providers have systems in place to prevent data leaks or access by third parties. Proper separation of duties should ensure that auditing or monitoring cannot be defeated, even by privileged users at the cloud provider.

- **Physical Control**

  Physical control of the Private Cloud equipment is more secure than having the equipment off site and under someone else's control. Having the ability to visually inspect the data links and access ports is required in order to ensure data links are not compromised.

- **Identity Management**

  Every enterprise will have its own identity management system to control access to information and computing resources. Cloud providers either integrate the customer's identity management system into their own infrastructure, using federation or SSO technology, or provide an identity management solution of their own.

- **Physical and Personnel Security**

  Providers ensure that physical machines are adequately secure and that access to these machines as well as all relevant customer data is not only restricted but that access is documented.

- **Availability**

  Cloud providers assure customers that they will have regular and predictable access to their data and applications.

- **Application Security**

  Cloud providers ensure that applications available as a service via the cloud are secure by implementing testing and acceptance procedures for outsourced or packaged application code. It also requires application security measures (application-level firewalls) be in place in the production environment.

- **Privacy**

  Finally, providers ensure that all critical data (credit card numbers, for example) are masked and that only authorized users have access to data in its entirety. Moreover, digital identities and credentials must be protected as should any data that the provider collects or produces about customer activity in the cloud.

- **Legal Issues**

  In addition, providers and customers must consider legal issues, such as Contracts and E-Discovery, and the related laws, which may vary by country.

4.3.3.2 Compliance

Numerous regulations pertain to the storage and use of data, including Payment Card Industry Data Security Standard (PCI DSS), the Health Insurance Portability and Accountability Act (HIPAA), the Sarbanes-Oxley Act, among others. Many of these regulations require regular reporting and audit trails. Cloud providers must enable their customers to comply appropriately with these regulations.

- **Business Continuity and Data Recovery**

  Cloud providers have business continuity and data recovery plans in place to ensure that service can be maintained in case of a disaster or an emergency and that any data loss will be recovered. These plans are shared with and reviewed by their customers.

- **Logs and Audit Trails**

  In addition to producing logs and audit trails, cloud providers work with their customers to ensure that these logs and audit trails are properly secured, maintained for as long as the customer requires, and are accessible for the purposes of forensic investigation (e.g., eDiscovery).

- **Unique Compliance Requirements**

  In addition to the requirements to which customers are subject, the data centers maintained by cloud providers may also be subject to compliance requirements. Using a cloud service provider (CSP) can lead to additional security concerns around data jurisdiction since customer or tenant data may not remain on the same system, or in the same data center or even within the same provider's cloud.

4.3.3.3 Legal and Contractual Issues

Aside from the security and compliance issues enumerated above, cloud providers and their customers will negotiate terms around liability (stipulating how incidents involving data loss or compromise will be resolved, for example), intellectual property, and end-of-service (when data and applications are ultimately returned to the customer.

4.4 CLOUD SECURITY ARCHITECTURE

- Cloud application developers and develops have been successfully developing applications for IaaS (Amazon AWS, Rackspace, etc) and PaaS (Azure, Google App Engine, Cloud Foundry) platforms.
- These platforms provide basic security features including support for authentication, DoS attack mitigation, firewall policy management, logging, basic user and profile management but security concerns continue to be the number one barrier for enterprise cloud adoption.
- Cloud security concerns range from securely configuring virtual machines deployed on an IaaS platform to managing user privileges in a PaaS cloud.
- Given that the cloud services can be delivered in many flavors i.e. in any combination of service delivery models, SaaS, PaaS and IaaS (SPI), and operational models, public, private and hybrid, the cloud security concerns and solutions are context (pattern) dependent.

- Hence, the solution architecture should match these concerns and build security safeguards (controls) into the cloud application architecture.

- So what are the architectural frameworks and tools that cloud application architects and develops have at their disposal when developing applications for IaaS andPaaS platforms? In this topic.

- We will learn the approach to baking "adequate" security into your application deployed in IaaS and PaaS clouds.

Cloud Security – Shared Responsibility

- First, let's talk about the cloud security operational model. By definition, cloud security responsibilities in a public cloud are shared between the cloud customer (your enterprise) and the cloud service provider where as in a private cloud, the customer is managing all aspects of the cloud platform.

- Cloud service providers are responsible for securing the shared infrastructure including routers, switches, load balancers, firewalls, hypervisors, storage networks, management consoles, DNS, directory services and cloud API.

- The figure below highlights the layers, within a cloud service, that are secured by the provider versus the customer.

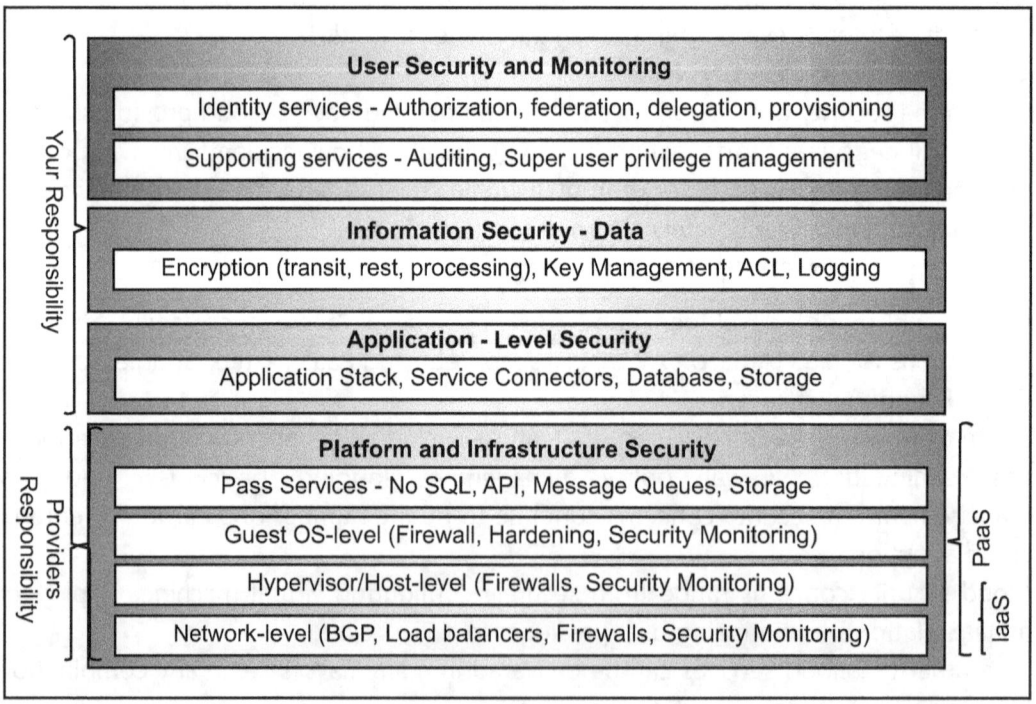

Fig. 4.3 : Cloud security architecture

- Prior to signing up with a provider, it is important to perform a gap analysis on the cloud service capabilities.

- This exercise should benchmark the cloud platform's maturity, transparency, compliance with enterprise security standards (e.g. ISO 27001) and regulatory standards such as PCI DSS, HIPAA and SOX.

- Cloud security maturity models can help accelerate the migration strategy of applications to the cloud. The following are a set of principles you can apply when evaluating a cloud service provider's security maturity :

- **Disclosure of Security Policies, Compliance and Practices :** The cloud service provider should demonstrate compliance with industry standard frameworks such as ISO 27001, SS 16 and CSA Cloud controls matrix. Controls certified by the provider should match control expectations from your enterprise data protection standard standpoint. When cloud services are certified for ISO 27001 or SSAE 16, the scope of controls should be disclosed. Clouds that host regulated data must meet compliance requirements such as PCI DSS, Sarbanes-Oxley and HIPAA.

- **Disclosure when Mandated :** The cloud service provider should disclose relevant data when disclosure is imperative due to legal or regulatory needs.

- **Security Architecture :** The cloud service provider should disclose security architectural details that either help or hinder security management as per the enterprise standard. For example, the architecture of virtualization that guarantees isolation between tenants should be disclosed.

- **Security Automation :** The cloud service provider should support security automation by publishing API(s) (HTTP/SOAP) that support :

  Export and import of security event logs, change management logs, user entitlements (privileges), user profiles, firewall policies, access logs in a XML or enterprise log standard format. Continuous security monitoring including support for emerging standards such as Cloud Audit.

- **Governance and Security Responsibility :** Governance and security management responsibilities of the customer versus those of the cloud provider should be clearly articulated.

4.4.1 Cloud Security Architecture – Plan

As a first step, architects need to understand what security capabilities are offered by cloud platforms (PaaS, IaaS). The figure below illustrates the architecture for building security into cloud services.

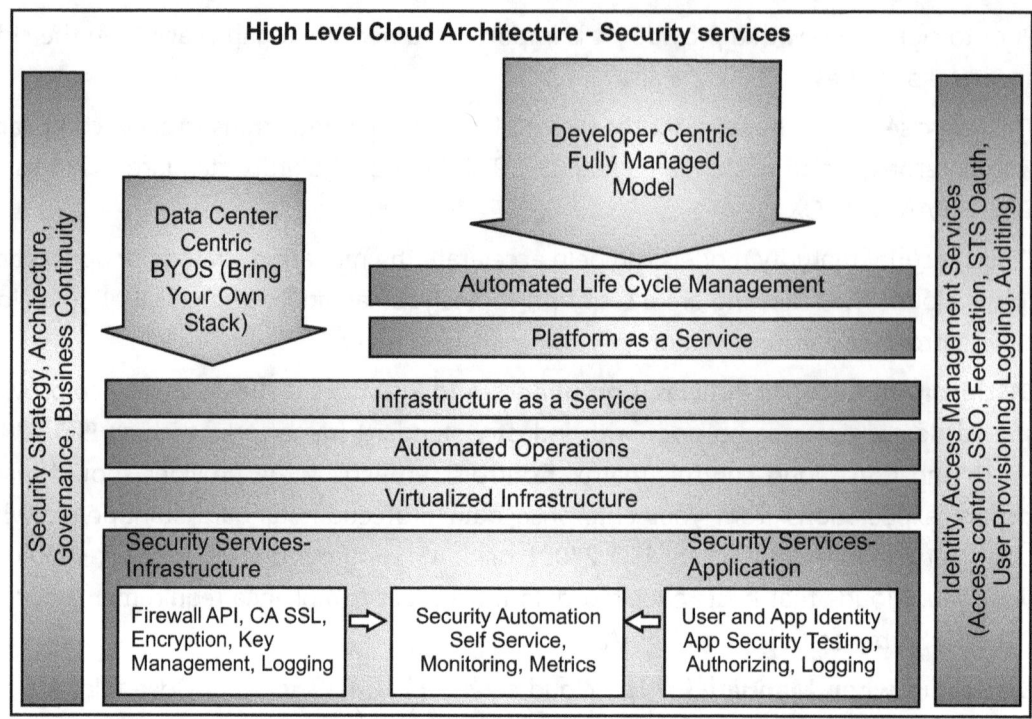

Fig. 4.4 : Cloud security Architecture - Plan

- Security offerings and capabilities continue to evolve and vary between cloud providers. Hence you will often discover that security mechanisms such as key management and data encryption will not be available.

- For example : the need for a AES 128 bit encryption service for encrypting security artifacts and keys escrowed to a key management service. For such critical services, one will continue to rely on internal security services.

- A "Hybrid cloud" deployment architecture pattern may be the only viable option for such applications that dependent on internal services. Another common use case is Single Sign-On (SSO).

- SSO implemented within an enterprise may not be extensible to the cloud application unless it is a federation architecture using SAML 1.1 or 2.0 supported by the cloud service provider.

The following are cloud security best practices to mitigate risks to cloud services :

- **Architect for Security-as-a-service :** Application deployments in the cloud involve orchestration of multiple services including automation of DNS, load balancer, network QoS, etc. Security automation falls in the same category which includes automation of firewall policies between cloud security zones, provisioning of certificates (for SSL), virtual machine system configuration, privileged accounts and log configuration. Application deployment processes that depend on security processes such as firewall policy creation, certificate provisioning, key distribution and application pen testing should be migrated to a self-service model. This approach will eliminate human touch points and will enable a security as a service scenario. Ultimately this will mitigate threats due to human errors, improve operational efficiency and embed security controls into the cloud applications.

- **Implement Sound Identity, Access Management Architecture and Practice :** Scalable cloud bursting and elastic architecture will rely less on network based access controls and warrant strong user access management architecture. Cloud access control architecture should address all aspects of user and access management lifecycles for both end users and privileged users – user provisioning anddeprovisioning, authentication, federation, authorization and auditing. A sound architecture will enable reusability of identity and access services for all use cases in public, private and hybrid cloud models. It is good practice to employ secure token services along with proper user and entitlement provisioning with audit trails. Federation architecture is the first step to extending enterprise SSO to cloud services. Refer to cloud security alliance, Domain 12 for detailed guidance here.

- **Leverage APIs to Automate Safeguards :** Any new security services should be deployed with an API (REST/SOAP) to enable automation. APIs can help automate firewall policies, configuration hardening, and access control at the time of application deployment. This can be implemented using open source tools such as puppet in conjunction with the API supplied by cloud service provider.

- **Always Encrypt or Mask Sensitive Data :** Today's private cloud applications are candidates for tomorrow's public cloud deployment. Hence architect applications to encrypt all sensitive data irrespective of the future operational model.

   Do not rely on an IP address for authentication services – IP addresses in clouds are ephemeral in nature so you cannot solely rely on them for enforcing network access control. Employ certificates (self-signed or from a trusted CA) to enable SSL between services deployed on cloud.

Log : Applications should centrally log all security events that will help create an end-to-end transaction view with non-repudiation characteristics. In the event of a security incident, logs and audit trails are the only reliable data leveraged by forensic engineers to investigate and understand how an application was exploited. Clouds are elastic and logs are ephemeral hence it is critical to periodically migrate log files to a different cloud or to the enterprise data center.

Continuously Monitor Cloud Services : Monitoring is an important function given that prevention controls may not meet all the enterprise standards. Security monitoring should leverage logs produced by cloud services, APIs and hosted cloud applications to perform security event correlation. Cloud audit (cloudaudit.org) from CSA can be leveraged towards this mission.

4.5 CLOUD SECURITY PRINCIPLES

- Every enterprise has different levels of risk tolerance and this is demonstrated by the product development culture, new technology adoption, IT service delivery models, technology strategy, and investments made in the area of security tools and capabilities.

- When a business unit within an enterprise decides to leverage SaaS for business benefits, the technology architecture should lend itself to support that model.
- Additionally the security architecture should be aligned with the technology architecture and principles.

Following is a sample of cloud security principles that an enterprise security architect needs to consider and customize :

- Services running in a cloud should follow the principles of least privileges.
- Isolation between various security zones should be guaranteed using layers of firewalls – Cloud firewall, hypervisor firewall, guest firewall and application container. Firewall policies in the cloud should comply with trust zone isolation standards based on data sensitivity.
- Applications should use end-to-end transport level encryption (SSL, TLS, IPSEC) to secure data in transit between applications deployed in the cloud as well as to the enterprise.
- Applications should externalize authentication and authorization to trusted security services. Single Sign-on should be supported using SAML 2.0.
- Data masking and encryption should be employed based on data sensitivity aligned with enterprise data classification standard.
- Applications in a trusted zone should be deployed on authorized enterprise standard VM images.
- Industry standard VPN protocols such as SSH, SSL and IPSEC should be employed when deploying virtual private cloud (VPC).
- Security monitoring in the cloud should be integrated with existing enterprise security monitoring tools using an API.

4.5.1 Cloud Security Architecture Patterns

- Architecting appropriate security controls that protect the CIA of information in the cloud can mitigate cloud security threats.
- Security controls can be delivered as a service (Security-as-a-Service) by the provider or by the enterprise or by a third party provider.
- Security architectural patterns are typically expressed from the point of security controls (safeguards) – technology and processes. These security controls and the service location (enterprise, cloud provider, 3rd party) should be highlighted in the security patterns.
- Security architecture patterns serve as the North Star and can accelerate application migration to clouds while managing the security risks.
- In addition, cloud security architecture patterns should highlight the trust boundary between various services and components deployed at cloud services.
- These patterns should also point out standard interfaces, security protocols (SSL, TLS, IPSEC, LDAPS, SFTP, SSH, SCP, SAML, OAuth, Tacacs, OCSP, etc.) and mechanisms available for authentication, token management, authorization, encryption methods (hash, symmetric, asymmetric), encryption algorithms (Triple DES, 128-bit AES, Blowfish, RSA, etc.), security event logging, source-of-truth for policies and user attributes and coupling models (tight or loose).

- Finally the patterns should be leveraged to create security checklists that need to be automated by configuration management tools like puppet.
- In general, patterns should highlight the following attributes (but not limited to) for each of the security services consumed by the cloud application :
- **Logical Location :** Native to cloud service, in-house, third party cloud. The location may have an implication on the performance, availability, firewall policy as well as governance of the service.
- **Protocol :** What protocol(s) are used to invoke the service? For example REST with X.509 certificates for service requests.
- **Service Function :** What is the function of the service? For example encryption of the artifact, logging, authentication and machine finger printing.
- **Input /Output :** What are the inputs, including methods to the controls, and outputs from the security service? For example, Input = XML doc and Output =XML doc with encrypted attributes.
- **Control Description :** What security control does the security service offer? For example, protection of information confidentiality at rest, authentication of user and authentication of application.
- **Actor :** Who are the users of this service? For example, End point, End user, Enterprise administrator, IT auditor and Architect.

Here is a subset of the cloud security architecture pattern published by open security architecture group (opensecurityarchitecturegroup.org).

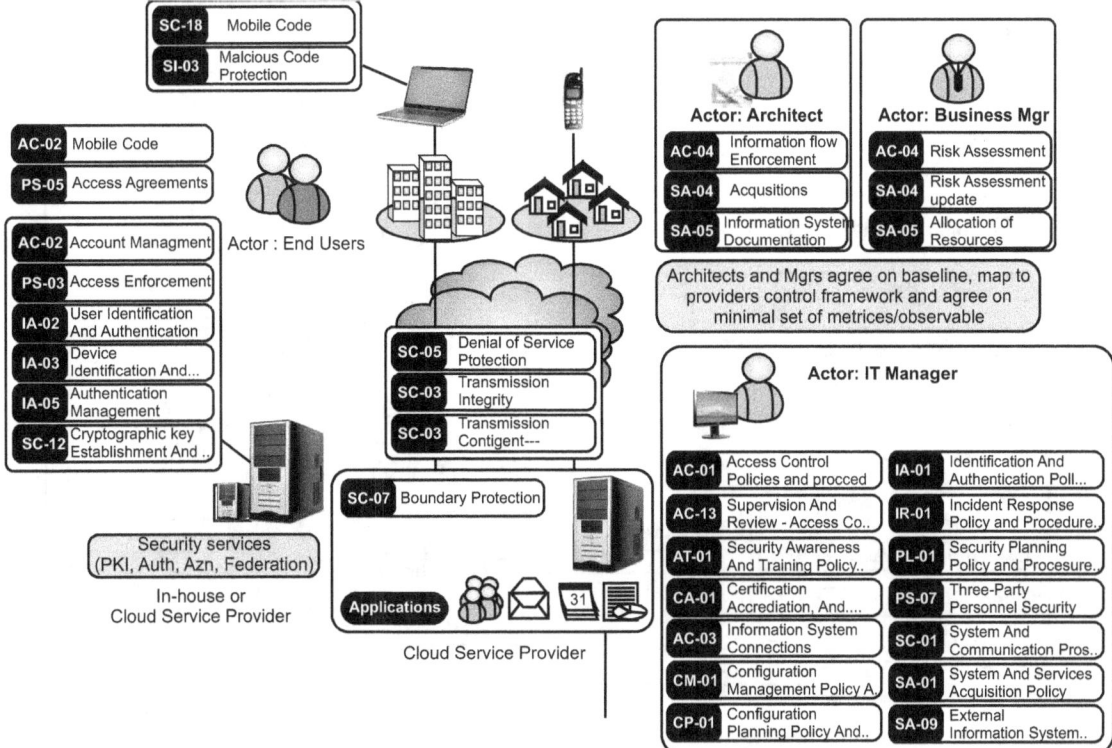

Fig. 4.5 : Cloud security architecture pattern

This pattern illustrates the actors (architect, end user, business manager, IT manager), interacting with systems (end point, cloud, applications hosted on the cloud, security services) and the controls employed to protect the actors and systems (access enforcement, DoS protection, boundary protection, cryptographic key & management, etc). Let's look at details communicated by the pattern.

4.5.2 Infrastructure Security Services (Controls) at Cloud Service Providers

- As per the pattern a cloud service provider is expected to provide security controls for DoS protection and protection of confidentiality and integrity for sessions originating from Mobile as well as PC.
- Typically these sessions initiated by browsers or client applications and are usually delivered using SSL/TLS terminated at the load balancers managed by the cloud service provider.
- Cloud service providers usually don't share the DoS protection mechanisms as hackers can easily abuse it.

Application Security Services (In-House or Cloud Service Provider)

- Security services such as user identification, authentication, access enforcement, device identification, cryptographic services and key management can be located either with the cloud service provider, within the enterprise data center or some combination of the two.
- The second pattern illustrated below is the identity and access pattern derived from the CSA identity domain.

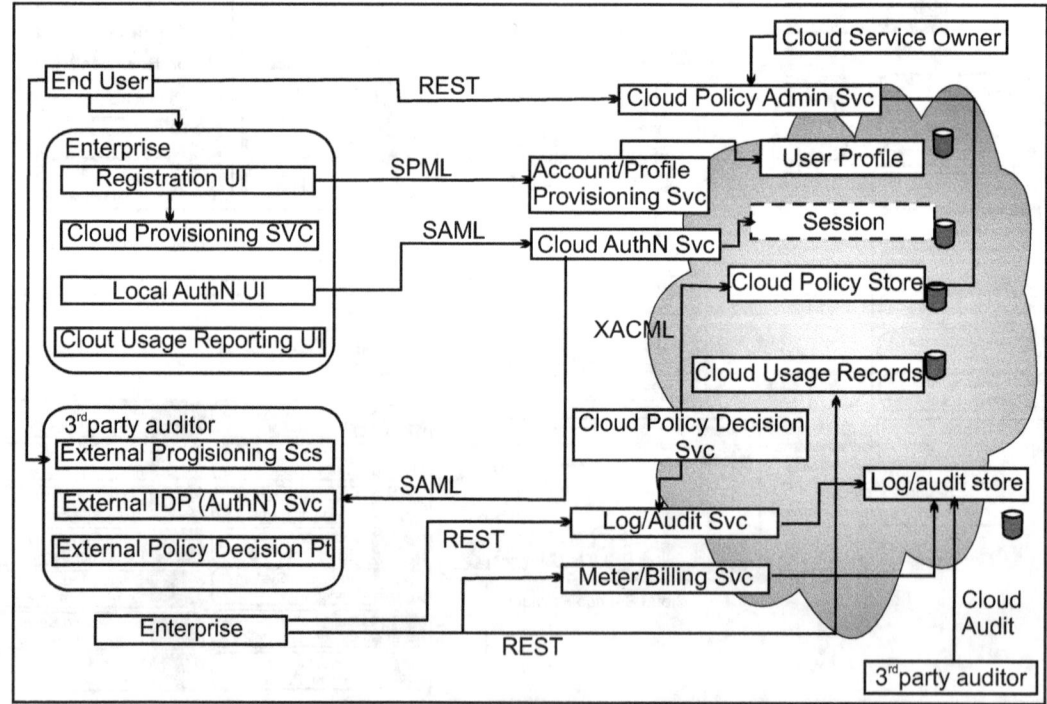

Fig. 4.6 : Cloud Identity/Access Architecture Pattern

- This pattern illustrates a collection of common cloud access control use cases such as user registration, authentication, account provisioning, policy enforcement, logging, auditing and metering.
- It highlights the actors (end user, enterprise business user, third party auditor, cloud service owner) interacting with services that are hosted in the cloud, in-house (enterprise) and in third party locations.

This pattern communicates the following :

4.5.3 Identity Security Services (Controls) at Cloud Service Providers

The cloud hosts the following services :

- Authentication service that supports user authentication originating from an enterprise portal (Local AuthN UI) and typically delivered using SAML protocol. The authenticated session state is maintained in a cloud session store.
- Account and profile provisioning service supports the provisioning of new accounts and user profiles, typically invoked via SPML (Service Provisioning Markup Language) or a cloud service provider specific API. Profiles are stored in the user profile store.
- Cloud policy admin service is used for managing policies that dictate which resources in the cloud can be accessed by end users. Using this service, cloud service owners (enterprise) can perform administrative functions and end users can request for access to cloud resources. Cloud policies are stored in the cloud policy store.
- Logging and auditing service supports dual functions. The first function is event logging, including security events, in the cloud and the second is for audit purposes. Cloud Audit protocols and APIs can be employed to access this service.
- Metering service keeps track of cloud resource usage. Finance departments can use this service for charge-back as well as for billing reconciliation.

4.5.4 Identity Security Services in the Enterprise

In this pattern, a subset of the applications is hosted in the enterprise :

- Cloud registration UI provides the UI service for end users to register, manage and provision new cloud resources. Authentication and Authorization is enforced by the cloud services.
- Cloud usage reporting UI is utilized by end users to generate usage reports.
- Cloud provisioning service is used to provision cloud resources (compute, storage, network, application services). Access control (AuthN, AuthZ) and session management are enforced at the cloud service end.

4.5.5 Identity Security Services at the Third Party Location

- In this pattern, cloud applications rely on identity services offered by a third party and hosted at their location. These services offer support for third party users who will need access to cloud resources to perform business functions on behalf of the enterprise.
- For example backup and application monitoring services. In this model, user provisioning, authentication and access enforcement functions are delegated to the third party service.

- By understanding what you can leverage from your cloud platform or service provider, one can build security into your application without reinventing the capability within your application boundary thus avoiding costly "bolt-on" safeguards.
- A good practice is to create security principles and architectural patterns that can be leveraged in the design phase. Architectural patterns can help articulate where controls are enforced (Cloud versus third party versus enterprise) during the design phase so appropriate security controls are baked into the application design.
- Keep in mind the relevant threats and the principle of "risk appropriate" when creating cloud security patterns. Ultimately cloud security architecture should support the developer's needs to protect the confidentiality, integrity and availability of data processed and stored in the cloud.

4.5.6 Trusted Cloud Computing

- The Trusted Cloud Initiative helps cloud providers develop industry-recommended, secure and interoperable identity, access and compliance management configurations, and practices.
- The Trusted Cloud Initiative will develop reference models and education in a vendor-neutral manner, inclusive of all CSA members and affiliates who wish to participate.
- The Trusted Cloud Initiative Reference Architecture is both a methodology and a set of tools that enable security architects, enterprise architects and risk management professionals to leverage a common set of solutions that fulfill their common needs to be able to assess where their internal IT and their cloud providers are in terms of security capabilities and to plan a roadmap to meet the security needs of their business.

4.6 IDENTITY MANAGEMENT AND ACCESS CONTROL

Before we get into cloud specific Identity Management and Access control, lets understand some basics of it.

4.6.1 Identity Management

- Identity management (IdM) describes the management of individual identities, their authentication, authorization, roles, and privileges/permissions within or across system and enterprise boundaries with the goal of increasing security and productivity while decreasing cost, downtime, and repetitive tasks.
- "Identity Management" and "Access and Identity Management" (or AIM) are terms that are used interchangeably under the title of Identity management while Identity management itself falls the umbrella of IT Security.
- Identity management systems, products, applications, and platforms are commercial Identity management solutions implemented for enterprises and organizations.
- Technologies, services, and terms related to Identity management include Active Directories, Service Providers, Identity Providers, Web Services, Access control, Digital Identities, Password Managers, Single Sign-on, Security Tokens, Security Token Services (STS), Workflows, OpenID, WS-Security, WS-Trust, SAML 2.0, OAuth, and RBAC.

- Identity management (IdM) is a term related to how humans are authenticated (identified) and authorized across computer networks. It covers issues such as how users are given an identity, the protection of that identity, and the technologies supporting that protection (e.g., network protocols, digital certificates, passwords, etc.).

4.6.2 Digital Identity

- Personal identifying information (PII) selectively exposed over a network. Thus the term management is appended to "identity" to indicate that there is technological and best practice framework around a somewhat intractable philosophical concept.
- Digital identity can be interpreted as the codification of identity names and attributes of a physical instance in a way that facilitates processing.
- In each organization there is normally a role or department that is responsible for managing the schema of digital identities of their staff and their own objects, these represented by object identities or object identifiers (OID).
- The SAML protocol is a prominent means used to exchange identity information between two identity domains.

Perspectives on IdM

In the real-world context of engineering online systems, identity management can involve three perspectives :

- **The Pure Identity Paradigm :** Creation, management and deletion of identities without regard to access or entitlements;
- **The User Access (log-on) Paradigm :** For example : a smart card and its associated data used by a customer to log on to a service or services (a traditional view);
- **The Service Paradigm :** A system that delivers personalized, role-based, online, on-demand, multimedia (content), presence-based services to users and their devices.

4.6.3 Pure Identity Paradigm

- A general model of identity can be constructed from a small set of axiomatic principles, for example that all identities in a given abstract namespace are unique and distinctive, or that such identities bear a specific relationship to corresponding entities in the real world.
- An axiomatic model of this kind can be considered to express "pure identity" in the sense that the model is not constrained by the context in which it is applied. In general, an entity can have multiple identities, and each identity can consist of multiple attributes or identifiers, some of which are shared and some of which are unique within a given name space.
- The diagram below illustrates the conceptual relationship between identities and the entities they represent, as well as between identities and the attributes they consist of.

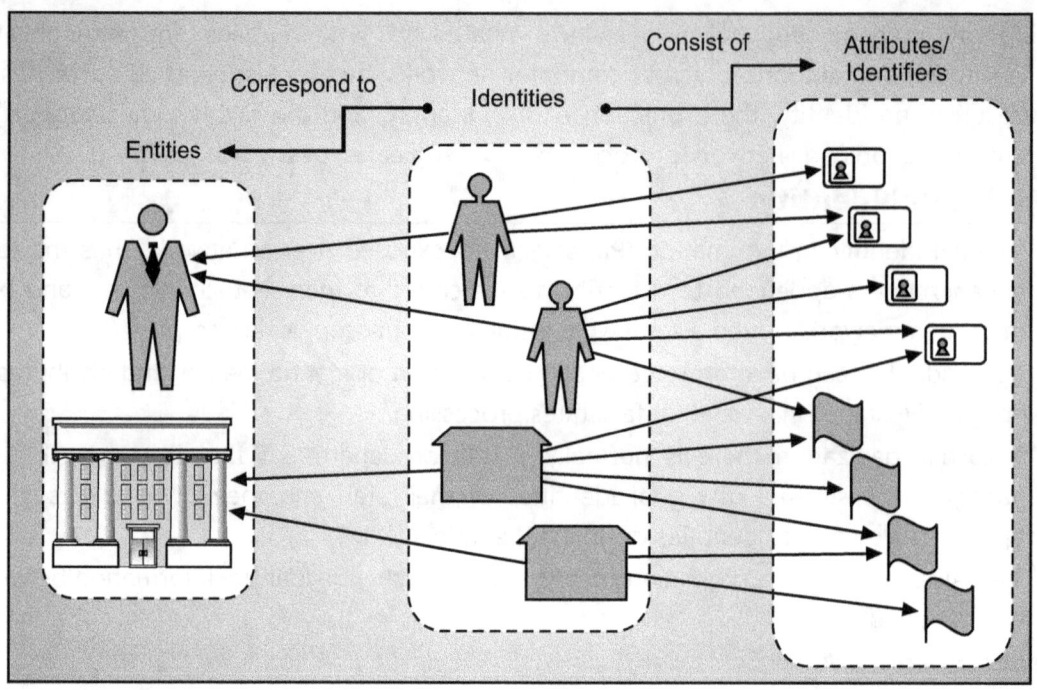

Fig. 4.7 : Identify Paradigms

- In most theoretical and all practical models of digital identity, a given identity object consists of a finite set of properties. These properties may be used to record information about the object, either for purposes external to the model itself or so as to assist the model operationally, for example in classification and retrieval.

- A "pure identity" model is strictly not concerned with the external semantics of these properties.

- The most common departure from "pure identity" in practice occurs with properties intended to assure some aspect of identity, for example a digital signature or software token which the model may use internally to verify some aspect of the identity in satisfaction of an external purpose.

- To the extent that the model attempts to express these semantics internally, it is not a pure model.

- Contrast this situation with properties which might be externally used for purposes of information security such as managing access or entitlement, but which are simply stored and retrieved, in other words not treated specially by the model. The absence of external semantics within the model qualifies it as a "pure identity" model.

- Identity management, then, can be defined as a set of operations on a given identity model, or as a set of capabilities with reference to it.

- In practice, identity management is often used to express how identity information is to be provisioned and reconciled between multiple identity models.

4.6.4 User Access Paradigm

- User access requires each user to assume a unique "digital identity" across applications and networked infrastructures, which enables access controls to be assigned and evaluate against this identity.

- Technically, the use of a unique identity across all systems ease the monitoring and verification of potential unauthorized access, and allows the organization to keep tabs of excessive privileges granted to any individual within the company.

- From the user lifecycle perspective, user access can be tracked from new hire, suspension to termination of employee.

4.6.5 Service Paradigm

- In the service paradigm perspective, where organizations evolve their systems to the world of converged services, the scope of identity management becomes much larger, and its application more critical.

- The scope of identity management includes all the resources of the company deployed to deliver online services. These may include devices, network equipment, servers, portals, content, applications and/or products as well as a user's credentials, address books, preferences, entitlements and telephone numbers. See Service Delivery Platform and Directory service.

- Today, many organizations face a major clean-up in their systems if they are to bring identity coherence into their influence.

- Such coherence has become a prerequisite for delivering unified services to very large numbers of users on demand, cheaply, with security and single-customer viewing facilities.

4.6.5 Access Control

- Access control refers to exerting control over who can interact with a resource. Often but not always, this involves an authority, who does the controlling. The resource can be a given building, group of buildings, or computer-based information system.

- But it can also refer to a restroom stall where access is controlled by using a coin to open the door.

- Access control is, in reality, an everyday phenomenon. A lock on a car door is essentially a form of access control. A PIN on an ATM system at a bank is another means of access control.

- The possession of access control is of prime importance when persons seek to secure important, confidential, or sensitive information and equipment.

- Similarly, in cloud as we are accessing services hosted remotely by some other enterprise, and on a shared basis, we have to implement access control practices to make our data more secure.

4.7 CLOUD COMPUTING SECURITY CHALLENGES

- Although virtualization and cloud computing can help companies accomplish more by breaking the physical bonds between an IT infrastructure and its users, heightened security threats must be overcome in order to benefit fully from this new computing paradigm.

- This is particularly true for the SaaS provider. Some security concerns are worth more discussion. For example, in the cloud, you lose control over assets in some respects, so your security model must be reassessed.

- Enterprise security is only as good as the least reliable partner, department, or vendor. Can you trust your data to your service provider?

- With the cloud model, you lose control over physical security. In a public cloud, you are sharing computing resources with other companies. In a shared pool outside the enterprise, you don't have any knowledge or control of where the resources run.

- Exposing your data in an environment shared with other companies could give the government "reasonable cause" to seize your assets because another company has violated the law.

- Simply because you share the environment in the cloud, may put your data at risk of seizure. Storage services provided by one cloud vendor may be incompatible with another vendor's services should you decide to move from one to the other.

- Vendors are known for creating what the hosting world calls "sticky services;" services that an end user may have difficulty transporting from one cloud vendor to another (e.g., Amazon's "Simple Storage Service" [S3] is incompatible with IBM's Blue Cloud, or Google, or Dell).

- If information is encrypted while passing through the cloud, who controls the encryption/decryption keys? Is it the customer or the cloud vendor? Most customers probably want their data encrypted both ways across the Internet using SSL (Secure Sockets Layer protocol). They also most likely want their data encrypted while it is at rest in the cloud vendor's storage pool. Be sure that you, the customer, control the encryption/decryption keys, just as if the data were still resident on your own servers.

- Data integrity means ensuring that data is identically maintained during any operation (such as transfer, storage, or retrieval). Put simply, data integrity is assurance that the data is consistent and correct. Ensuring the integrity of the data really means that it changes only in response to authorized transactions. This sounds good, but you must remember that a common standard to ensure data integrity does not yet exist.

- Using SaaS offerings in the cloud means that there is much less need for software development. For example, using a web-based customer relationship management (CRM) offering eliminates the necessity to write code and "customize" a vendor's application. If you plan to use internally developed code in the cloud, it is even more important to have a formal secure software development life cycle (SDLC).

- The immature use of mashup technology (combinations of web services), which is fundamental to cloud applications, is inevitably going to cause unwitting security vulnerabilities in those applications.
- Your development tool of choice should have a security model embedded in it to guide developers during the development phase and restrict users only to their authorized data when the system is deployed into production.
- As more and more mission-critical processes are moved to the cloud, SaaS suppliers will have to provide log data in a real-time, straightforward manner, probably for their administrators as well as their customers' personnel.
- Someone has to be responsible for monitoring for security and compliance, and unless the application and data are under the control of end users, they will not be able to.
- Will customers trust the cloud provider enough to push their mission-critical applications out to the cloud? Since the SaaS provider's logs are internal and not necessarily accessible externally or by clients or investigators, monitoring is difficult.
- Since access to logs is required for Payment Card Industry Data Security Standard (PCI DSS) compliance and may be requested by auditors and regulators, security managers need to make sure to negotiate access to the provider's logs as part of any service agreement.
- Cloud applications undergo constant feature additions, and users must keep up to date with application improvements to be sure they are protected. The speed at which applications will change in the cloud will affect both the SDLC and security.
- For example, Microsoft's SDLC assumes that mission-critical software will have a three- to five-year period in which it will not change substantially, but the cloud may require a change in the application every few weeks.
- Even worse, a secure SLDC will not be able to provide a security cycle that keeps up with changes that occur so quickly. This means that users must constantly upgrade, because an older version may not function, or protect the data.
- Having proper fail-over technology is a component of securing the cloud that is often overlooked. The company can survive if a non-mission-critical application goes offline, but this may not be true for mission-critical applications.
- Core business practices provide competitive differentiation. Security needs to move to the data level, so that enterprises can be sure their data is protected wherever it goes.
- Sensitive data is the domain of the enterprise, not the cloud computing provider. One of the key challenges in cloud computing is data-level security.
- Most compliance standards do not envision compliance in a world of cloud computing. There is a huge body of standards that apply for IT security and compliance, governing most business interactions that will, over time, have to be translated to the cloud.
- SaaS makes the process of compliance more complicated, since it may be difficult for a customer to discern where its data resides on a network controlled by its SaaS provider, or a partner of that provider, which raises all sorts of compliance issues of data privacy, segregation, and security.

- Many compliance regulations require that data not be intermixed with other data, such as on shared servers or databases. Some countries have strict limits on what data about its citizens can be stored and for how long, and some banking regulators require that customers' financial data remain in their home country.

- Compliance with government regulations such as the Sarbanes-Oxley Act (SOX), the Gramm-Leach-Bliley Act (GLBA), and the Health Insurance Portability and Accountability Act (HIPAA), and industry standards such as the PCI DSS, will be much more challenging in the SaaS environment.

- There is a perception that cloud computing removes data compliance responsibility; however, it should be emphasized that the data owner is still fully responsible for compliance. Those who adopt cloud computing must remember that it is the responsibility of the data owner, not the service provider, to secure valuable data.

- Government policy will need to change in response to both the opportunity and the threats that cloud computing brings. This will likely focus on the off-shoring of personal data and protection of privacy, whether it is data being controlled by a third party or off-shored to another country.

- There will be a corresponding drop in security as the traditional controls such as VLANs (virtual local-area networks) and firewalls prove less effective during the transition to a virtualized environment.

- Security managers will need to pay particular attention to systems that contain critical data such as corporate financial information or source code during the transition to server virtualization in production environments.

- Outsourcing means losing significant control over data, and while this isn't a good idea from a security perspective, the business ease and financial savings will continue to increase the usage of these services. Security managers will need to work with their company's legal staff to ensure that appropriate contract terms are in place to protect corporate data and provide for acceptable service-level agreements.

- Cloud-based services will result in many mobile IT users accessing business data and services without traversing the corporate network. This will increase the need for enterprises to place security controls between mobile users and cloud-based services.

- Placing large amounts of sensitive data in a globally accessible cloud leaves organizations open to large distributed threats-attackers no longer have to come onto the premises to steal data, and they can find it all in the one "virtual" location.

- Virtualization efficiencies in the cloud require virtual machines from multiple organizations to be co-located on the same physical resources. Although traditional data center security still applies in the cloud environment, physical segregation and hardware-based security cannot protect against attacks between virtual machines on the same server.

- Administrative access is through the Internet rather than the controlled and restricted direct or on-premises connection that is adhered to in the traditional data center model.

This increases risk and exposure and will require stringent monitoring for changes in system control and access control restriction.

- The dynamic and fluid nature of virtual machines will make it difficult to maintain the consistency of security and ensure that records can be audited. The ease of cloning and distribution between physical servers could result in the propagation of configuration errors and other vulnerabilities.

- Proving the security state of a system and identifying the location of an insecure virtual machine will be challenging. Regardless of the location of the virtual machine within the virtual environment, the intrusion detection and prevention systems will need to be able to detect malicious activity at virtual machine level.

- The co-location of multiple virtual machines increases the attack surface and risk of virtual machine-to-virtual machine compromise.

- Localized virtual machines and physical servers use the same operating systems as well as enterprise and web applications in a cloud server environment, increasing the threat of an attacker or malware exploiting vulnerabilities in these systems and applications remotely.

- Virtual machines are vulnerable as they move between the private cloud and the public cloud. A fully or partially shared cloud environment is expected to have a greater attack surface and therefore can be considered to be at greater risk than a dedicated resources environment.

- Operating system and application files are on a shared physical infrastructure in a virtualized cloud environment and require system, file, and activity monitoring to provide confidence and auditable proof to enterprise customers that their resources have not been compromised or tampered with. In the cloud computing environment, the enterprise subscribes to cloud computing resources, and the responsibility for patching is the subscriber's rather than the cloud computing vendor's.

- The need for patch maintenance vigilance is imperative. Lack of due diligence in this regard could rapidly make the task unmanageable or impossible, leaving you with "virtual patching" as the only alternative.

- Enterprises are often required to prove that their security compliance is in accord with regulations, standards, and auditing practices, regardless of the location of the systems at which the data resides.

- Data is fluid in cloud computing and may reside in on-premises physical servers, on-premises virtual machines, or off-premises virtual machines running on cloud computing resources, and this will require some rethinking on the part of auditors and practitioners alike.

- In the rush to take advantage of the benefits of cloud computing, not least of which is significant cost savings, many corporations are likely rushing into cloud computing without a serious consideration of the security implications.

- To establish zones of trust in the cloud, the virtual machines must be self-defending, effectively moving the perimeter to the virtual machine itself.

- Enterprise perimeter security (i.e., firewalls, demilitarized zones [DMZs], network segmentation, intrusion detection and prevention systems [IDS/IPS], monitoring tools, and the associated security policies) only controls the data that resides and transits behind the perimeter.
- In the cloud computing world, the cloud computing provider is in charge of customer data security and privacy.
- In short, in order to ensure that data is secure (that it cannot be accessed by unauthorized users or simply lost) and that data privacy is maintained, cloud providers attend to the following areas :
- **Data Protection**
- To be considered protected, data from one customer must be properly segregated from that of another; it must be stored securely when "at rest" and it must be able to move securely from one location to another.
- Cloud providers have systems in place to prevent data leaks or access by third parties. Proper separation of duties should ensure that auditing or monitoring cannot be defeated, even by privileged users at the cloud provider.
- **Physical Control**
  Physical control of the Private Cloud equipment is more secure than having the equipment off site and under someone else's control. Having the ability to visually inspect the data links and access ports is required in order to ensure data links are not compromised.
- **Identity Management**
  Every enterprise will have its own identity management system to control access to information and computing resources. Cloud providers either integrate the customer's identity management system into their own infrastructure, using federation or SSO technology, or provide an identity management solution of their own.
- **Physical and Personnel Security**
  Providers ensure that physical machines are adequately secure and that access to these machines as well as all relevant customer data is not only restricted but that access is documented.
- **Availability**
  Cloud providers assure customers that they will have regular and predictable access to their data and applications.
- **Application Security**
  Cloud providers ensure that applications available as a service via the cloud are secure by implementing testing and acceptance procedures for outsourced or packaged application code. It also requires application security measures (application-level firewalls) be in place in the production environment.
- **Privacy**
  Finally, providers ensure that all critical data (credit card numbers, for example) are masked and that only authorized users have access to data in its entirety. Moreover,

digital identities and credentials must be protected as should any data that the provider collects or produces about customer activity in the cloud.

- **Virtualization Security Management**

  Virtualization security management mainly includes what mistakes people generally make while creating virtualized servers and what all the preventive measures we should take while implementing it.

Virtualization Threats and Preventative Measures

- Virtualization of IT resources now spans production Web and database servers, storage, and networking. Organizations also need to consider that users may be installing virtual machines on their desktops, as well.

- VM technology adds an additional layer to host operating systems that sits beneath the kernel. This layer consists of a stripped down operating system the virtual machine manager (VMM), such as VMWare's Hypervisor that manage what can be dozens of virtual machines on a single host. While there are risk areas in the VMMs themselves, most of the discussion in this paper relates to server and networking virtualization security issues and suggestions because that is what IT organizations can control. Beyond accepting vendor patches and keeping VMMs hardened, these virtual machine managers are primarily reliant on vendor support to keep them secure.

- Virtual technologies are often used by many of the leading cloud computing platforms and services to provide scalability and deliver cost-effective and dedicated virtual services. This paper doesn't go into detail on cloud security issues.

- However, the same rules for monitoring, configuration and risk management apply in the cloud. Cloud computing customers must adequately assess security risks (including virtualization issues) posed by cloud services and ensure that necessary controls and access to security- and regulatory-related data within their clouds is accessible when required.

Mistake #1 : Misconfiguring Virtual Hosting Platforms, Guests, and Networks

- Creating secure default configurations for virtual machines is much the same as configuring physical machine defaults. In the case of virtual servers, configuration problems are magnified.

- If a machine build starts out with poor default configurations, including unnecessary ports and services and other such items, those vulnerabilities will extend to each instance of the virtual machine that is replicated from that build. In light of the virtual machine hacks demonstrated at Black Hat, it is also important to note where virtual applications call to the host and vice versa.Virtual network configuration is another area where organizations make mistakes.

- On a virtual network, for example, some organizations still host their Web servers and database servers without proper segmentation. Some popular virtualization platforms provide only three virtual switch security configuration settings : promiscuous mode, forged transmits, and MAC address changes.
- What about when virtual systems make connections to other parts of your network? Moving from virtual to physical switches (and vice versa) makes it difficult to carry over policy and configuration controls between them.

Best Security Practices

- Leverage default secure gold builds, then clone other virtual systems from this base. Examples of secure by default configurations are listed at the Center for Internet Security (including benchmarks for popular virtualization platforms) and at the Information Assurance Support Environment.
- Manage the virtual machine's configuration lifecycle from cradle to grave with tools native to the virtual machine, and use outside tools where required. Monitoring tools should be virtual-machine-aware and able to detect and take action (alert/block/sandbox/move to remediation) on assets that deviate from the gold build. They should work with the VMM to correlate changes in VM and virtual network configuration, including on virtual systems behind virtual firewalled switches (which can't be done without working with the Hypervisor/VMM).
- Examine closely any virtualization platform capabilities that enable communication between guest and host operating systems, such as device drivers, copy/paste functions, leaks in memory, and so on. Where possible, these should be identified and disabled. System monitoring tools and virtualization-aware monitoring tools should be tuned to locate and monitor these communications paths. In addition, keep an eye on virtualization vendor security advisories for new vulnerabilities and patches.

Mistake #2 : Failure to Properly Separate Duties and Deploy Least Privilege Controls

- Creating separation of duties and providing the least amount of privilege necessary for users to perform their authorized tasks are basic tenets of information security that apply to both physical and virtual resources.
- Some virtualization platforms collapse the functions of system and network administration so that separating these duties, is difficult.
- As such, they give too much privilege and capability to virtual administrators. This level of privilege conflicts with compliance regulations including PCI DSS, FISMA, and others that require separation of duties and least privilege to protect sensitive data.
- Moreover, high privilege access raises the risk of abuse by privileged insiders, which accounted for 22 percent of breaches investigated by Verizon Business last year, according to the Verizon 2009 Data Breach Investigations Report.
- Beyond the insider issue, compromise of the virtual administrator's login credentials would yield a powerful set of capabilities for outside attackers.

Best Practices

- Use tried and true security mechanisms, such as requiring SSH for administrative console access.
- Use firewall alter rules to limit administrative virtualization console access to predetermined, authorized, internal network addresses to protect against an outside attacker gaining access to the virtualization administrative console.
- Employ a system of checks and balances, with processes to split functions and enforce dual controls for critical tasks.
- Set up approval processes for creating new virtual machines and moving new applications to new virtual machines.
- Monitor and audit logs for virtual machine usage activity in the data center and on end points. Look to VMaware monitoring tools that can also monitor in non-virtual environments to compare and report per policy.
- Security tools, such as host-based firewalls and host intrusion prevention, may also prove useful here.

Mistake #3 : Failure to Integrate into Change/Lifecycle Management

- Some specific problems in this category include failure to manage vulnerabilities and patches across virtual systems and failure to conduct system integrity checking for virtual systems.
- However, with the right combination of controls, organizations may be able to manage their virtual machine lifecycles more easily than their physical environments. Patch management is an area where virtualization is a mixed blessing.
- On the negative side, applying patches to the host OS VMM for physical hardware that's supporting numerous virtual systems can cause problems and interruptions with the virtual machines running in production, particularly if a system reboot is required.
- Of course, a reboot can be done during off hours (just as in the physical realm). And, on the positive side, virtualization can be used to avoid interruption by migrating live applications to other running virtual machines while virtual systems are patched sequentially.

Best Practices

- The same processes used for events that might trigger patching requirements, including monitoring vendor security advisories, apply in virtual systems. Test patches and follow a change control process.
- Look to native management capabilities provided by virtualization vendors as well as third party tools that can scan for vulnerabilities in virtual machines and work independent of and with the VMM (for example to see VMs behind firewalled switches).
- Use management agents that are part of default physical server configurations for your virtual servers as well, so that existing change management systems and processes are provided, along with visibility into virtual servers.

Mistake #4 : Failure to Coordinate Policy Between Virtual Machines and Network Connections

- With physical systems and network connections, we can be fairly sure that once we establish policies and physically connect servers, routers, switches and network security devices, things will remain static and change control policies will govern how policy and network configurations may be changed.
- It is the opposite with virtualization, which makes the creation and movement of virtual machines highly dynamic.
- This dynamic nature is the beauty of virtualization, but it is also problematic when it comes to attaching and enforcing security policy for virtual machines as they are moved around.
- VMs can also be modified in ways that their physical counterparts rarely would. Changes to network interfaces and port-group memberships can be made quickly and can therefore easily undo established network security zoning.
- The kind of isolation and security zones created through the use of firewalls, routers, switches, IPS devices, and other such physical devices on the network can be created in virtualization environments. The trouble is in getting the rules to follow the virtual machines as they move around.
- In addition, providing access control protections for the host OS platform is a highly desirable defense-in-depth strategy that can be achieved through the use of tools such as TCP Wrappers, pluggable authentication modules (PAM) and iptables.
- These technologies can provide access control capabilities for the virtualization host, allowing access control by hostname, IP address, time of day, group membership and username.

Best Practices

- Use security policy management tools, along with processes governing the management of virtual machines, to ensure that changing the location of VMs will trigger replication of required security functions to the new location.
- Ensure that physical infrastructure such as routers and switches, or their virtual environment equivalents, are bound to virtual machines. Create policies that move network associations required for virtual machines around with the virtual machines themselves. Seek virtualization-aware solutions that can help manage network security policies and work with the VMM/Hypervisor for added visibility and control.
- In the longer term, look for integrated and virtualization-aware solutions to more tightly couple security functions to virtual machines. Standards such as SR-IOV, mentioned earlier, will help make this a reality because they allow network security policy and capability to be bound to virtual machines.

Trust   **(Nov. 16, May 17)**

- Regarding scientific texts existed in different fields; a widely accepted definition about trust can be mentioned as followers. "Trust is a psychological state comprising the intention to accept vulnerability based upon positive expectations of the intentions or behavior of another". However the definition does not include all, its dynamic and various dimensions and capacity.

- Trust is an expanded concept of security which includes mental and practical criteria. Trust can be divided into hard trust (security-oriented) and soft trust (non-security) oriented trust.

- The hard trust includes parts and operations such as validity, encoding and security in processes however the soft trust covers dimensions like human psychology, loyalty to trade mark (brand loyalty) and user-friendliness. Fame is an example of soft trust which is part of online trust and can be most valuable asset of a company.

- A company's brand is liked with trust. If it cannot perform successfully in matters like trust and privacy, it will fail and be defeated.

- However people still have less confidence to the services provided online in comparison with the offline ones due to the lack of physical cues in digital world.

- So the infield of online service providing, lack of trust in them can have a negative effect in entering and competitive competence of the firms and old organization which were trust worthy for a longtime into the digital world.

- Some argue that there is no relation between security and trust. Nissenbaum argues that the security level does not affect trust.

- On the other hand if for example the people, who have more intention to invest on E-commerce, are assured their credit-card number and private information is protected through encoding methods, will increase the amount of trust among them.

- Now, following especial and technical meaning of trust, a simple definition of it can be summarized as such : if we have control over our data we trust in the system.

- For example, we rely on ATM because we are sure it pays the exact amount of money we withdraw, so we have control over our money. So every system needs to create trust.

- This is trust in cloud environment too as all information of the service users is available for CSP. The level of trust in cloud computing is regarded the basic or primary trust because the cloud computing is a recent technology and its role players do not have much valid and meaningful knowledge about each other.

- Therefore, trust has a positive impact on the understanding of the cloud computing application. May be distinction between the social-based and technical meaning of trust will be useful in presenting durable and dynamic trust while trust in cloud computing of course in case of trust being necessary in all considerations.

- Persistent trust is the long run trust on the essential features or infra-structures. This is because of rather stable social and technological mechanisms.

- Dynamic trust is the trust on special mods, contexts or on the summary or variable information which can be achieved through context-based social and technological mechanisms.
- Persistent social-based trust in hardware or software system is tool or device to create assurance on technological-based trust because persistent social-based trust guarantees application and maintenance of the hardware or software system.
- Also there is a connection between social-based trust and technological-based trust through vouching mechanisms because it is important to know who is vouching for something as well as what they are vouching; so the social-based trust should it be ignored of anytime.
- **Challenges in Trust**

Diminishing Control

- SoftCom finds that the moment its images leave its perimeter, it does not have much control over them or the processes that manipulate them. It does not know who can access the images which are stored on various disks in multiple locations and possibly managed by third-party providers.
- In cloud computing, this lack of control over the data and processes triggers the risk of losing data confidentiality, integrity, and availability.
- Cloud computing virtually requires consumers to relinquish control of running their applications and storing their data.
- The degree of lost control over the data and processes depends on the cloud service model. For example, in IaaS and PaaS, the provider usually has complete control of the server, storage facility, and network.
- It is the same with SaaS, but the provider also controls the applications. Enterprises retain only partial control of their data, which they often find quite alarming.

Lack of Transparency

- The consumer's perception is that a cloud is generally less secure than an in-house system, but better transparency could help address this issue. Data stored in a cloud provider's devices is not located on a single machine in a single location or country.
- Rather, the data is stored and processed across the entire virtual layer.
- There are two issues involved in transparency : one is the physical location of the storage and processing sites, and the other is the security profiles of these sites.
- In our example, SoftCom has lost visibility of its applications and storage sites. It should know where its images are processed and stored, because in some countries, the laws might not support SoftCom should a data breach or loss occur. In this highly fluid distributed environment, SoftCom needs to know how its images are protected while being moved within the system or across multiple sites owned by multiple independent software vendors.
- It should also know what data manipulation and access privileges third-party employees have and if audit trails are available. Without transparency, SoftCom does not know if there is any mismatch between its enterprise security requirements and CloudX's security

assurances. SoftCom's clients also need to know where their images are processed and stored and the security assurances of those sites.

- At the end of day, SoftCom is accountable to its own clients and thus must supply them with sufficient information for trusting CloudX.

Operating System Security   **(Nov. 16, May 17)**

- The proposed cloud operating system offers variety of selected applications that allow the users to write documents, draw graphs, compile classes and programs. We use mobile phones in that we use Drop Box Type software.
- It is Cloud based software to run that particular software we need special type of operating system which support cloud features for us. "Powerful services and applications are being integrated and packaged on the web in what the industry now calls cloud computing".
- The cloud can be established on either a single computer or with multiple computers. The first step towards building the cloud begins with a go through the available of documentation for single machine installation. Today, virtual machines on the cloud typically run the same traditional operating systems that were used on physical machines, e.g., Linux, Windows.
- Operating system is a platform for software under hardware. Operating system is a program that acts as an intermediary between a user of a computer and the computer hardware. Operating system controls and coordinates the use of the hardware among the various application programs for the various users.
- Operating System defines Resource allocator that manages and allocates resources. Operating System defines Control program as controls the execution of user programs and operation of I/O devices. Operating System defines Kernel as the one program running at all time.
- OS features needed for multiprogramming I/O routine supplied by the system. Memory management the system must allocate the memory to several jobs.
- CPU scheduling the system must choose among several jobs ready to run. Allocation of devices. Operating systems were originally developed to provide a set of common system services, such as I/O, communication and persistent storage to simplify application programming.
- With the advent of multiprogramming, this charter expanded to include abstracting shared resources that they were as easy to use as dedicated physical resource.

Various Operating System

- **Mobile cloud computing service (MCCS) :** It is an established perception that aspires at utilizing some techniques in cloud computing for the dispensation and storage of data on Smartphones. The Android OS is Linux-based and has the benefit of being used on various smartphones. The openness of the Android OS will aid user experience that will create future opportunity to get into other sections The authors argue that the openness of an operating system cannot be made at the expense of the system's security. As much as the authors see the openness of the Android OS as being a threat to its security.

- **TRANSOS :** Architecture operating system that gets their machines up and running, whether that is the Microsoft Windows, Apple Mac, Linux, Chrome, operating systems seem firmly entrenched in the personal computer and their files, documents, movies, sounds and images, sit deep within the hard drive.

- **HPCLOUD :** Simplify your data centre by pooling server, storage, and networking resources together with h Accelerate cloud innovation with the world's first software-defined server that delivers breakthrough efficiency and scale easy-to-use HPC resources built on a scalable platform delivering peak performance in an easy to use self-service model.

- **MIRAGE OS :** Framework is fully event driven GUI app. We can create application like chemical sensors in your fridge 1 click for share your data with other device.

- **OSPREY :** In the mid-term future we plan to port Osprey to Power PC, ARM, and possibly MIPS, and to provide a Linux compatibility layer, we adopt the multi kernel design in Osprey by partitioning most of the kernel state, running an independent scheduler on each core, and using message.

- **MEGAHA OS :** Megha OS is divided into three parts. They are cloud platforms (CP), cloud services(CS) and cloud storage (CSt). For the users cloud platform is provided by Megha OS.

- **VSTARE CLOUD :** VStar cloud architecture mainly composed of two parts, terminal operating system and a cloud operating system. Traditional operating system is not sufficient for supporting network computing environment.

- **JEOS OS :** Just Enough Operating System (JeOS), Ubuntu and other Linux architect, Linux's open source licensing also makes it a natural fit for developers who want to distribute their software as an appliance without worrying about OS licensing costs and constrictions.

- **XOS :** Xtreemoslinux , For mobile devices, XtreemOS provides the XtreemOS-MD flavour with VO support and specially-tailored, lightweight services for application execution, XtreemOS services should be designed to scale with the number of entities and their geographical distribution.

- **MIDORY :** Microkernel Architecture---these mechanisms included low level address ,only software executing At most level Midori handles all the latest web technologies like HTML5 and CSS3 GUI based launch by Microsoft Corporation in 20 November 1985. Software-isolated processes.

- **GLIDE OS :** The Glide OS provides automatic file and application compatibility across devices and operating systems. With Glide OS you also get the Glide Sync App which helps you to synchronize your home and work files. Glide OS 4.0 is a comprehensive AdFree cloud computing solution. 30 GB storage capacity

- **AMOEBA :** Amoeba OS is an advanced Online Operating System. Log in to your free account and join a cloud computing revolution that begins with great apps like Shutter Borg, Extreme and Surf.

4.8 SECURITY OF VIRTUALIZATION

- 2011 ended with the popularization of an idea : Bringing VMs (virtual machines) onto the cloud. Recent years have seen great advancements in both cloud computing and virtualization.

- On one hand there is the ability to pool various resources to provide software-as-a-service, infrastructure-as-a-service and platform-as-a-service.

- At its most basic, this is what describes cloud computing. On the other hand, we have virtual machines that provide agility, flexibility, and scalability to the cloud resources by allowing the vendors to copy, move, and manipulate their VMs at will.

- The term *virtual machine* essentially describes sharing the resources of one single physical computer into various computers within itself. *VMware* and *virtual box* are very commonly used virtual systems on desktops. Cloud computing effectively stands for many computers pretending to be one computing environment. Obviously, cloud computing would have many virtualized systems to maximize resources.

- Keeping this information in mind, we can now look into the security issues that arise within a cloud-computing scenario. As more and more organizations follow the "Into the Cloud" concept, malicious hackers keep finding ways to get their hands on valuable information by manipulating safeguards and breaching the security layers (if any) of cloud environments.

- One issue is that the cloud-computing scenario is not as transparent as it claims to be. The service user has no clue about how his information is processed and stored. In addition, the service user cannot directly control the flow of data/information storage and processing.

- The service provider usually is not aware of the details of the service running on his or her environment. Thus, possible attacks on the cloud-computing environment can be classified in to :

- **Resource attacks :** These kinds of attacks include manipulating the available resources into mounting a large-scale botnet attack. These kinds of attacks target either cloud providers or service providers.

- **Data Attacks :** These kinds of attacks include unauthorized modification of sensitive data at nodes, or performing configuration changes to enable a sniffing attack via a specific device etc. These attacks are focused on cloud providers, service providers, and also on service users.

- **Denial of Service attacks :** The creation of a new virtual machine is not a difficult task, and thus, creating rogue VMs and allocating huge spaces for them can lead to a Denial of Service attack for service providers when they opt to create a new VM on the cloud. This kind of attack is generally called virtual machine sprawling.

- **Backdoor :** Another threat on a virtual environment empowered by cloud computing is the use of backdoor VMs that leak sensitive information and can destroy data privacy.

- Having virtual machines would indirectly allow anyone with access to the host disk files of the VM to take a snapshot or illegal copy of the whole System. This can lead to corporate espionage and piracy of legitimate products.

- With so many obvious security issues (and a lot more can be added to the list), we need to enumerate some steps that can be used to secure virtualization in cloud computing. The most neglected aspect of any organization is its physical security.

- An advanced social engineer can take advantage of weak physical-security policies an organization has put in place. Thus, it' is important to have a consistent, context-aware security policy when it comes to controlling access to a data center.

- Traffic between the virtual machines needs to be monitored closely by using at least a few standard monitoring tools.

- After thoroughly enhancing physical security, it is time to check security on the inside. A well-configured gateway should be able to enforce security when any virtual machine is reconfigured, migrated, or added. This will help to prevent VM sprawls and rogue VMs. Another approach that might help enhance internal security is the use of third-party validation checks, performed in accordance with security standards.

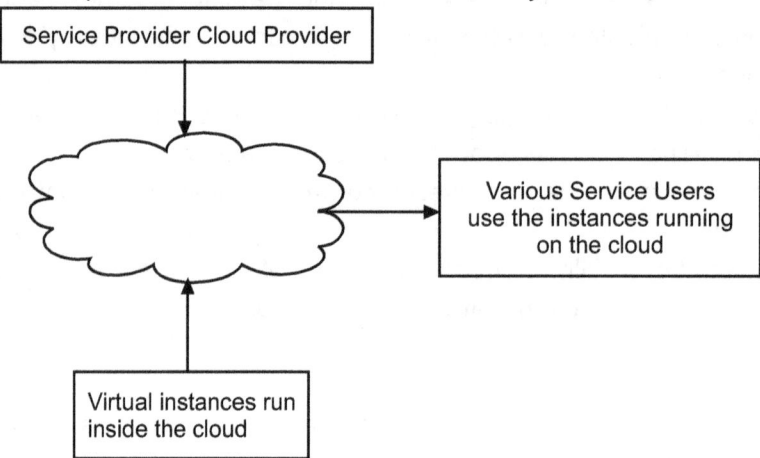

Fig. 4.8 : Service level agreement

- In the above figure, we see that the service provider and cloud provider work together and are bound by the *Service Level Agreement*.

- The cloud is used to run various instances, whereas the service end users pay for each use instant the cloud is used. The following section tries to explain an approach that can be used to check the integrity of virtual systems running inside the cloud.

- Checking virtual systems for integrity increases the capabilities for monitoring and securing environments. One of the primary focuses of this integrity check should the seamless integration of existing virtual systems like VMware and virtual box.

- This would lead to file integrity checking and increased protection against data losses within VMs. Involving agentless anti-malware intrusion detection and prevention in one single virtual appliance (unlike isolated point security solutions) would contribute greatly towards VM integrity checks. This will greatly reduce operational overhead while adding zero footprints.
- A server on a cloud may be used to deploy web applications, and in this scenario an OWASP top-ten vulnerability check will have to be performed. Data on a cloud should be encrypted with suitable encryption and data-protection algorithms.
- Using these algorithms, we can check the integrity of the user profile or system profile trying to access disk files on the VMs. Profiles lacking in security protections can be considered infected by malwares.
- Working with a system ratio of one user to one machine would also greatly reduce risks in virtual computing platforms.
- To enhance the security aspect even more, after a particular environment is used, it is best to sanitize the system (reload) and destroy all the residual data. Using incoming IP addresses to determine scope on Windows-based machines, and using SSH configuration settings on Linux machines, will help maintain a secure one-to-one connection.

4.8.1 Virtualization Components

- Virtualization is one of most important elements that makes cloud computing. Virtualization is a technology to help. IT organizations optimize their application performance in a cost-effective manner, but it can also present its share of application delivery challenges that cause some security difficulties.
- Most of the current interest in virtualization revolves around virtual servers in part because virtualizing servers can result in significant cost savings. The phrase virtual machine refers to a software computer that, like a physical computer, runs an operating system and applications.
- An operating system on a virtual machine is called a guest operating system. In addition, there is a management layer called a virtual machine monitor or manager (VMM) that creates and controls the all virtual machines' in virtual environment.
- A hypervisor is one of many virtualization techniques which allow multiple operating systems, termed guests, to run concurrently on a host computer, a feature called hardware virtualization.
- It is so named because it is conceptually one level higher than a supervisor. The hypervisor presents to the guest operating systems a virtual operating platform and monitors the execution of the guest OS (guest operating systems).
- Multiple instances of a variety of operating systems may share the virtualized hardware resources. Hypervisor is installed on server hardware whose only task is to run guest operating systems.

4.8.2 Virtualization Approaches

- In a traditional environment consisting of physical servers connected by a physical switch, IT organizations can get detailed management information about the traffic that goes between the servers from that switch.

- Unfortunately, that level of information management is not typically provided from a virtual switch. Basically, the virtual switch has links from the physical switch via the physical NIC that attaches to Virtual Machines.

- The resulting lack of oversight of the traffic flows between and among the Virtual Machines on the same physical level affects security and performance surveying. There are several common approaches to virtualization with differences between how each controls the virtual machines. The architecture of these approaches is illustrated in Fig. 4.9.

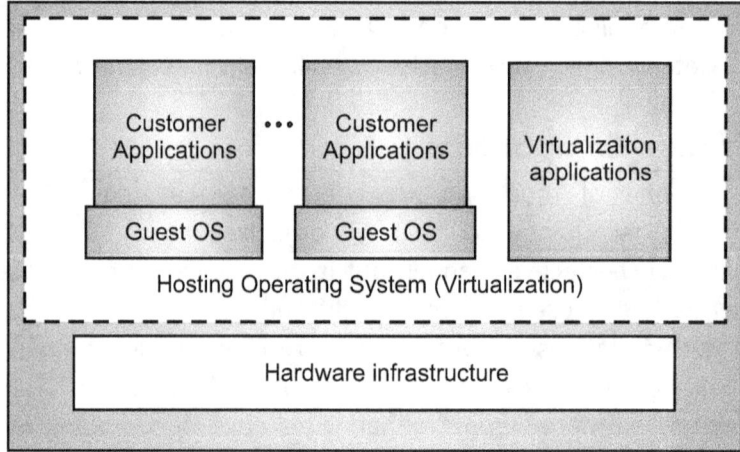

Fig. 4.6 : Operating System based Virtualization

Operating System-Based Virtualization :

- In this approach (Fig. 4.9), virtualization is enabled by a host operating system that supports multiple isolated and virtualized guest OSs on a single physical server with the characteristic that all are on the same operating system kernel with exclusive control over the hardware infrastructure.

- The host operating system can view and has control over the Virtual Machines. This approach is simple, but it has vulnerabilities, such as when an attacker injects controlling scripts into the host operating system that causes all guest OSs to gain control over the host OS on this kernel.

- The result is that the attacker will have control over all VMs that exist or will be established in the future.

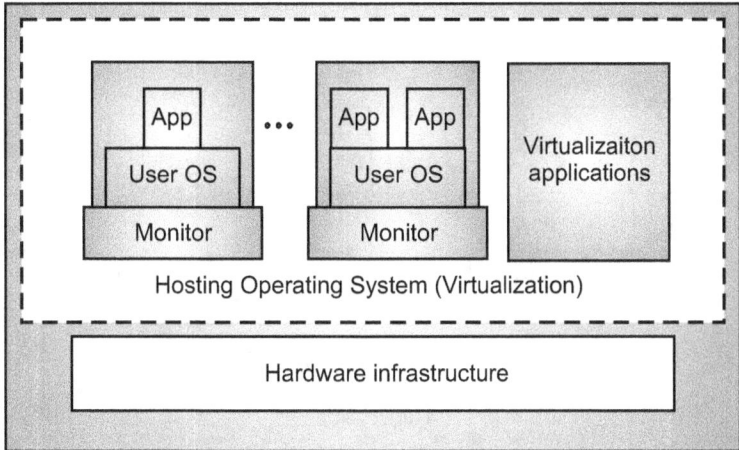

Fig. 4.10 : Application based Virtualization

Application Based Virtualization

- An application-based virtualization is hosted on top of the hosting operating system (Fig. 4.10). This virtualization application then emulates each VM containing its own guest operating system and related applications.

- This virtualization architecture is not commonly used in commercial environments. Security issues of this approach are similar to Operating system-based.

Hypervisor-Based Virtualization

- The hypervisor is available at the boot time of machine in order to control the sharing of system resources across multiple VMs.

- Some of these VMs are privileged partitions which manage the virtualization platform and hosted Virtual Machines. In this architecture, the privileged partitions view and control the Virtual Machines.

- This approach establishes the most controllable environment and can utilize additional security tools such as intrusion detection systems.

- However, it is vulnerable because the hypervisor has a single point of failure. If the hypervisor crashes or the attacker gains control over it, then all VMs are under the attacker's control.

- However, taking control over the hypervisor from the virtual machine level is difficult, though not impossible. According to this characteristic, this layer chose for implementing proposed security architecture.

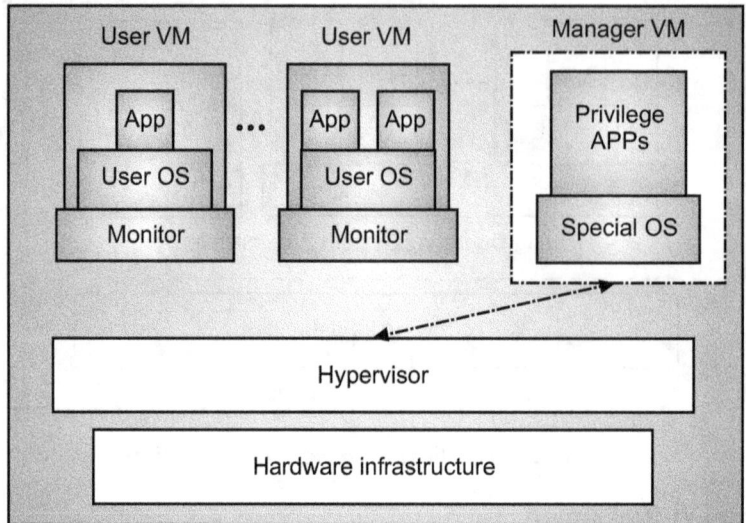

Fig. 4.11 : Hypervisor based virtualization

Trusted Virtual Machine Monitor

- Generally, encryption is used by most of users and it is not possible to ask users not to encrypt their data. In my proposed architecture, there are not any requirements to reveal user data or encryption key to cloud providers. There are also added some new features to increase security performance in virtualization technology such as security and reliability monitoring units (VSEM and VREM).

- HSEM and HREM are the main components of the security system, and all the other parts of the security system communicate with them, but HSEM decides if the VM is an attacker or a victim. Actually, HSEM receives behavioural information from VSEM and HREM and never collects any information itself.

- In addition, HSEM notifies the hypervisor about which VM is under Level-2 monitoring in order to set service limits until the status is determined. Fig. 4.13 illustrates the new secure architecture and the new units in VMs level, VSEM and VREM, which is available for all VMs (and also in Management VM).

- In addition, there are two other new units, HSEM and HREM, which is available in the hypervisor level. VSEM and VREM consume low resources of the VM, but they help to secure VMs against attacks.

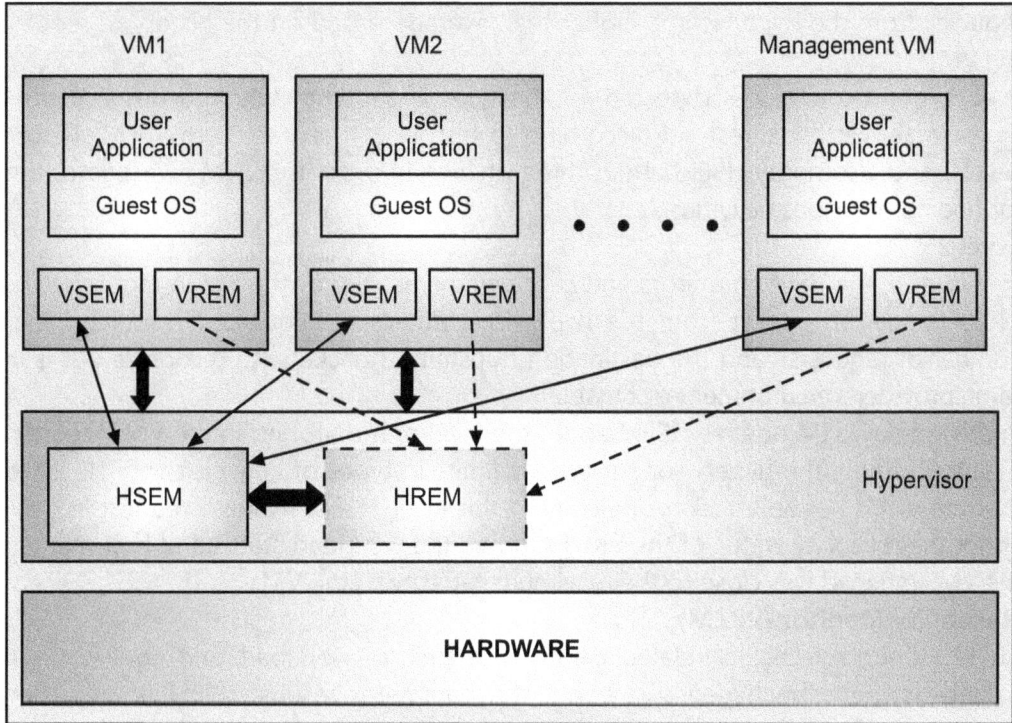

Fig. 4.12 : Hypervisor trusted virtual machine monitor

VM Security Monitor (VSEM)

- There is a VSEM within every VM that is running in a virtual environment. These monitors acts as sensors, but are different from sensors. In fact, VSEM is a two-level controller and behaviour recorder in the cloud system that helps HSEM identify attacks and malicious behaviour with less processing.

- VSEM monitors the security-related behaviours of VMs and reports them to HSEM. Because there are a large number of transmissions in cloud, and sending all of them to HSEM consumes a lot of bandwidth and processing resources, which can affect general hypervisor activity, some tasks were done by VSEMs in VMs such as collecting information that is asked by HSEM.

- In addition, because users do not want to consume their resources, which they paid for it, VSEMs have two levels of monitoring that consume more resource only when it is necessary. Actually, each level of VSEM is monitored almost the same events but at different detail levels.

(1) Level 1

- In this level, the VSEMs monitor their own VMs. In this level VSEM collects of the source and destination addresses which are in head of data, number of unsuccessful and successful tries in sending data, and number of requests that were sent to the hypervisor.

- At this level, VSEM, according to the brief history of the VM which provided by HSEM, looks for anomaly behaviour (HSEM has had history of VMs in more details). For instance, the system identifies the VM as a potential attacker or victim if the number of service requests from the hypervisor is higher than average based on the history of requests of the VM.

- If abnormal behaviour is detected, or the type of sending data and unsuccessful tries increase above that threshold (according to history of the VM), then VSEM switches to Level 2 and also notify HSEM about this switching in order to HSEM investigates the VM for finding malicious activities.

(2) Level 2
- In this level, the VSEM monitors and captures the activity of the VM in more detail, such as VM's special request from the hypervisor, details of requested resources (e.g. the number of requests), and the destination transmitted packets (to recognize if it is in the same provider's environment or outside).
- In this mode VSEM notifies HSEM about the level of monitoring in the VM. According to this notification, the hypervisor set activity limits in types of activities until HSEM learns that the VM is not an attacker or victim. At this level, HSEM makes a request from VREM about the reliability status of the VM, including the workload status and how many times the VM workload was close to the maximum capacity of the VM.

VM Reliability Monitor (VREM)
- VREM monitors reliability-related parameters, such as workload, and notifies the load-balancer (within the hypervisor) about the parameter results. VREM is also used for security purposes.
- The VREM will send useful information such as workload status to HREM and requests the status of the VM from HSEM, and then it decides whether to give the VM more resources.
- Actually, if the VM requests as many resources as it can (that is different behaviour according to its usage history), it may signify an overflow attack victim. Therefore, proposed HREM can detect overflow attacks and notify the HSEM about it.

QUESTIONS

1. Explain the cloud security fundamentals.
2. What are the risks involved in cloud security ?
3. Draw and explain CSA cloud reference model.
4. Write short note on privacy and security in cloud.
5. Draw and explain cloud security architecture.
6. What are the principals of cloud security?
7. Write short note on identity management and access control.
8. Write short note on security of virtualization components.

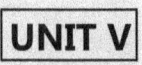

CLOUD IMPLEMENTATION AND APPLICATIONS

5.1 AMAZON EC2 AND S3

- Amazon Elastic Compute Cloud (Amazon EC2) is a web service that provides resizable compute capacity in the cloud. It is designed to make web-scale cloud computing easier for developers. Amazon EC2s simple web service interface allows you to obtain and configure capacity with minimal friction. It provides you with complete control of your computing resources and lets you run on Amazon's proven computing environment. Amazon EC2 reduces the time required to obtain and boot new server instances to minutes, allowing you to quickly scale capacity, both up and down, as your computing requirements change.

- Amazon EC2 changes the economics of computing by allowing you to pay only for capacity that you actually use. Amazon EC2 provides developers the tools to build failure resilient applications and isolate themselves from common failure scenarios.

5.2 BENEFITS OF AMAZON EC2 AND S3   (Nov. 16, May 17)

Elastic Web-Scale Computing

- Amazon EC2 enables you to increase or decrease capacity within minutes, not hours or days. You can commission one, hundreds or even thousands of server instances simultaneously.

- Of course, because this is all controlled with web service APIs, your application can automatically scale itself up and down depending on its needs.

- **Completely Controlled**

You have complete control of your instances. You have root access to each one, and you can interact with them as you would any machine. You can stop your instance while retaining the data on your boot partition and then subsequently restart the same instance using web service APIs. Instances can be rebooted remotely using web service APIs. You also have access to console output of your instances.

- **Flexible Cloud Hosting Services**

You have the choice of multiple instance types, operating systems, and software packages. Amazon EC2 allows you to select a configuration of memory, CPU, instance storage, and the boot partition size that is optimal for your choice of operating system and application. For example, your choice of operating systems includes numerous Linux distributions, and Microsoft Windows Server.

- **Designed for use with other Amazon Web Services**

Amazon EC2 works in conjunction with Amazon Simple Storage Service (Amazon S3), Amazon Relational Database Service (Amazon RDS), Amazon SimpleDB and Amazon Simple Queue Service (Amazon SQS) to provide a complete solution for computing, query processing and storage across a wide range of applications.

- **Reliable**

Amazon EC2 offers a highly reliable environment where replacement instances can be rapidly and predictably commissioned. The service runs within Amazon's proven network infrastructure and data centers. The Amazon EC2 Service Level Agreement commitment is 99.95% availability for each Amazon EC2 Region.

- **Secure**
    - Amazon EC2 works in conjunction with Amazon VPC to provide security and robust networking functionality for your compute resources.
    - Your compute instances are located in a Virtual Private Cloud (VPC) with an IP range that you specify. You decide which instances are exposed to the Internet and which remain private.
    - Security Groups and networks ACLs allow you to control inbound and outbound network access to and from your instances.
    - You can connect your existing IT infrastructure to resources in your VPC using industry-standard encrypted IPsec VPN connections.
    - You can provision your EC2 resources as Dedicated Instances. Dedicated Instances are Amazon EC2 Instances that run on hardware dedicated to a single customer for additional isolation.
    - For more information on Amazon EC2 security refer to our Amazon Web Services: Overview of Security Process document.
    - If you do not have a default VPC you must create a VPC and launch instances into that VPC to leverage advanced networking features such as private subnets, outbound security group filtering, network ACLs, Dedicated Instances, and VPN connections.

- **Inexpensive**
    - Amazon EC2 passes on to you the financial benefits of Amazon's scale. You pay a very low rate for the compute capacity you actually consume. See Amazon EC2 Instance Purchasing Options for a more detailed description.
    - **On-Demand Instances :** On-Demand Instances let you pay for compute capacity by the hour with no long-term commitments. This frees you from the costs and complexities of planning, purchasing, and maintaining hardware and transforms what are commonly large fixed costs into much smaller variable costs. On-Demand Instances also remove the need to buy "safety net" capacity to handle periodic traffic spikes.
    - **Reserved Instances :** Reserved Instances provide you with a significant discount (up to 75%) compared to On-Demand Instance pricing. There are three Reserved

Instance payment options (No Upfront, Partial Upfront, All Upfront) that enable you to balance the amount you pay upfront with your effective hourly price. The Reserved Instance Market place is also available, which provides you with the opportunity to sell Reserved Instances if your needs change (i.e. want to move instances to a new AWS Region, change to a new instance type, or sell capacity for projects that end before your Reserved Instance term expires).

- **Spot Instances :** Spot Instances allow customers to bid on unused Amazon EC2 capacity and run those instances for as long as their bid exceeds the current Spot Price. The Spot Price changes periodically based on supply and demand, and customers whose bids meet or exceed it gain access to the available Spot Instances. If you have flexibility in when your applications can run, Spot Instances can significantly lower your Amazon EC2 costs.

- **Easy to Start**

Quickly get started with Amazon EC2 by visiting AWS Marketplace to choose preconfigured software on Amazon Machine Images (AMIs). You can quickly deploy this software to EC2 via 1-Click launch or with the EC2 console.

- **What is AMI?**

An Amazon Machine Image (AMI) provides the information required to launch an instance, which is a virtual server in the cloud. You specify an AMI when you launch an instance, and you can launch as many instances from the AMI as you need. You can also launch instances from as many different AMIs as you need.

An AMI includes the following:

- A template for the root volume for the instance (for example, an operating system, an application server, and applications).
- Launch permissions that control which AWS accounts can use the AMI to launch instances.
- A block device mapping that specifies the volumes to attach to the instance when it is launched.

- **Root Device Storage Concepts**

You can launch an instance from one of two types of AMIs: an instance store-backed AMI or an Amazon EBS-backed AMI. The description of an AMI includes which type of AMI it is; you will see the root device referred to in some places as either ebs (for Amazon EBS-backed) or instance store (for instance store-backed). This is important because there are significant differences between what you can do with each type of AMI. For more information about these differences.

- **Instance Store-backed Instances**

- Instances that use instance stores for the root device automatically have instance store volumes available, with one serving as the root device volume. When an instance is launched, the image that is used to boot the instance is copied to the root volume (typically sda1). Any data on the instance store volumes persists as long as the instance is running, but this data is deleted when the instance is terminated (instance store-backed instances do not support the Stop action) or if it fails (such as if an underlying drive has issues).

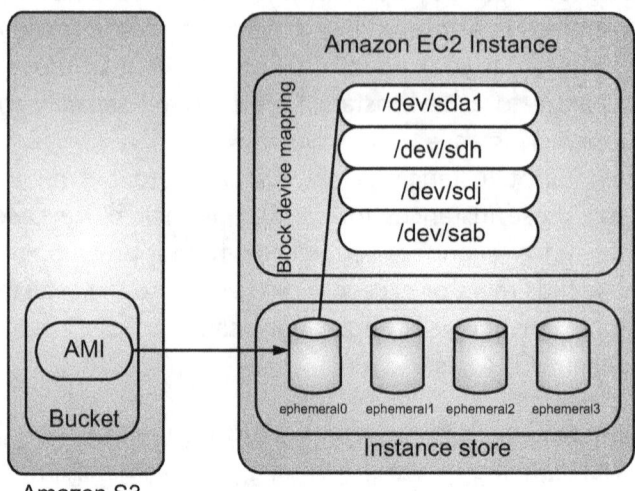

Fig. 5.1

- After an instance store-backed instance fails or terminates, it cannot be restored. If you plan to use Amazon EC2 instance store-backed instances, we highly recommend that you distribute the data on your instance stores across multiple Availability Zones. You should also back up the data on your instance store volumes to persistent storage on a regular basis.

Amazon EBS-backed Instances

- Instances that use Amazon EBS for the root device automatically have an Amazon EBS volume attached.
- When you launch an Amazon EBS-backed instance, we create an Amazon EBS volume for each Amazon EBS snapshot referenced by the AMI you use. You can optionally use other Amazon EBS volumes or instance store volumes.

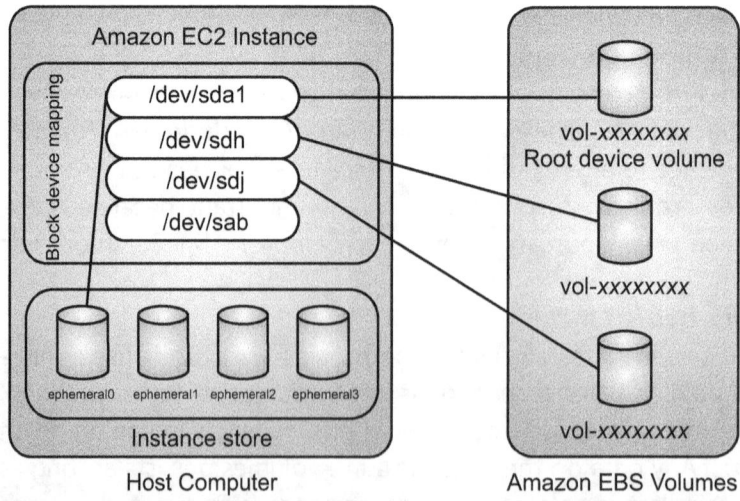

Fig. 5.2

- An Amazon EBS-backed instance can be stopped and later restarted without affecting data stored in the attached volumes. There are various instance and volume-related tasks you can do when an Amazon EBS-backed instance is in a stopped state.
- For example, you can modify the properties of the instance, you can change the size of your instance or update the kernel it is using, or you can attach your root volume to a different running instance for debugging or any other purpose.
- By default, the root device volume and the other Amazon EBS volumes attached when you launch an Amazon EBS-backed instance are automatically deleted when the instance terminates. For information about how to change this behavior when you launch an instance

How to Create an AMI?

Creating an instance store-Backed Linux AMIWU1

- To create an instance store-backed Linux AMI, start from an instance that you have launched from an existing instance store-backed Linux AMI.
- After you've customized the instance to suit your needs, bundle the volume and register a new AMI, which you can use to launch new instances with these customizations.
- The AMI creation process is different for instance store-backed AMIs. For more information about the differences between Amazon EBS-backed and instance store-backed instances, and how to determine the root device type for your instance, see Storage for the Root Device.
- If you need to create an Amazon EBS-backed Linux AMI, see Creating an Amazon EBS-Backed Linux AMI.

Overview of the Creation Process for Instance Store-Backed AMIs

The following diagram summarizes the process of creating an AMI from an instance store-backed instance.

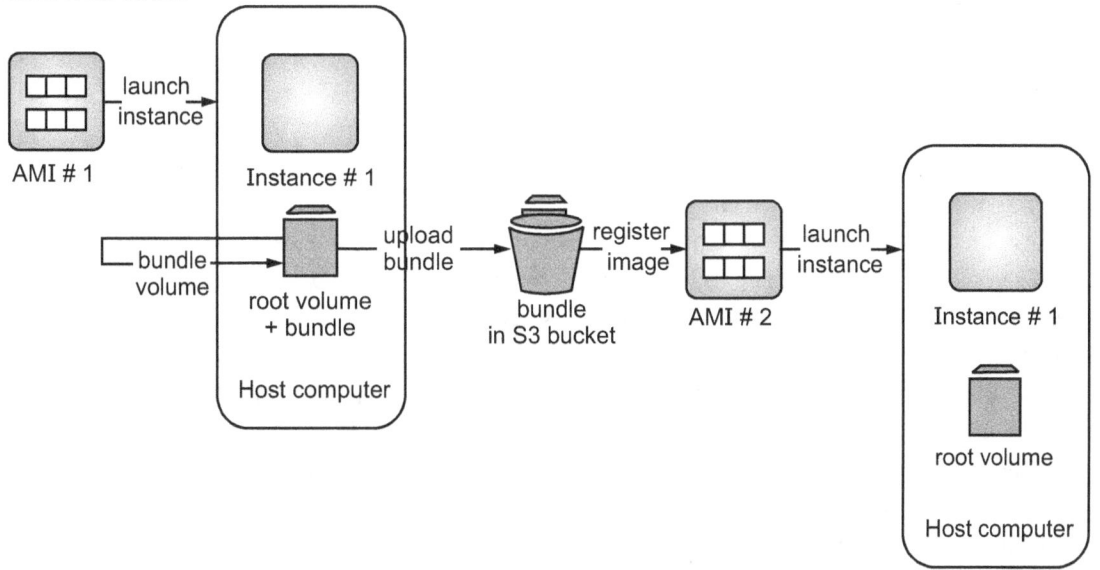

Fig. 5.3

- First, launch an instance from an AMI that is similar to the AMI that you had like to create. You can connect to your instance and customize it. When the instance is set up the way you want it, you can bundle it. It takes several minutes for the bundling process to complete.

- After the process completes, you have a bundle, which consists of an image manifest (image.manifest.xml) and files (image.part.xx) that contain a template for the root volume. Next you upload the bundle to your Amazon S3 bucket and then register your AMI.

- When you launch an instance using the new AMI, we create the root volume for the instance using the bundle that you uploaded to Amazon S3. The storage space used by the bundle in Amazon S3 incurs charges to your account until you delete it. For more information, see Deregistering Your AMI.

- If you add instance store volumes to your instance in addition to the root device volume, the block device mapping for the new AMI contains information for these volumes, and the block device mappings for instances that you launch from the new AMI automatically contain information for these volumes. For more information.

Prerequisites

Before you can create the AMI, you must complete the following tasks:

- Install the AMI tools.
- Install the API tools.
- Ensure that you have an Amazon S3 bucket for the bundle. To create an Amazon S3 bucket, open the Amazon S3 console and click **Create Bucket**.
- Ensure that you have the following credentials:
- Your AWS account ID. To retrieve your account ID, go to Your Security Credentials and expand **Account Identifiers**.
- An X.509 certificate and private key. If you need to create an X.509 certificate, go to Your Security Credentials, expand X.509 Certificates, and click Create New Certificate. The X.509 certificate and private key are used to encrypt and decrypt your AMI.
- Your access key ID. If you need to retrieve or create an access key ID, go to Your Security Credentials, and expand Access Keys.
- Your secret access key. You can't retrieve your secret access key. Therefore, if you can't find your secret access key, you'll need to create a new one. To create a secret access key, go to Your Security Credentials, expand **Access Keys**, and click **Create New Access Key**.
- Connect to your instance and customize it. For example, you can install software and applications, copy data, delete temporary files, and modify the Linux configuration.

To prepare to use the Amazon EC2 AMI Tools (HVM instances only)

- The Amazon EC2 AMI tools require GRUB Legacy to boot properly. Some AMIs (most notably, Ubuntu) is configured to use GRUB 2. You must check to see that your instance uses GRUB Legacy, and if not, you need to install and configure it.

- HVM instances also require partitioning tools to be installed for the AMI tools to work properly.

Check to see if your instance uses GRUB Legacy.

List the block devices to find the root block device.

[ec2-user ~]$ lsblk

NAME MAJ:MIN	RM	SIZE	ROTYPE	MOUNTPOINT
xvda	202:0 0	8G	0	disk
xvda1	202:1 0	8G	0	part /
xvdb	202:16 0	30G	0	disk /media/ephemeral0

In this example, the root device (indicated by a MOUNTPOINT of /) is /dev/xvda1. The root block device is its parent, /dev/xvda.

(a) Determine the GRUB version on the root block device.

[ec2-user ~]$ sudo file -s /dev/xvda

/dev/xvda: x86 boot sector; GRand Unified Bootloader, stage1 version 0x3, stage2 address 0x2000, 1st sector stage2 0x800, stage2 segment 0x200, GRUB version 0.94; partition 1: ID=0xee, starthead 254, startsector 1, 16777215 sectors, extended partition table (last)\011, code offset 0x48

In the above example, the GRUB version is 0.94, which is GRUB Legacy. If your GRUB version is 0.9x or less, you may move on to **Step** 3. If you do not see a GRUB version in this output, try the **grub-install -v** command.

ubuntu:~$ grub-install -v

grub-install (GRUB) 1.99-21ubuntu3.10

In this example, the GRUB version is greater than 0.9x, so GRUB Legacy must be installed.

(b) Install the grub package using the package manager for your distribution to install GRUB Legacy. For Ubuntu instances, use the following command.

ubuntu:~$ sudo apt-get install -y grub

You can verify that your instance is using GRUB Legacy with the **grub --version** command.

ubuntu:~$ grub --version

grub (GNU GRUB 0.97)

Install the following partition management packages using the package manager for your distribution.

gdisk (some distributions may call this package gptfdisk instead)

kpartx

For Ubuntu instances, use the following command.

ubuntu:~$ sudo apt-get install -y gdisk kpartx

Check the kernel parameters for your instance.

```
ubuntu:~$ cat /proc/cmdline
BOOT_IMAGE=/boot/vmlinuz-3.2.0-54-virtual          root=UUID=4f392932-ed93-4f8f-aee7-
72bc5bb6ca9d ro console=ttyS0 xen_emul_unplug=unnecessary
```

Note the options following the kernel and root device parameters,

```
console=ttyS0 and xen_emul_unplug=unnecessary.
```

Check the kernel entries in /boot/grub/menu.lst.

```
ubuntu:~$ grep ^kernel /boot/grub/menu.lst
kernel/boot/vmlinuz-3.2.0-54-virtual root=LABEL=cloudimg-rootfs ro console=hvc0
kernel/boot/vmlinuz-3.2.0-54-virtual root=LABEL=cloudimg-rootfs ro single
kernel  /boot/memtest86+.bin
```

Note that the console parameter is pointing to hvc0 instead of ttyS0 and that the xen_emul_unplug=unnecessary parameter is missing.

Edit the /boot/grub/menu.lst file with your favorite text editor (such as **vim** or **nano**) to change the console and add the parameters you identified earlier to the boot entries.

TitleUbuntu 12.04.3 LTS, kernel 3.2.0-54-virtual

```
Root(hd0)
kernel    /boot/vmlinuz-3.2.0-54-virtual    root=LABEL=cloudimg-rootfs    ro    console=ttyS0
xen_emul_unplug=unnecessary
initrd /boot/initrd.img-3.2.0-54-virtual
title Ubuntu 12.04.3 LTS, kernel 3.2.0-54-virtual (recovery mode)
root (hd0)
kernel  /boot/vmlinuz-3.2.0-54-virtual  root=LABEL=cloudimg-rootfs  ro  single  console=ttyS0
xen_emul_unplug=unnecessary
initrd /boot/initrd.img-3.2.0-54-virtual
titleUbuntu 12.04.3 LTS, memtest86+
root (hd0)
kernel/boot/memtest86+.bin
```

Verify that your kernel entries now contain the correct parameters.

```
ubuntu:~$ grep ^kernel /boot/grub/menu.lst
kernel/boot/vmlinuz-3.2.0-54-virtual       root=LABEL=cloudimg-rootfs      ro      console=ttyS0
xen_emul_unplug=unnecessary
kernel/boot/vmlinuz-3.2.0-54-virtual   root=LABEL=cloudimg-rootfs   ro   single   console=ttyS0
xen_emul_unplug=unnecessary
kernel /boot/memtest86+.bi
```

Creation of AMI

This procedure assumes that you have satisfied the prerequisites in Prerequisites.

1. Upload your credentials to your instance. We use these credentials to ensure that only you and Amazon EC2 can access your AMI.

(a) Create a temporary directory on your instance for your credentials as follows:

[ec2-user ~]$ mkdir /tmp/cert

This enables you to exclude your credentials from the created image.

(b) Copy your X.509 certificate and private key from your computer to the /tmp/cert directory on your instance, using a secure copy tool such as scp. The -i my-private-key.pem option in the following scp command is the private key you use to connect to your instance with SSH, not the X.509 private key.

2. Prepare the bundle to upload to Amazon S3 using the ec2-bundle-vol command. Be sure to specify the -e option to exclude the directory where your credentials are stored. By default, the bundle process excludes files that might contain sensitive information. These files include *.sw, *.swo, *.swp, *.pem, *.priv, *id_rsa*, *id_dsa* *.gpg, *.jks,*/.ssh/authorized_keys, and */.bash_history. To include all of these files, use the --no-filter option. To include some of option.

3. By default, the AMI bundling process creates a compressed, encrypted collection of files in the /tmp directory that represent your root volume. If you do not have enough free disk space in /tmp to store the bundle, you need to specify a different location for the bundle to be stored with the -d /path/to/bundle/storage option. Some instances have ephemeral storage mounted at /mnt or /media/ephemeral0 that you can use, or you can also create, attach, and mount a new Amazon EBS volume to store the bundle.

The ec2-bundle-vol command needs to run as root. For most commands, you can use sudo to gain elevated permissions, but in this case, you should run sudo -E su to keep your environment variables.

[ec2-user ~]$ sudo -E su

Run the ec2-bundle-vol command with the following arguments. If you do not have enough available disk space in/tmp to store your bundle, specify a location that has available space with the -d /path/to/bundle/storage option. For HVM instances, be sure to add the --partition flag; otherwise, your AMI will not boot.

[root   ec2-user]# $EC2_AMITOOL_HOME/bin/ec2-bundle-vol   -k   /tmp/cert/pk-HKZYKTAIG2ECMXYIBH3HXV4ZBEXAMPLE.pem -c /tmp/cert/cert-HKZYKTAIG2ECMXYIBH3HXV4ZBEXAMPLE.pem -u

your_aws_account_id -r x86_64 -e /tmp/cert. It can take a few minutes to create the image. When this command completes, your tmp directory contains the bundle (image.manifest.xml, plus multiple image.part.xx files).

Exit from the root shell.

[root ec2-user]# exit

4. Upload your bundle to Amazon S3 using the ec2-upload-bundle command. Note that if the bundle prefixes (directories) don't exist in the bucket, this command creates them.

Note :

If you specified a path with the -d /path/to/bundle/storage option in Step 2., use that same path in the -moption below, instead of /tmp.

```
[ec2-user   ~]$   ec2-upload-bundle   -b   my-s3-bucket/bundle_folder/bundle_name   -m
/tmp/image.manifest.xml -a your_access_key_id -s your_secret_access_key --region us-west-2
(Optional)
```

After the bundle is uploaded to Amazon S3, you can remove the bundle from the /tmp directory on the instance using the following rm command:

Note :

If you specified a path with the -d /path/to/bundle/storage option, use that same path below, instead of /tmp.

```
[ec2-user ~]$ sudo rm /tmp/image.manifest.xml /tmp/image.part.* /tmp/image
```

Register your AMI using the ec2-register command. Note that you don't need to specify the -O and -W options if you've set the AWS_ACCESS_KEY and AWS_SECRET_KEY environment variables.

Important

For HVM AMIs, add the --virtualization-type hvm flag.

```
[ec2-user   ~]$   ec2-register  my-s3-bucket/bundle_folder/bundle_name/image.manifest.xml  -n
AMI_name -O your_access_key_id -W your_secret_access_key --region us-west-2
```

5.2 APACHE CLOUDSTACK

5.2.1 What is Apache CloudStack?

Apache CloudStack is a top-level project of the Apache Software Foundation (ASF). The project develops open source software for deploying public and private Infrastructure-as-a-Service (IaaS) clouds.

CloudStack provides an open and flexible cloud orchestration platform to deliver reliable and scalable private and public clouds. What's that mean, exactly?

Features and Functionality

Apache CloudStack is a Java-based project that provides a management server and agents (if needed) for hypervisor hosts so that you can run an IaaS cloud. Some, but not all, of the features and functionality provided by CloudStack:

- Works with hosts running XenServer/XCP, KVM, Hyper-V, and/or VMware ESXi with vSphere.
- Provides a friendly Web-based UI for managing the cloud.
- Provides a native API.
- May provide an Amazon S3/EC2 compatible API (optional).
- Manages storage for instances running on the hypervisors (primary storage) as well as templates, snapshots, and ISO images (secondary storage).
- Orchestrates network services from the data link layer (L2) to some application layer (L7) services, such as DHCP, NAT, firewall, VPN, and so on.
- Accounting of network, compute, and storage resources.

- Multi-tenancy/account separation.
- User management.

In short, organizations can use Apache CloudStack to deploy a full-featured public or private IaaS cloud.

Choosing a Deployment Architecture

The architecture used in a deployment will vary depending on the size and purpose of the deployment. This section contains examples of deployment architecture, including a small-scale deployment useful for test and trial deployments and a fully redundant large-scale setup for production deployments.

Small-Scale Deployment

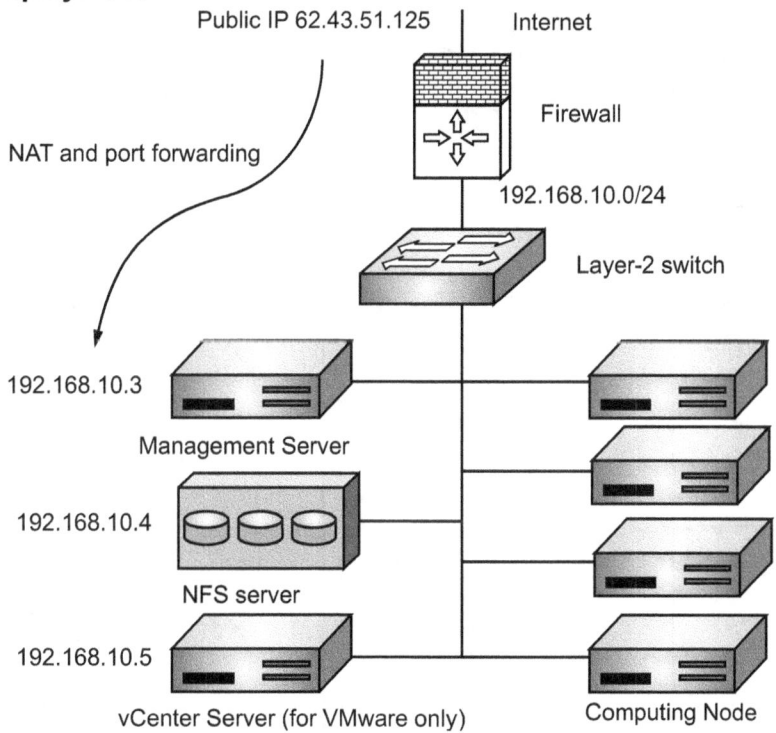

Fig. 5.4 : Small-scale deployment

This diagram illustrates the network architecture of a small-scale CloudStack Deployment :

- A firewall provides a connection to the Internet. The firewall is configured in NAT mode. The firewall forwards HTTP requests and API calls from the Internet to the Management Server. The Management Server resides on the management network.
- A layer-2 switch connects all physical servers and storage.
- A single NFS server functions as both the primary and secondary storage.
- The Management Server is connected to the management network.

Large-Scale Redundant Setup

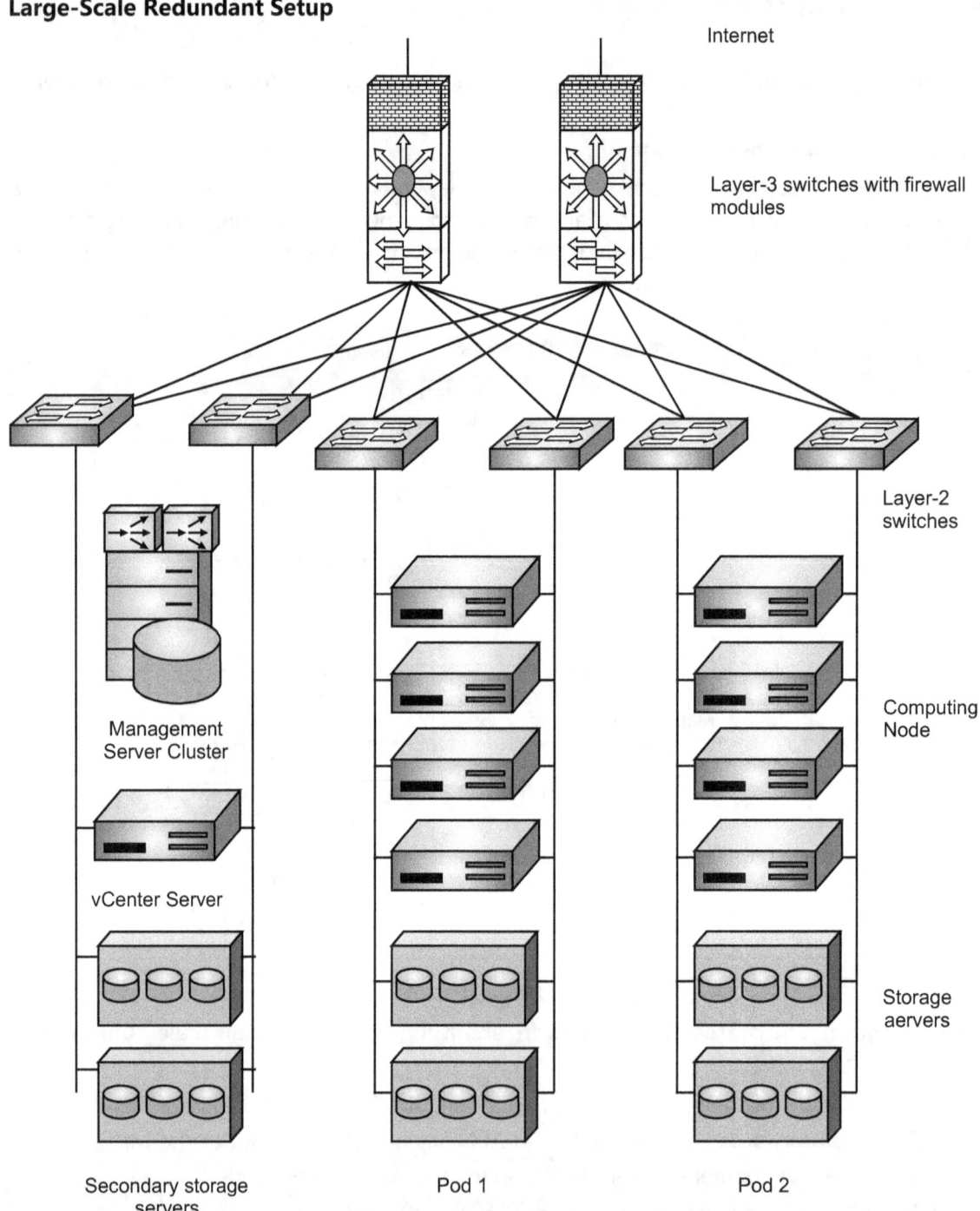

Fig. 5.5 : Large-scale redundant deployment

Fig. 5.5 illustrates the network architecture of a large-scale CloudStack deployment.

- A layer-3 switching layer is at the core of the data center. A router redundancy protocol like VRRP should be deployed. Typically high-end core switches also include firewall modules. Separate firewall appliances may also be used if the layer-3 switch does not have integrated firewall capabilities.
- The firewalls are configured in NAT mode. The firewalls provide the following functions:
- Forwards HTTP requests and API calls from the Internet to the Management Server. The Management Server resides on the management network.
- When the cloud spans multiple zones, the firewalls should enable site-to-site VPN such that servers in different zones can directly reach each other.
- A layer-2 access switch layer is established for each pod. Multiple switches can be stacked to increase port count. In either case, redundant pairs of layer-2 switches should be deployed.
- The Management Server cluster (including front-end load balancers, Management Server nodes, and the MySQL database) is connected to the management network through a pair of load balancers.
- Secondary storage servers are connected to the management network.
- Each pod contains storage and computing servers. Each storage and computing server should have redundant NICs connected to separate layer-2 access switches.

Separate Storage Network

In the large-scale redundant setup described in the previous section, storage traffic can overload the management network. A separate storage network is optional for deployments. Storage protocols such as iSCSI are sensitive to network delays. A separate storage network ensures guest network traffic contention does not impact storage performance.

Multi-Node Management Server

The CloudStack Management Server is deployed on one or more front-end servers connected to a single MySQL database. Optionally a pair of hardware load balancers distributes requests from the web. A backup management server set may be deployed using MySQL replication at a remote site to add DR capabilities.

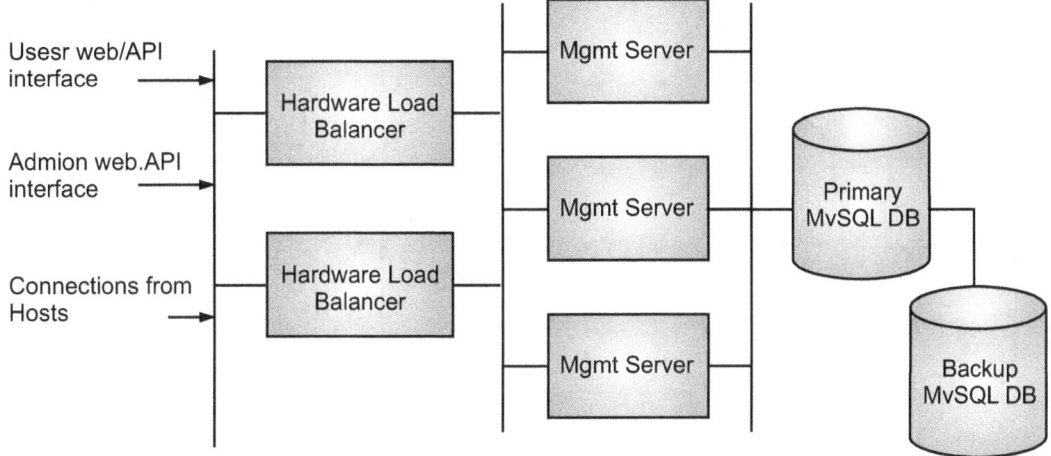

Fig. 5.6 : Multi-Node management server deployment

The administrator must decide the following.

● Whether or not load balancers will be used.

● How many Management Servers will be deployed?

● Whether MySQL replication will be deployed to enable disaster recovery.

Multi-Site Deployment

The CloudStack platform scales well into multiple sites through the use of zones. The following diagram shows an example of a multi-site deployment.

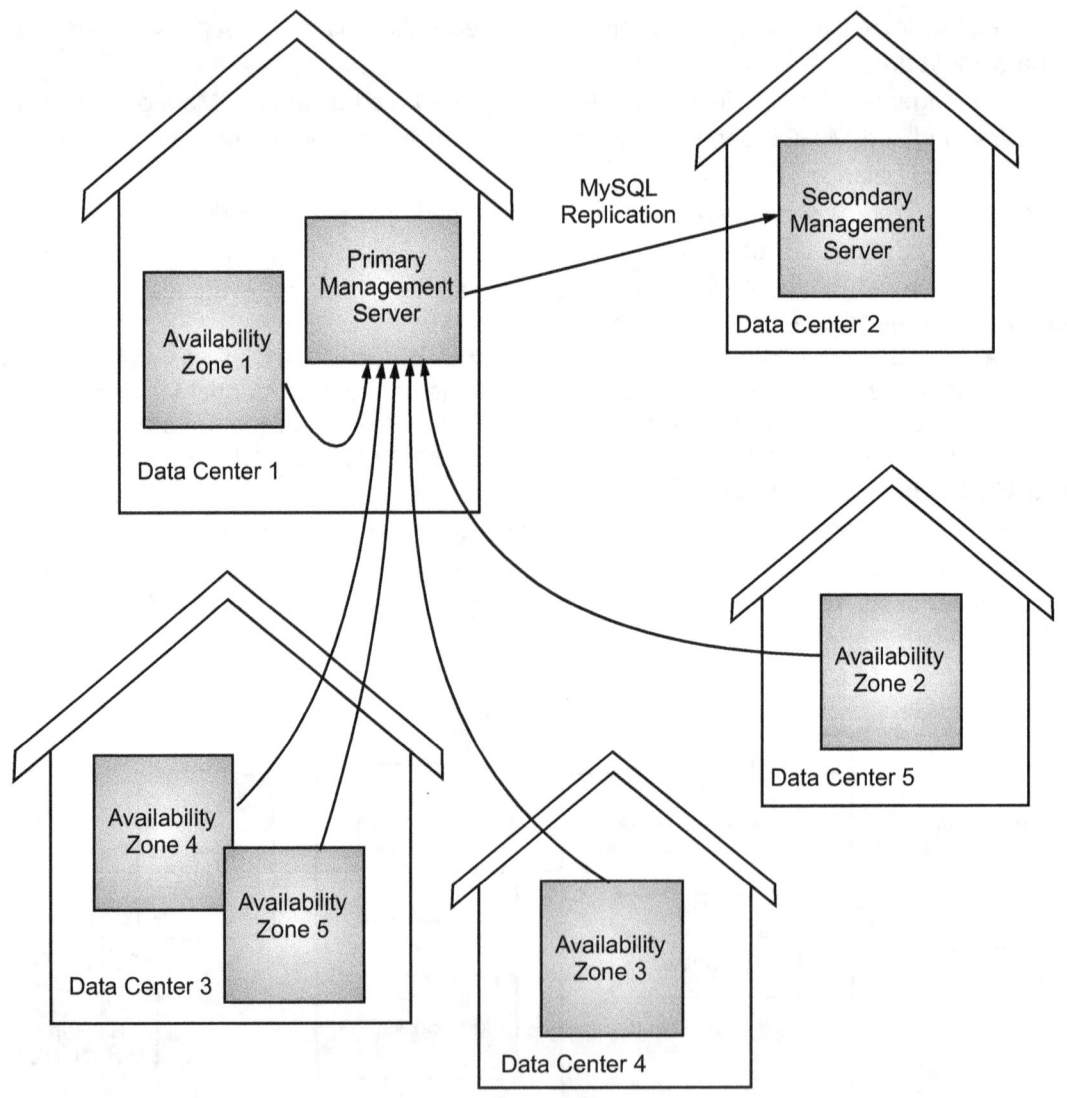

Fig. 5.7 : Example of a Multi-site deployment

Data Center 1 houses the primary Management Server as well as zone 1. The MySQL database is replicated in real time to the secondary Management Server installation in Data Center 2.

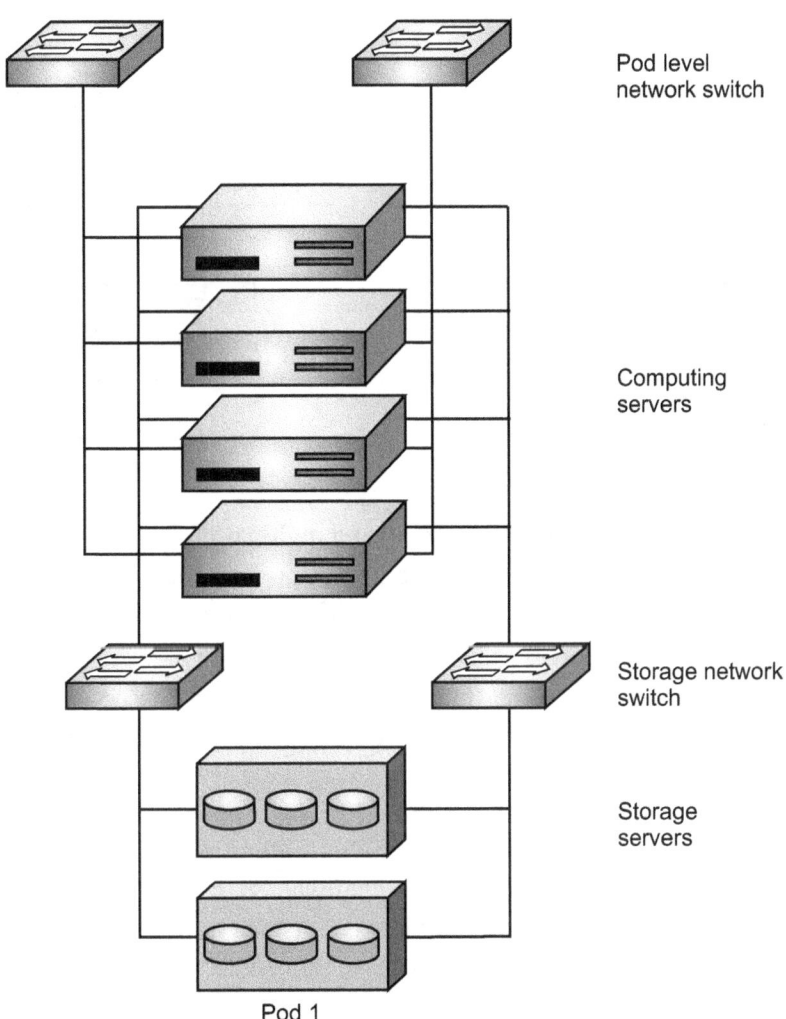

Pod level
network switch

Computing
servers

Storage network
switch

Storage
servers

Pod 1

Fig. 5.8 : Separate storage network

This diagram illustrates a setup with a separate storage network. Each server has four NICs, two connected to pod-level network switches and two connected to storage network switches.

There are two ways to configure the storage network:

- Bonded NIC and redundant switches can be deployed for NFS. In NFS deployments, redundant switches and bonded NICs still result in one network (one CIDR block + default gateway address).

- iSCSI can take advantage of two separate storage networks (two CIDR blocks each with its own default gateway). Multipath iSCSI client can failover and load balance between separate storage networks.

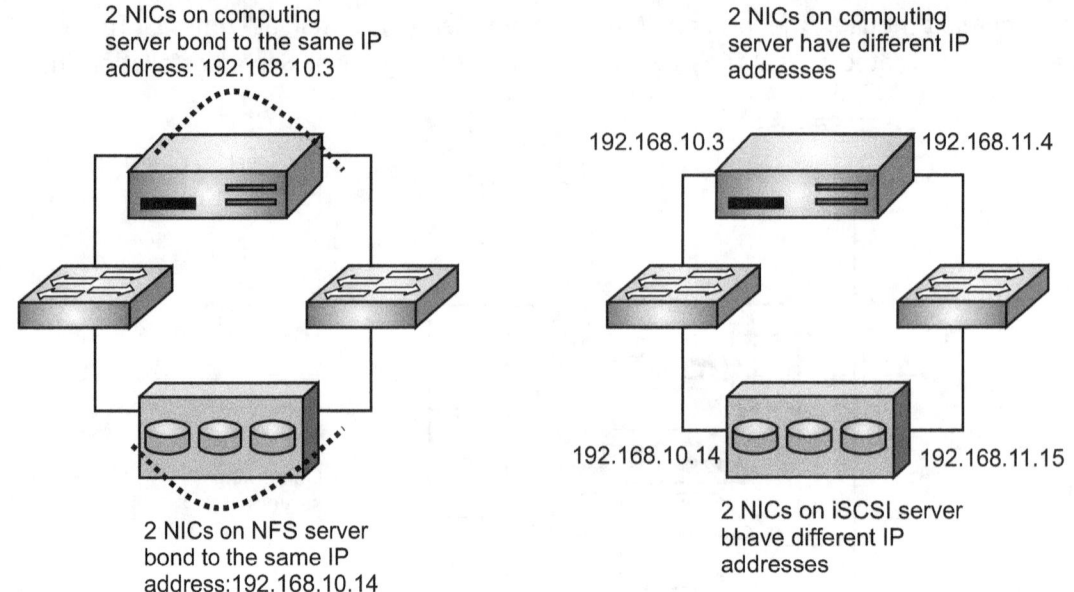

Fig. 5.9 : NIC bonding and multipath I/O

This diagram illustrates the differences between NIC bonding and Multipath I/O (MPIO). NIC bonding configuration involves only one network. MPIO involves two separate networks.

Choosing a Hypervisor

- CloudStack supports many popular hypervisors. Your cloud can consist entirely of hosts running a single hypervisor, or you can use multiple hypervisors. Each cluster of hosts must run the same hypervisor.

- You might already have an installed base of nodes running a particular hypervisor, in which case, your choice of hypervisor has already been made. If you are starting from scratch, you need to decide what hypervisor software best suits your needs. A discussion of the relative advantages of each hypervisor is outside the scope of our documentation. However, it will help you to know which features of each hypervisor are supported by CloudStack. The following table provides this information.

Feature	XenServer	vSphere	KVM - RHEL	LXC	HyperV	Bare Metal
Network Throttling	Yes	Yes	No	No	?	N/A
Security groups in zones that use basic networking	Yes	No	Yes	Yes	?	No
iSCSI	Yes	Yes	Yes	Yes	Yes	N/A
FibreChannel	Yes	Yes	Yes	Yes	Yes	N/A
Local Disk	Yes	Yes	Yes	Yes	Yes	Yes

Contd...

HA	Yes	Yes (Native)	Yes	?	Yes	N/A
Snapshots of local disk	Yes	Yes	Yes	?	?	N/A
Local disk as data disk	Yes	No	Yes	Yes	Yes	N/A
Work load balancing	No	DRS	No	No	?	N/A
Manual live migration of VMs from host to host	Yes	Yes	Yes	?	Yes	N/A
Conserve management traffic IP address by using link local network to communicate with virtual router	Yes	No	Yes	Yes	?	N/A

Hypervisor Support for Primary Storage

The following table shows storage options and parameters for different hypervisors.

Primary Storage Type	XenServer	vSphere	KVM - RHEL	LXC	HyperV
Format for Disks, Templates, and Snapshots	VHD	VMDK	QCOW2		VHD
iSCSI support	CLVM	VMFS	Yes via Shared Mountpoint	Yes via Shared Mountpoint	No
Fiber Channel support	Yes, Via existing SR	VMFS	Yes via Shared Mountpoint	Yes via Shared Mountpoint	No
NFS support	Yes	Yes	Yes	Yes	No
Local storage support	Yes	Yes	Yes	Yes	Yes
Storage over-provisioning	NFS	NFS and iSCSI	NFS		No
SMB/CIFS	No	No	No	No	Yes

- XenServer uses a clustered LVM system to store VM images on iSCSI and Fiber Channel volumes and does not support over-provisioning in the hypervisor. The storage server itself, however, can support thin-provisioning.
- As a result the CloudStack can still support storage over-provisioning by running on thin-provisioned storage volumes.
- KVM supports "Shared Mountpoint" storage. A shared mountpoint is a file system path local to each server in a given cluster. The path must be the same across all Hosts in the cluster, for example /mnt/primary1. This shared mountpoint is assumed to be a clustered filesystem such as OCFS2. In this case the Cloud Stack does not attempt to mount or unmount the storage as is done with NFS. The CloudStack requires that the administrator insure that the storage is available.

- With NFS storage, CloudStack manages the overprovisioning. In this case, the global configuration parameter storage.overprovisioning.factor controls the degree of overprovisioning. This is independent of hypervisor type.
- Local storage is an option for primary storage for vSphere, XenServer, and KVM. When the local disk option is enabled, a local disk storage pool is automatically created on each host.
- To use local storage for the System Virtual Machines (such as the Virtual Router), set system.vm.use.local.storage to true in global configuration.
- CloudStack supports multiple primary storage pools in a Cluster. For example, you could provision 2 NFS servers in primary storage. Or you could provision 1 iSCSI LUN initially and then add a second iSCSI LUN when the first approaches capacity.

Best Practices

- Deploying a cloud is challenging. There are many different technology choices to make, and CloudStack is flexible enough in its configuration that there are many possible ways to combine and configure the chosen technology. This section contains suggestions and requirements about cloud deployments.
- These should be treated as suggestions and not absolutes. However, we do encourage anyone planning to build a cloud outside of these guidelines to seek guidance and advice on the project mailing lists.

Process Best Practices

- A staging system that models the production environment is strongly advised. It is critical if customizations have been applied to CloudStack.
- Allow adequate time for installation, a beta, and learning the system. Installs with basic networking can be done in hours. Installs with advanced networking usually take several days for the first attempt, with complicated installations taking longer. For a full production system, allow at least 4-8 weeks for a beta to work through all of the integration issues. You can get help from fellow users on the cloudstack-users mailing list.

Setup Best Practices

- Each host should be configured to accept connections only from well-known entities such as the CloudStack Management Server or your network monitoring software.
- Use multiple clusters per pod if you need to achieve a certain switch density.
- Primary storage mountpoints or LUNs should not exceed 6 TB in size. It is better to have multiple smaller primary storage elements per cluster than one large one.
- When exporting shares on primary storage, avoid data loss by restricting the range of IP addresses that can access the storage. See "Linux NFS on Local Disks and DAS" or "Linux NFS on iSCSI".
- NIC bonding is straightforward to implement and provides increased reliability.
- 10G networks are generally recommended for storage access when larger servers that can support relatively more VMs are used.

- Host capacity should generally be modeled in terms of RAM for the guests. Storage and CPU may be overprovisioned. RAM may not. RAM is usually the limiting factor in capacity designs.
- (XenServer) Configure the XenServer dom0 settings to allocate more memory to dom0. This can enable XenServer to handle larger numbers of virtual machines. We recommend 2940 MB of RAM for XenServer dom0. For instructions on how to do this, see http://support.citrix.com/article/CTX126531. The article refers to XenServer 5.6, but the same information applies to XenServer 6.0.

Maintenance Best Practices

- Monitor host disk space. Many host failures occur because the host's root disk fills up from logs that were not rotated adequately.
- Monitor the total number of VM instances in each cluster, and disable allocation to the cluster if the total is approaching the maximum that the hypervisor can handle. Be sure to leave a safety margin to allow for the possibility of one or more hosts failing, which would increase the VM load on the other hosts as the VMs are redeployed.
- Consult the documentation for your chosen hypervisor to find the maximum permitted number of VMs per host, then use CloudStack global configuration settings to set this as the default limit. Monitor the VM activity in each cluster and keep the total number of VMs below a safe level that allows for the occasional host failure.
- For example, if there are N hosts in the cluster, and you want to allow for one host in the cluster to be down at any given time, the total number of VM instances you can permit in the cluster is at most (N-1) * (per-host-limit). Once a cluster reaches this number of VMs, use the CloudStack UI to disable allocation to the cluster.

5.3 INTERCLOUD

Following figure represents an overview of the Cisco Intercloud Fabric architecture.

Cisco Intercloud Fabric Solution Overview

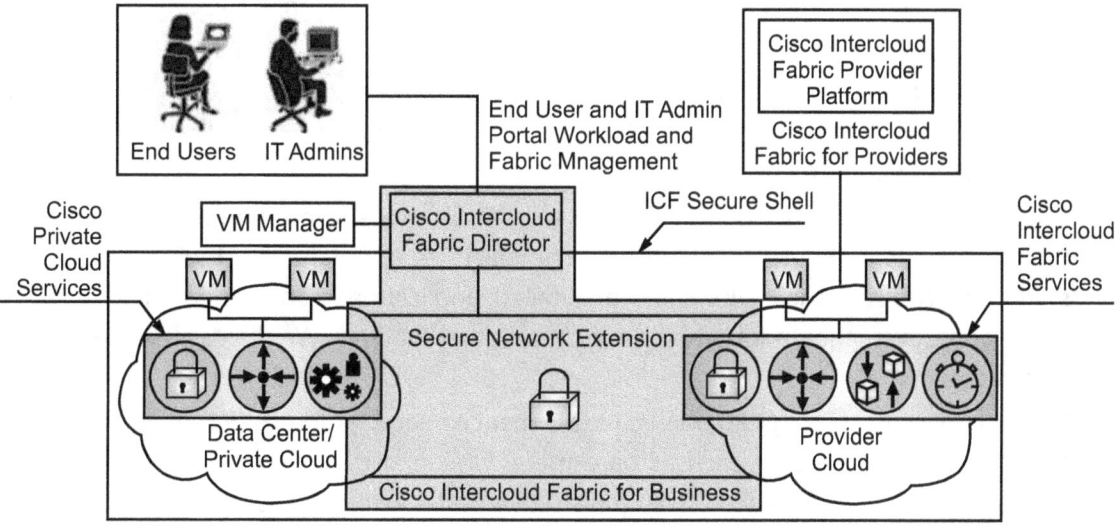

Fig. 5.10

The Cisco Intercloud Fabric architecture provides two product configurations to address the following two consumption models:

- Cisco Intercloud Fabric for Business
- Cisco Intercloud Fabric for Providers.

5.3.1 Cisco Intercloud Fabric for Business

- Cisco Intercloud Fabric for Business is intended for enterprise customers who want to be able to transparently extend their private clouds into public cloud environments, while keeping the same level of security and policy across environments. Cisco Intercloud Fabric for Business consists of the following components:
- Cisco Intercloud Fabric Director
- Cisco Intercloud Fabric Secure Fabric
- Cisco Intercloud Fabric Director
- Workload management in a hybrid environment goes beyond the capability to create and manage virtual services in a private or public and provider cloud and network extension. Both capabilities are part of the overall hybrid cloud solution, which also needs to provide different types of services, such as policy capabilities (placement, quotas, etc.), capabilities to manage workloads in heterogeneous environments, and other capabilities as discussed here.
- Cisco Intercloud Fabric Director (ICFD) provides to the end user and IT administrator a seamless experience to create and manage workloads across multiple clouds, it is the single point of management and consumption for hybrid cloud solutions.
- Heterogeneous cloud platforms are supported by Cisco ICFD in the private cloud, which operationally unifies workload management in a cloud composed of different cloud infrastructure platforms, such as VMware vSphere and vCloud, Microsoft Hyper-V and System Center Virtual Machine Manager (SCVMM), OpenStack, and CloudStack.
- This unification provides a holistic workload management experience and multiple options for cloud infrastructure platforms for our customers. Cisco ICFD provides the required software development kit (SDK) and APIs to integrate with the various cloud infrastructure platforms.
- Cisco ICFD exposes northbound APIs that allows customers to programmatically manage their workloads in the hybrid cloud environment or to integrate with their management system of choice, which allows more detailed application management that includes policy and governance, application design, and other features. We discuss this later in the document.
- Future releases of Cisco ICFD will include enhanced services that differentiate the Cisco Intercloud Fabric solution, such as bare-metal workload deployment in a hybrid cloud environment and an enhanced IT administrative portal with options to configure disaster recovery and other services.

Self-Service IT Portal and Service Catalog

- The Cisco ICFD self-service IT portal makes it easy for IT administrators to manage and consume hybrid cloud offers, and for the end users to consume services. For end users, Cisco ICFD provides a service catalog that combines offers from multiple clouds and a single self-service IT portal for hybrid workloads.

- For IT administrators, Cisco ICFD has an IT administrative portal from which administrators can perform the following administrative tasks:

- Configure connection to public and enterprise private clouds.

- Configure roles and permissions and enterprise Lightweight Directory Access Protocol (LDAP) integration.

- Add and manage tenants.

- Configure basic business policies that govern workload placement between the enterprise and public clouds; advanced policies are available in the management layer.

- Customize portal branding.

- Monitor capacity and quota use.

- Browse and search the service catalog and initiate requests to provision and manage workloads in the cloud.

- View the workload across multiple clouds and migrate workloads as necessary.

- Manage user information and preferences.

- Configure catalog and image entitlement.

- Configure virtual machine template and image import, categorization, and entitlement.

- Perform Cisco Intercloud Fabric Secure Extension management.

- Future capabilities can be added through the end-user or IT administrative portal.

Ease of Installation

Cisco ICFD provides a simplified installation experience, allowing customers to set up the initial environment and connect to a service provider within hours. As a single pane for workload management in the hybrid environment, Cisco ICFD also improves Day 1 and Day 2 operations, making it easier to configure provider cloud access and manage the environment.

Cisco Intercloud Fabric Secure Extension

All data in motion is cryptographically isolated and encrypted within the Cisco Intercloud Fabric Secure Extender. This data includes traffic exchanged between the private and public clouds (site to site) and the virtual machines running in the cloud (VM to VM). A Datagram Transport Layer Security (DTLS) tunnel is created between these endpoints to more securely transmit this data. DTLS is a User Datagram Protocol (UDP)-based highly secure transmission protocol. The Cisco Intercloud Fabric Extender always initiates the creation of a DTLS tunnel.

The encryption algorithm used is configurable, and different encryption strengths can be used depending on the level of security desired.

The supported encryption algorithms are:

- AES-128-GCM
- AES-128-CBC
- AES-256-GCM (Suite B)
- AES-256-CBC
- None

The supported hashing algorithms are:

- SHA-1
- SHA-256
- SHA-384

Cisco Intercloud Fabric Core Services

- Cisco Intercloud Fabric includes a set of services that are crucial for customers to successfully manage their workloads across the hybrid cloud environment. These services are identified as Intercloud Fabric Core Services and can be described as follow:
- **Cloud Security :** Security enforcement for site to site and VM to VM communications.
- **Networking :** Switching, routing and other advanced network-based capabilities.
- **VM Portability :** VM format conversion and mobility.
- **Management and Visibility :** Hybrid cloud monitoring capabilities.
- **Automation :** VM lifecycle management, automated operations and programmatic API.

Future releases of Cisco Intercloud Fabric will include an extended set of services, including support for 3 rd party appliances.

Cisco Intercloud Fabric Firewall Services

- In traditional data center deployments, virtualization presents a need to secure traffic between virtual machines; this traffic is generally referred to as east-west traffic. Instead of redirecting this traffic to the edge firewall for lookup, data centers can handle the traffic in the virtual environment by deploying a zone-based firewall.
- Cisco Intercloud Fabric includes a zone-based firewall that can be deployed to provide policy enforcement for communication between virtual machines and to protect east-west traffic in the provider cloud.

The virtual firewall is integrated with Cisco Virtual Path (vPath) technology, which enables intelligent traffic steering and service chaining. The main features of the zone-based firewall include:

Policy definition based on network attributes or virtual machine attributes such the virtual machine name.

- Zone-based policy definition, which allows the policy administrator to partition the managed virtual machine space into multiple logical zones and write firewall policies based on these logical zones.

- Enhanced performance due to caching of policy decisions on the local Cisco vPath module after the initial flow lookup process.

Cisco Intercloud Fabric Routing Services

- Cisco Intercloud Fabric Secure Extender provides a Layer 2 extension from the enterprise data center to the provider cloud. To support Layer 3 functions without requiring traffic to be redirected to the enterprise data center, Cisco Intercloud Fabric also includes a virtual router.

- The virtual router is based on proven Cisco IOS® XE Software and runs as a virtual machine in the provider cloud.

- The router deployed in the cloud by Intercloud Fabric serves as a virtual router and firewall for the workloads running in the provider cloud and works with Cisco routers in the enterprise to deliver end-to-end Cisco optimization and security. The main functions provided by the virtual router include:

- Routing between VLANs in the provider cloud.

- Direct access to cloud virtual machines.

- Connectivity to enterprise branch offices through a direct VPN tunnel to the service provider's data center.

- Access to native services supported by a service provider: for example, use of Amazon Simple Storage Service (S3) or Elastic Load Balancing services.

Cisco Secure Intercloud Fabric Shell

Cisco Secure Intercloud Fabric Shell (Secure ICF Shell) is a high level construct that identifies a group of VMs and the associated Cloud Profiles, and it is designed to be portable and secure across clouds. A cloud profile includes the following configurations:

- **Workload Policies :** a set of policies that are created by the enterprise IT admin via Intercloud Fabric Director portal to define what networks will be extend, security enforcements to be applied to the workloads in the cloud, and other characteristics such as DNS configuration.

- **Definition of the Site-to-Site and VM to VM Secure Communication :** IT admins can manage, enable, or disable secure tunnel configurations between the private and public clouds and/or between the VMs in the cloud.

- **VM Identity :** Intercloud Fabric creates an identity for all the VMs that it manages to ensure only trusted VMs are allowed to participate of the networks extended to the cloud, communicate to other VMs in the same circle of trust in the public cloud, or to communicate to other VMs in the private cloud.

- **Cloud VM Access Control :** Intercloud Fabric helps to control the access to the cloud VMs via the secure tunnel established between private and public clouds, or directly via the VM public IP defined and managed via Intercloud Fabric.

5.3.2 Cisco Intercloud Fabric for Providers

- Cisco Intercloud Fabric for Providers is intended for provider cloud environments, allowing their enterprise customers to transparently extend their private cloud environments into the provider's public cloud, while keeping the same level of security and policy across cloud environments.
- There are two Cisco Intercloud Fabric offers for providers; those who offer managed services, or those who are just targets for Intercloud Fabric hybrid workloads.
- Cisco Intercloud Fabric for Providers that want to offer managed services consists of the following components:
  - Cisco Intercloud Fabric Director
  - Cisco Intercloud Fabric Secure Fabric
  - Cisco Intercloud Fabric Provider Platform
- Cisco Intercloud Fabric for Providers that want to just be a target for Intercloud Fabric hybrid workloads consists of the following component:
- Cisco Intercloud Fabric Provider Platform

Cisco Intercloud Fabric Provider Platform

- Cisco Intercloud Fabric Provider Platform (ICFPP) simplifies and abstracts the complexity involved in working with a variety of public cloud APIs, and it enables cloud API support for service providers that currently do not have it.
- Cisco ICFPP provides an extensible adapter framework to allow integration with a variety of provider cloud infrastructure management platforms, such as OpenStack, Cloudstack, VMware vCloud Director and virtually any other APIs that can be integrated through an SDK provided by Cisco.
- Currently, service providers have their own proprietary cloud APIs (Amazon Elastic Compute Cloud [EC2], Microsoft Windows Azure, VMware vCloud Director, OpenStack, etc.), giving customers limited choices and no easy option to move from one provider to another.
- Cisco ICFPP abstracts this complexity and translates Cisco Intercloud Fabric API calls to different provider infrastructure platforms, giving customers the choice to move their workloads regardless of the cloud API exposed by the service provider.
- Many service providers do not provide cloud APIs that Cisco Intercloud Fabric can use to deploy customer's workloads. One option for these providers is to provide direct access to their virtual machine manager's SDKs and APIs (for example, through VMware vCenter or Microsoft System Center), which exposes the provider environment and in many cases is not a preferred option for service providers because of security concerns, for example, Cisco ICFPP, as the first point of authentication for the customer cloud that allows it to consume provider cloud resources, enforces highly secure access to the provider environment and provides the cloud APIs that are required for service providers to be part of the provider ecosystem for Cisco Intercloud Fabric.

- As the interface between the Cisco Intercloud Fabric from customer's cloud environments and provider clouds (public and virtual private clouds), Cisco ICFPP provides a variety of benefits, as described below:

- Brings standardization and uniformity to cloud APIs, making it easier for Cisco Intercloud Fabric to consume cloud services from service providers that are part of the Cisco Intercloud Fabric ecosystem.

- Helps secure access to service provider's underlying cloud platforms.

- Limits the utilization rate per customer and tenant environment.

- Provides northbound APIs for service providers to integrate with existing management platforms.

- Supports multitenancy.

- Provides tenant-level resource monitoring.

- In the future, it will help build Cisco infrastructure-specific differentiation.

- In the future, support will be provided for enterprises to deploy bare-metal workloads in the provider cloud.

Cisco ICFPP Architecture

- Cisco ICFPP is a virtual appliance deployed in the service provider cloud data center to enable service provider customers to access cloud resources using Cisco Intercloud Fabric APIs. The virtual appliance provides a virtual network interface to allow customer's Cisco Intercloud Fabric to reach the Cisco ICFPP appliance instance from public networks, and to allow the Cisco ICFPP appliance to connect with the service provider cloud platforms following Fig. 5.11shows the Cisco ICFPP appliance architecture.

Cisco Intercloud Fabric Provider Platform Architecture

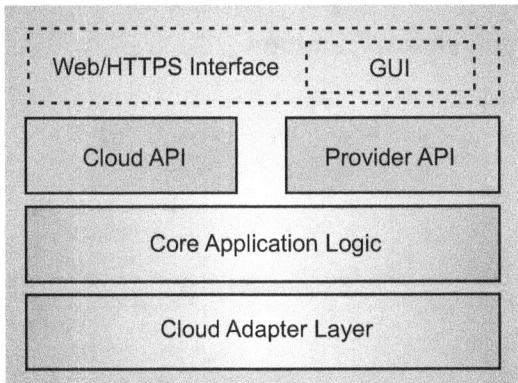

Fig. 5.11

Cisco ICFPP architecture includes four major interface modules:

- **Northbound Cloud API :** This module implements the Cisco Intercloud Fabric cloud API, which is consumed by Cisco Intercloud Fabric (customer cloud) for workload provisioning.

- **Northbound Provider API :** This module implements a set of APIs for the service provider administrator to use to configure the Cisco ICFPP appliance, provision tenants and users, and monitor tenant operations.
- **Core Application Logic :** This module implements translation logic between Cisco Intercloud Fabric cloud APIs and cloud platform-specific APIs.
- **Cloud Adapter Layer :** This module implements the various cloud platform interface adapters, each of which is responsible for interfacing with a specific cloud platform such as OpenStack, Cloudstack, or custom.

When to Deploy Cisco ICFPP?

Cisco ICFPP should be implemented for all service providers that interface with Cisco Intercloud Fabric. The only exceptions to this rule are Amazon EC2, Microsoft Windows Azure and IBM SoftLayer, which are available to Cisco Intercloud Fabric through their native public cloud APIs.

Cisco ICFPP Deployment Topology

- To access the service provider's cloud resources, Cisco Intercloud Fabric needs to access the Cisco ICFPP appliance from the public network; therefore, the network interface of the appliance needs to be deployed in a provider network that is exposed to the service provider's edge router. The network interface needs also to connect to the private provider network that accesses the service provider cloud platform (for example, OpenStack or Cloudstack).

The Cisco ICFPP deployment topology varies for different service providers and cloud platforms.

Following Fig. 5.12 shows a deployment with a VMware vCloud Director environment in the service provider.

Cisco ICFPP Appliance Deployment Topology

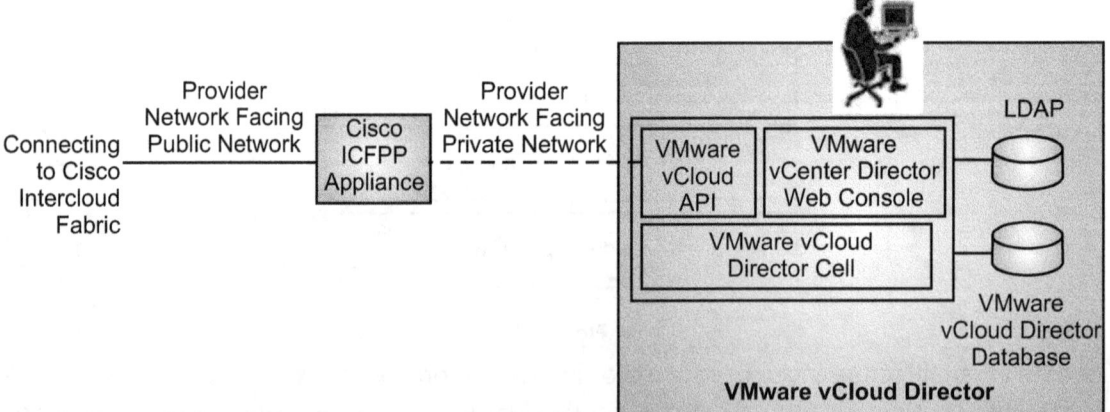

Fig. 5.12

- The Cisco ICFPP appliance uses HTTPS connections to communicate with the Cisco Intercloud Fabric and the service provider cloud platform.

- A firewall is not required in the network path between the Cisco Intercloud Fabric and the Cisco ICFPP appliance, or between the Cisco ICFPP appliance and the cloud platform endpoints, but can be used to reinforce only expected traffic flows to and from ICFPP.

Cisco ICFPP Operating Model

The following example describes Day 0 and Day 1 operations for the Cisco ICFPP appliance.

Day 0 Operation: Deployment and Initialization

- The Cisco ICFPP appliance is deployed in the service provider data center as part of the service provider's cloud platform. In Day 0 operation, the service provider administrator deploys the appliance in the provider network and provides the appliance with the following configurations:
- Appliance IP address.
- Administrator user credentials and privileges.
- Cloud platform type and endpoint address.
- The service provider administrator provisions service provider tenants and users for the appliance. After the Cisco ICFPP appliance is deployed, the service provider administrator publishes the URL of the appliance to the provider's customers so that they can reach it.

Day 1 Operation: Tenant Sign-On and Query

- After the Cisco ICFPP appliance is operational in the service provider data center and its URL has been posted publicly, the provider's customers can start to reach the appliance, and the Cisco Intercloud Fabric component can start to access the Cisco ICFPP appliance with a sign-on API request.

Cisco Intercloud Fabric and Cisco Validated Designs

- For Cisco Powered Cloud Providers or large enterprise customers that deploy VMDC (Virtualized Multiservice Data Center) validated design, Intercloud Fabric is complementary to it and does not have dependency on specific configuration or version.
- For cloud providers, Cisco Intercloud Fabric for Provider can integrate with the cloud management platform of choice, and for large enterprise VMDC customers, Intercloud Fabric for Business also integrates with the environment, interfacing with the VM Manager and the cloud management platform of choice, if needed, allowing workload mobility and management across multiple clouds.
- For customers that deploy FlexPod or other Cisco Validated Designs in their data centers, and are willing to securely move and manage their workloads across multiple clouds, Intercloud Fabric for Business complements the solution and augment its value with the capabilities discussed previously in this document.
- Intercloud Fabric for Business interfaces with the VM Manager of the converged infrastructure and provides all the resources needed to manage the workload in hybrid cloud environment.

Cisco Intercloud Fabric and Management Cloud Platforms Integration

- The seemingly borderless environment created by Cisco Intercloud Fabric between private and public resources provides numerous features and benefits.

- To also provide the benefits of automated placement decisions for cloud services, application visibility and orchestration, application blueprints or deployment profiles, enterprises can use a management cloud platform of choice integrated with Cisco Intercloud Fabric through its Northbound APIs.

- The management cloud platform connects to Cisco ICFD through the available northbound REST (Representational State Transfer) API, which enables it to perform operations on ICFD resources and to integrate with upstream portal and orchestration systems. As of today, ICFD supports the following API operations:
  - Policy Management
  - VDC Management
  - Catalog Operations
  - Charge-Back Management
  - Workflow Management
  - Auditing Management
  - Virtual Machine Operations

Other API operations will be added in future releases of the product. Cisco ICFD REST API is compatible with HTTP and HTTPS protocols, and supports code formatted in JSON and XML. A Java API is also available. The APIs document is available at cisco.com/go/intercloudfabric.

5.4 GOOGLE APP ENGINE　　　　　　(Nov. 16, May 17)

5.4.1 Installing and Running the Google App Engine on Windows

- This document describes the installation of the Google App Engine Software Development Kit (SDK on a Microsoft Windows and running a simple "hello world" application.

- The App Engine SDK allows you to run Google App Engine Applications on your local computer. It simulates the runGtime environment of the Google App Engine infrastructure.

Pre9Requisites: Python 2.5.4

If you don't already have Python 2.5.4 installed in your computer, download and Install Python 2.5.4 from:

http://www.python.org/download/releases/2.5.4/

Download and Install

You can download the Google App Engine SDK by going to:

http://code.google.com/appengine/downloads.html

and download the appropriate install package.

5.4.2 Download the Google App Engine SDK

Before downloading, please read the Terms that govern your use of the App Engine SDK.

Please Note the App Engine SDK is under active development, please keep this in mind as you explore its capabilities.

See the SDK release notes for the information on the most recent changes to the App Engine SDK, if you discover any issues, please feel free top notify us via our issue Tracker.

Platform	Version	Package	Size	SHA1 Checksum
Windows	1.15-10/03/08	GoogleAppEngine 1.1.5 msi	2.5 MB	e7431b4aefc0b3873ff0d93ed4c525d5e88c30
Max OS \X	1.1.5-10/03/08	GoogleAppEngineLaucher 1.1.5 dmg	3.6 MB	f62208ac01c1b3e3976e58100d5f0523d3e7

Download the Windows installer – the simplest thing is to download it to your Desktop or another folder that you remember.

Double Click on the **GoogleApplicationEngine** installer.

Click through the installation wizard, and it should install the App Engine. If you do not have Python 2.5, it will install Python 2.5 as well.

Once the install is complete you can discard the downloaded installer

Fig. 5.13

5.4.3 Making your First Application

Now you need to create a simple application. We could use the "+" option to have the launcher make us an application but instead we will do it by hand to get a better sense of what is going on.

Make a folder for your Google App Engine applications. I am going to make the Folder on my Desktop called "apps" – the path to this folder is:

C:\Documents and Settings\csev\Desktop\apps

And then make a sub folder in within apps called "ae9019trivial", the path to this folder would be:

C:\ Documents and Settings \csev\Desktop\apps\ae9019trivial

Using a text editor such as JEdit (www.jedit.org), create a file called app.yaml in the ae9019trivial folder with the following contents:

application: ae-01-trivial version: 1

runtime: python api_version: 1

handlers:

url: /.* script: index.py

Note: Please do not copy and paste these lines into your text editor, you might end up with strange characters, simply type them into your editor.

Then create a file in the ae9019trivial folder called index.py with three lines in it:

print 'Content-Type: text/plain' print ' '

print 'Hello there Chuck'

Then start the GoogleAppEngineLauncher program that can be found under Applications. Use the File 9> Add Existing Application command and navigate into the apps directory and select the ae9019trivial folder. Once you have added the application, select it so that you can control the application using the launcher.

Once you have selected your application and press run. After a few moments your application will start and the launcher will show a little green icon next to your application. Then press Browse to open a browser pointing at your application which is running at http://localhost:8080/

Paste http://localhost:8080 into your browser and you should see your application as follows:

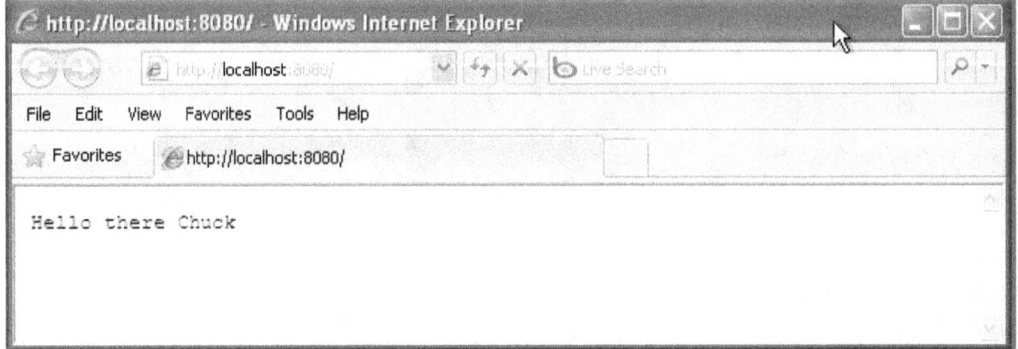

Fig. 5.14

Just for fun, edit the index.py to change the name "Chuck" to your own name and press Refresh in the browser to verify your updates.

Watching the Log

- You can watch the internal log of the actions that the web server is performing when you are interacting with your application in the browser. Select your application in the Launcher and press the Logs button to bring up a log window:

- Each time you press Refresh in your browser, you can see it retrieving the output with a GET request.

Dealing with Errors

With two files to edit, there are two general categories of errors that you may encounter. If you make a mistake on the **app.yaml** file, the App Engine will not start and your launcher will show a yellow icon near your application.

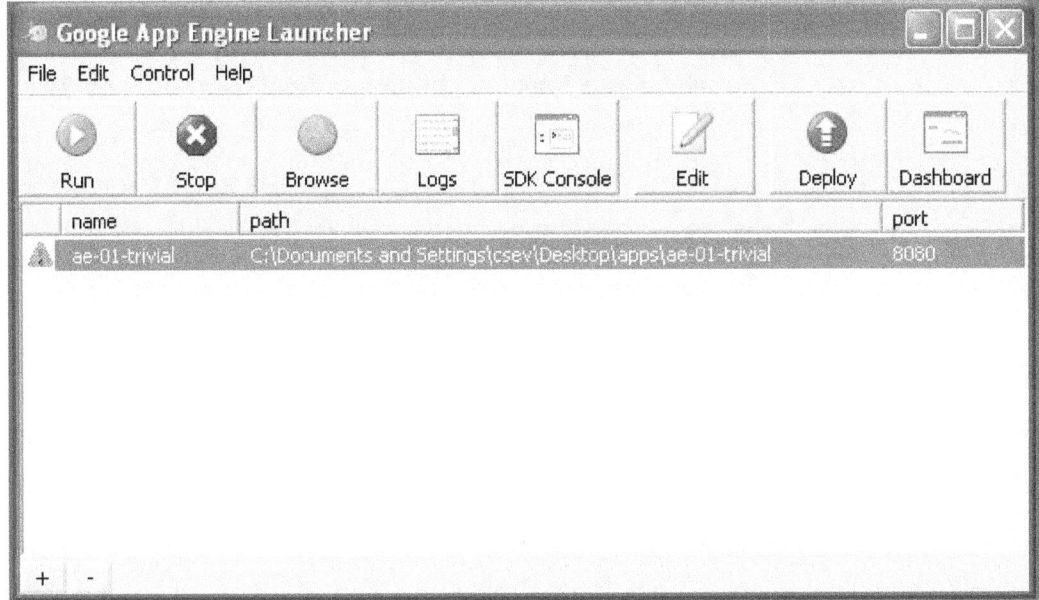

Fig. 5.15

To get more detail on what is going wrong, take a look at the log for the application.

```
Log Console (ae-01-trivial)
Invalid object:
Unknown url handler type.
<URLMap
    static_dir=None
    secure=default
    script=None
    url=/.*
    static_files=None
    upload=None
    mime_type=None
    login=optional
    require_matching_file=None
    auth_fail_action=redirect
    expiration=None
    >
    in "C:\Documents and Settings\csev\Desktop\apps\ae-01-trivial\app.yaml", line 8,
column 1
```

Fig. 5.16

- In this instance, the mistake is misGindenting the last line in the app.yaml (line 8). If you make a syntax error in the index.py file, a Python trace back error will appear in your browser.

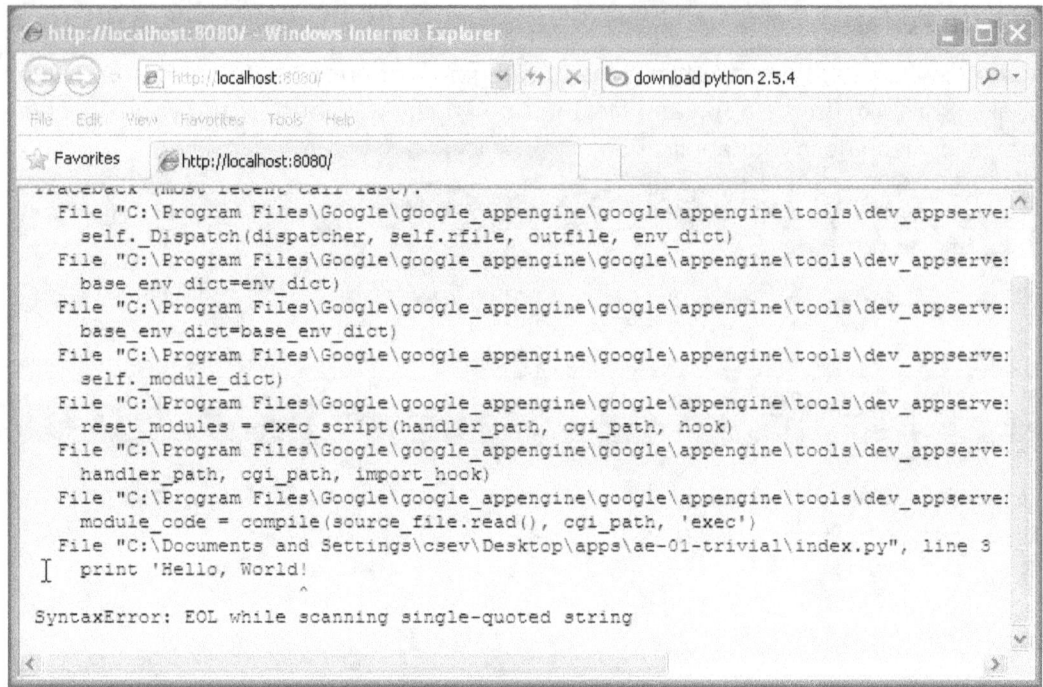

Fig. 5.17

- The error you need to see is likely to be the last few lines of the output – in this case I made a Python syntax error on line one of our oneGline application.

  Reference: http://en.wikipedia.org/wiki/Stack_trace

When you make a mistake in the app.yaml file, you must fix the mistake and attempt to start the application again.

If you make a mistake in a file like index.py, you can simply fix the file and press refresh in your browser, there is no need to restart the server.

Shutting Down the Server

To shut down the server, use the Launcher, select your application and press the Stop button.

5.5 OPEN SOURCE EUCALYPTUS CLOUD

5.5.1 The Eucalyptus Open-Source Private Cloud

- Eucalyptus is a Linux-based open-source software architecture that implements efficiency-enhancing private and hybrid clouds within an enterprise's existing IT infrastructure. Eucalyptus is an acronym for "Elastic Utility Computing Architecture for Linking Your Programs to Useful Systems."

- A Eucalyptus private cloud is deployed across an enterprise's "on premise" data center infrastructure and is accessed by users over enterprise intranet. Thus, sensitive data remains entirely secure from external intrusion behind the enterprise firewall.

- Initially, developed to support the high performance computing (HPC) research of Professor Rich Wolski's research group at the University of California, Santa Barbara. Eucalyptus is engineered according to design principles that ensure compatibility with existing Linux-based data center installations.
- Eucalyptus can be deployed without modification on all major Linux OS distributions, including Ubuntu, RHEL, Centos, and Debian.
- And Ubuntu distributions now include the Eucalyptus software core as the key component of the Ubuntu Enterprise Cloud.

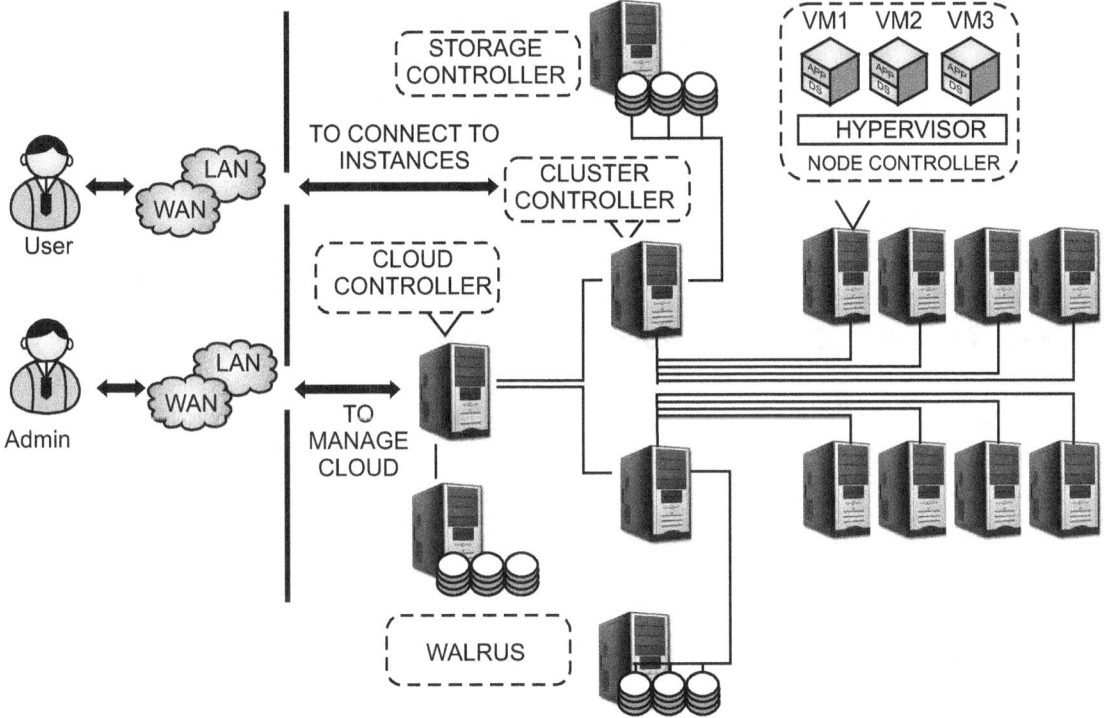

Fig. 5.18

5.5.2 Eucalyptus Components

- Each Eucalyptus service component exposes a well-defined language agnostic API in the form of a WSDL document containing both the operations that the service can perform and the input/output data structures.
- Inter-service authentication is handled via standard WS-Security mechanisms. There are five high-level components, each with its own Web-service interface, that comprise a Eucalyptus installation (Fig. 5.18).

A brief description of the components within the Eucalyptus system follows.

1. Cloud Controller

- Cloud Controller (CLC) is the entry-point into the cloud for administrators, developers, project managers, and end-users. The CLC is responsible for querying the node managers for information about resources, making high level scheduling decisions, and implementing them by making requests to cluster controllers.

- The CLC is also the interface to the management platform. In essence, the CLC is responsible for exposing and managing the underlying virtualized resources (servers, network, and storage) via a well-defined industry standard API (Amazon EC2) and a Web-based user interface.

Functions:

1. Monitor the availability of resources on various components of the cloud infrastructure, including hypervisor nodes that are used to actually provision the instances and the cluster controllers that manage the hypervisor nodes.

2. Resource arbitration : deciding which clusters will be used for provisioning the instances.

3. Monitoring the running instances.

In short, CLC has a comprehensive knowledge of the availability and usage of resources in the cloud and the state of the cloud.

2. Cluster Controller

- Cluster Controller (CC) generally executes on a cluster front-end machine or any machine that has network connectivity to both the nodes running NCs and to the machine running the CLC. CCs gather information about a set of VMs and schedules VM execution on specific NCs.

- The CC also manages the virtual instance network and participates in the enforcement of SLAs as directed by the CLC. All nodes served by a single CC must be in the same broadcast domain (Ethernet).

Functions

1. To receive requests from CLC to deploy instances.
2. To decide which NCs to use for deploying the instances on.
3. To control the virtual network available to the instances.
4. To collect information about the NCs registered with it and report it to the CLC.

3. Node Controller

- Node Controller (NC) is executed on every node that is designated for hosting VM instances. A UEC node is a VT-enabled server capable of running KVM as the hypervisor. UEC automatically installs KVM when the user chooses to install the UEC node.

- The VMs running on the hypervisor and controlled by UEC are called instances. Eucalyptus supports other hypervisors like Xen apart from KVM, but Canonical has chosen KVM as the preferred hypervisor for UEC.

- The NC runs on each node and controls the life cycle of instances running on the node. The NC interacts with the OS and the hypervisor running on the node on one side and the CC on the other side.

- NC queries the operating system running on the node to discover the node's physical resources, the number of cores, the size of memory, and the available disk space. It also learns about the state of VM instances running on the node and propagates this data up to the CC.

Functions

1. Collection of data related to the resource availability and utilization on the node and reporting the data to CC.

2. Instance life cycle management.

4. Storage Controller

- Storage Controller (SC) implements block-accessed network storage (e.g., Amazon Elastic Block Storage - EBS) and is capable of interfacing with various storage systems (NFS, iSCSI, etc.).

- An elastic block store is a Linux block device that can be attached to a virtual machine but sends disk traffic across the locally attached network to a remote storage location. An EBS volume cannot be shared across instances but does allow a snapshot to be created and stored in a central storage system such as Walrus, the Eucalyptus storage service.

Functions

1. Creation of persistent EBS devices.

2. Providing the block storage over AoE or iSCSI protocol to the instances.

3. Allowing creation of snapshots of volumes.

Walrus

- Walrus (put/get storage) allows users to store persistent data, organized as eventually-consistent buckets and objects. It allows users to create, delete, list buckets, put, get, and delete objects, and set access control policies.

- Walrus is interface compatible with Amazon's S3, and supports the Amazon Machine Image (AMI) image-management interface, thus providing a mechanism for storing and accessing both the virtual machine images and user data.

- Using Walrus, users can store persistent data, which is organized as buckets and objects. WS3 is a file-level storage system, as compared to the block-level storage system of Storage Controller.

- For using Walrus to manage Eucalyptus VM images, you can use Amazon's tools to store/register/delete them from Walrus. Other third-party tools can also be used to interact with Walrus directly.

Third-Party Tools for Interacting with Walrus

1. S3curl: a command line tool that is a wrapper around curl.
   http://open.eucalyptus.com/wiki/s3curl

2. S3cmd: a tool that allows command line access to storage that supports the S3 API.
   http://open.eucalyptus.com/wiki/s3cmd

3.   S3fs: a tool that allows users to access S3 buckets as local directories.
     http://open.eucalyptus.com/wiki/s3fs

Management Platform

Management Platform provides an interface to various Eucalyptus services and modules. These features can include VM management, storage management, user/group management, accounting, monitoring, SLA definition and enforcement, cloud-bursting, provisioning, etc.

Euca2ool

Euca2ools are command-line tools for interacting with Web services that export a REST/Query-based API compatible with Amazon EC2 and S3 services. The tools can be used with both Amazon's services and with installations of the Eucalyptus open-source cloud-computing infrastructure. The tools were inspired by command-line tools distributed by Amazon (api-tools and ami-tools) and largely accept the same options and environment variables. However, these tools were implemented from scratch in Python, relying on the Boto library and M2Crypto toolkit.

Features

1.   Query of availability zones (i.e., clusters in Eucalyptus).
2.   SSH key management (add, list, delete).
3.   VM management (start, list, stop, reboot, get console output).
4.   Security group management.
5.   Volume and snapshot management (attach, list, detach, create, bundle, delete).
6.   Image management (bundle, upload, register, list, deregister).
7.   IP address management (allocate, associate, list, release).

Key Benefits

•   Build and manage self-service heterogeneous on-premise IaaS clouds using either existing infrastructure or dedicated compute, network and storage resources.

•   Support high-availability IaaS for the most demanding cloud deployments.

•   Gain precise control of private cloud resources via enterprise-ready user and group identity management along with resource quotas.

•   Pool dynamic resources with built-in elasticity, allowing organizations to scale up and down virtual compute, network and storage resources.

•   Integrate robust storage, enabling IT to easily connect and manage existing storage systems from within Eucalyptus clouds.

•   Build hybrid clouds between on-premise Eucalyptus clouds and AWS and AWS-compatible public clouds.

•   Run Eucalyptus or Amazon Machine Images as virtual cloud instances on Eucalyptus and AWS-compatible clouds.

•   Leverage vibrant AWS ecosystem and management tools to manage Eucalyptus IaaS clouds.

5.6 OPENSTACK

- OpenStack is a collection of open source software projects that can be collectively utilized to operate a cloud network infrastructure in order to provide IaaS. The OpenStack project began as a collaboration of Rackspace Hosting and NASA as an open source project.

- NASA was a user of the Eucalyptus open source cloud project before scalability issues in their Nebula project meant that they needed to develop their own technologies in this space. A contribution of their Cloud Files platform by Rackspace, combined with the Nebula computing software from NASA led to the initial birth of OpenStack.

- In the time since it's inception, the OpenStack consortium has managed to bring in over 100 members, including high profile industry names such as Citrix, Canonical and Dell.

- Since Amazon's AWS was the first majorly used cloud service, OpenStack also makes its services available via Amazon EC2 and S3 compatible APIs. This ensures that all the existing tools that work with Amazon's cloud offerings, can work with deployments of OpenStack as well.

The OpenStack project is combination of three main components:

- OpenStack Compute (Nova) : It is used to orchestrate, manage and offer virtual machines upon many hypervisors, including QEMU and KVM. This is analogous to the Amazon Elastic Compute Cloud (EC2).

- OpenStack Object Store (Swift) : Provides redundant storage for static objects. This serviceis scalable to massive data sizes and theoretically can provide infinite storage. It is analogous to the Amazon Simple Storage Service (S3).

- OpenStack Image Service (Glance) : Provides storage for virtual disk, kernel and images. Glance is also used to provide image registration and querying services. It is able to accept images in many formats, including the popular Amazon Machine Image (AMI), Amazon Kernel Image (AKI) and Amazon Ramdisk Image (ARI).

- Installing, configuring and working with Nova and Glance are covered as part of this tutorial. However, Swift is beyond the scope. Nonetheless, setting up Swift should not be a hard task for anyone who completes this tutorial.

- It should also be noted that this tutorial is based upon the OpenStack Diablo release and uses an Ubuntu 11.10 Oneiric Ocelot server environment to setup all necessary packages. However, this is only because Ubuntu provides prebuilt packages for OpenStack Diablo. As such, the configuration of OpenStack can be performed on any flavor of Linux by using this tutorial as a basic guide.

5.6.1 OpenStack Compute (Nova)

Nova takes up the role of providing computing services within the OpenStack cloud. As such, any activity needed to support the life cycle of a virtual machine instance within the cloud is handled by Nova.

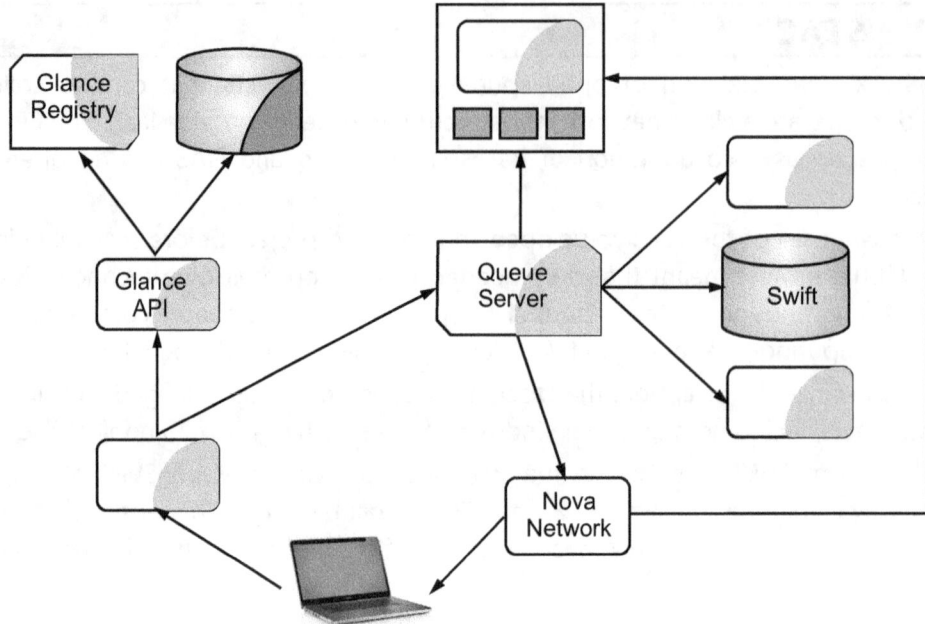

Fig. 5.19

- An overview of the OpenStack architecture is shown as in Fig. The client interacts with Nova API services. This uses Glance API for image registration and retrieval. All other requests are sent to the queue server, which passes them off to the Compute, Volume, Schedule or Network nodes, as the need be.
- This includes things like managing block storage, networking, scheduling, computing resources, authorization and hypervisors.
- However, Nova does not provide any virtualization capabilities by itself. It is designed to use libvirt APIs to interact with any supported hypervisors.
- This means that Nova is hypervisor agnostic and provides support for Xen, XenServer/XCP, KVM, UML, VMware vSphere and Hyper-V amongst others.
- All services provided by Nova are accessible via an API that is compatible with the AWS EC2. The main components of Nova are nova-api, rabbitmq-server, nova-compute, nova-network, nova-volume and nova-scheduler.
- An overview of the OpenStack architecture can be seen in Fig. 5.19. As can be seen, the client interacts with the Nova API server. In case requests dealing with registration or querying of images are sent, the API forwards these requests to the Glance API, which can perform queries within the Glance registry (stored in a SQL database).
- However, if the request deals with managing an instance, then this is forwarded to the queue server, which in turn distributes the requests to appropriate components. Network address allocation, association and deallocation requests are handled by nova-network.
- On the other hand, block storage creation, deletion and association requests are handled by nova-volume. Similarly, virtual machine instance related queries are processed by nova-compute.

API Services (nova-api)

- The nova-api service provides an interface to the outside world to interact with the cloud infrastructure. The API server is the only component that the outside world uses to manage the infrastructure. Management is done through RESTful calls using the EC2 API. The API server then, in turn, communicates with the relevant components of the cloud infrastructure by using the Message Queue.

Message Queuing (rabbitmq-server)

- The OpenStack Cloud Controller communicates with other nova components such as the Scheduler, Network Controller, and Volume Controller by using AMQP (Advanced Message Queue Protocol). OpenStack uses the rabbitmq-server for this purpose.

- Nova uses asynchronous calls for request-response, with a call-back that gets triggered once a response is received. Since asynchronous communication is used, none of the user actions get stuck for long in a waiting state. This is especially true since many actions expected by the API calls such as launching an instance or uploading an image are time consuming.

Computing Services (nova-compute)

- Servers providing computing services via nova-compute deal with instance management life cycle. They receive requests for life cycle management via the Message Queue and carry out appropriate operations.

- There are several servers providing computing services in a typical production cloud deployment. An instance is deployed on any of the available compute workers based on the scheduling algorithm used by Nova.

Network Services (nova-api)

- The network services provided by nova-api deals with the network configuration of host machines. It does operations like allocating IP addresses, configuring VLANs for projects, implementing security groups and configuring networks for compute nodes.

Block Storage Services (nova-volume)

- Block storage services performed by nova-volume include creation, deletion, attaching a volume to an instance, and detaching a volume from an instance.

- Volumes provide a way of providing persistent storage for use by instances, as the main disk attached to an instance is non-persistent and any changes made to it are lost when the volume is detached or the instance is terminated.

- When a volume is detached from an instance or when an instance, to which the volume is attached, is terminated, it retains the data that was stored on it when it was attached to an instance earlier.

- This data can be accessed by reattaching the volume to the same instance or by attaching it to another instances.

- As such, any valuable data that gets accumulated during the life cycle of an instance should be written to a volume, so that it can be accessed later.

Scheduling Services (nova-scheduler)

- The nova-scheduler maps API calls to the appropriate OpenStack components. It picks a server from a pool depending upon the scheduling algorithm in place. A scheduler can base its decisions on various factors such as load, memory, physical distance of the availability zone, CPU architecture, etc.

5.6.2 OpenStack Image Service (Glance)

- OpenStack Imaging Service is a lookup and retrieval system for virtual machine images. While it can be configured to use Swift or S3 storage to store the images, it normally uses a regular filesystem on the host for the glance service.

- The information regarding registered images is stored in an SQL database, which can be either MySQL, PostgreSQL, SQLite or many other varieties as well.

Installation and Configuration

- The distributed architecture of OpenStack means that all components can be installed on either a single or multiple systems. This means that a single computer could be used to provide API, Scheduler, Network, Compute, Volume, Message Queuing and Glance services.

- On the other hand, any of these services could be installed on separate hosts as well. In fact, some services, like Volume and Compute, can be installed on multiple servers for load balancing purposes.

- In this tutorial, installation on a single server will be covered, however, by simple extension of the configuration file this can be extended to any configuration necessary. An Ubuntu 11.10 server install with OpenSSH and Virtual Machine Host tasks is used as the base.

- In case you miss choosing OpenSSH and/or Virtual Machine Host tasks, make sure to install the openssh and qemu packages before proceeding. This can be done by using apt-get:

```
$ sudo apt-get install openssh-server qemu libvirt0
```

- It is assumed that the host has a single network interface named eth0 with an IP address 172.16.4.10.

- In order to work with nova-volume, the host also has two hard drives; the first contains the base OS installation, while the second one will be used to create LVM volumes used by virtual machine instances.

3. **Install MySQL**

- The Nova installation uses a SQL database to store all metadata and operation information. We will use MySQL, however, you may use any other flavor as well.

Install MySQL server and set the root password as "nova".

```
$ sudo apt-get install mysql-server
```

- Open /etc/mysql/my.cnf and change the bind-address property to look like:
  bind-address = 0.0.0.0

Now restart the server.

```
$ sudo restart mysql
```

- Once this is done, you must create the Nova database and give permissions to the root user to access this database from any connecting IP address, so that if you decide to add more nodes or create a multi-node setup, it will still work without any troubles.

```
$ mysqladmin -u root -p create nova Enter password:
$ mysql -u root -p -e "GRANT ALL PRIVILEGES ON *.* TO 'root'@'%' WITH GRANT OPTION;" Enter password:
$ mysql -uroot -p -e "SET PASSWORD FOR 'root'@'%' = PASSWORD('nova');" Enter password:
```

- Now that MySQL is setup and ready for Nova, we can proceed with installing the other services.

4. Install RabbitMQ

- Before installing RabbitMQ, make sure that your hostname is set to your correct IP address in your /etc/hosts file. Without this correctly entered, RabbitMQ will refuse to start.

Once this is done, install RabbitMQ.

```
$ sudo apt-get install rabbitmq-server
```

5. Install Glance

- Nova can use Glance service to manage Operating System images that it needs for bringing up instances. Installing this is also easy.

```
$ sudo apt-get install glance
```

- There is no need to make any further configuration changes since we are going to let Glance use the local file system for storing images and a default SQLite database for metadata.

6. Setup the Nova Cloud Controller

- The cloud controller is responsible for the API, Scheduling and Network services. As such, install these along with some other dependencies.

```
$ sudo apt-get install nova-common nova-doc nova-api
$ sudo apt-get install nova-network nova-objectstore nova-scheduler $ sudo apt-get install python-nova unzip
```

- These install commands added all the packages needed on the cloud controller, along with a large number of dependencies. In addition, the package installation scripts have added a system user nova and added it to the appropriate groups.
- A minimal configuration file for Nova is also created during the installation procedure, but this needs to be edited in order to suit our installation environment. As such, edit the /etc/nova/nova.conf file to reflect the following:

```
--daemonize=1
--dhcpbridge_flagfile=/etc/nova/nova.conf        --dhcpbridge=/usr/bin/nova-dhcpbridge        --logdir=/var/log/nova --state_path=/var/lib/nova
```

```
--verbose --libvirt_type=qemu

--sql_connection=mysql://root:nova@172.16.4.10/nova --s3_host=172.16.4.10
--rabbit_host=172.16.4.10 --ec2_host=172.16.4.10 --ec2_dmz_host=172.16.4.10

--ec2_url=http://172.16.4.10:8773/services/Cloud --fixed_range=10.0.0.0/8

--network_size=64   --num_networks=1   --FAKE_subdomain=ec2   --public_interface=eth0   --
state_path=/var/lib/nova --lock_path=/var/lock/nova --glance_host=172.16.4.10
--image_service=nova.image.glance.GlanceImageService --glance_api_servers=172.16.4.10:9292 -
-vlan_start=100

--vlan_interface=eth0 --iscsi_ip_prefix=172.16.4 --iscsi_helper=tgtadm
```

- Please note that in our single-node setup the IP address of the host node is 172.16.4.10, however, this may differ in your case. As such, substitute this with your cloud controller's IP address.

- As is evident from the above, we are instructing Nova to use QEMU as the hypervisor of choice. It is then instructed to use the nova MySQL database sitting on the cloud controller.

- The --s3_host configuration parameter is used to instruct Nova where the Swift services are installed (omitted in this tutorial). The --rabbit_host parameter tells Nova where the RabbitMQ server is installed; in our case it is on the cloud controller. The –ec2_host parameter is used to configure the target API server, as are all the other ec2 parameters.

- Nova is then instructed to use the 10.0.0.0/8 network for its private network between the instances. This network is referred to the fixed network by Nova.

- A network size of 64 means that Nova should use up to 64 IPs from the 10.0.0.0/8 network and it is also instructed to create only a single network.

- There is only one interface on the host interface, which provides access to the public network. As such, Nova is instructed to use the eth0 interface for all public traffic via the--public_interface option.

- It is also essential for Nova to know where Glance is installed, so that it can successfully register and retrieve images when necessary. In our case, this is the same as the cloud controller, and Nova is instructed to use the Glance image service located on the cloud controller via the Glance related switches, i.e. --glance_host, --image_service and --glance_api_servers.

- Nova uses VLANs to setup communication between the nova-network host and the virtual machine instances. The --vlan_start option instructs Nova to start numbering the VLANs at 100. Please note that this is the minimum number recommended. The --vlan_interface option should be set to the interface that can provide connectivity between the cloud controller, volume host and compute host. In our case, this is eth0.

- Lastly, since it is essential to have persistent storage in the virtual machine instances, nova-volume is used and must be configured. The nova-volume service uses ISCSI to export LVM volumes and attach these to instances. These may then be used for block storage inside instances. The --iscsi_prefix option must be set to the IP prefix of the network which can be used to reach the volume host. The --iscsi_helper option instructs nova-volume and nova-compute to use the tgtadm package for administering the ISCSI volumes.

- Please note that in a multi-host setup, the nova.conf file must be existent on every host that has any Nova services on it.

7. Setup the Volume Host

- The volume host provides block storage services to the virtual machine instances by installing the nova-compute package along with the ISCSI tools.

```
$ sudo apt-get install nova-volume iscsitarget iscsitarget-dkms tgt
```

Once these are installed, you must enable the iscsitarget service to start by default.

```
$ sudo sed -i 's/false/true/g' /etc/default/iscsitarget
```

- It is advisable for the volume host to have an additional hard drive that can be used to setup the necessary LVM volumes. In our single node environment, the cloud controller is the volume host as well and has a second hard drive, which is visible to the system at /dev/sdb. As such, a physical volume and volume group named nova-volumes must be created on /dev/sdb.

```
$ sudo pvcreate /dev/sdb
$ sudo vgcreate nova-volumes /dev/sdb
```

8. Setup the Compute Host

- The compute host uses the nova-compute package to provide virtual machine instantiation services. It is also uses the ISCSI tools to discover available appropriate targets and attach them to relevant virtual machines. As such, install the following packages on the compute host.

```
$ sudo apt-get install nova-compute qemu
$ sudo apt-get install iscsitarget iscsitarget-dkms tgt open-iscsi
```

- It is also important to note that when working along with the tgt ISCSI packages, which are the default as well, Nova has a bug that causes it to fail attaching ISCSI volumes to a virtual machine instance. This can be fixed by editing the /usr/lib/python2.7/dist-packages/nova/volume/driver.py file.

Change the following line:

```
mount_device = ("/dev/disk/by-path/ip-%s-iscsi-%s-lun-0" %
```

To:

```
mount_device = ("/dev/disk/by-path/ip-%s-iscsi-%s-lun-1" %
```

This should be located on, or around, line 536.

9. Create Network Schema

- It is recommended that you now reboot all your Nova hosts, before setting up the networking schema necessary to instantiate virtual machines. After rebooting, create the schema on the cloud controller:

```
$ sudo nova-manage db sync
```

- Now that the basic database schema has been created, it is important for all services to be restarted. Since there are too many services to restart by hand, reboot all your Nova hosts once again. After the reboot, check if all the nova services have started up correctly:

```
$ sudo nova-manage service list
```

Binary	Host	Zone	Status	State Updated_At	
nova-compute	cloud-controller	nova	enabled	:-)	2012-06-02 15:05:14
nova-volume	cloud-controller	nova	enabled	:-)	2012-06-11	08:40:21
nova-scheduler	cloud-controller	nova	enabled	:-)	2012-06-11	08:40:21
nova-network	cloud-controller	nova	enabled	:-)	2012-06-11	08:40:21

- If you see smiley faces, ":-)", against all service names, it means that all services started up correctly after the reboot. If not, you should wait for some time and try to check the service list once again, since sometimes it can take a little while before a service comes up.

- However, even after waiting, if a service does not get a smiley face next to it, but only "XXX", then a manual start of that particular service can at times help. For example, if the nova-network service is the one that has not started, then restart it manually with "/etc/init.d/nova-network restart".

- After a few moments, you should now see a smiley face. If, however, this too does not work, it is recommended that you check the nova.conf configuration file and log files located in

/var/log/nova/.

Once all the services have started up correctly, you can create the network schema:

```
$ sudo nova-manage network create vmnet --fixed_range_v4=10.0.0.0/8 \

--network_size=64  --bridge_interface=eth0  $  sudo  nova-manage  floating  create  --
ip_range=172.16.4.224/27
```

- The vmnet (or fixed network) is the VLAN created for use between the Nova network host and the virtual machines on the compute node. The parameters used here are the same as in the nova.conf file.
- On the other hand, the floating network is the block of public IP addresses that are reachable on the eth0 interface and can be handed out to virtual machines on demand.
- At this point your basic OpenStack Nova and Glance setup is complete. The following section will cover some important details regarding working with OpenStack. Registering and uploading images to Glance, creating VM instances, configuring network firewall policies, associating public IP addresses, creating persistent block storage and attaching it to VMs is covered.

```
$ sudo    nova-manage user create aimsuser
export    EC2_ACCESS_KEY=d77406c3-cea1-45af-bbd9-acfd16ff49e3
export    EC2_SECRET_KEY=b9c6ab50-65d7-4185-a1a9-267a2afe30f9
```

- At this point, it is important to note that a minor bug in the way the nova-manage command works, causes the environment variables to be setup incorrectly.
- As such, it is important for you to make a note of the value the EC2_ACCESS_KEY shell variable has after the above command is issued. Once you have made a note of it, you can continue assigning roles to the user and creating associated projects:

```
$ sudo nova-manage role add aimsuser cloudadmin
$ sudo nova-manage project create aimsproj aimsuser $ sudo nova-manage project zipfile aimsproj aimsuser
```

- You shall now have a nova.zip file, which contains the credentials necessary to work with the Nova. Copy this zip file to your client machine and expand it.
- Once expanded, you will need to open the novarc file in an editor, with super-user privileges, and change the following line:

```
export EC2_ACCESS_KEY="aimsuser:aimsproj"
```

- Instead of the user name, aims user, which is currently in this line, you must replace it with the value of the variable that you noted before. As such, in our example, this will change to:

```
export EC2_ACCESS_KEY="d77406c3-cea1-45af-bbd9-acfd16ff49e3:aimsproj"
```

- On your client machines, once the zip file is expanded and the above mentioned edit to the novarc file made, setup the environment variables included in the novarc file.

```
$ source ./novarc
```

- You might want to add it to your shell profile to have it automatically sourced on login.

11. Uploading Images

- Before you can actually instantiate a virtual machine, you will need to upload and register an image with Glance. For the purposes of our test server setup, let's use Ubuntu's Enterprise Cloud images.

```
$ wget \
http://uec-images.ubuntu.com/releases/lucid/release/\
ubuntu-10.04-server-cloudimg-i386.tar.gz
```

- Once this is done, you can upload the image to Glance.

```
$ cloud-publish-tarball ubuntu-10.04-server-cloudimg-i386.tar.gz images
Sun May 5 15:48:19 PDT 2012: ====== extracting image ======
Warning: no ramdisk found, assuming '--ramdisk none' kernel : natty-server-uec-amd64-vmlinuz-
virtual ramdisk: none
image : natty-server-uec-amd64.img
Sun May 5 15:48:45 PDT 2012: ====== bundle/upload kernel ======
Sun May 5 15:49:52 PDT 2012: ====== bundle/upload image ======
Sun May 5 15:54:19 PDT 2012: ====== done ======
emi="ami-00000002"; eri="none"; eki="aki-00000001";
```

- Once you have the ami number, then you are ready to start instances.

12. Launching Instances

- With the ami number available, you can not have ami number, you can use the images. euca-describe-images use the euca2ools package to launch instances. In case, you do command to get a list of all available.

- However, before launching an instance, it is useful to create your keypair so that you can later access this instance via ssh.

```
$ euca-add-keypair aimsuser > aimsuser.pem; chmod 600 aimsuser.pem
```

- Now launch an instance by using the euca-run-instances command, your keypair and providing a system type.

```
$ euca-run-instance -k aimsuser -t m1.tiny ami-00000002
```

- You can view a list of running instances using the euca-describe-instances command. If an instance has not been marked as running after 10-15 minutes, it is likely that something has gone awry and you should look at Nova log files.

13. Network Connectivity

- Configuring network access to the virtual machine is important since that makes it usable. By default Nova sets up the iptables firewall to not allow access to the machine in any form. It makes sense to enable at least ICMP and SSH traffic.

```
$ euca-authorize default -P tcp -p 22 -s 0.0.0.0/0 $ euca-authorize default -P icmp -t -1:-1
```

- Once the traffic is permitted to the instance, you can allocate and associate an address with the instance. The example below associates the allocated IP with instance i-00000001.

```
$ euca-allocate-address
ADDRESS           172.16.4.224
```

```
$ euca-associate-address          -i i-00000001 172.16.4.224

ADDRESS              172.16.4.224 i-00000001
```

To access the instance via SSH, just use the created keypair and the recently associated floating IP address.

```
$ ssh –i aimsuser.pem  ubuntu@172.16.4.224
```

- It is important to note that the initially assigned fixed address is not routeable from outside the Nova hosts, as such you must associate a floating address with an instance before it is reachable.

- It is important to turn on IPv4 forwarding on the nova-network and nova-compute hosts so that the virtual machines can reach the public Internet.

Attaching Volumes

- Before a volume can be attached to an instance, it must be created. Volumes should be created in the zone named nova.

```
$ euca-create-volume -s 1 -z nova
```

- Once the volume is successfully created, you can get a list of all volumes and their status using the euca-describe-volumes command. Use the euca-attach-volume command to associate an available volume to an instance.

- In the example below, the volume vol-00000001 is attached to instance i-00000001 as a raw block device at /dev/vdb.

```
$ euca-attach-volume vol-00000001 -i i-00000001 -d /dev/vdb
```

- Once the volume is attached, you can use fdisk to format it. Following that you may mount it and store files for persistent storage.

- If you encounter troubles, you can use the euca-describe-availability-zones verbose command to get an overview of which servers are running without problems.

5.7 OPENNEBULA   (Nov. 16, May 17)

- OpenNebula is an open-source cloud computing toolkit for managing heterogeneous distributed data center infrastructures. The OpenNebula toolkit manages a data center's virtual infrastructure to build private, public and hybrid IaaS (Infrastructure as a Service) clouds.

- OpenNebula orchestrates storage, network, virtualization, monitoring, and security technologies to deploy multi-tier services (e.g. compute clusters) as virtual machines on distributed infrastructures, combining both data center resources and remote cloud resources, according to allocation policies.

- According to the European Commission's report about the future of cloud computing from a group of experts "... only few cloud dedicated research projects in the widest sense have been initiated – most prominent amongst them probably OpenNebula ...".
- The toolkit includes features for integration, management, scalability, security and accounting.
- It also emphasizes standardization, interoperability and portability, providing cloud users and administrators with a choice of several cloud interfaces (EC2 Query, OGF OCCI and vCloud) and hypervisors (Xen, KVM and VMware), and a flexible architecture that can accommodate multiple hardware and software combinations in a data center.
- OpenNebula was a mentoring organization in Google Summer of Code 2010. OpenNebula is sponsored by C12G.

5.7.1 OpenNebula Features

Powerful User Security Management

- Secure and efficient Users and Groups Subsystem for authentication and authorization of requests with complete functionality for user management: create, delete, show...
- Pluggable authentication and authorization based on passwords, ssh rsa keypairs, X509 certificates or LDAP
- Special authentication mechanisms for SunStone (OpenNebula GUI) and the Cloud Services (EC2 and OCCI)
- Authorization framework with fine-grained ACLs that allows multiple-role support for different types of users and administrators, delegated control to authorized users, secure isolated multi-tenant environments, and easy resource (VM template, VM image, VM instance, virtual network and host) sharing

Advanced Multi-tenancy with Group Management

Administrators can groups users into organizations that can represent different projects, division...

- Each group have configurable access to shared resources so enabling a multi-tenant environment with multiple groups sharing the same infrastructure.
- Configuration of special users that are restricted to public cloud APIs (e.g. EC2 or OCCI).
- Complete functionality for management of groups: create, delete, show

On-demand Provision of Virtual Data Centers

- A Virtual Data Centers (VDC) is a fully-isolated virtual infrastructure environment where a group of users, under the control of the VDC administrator, can create and manage compute, storage and networking capacity

- Advanced multi-tenancy with complete functionality for management of VDCs: create, delete, show...

Advanced Control and Monitoring of Virtual Infrastructure

- Image Repository Subsystem with catalog and complete functionality for VM image management: list, publish, unpublish, show, enable, disable, register, update, saveas, delete...

- Template Repository Subsystem with catalog and complete functionality for VM template management: add, delete, list...

- Full control of VM instance life-cycle and complete functionality for VM instance management: submit, deploy, migrate, livemigrate, stop, save, resume, cancel, shutdown, restart, delete, monitor, list...

- Broad network virtualization capabilities with traffic isolation, ranged or fixed networks, definition of generic attributes to define multi-tier services consisting of groups of inter-connected VMs, and complete functionality for virtual network management to interconnect VM instances: create, delete, monitor, list...

- Configurable system usage statistics to visualize and report resource usage data, to allow their integration with chargeback and billing platforms, or to guarantee fair share of resources among users

- Tagging of users, VM images and virtual networks with arbitrary metadata that can be later used by other components.

Virtual Machine Configuration

- Complete definition of VM attributes and requirements.

- Support for automatic configuration of VMs with advanced contextualization mechanisms.

- Hook Manager to trigger administration scripts upon VM state change.

- Wide range of guest operating system including Microsoft Windows and Linux.

- Flexible network definition.

- Configuration of firewall for VMs to specify a set of black/white TCP/UDP ports.

Advanced Control and Monitoring of Physical Infrastructure

- Configurable to deploy public, private and hybrid clouds.

- Host Management Subsystem with complete functionality for management of physical hosts: create, delete, enable, disable, monitor, list...

- Dynamic creation of logical clusters to serve different types of service workloads.

- Powerful and extensible built-in monitoring subsystem.

Broad Commodity and Enterprise Platform Support

- Hypervisor agnostic Virtualization Subsystem with broad hypervisor support (Xen, KVM and VMware), centralized management of environments with multiple hypervisors, and support for multiple hypervisors within the same physical box.

- Storage Subsystem supporting any backend configuration, from non shared file systems with image transferring with SSH to shared file systems (NFS, GlusterFS, Lustre...) or LVM with CoW, and any storage server, from using commodity hardware to enterprise-grade solutions.

- Flexible Network Subsystem with integration with Ebtable, Open vSwitch and 802.1Q tagging.

- Optional integration with datacenter monitoring tools like Ganglia.

Distributed Resource Optimization

- Powerful and flexible requirement/rank matchmaker scheduler providing automatic initial VM placement for the definition of workload and resource-aware allocation policies such as packing, striping, load-aware, affinity-aware...

- Resource quota management to allocate, track and limit resource utilization.

Centralized Management of Multiple Zones

- Single access point and centralized management for multiple instances of OpenNebula.

- Federation of multiple OpenNebula zones for scalability, isolation or multiple-site support.

- Complete functionality for management of zones: create, delete, show, list...

High Availability

- Persistent database backend with support for high availability configurations.

- Configurable behavior in the event of host, VM, or OpenNebula instance failure to provide an easy to use and cost-effective failover solution.

- Support for high availability architectures.

Hybrid Cloud Computing and Cloudbursting

- Extension of the local private infrastructure with resources from remote clouds.

- Support for Amazon EC2 and for simultaneous access to multiple remote clouds.

Interfaces for Cloud Consumers

- Transform your local infrastructure into a public cloud by exposing REST-based interfaces.

- OGF OCCI service, the emerging cloud API standard, and client tools.

- AWS EC2 API service, the de facto cloud API standard, with compatibility with EC2 ecosystem tools and client tools.
- Support for simultaneously exposing multiple cloud APIs.
- Easily-customizable self-service portal.

Rich Operation Interfaces and User Self-Service Portal

- Unix-like Command Line Interface to manage all resources: users, VM images, VM templates, VM instances, virtual networks, zones, VDCs, physical hosts, accounting, authentication, authorization...
- Easy-to-use Sunstone Graphical Interface providing usage graphics and statistics with cloudwatch-like functionality, VNC support, different system views for different roles, catalog access, multiple-zone management...

Deployment Options

- Easy to install with packages for most common Linux distributions.
- Available in most popular Linux distributions.
- Optional building from source code.
- System features a small footprint, less than 10Mb.
- Detailed log files for the different components that maintain a record of significant changes.

Extension and Integration

- Modular and extensible architecture to fit into any existing datacenter.
- Customizable drivers for the main subsystems to easily leverage existing IT infrastructure and system management products: Virtualization, Storage, Monitoring, Image Repository, Network, Auth and Hybrid Cloud.
- New drivers can be easily written in any language.
- Plugin support to easily extend SunStone Graphical Interface with additional tabs to better integrate Cloud and VM management with each site own operations and tools.
- Easily customizable self-service portal for cloud consumers.
- Configuration and tuning parameters to adjust behavior of the cloud management instance to the requirements of the environment and use cases.
- Fully open-source technology available under Apache license.
- Well-documented database schema for accounting.
- Powerful and extensible low-level cloud API in Ruby and JAVA and XMLRPC API.
- A Ruby API to build applications on top of the Zones/VDC component ZONA, the ZONes Api.

- OpenNebula ecosystem with experimental components enhancing the functionality provided by OpenNebula.

Reliability, Efficiency and Massive Scalability

- Automated testing process for functionality, scalability, performance, robustness and stability.
- Technology matured through an active and engaged community.
- Proven on large scale infrastructures consisting of tens of thousands of cores and VMs.
- Highly scalable database back-end with support for MySQL and SQLite.
- Virtualization drivers adjusted for maximum scalability.
- Very efficient core developed in C++ language. Cv

QUESTIONS

1. Explain the benefits of Amazon EC2 and S3.

2. Explain in detail Amazon Machine Image (AMI) How AMI is created?

3. Write short note on Apache Cloudstack.

4. Explain the concept of Intercloud in detail.

5. Write short note on Google App engine.

6. Explain the Open Source Eucalyptus cloud in detail.

7. Explain the concept of openstakc, also explain the openstack compute NOVA.

8. Write short note on open Nebula.

UBIQUITOUS COMPUTING

6.1 BASIC AND VISION

- We inhabit an increasingly digital world, populated by a profusion of digital devices designed to assist and automate more human tasks and activities, to enrich human social interaction and enhance physical world interaction. The physical world environment is being increasingly digitally instrumented and strewn with embedded sensor-based and control devices. These can sense our location and can automatically adapt to it, easing access to localized services, e.g., doors open and lights switch on as we approach them. Positioning systems can determine our current location as we move.

- They can be linked to other information services, i.e., to propose a map of a route to our destination. Devices such as contactless keys and cards can be used to gain access to protected services, situated in the environment.

- E-paper and e-books allow us to download current information onto flexible digital paper, over the air, without going into any physical bookshop. Even electronic circuits may be distributed over the air to special printers, enabling electronic circuits to be printed on a paper-like substrate.

- In many parts of the world, there are megabits per second speed wired and wireless networks for transferring multimedia (alpha-numeric text, audio and video) content, at work and at home and for use by mobile users and at fixed locations. The increasing use of wireless networks enables more devices and infrastructure to be added piecemeal and less disruptively into the physical environment.

- Electronic circuits and devices can be manufactured to be smaller, cheaper and can operate more reliably and with less energy. There is a profusion of multi-purpose smart mobile devices to access local and remote services. Mobile phones can act as multiple audio-video cameras and players, as information appliances and games consoles. Interaction can be personalized and be made user context-aware by sharing personalization models in our mobile devices with other services as we interact with them, e.g., audio-video devices can be pre-programmed to show only a person's favorite content selections.

- Many types of service provision to support everyday human activities concerned with food, energy, water, distribution and transport and health are heavily reliant on computers. Traditionally, service access devices were designed and oriented towards human users who are engaged in activities that access single isolated services, e.g., we access information vs we watch videos vs we speak on the phone. In the past, if we wanted to access and combine multiple services to support multiple activities, we needed to use separate access devices.

- In contrast, service offerings today can provide more integrated, interoperable and ubiquitous service provision, e.g., use of data networks to also offer video broadcasts and voice services, so-called triple-play service provision. There is great scope to develop these further.

- The term 'ubiquitous', meaning appearing or existing everywhere, combined with computing to form the term Ubiquitous Computing (UbiCom) is used to describe ICT (Information and Communication Technology) systems that enable information and tasks to be made available everywhere, and to support intuitive human usage, appearing invisible to the user.

1. Application of Ubiquitous Computing

- The following applications situated in the human and physical world environments illustrate the range of benefits and challenges for ubiquitous computing. A personal memories scenario focuses on users recording audio-video content, automatically detecting user contexts and annotating the recordings.

- A twenty-first-century scheduled transport service scenario focuses on the transport schedules, adapting their preset plans to the actual status of the environment and distributing this information more widely.

- A foodstuff management scenario focuses on how analogue non-electronic objects such as foodstuffs can be digitally interfaced to a computing system in order to monitor their human usage. A fully automated foodstuff management system could involve robots which can move physical objects around and is able to quantify the level of a range of analogue objects.

- A utility management scenario focuses on how to interface electronic analogue devices to an UbiCom system and to manage their usage in a user-centred way by enabling them to cooperate to achieve common goals.

2. Personal Memories

- As a first motivating example, consider recording a personal memory of the physical world (Fig. 6.1). Up until about the 1980s, before the advent of the digital camera, photography would entail manually taking a light reading and then manually setting the aperture and shutter speed of the camera in relation to the light reading so that the light exposure on to a light-sensitive chemical film was correct. It involved manually focusing the lens system of the camera.

- The camera film behaved as a sequential recording media : A new recording requires winding the film to the next empty section. It involved waiting for the whole film of a set of images, typically 12 to 36, to be completed before sending the recorded film to a specialist film processing company with specialist equipment to convert the film into a specialist format that could be viewed. The creation of additional copies would also require the services of a specialist film processing company.

- A digital camera automatically captures a visual of part of the physical world scene on an inbuilt display. The use of digital cameras enables photography to be far less intrusive for the subject than using film cameras.

- The camera can autofocus and auto-expose recorded images and GPS Transmitter Location Determination AV-Capture Projector Automatic face detection, recognition, etc Printer Removable Memory Communication AVplayer Display Clock UbiComp System Image Processing AV database GIS dd/mm/yy.

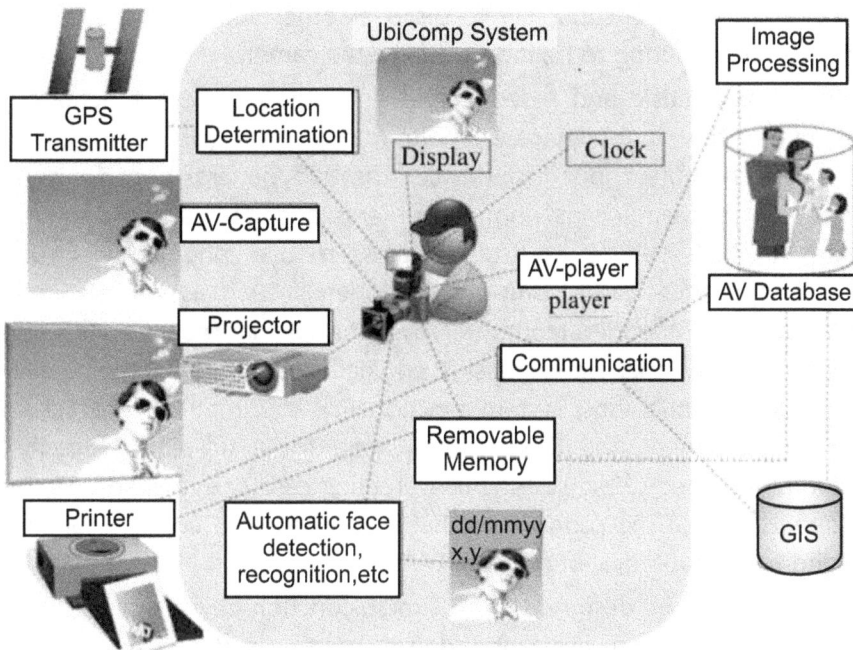

Fig. 6.1 : Example of a ubiquitous computing application

The AV-recording is person-aware, location-aware (via GPS), time-aware and networked to interact with other ICT devices such as printers and a family-and-friends database video so that recordings are automatically in focus and selected parts of the scene are lit to the optimum degree. The context of the recording such as the location and date/time is also automatically captured using inbuilt location and clock systems.

- The camera is aware that the person making a recording is perhaps interested in capturing people in a scene, in focus, even if they are off centre. It uses an enhanced user interface to do this which involves automatically overlaying the view of the physical world, whether on an inbuilt display or through a lens or viewfinder, with markers for parts of the face such as the eyes and mouth.

- It then automatically focuses the lens so faces are in focus in the visual recording.

- The recorded content can be immediately viewed, printed and shared among friends and family using removable memory or exchanged across a communications network.

- It can be archived in an external Audio-Visual (AV) content database. When the AV content is stored, it is tagged with the time and location (the GIS database is used to convert the position to a location context). Image processing can be used to perform face recognition to automatically tag any people who can be recognised using the friends and family database.

- Through the use of micro electromechanical systems (MEMS) what previously needed to be a separate decimetre-sized device, e.g., a projector, can now be inbuilt. The camera is networked and has the capability to discover other specific types of ICT devices, e.g., printers, to allow printing to be initiated from the camera.

- Network access, music and video player and video camera functions could also be combined into this single device. Ubiquitous computing (UbiCom) encompasses a wide spectrum of computers, not just devices that are general purpose computers, multi-function ICT devices such as phones, cameras and games consoles, Automatic Teller Machines (ATMs), vehicle control systems, mobile phones, electronic calculators, household appliances, and computer peripherals such as routers and printers. The characteristics of embedded (computer) systems are that they are self-contained and run specific predefined tasks. Hence, design engineers can optimize them as follows. There is less need for full operating system functionality, e.g., multiple process scheduling and memory management and there is less need for a full CPU, e.g., the simple 4-bit microcontrollers used to play a tune in a greeting card or in a children's toy. This reduces the size and cost of the product so that it can be more economically mass-produced, benefiting from economies of scale.

- Many objects could be designed to be a multi-function device supporting AV capture, an AV player, communicator, etc. Embedded computing systems may be subject to a real-time constraint, real-time embedded systems, e.g., anti-lock brakes on a vehicle may have a real-time constraint that brakes must be released within a short time to prevent the wheels from locking.

- ICT Systems are increasing in complexity because we connect a greater diversity and number of individual systems in multiple dynamic ways.

- For ICT systems to become more useful, they must in some cases become more strongly interlinked to their physical world locale, i.e., they must be context-aware of their local physical world environment. For ICT systems to become more usable by humans, ICT systems must strike the right balance between acting autonomously and acting under the direction of humans. Currently it is not possible to take humans completely out of the loop when designing and maintaining the operation of significantly complex systems. ICT systems need to be designed in such a way that the responsibilities of the automated ICT systems are not clear and the responsibilities of the human designers, operators and maintainers are clear and in such a way that human cognition and behavior are not overloaded.

3. Adaptive Transport Scheduled Service

- In a twentieth-century scheduled transport service, timetables for a scheduled transport service, e.g., taxi, bus, train, plane, etc. to pick up passengers or goods at fixed or scheduled point are only accessible at special terminals and locations. Passengers and controllers have a limited view of the actual time when vehicles arrive at designated way-points on the route. Passengers or goods can arrive and wait long times at designated pick-up points.

- A manual system enables vehicle drivers to radio in to controllers their actual position when there is a deviation from the timetable. Controllers can often only manually notify passengers of delays at the designated pick-up points. By contrast, in a twenty-first-century scheduled transport service, the position of transport vehicles is determined using automated positioning technology, e.g., GPS. For each vehicle, the time taken to travel to designated pick-up points, e.g., next stop, final stop, is estimated partly based on current vehicle position, progress and historical data of route users. Up-to-date vehicle arrival times can then be accessed ubiquitously using mobile phones enabling JIT (Just-In-Time) arrival at passenger and goods collection points. Vehicles on the route can tag locations that they anticipate will change the schedule of other vehicles in that vicinity. Anticipated schedule change locations can be reviewed by all subsequent vehicles.

- Vehicles can then be re-routed and re-scheduled dynamically, based upon 'schedule change' locations, current positions and the demand for services.

- If the capacity of the transport vehicles was extensible, the volume of passengers waiting on route could determine the capacity of the transport service to meet demand.

- The transport system may need to deal with conflicting goals such as picking up more passengers and goods to generate more revenue for services rendered versus minimizing how late the vehicle arrives at pre-set points along its route.

4. Foodstuff Management

- A ubiquitous home environment is designed to support healthy eating and weight regulation for food consumers. A conventional system performs this manually.

- A next generation system (semi-)automates this task using networked physical devices such as fridges and other storage areas for food and drink items which can monitor the food in and out. Sensors are integrated in the system, e.g., to determine the weight of food and of humans. Scanners can be used to scan the packaging of food and drink items for barcodes, text tables, expiry dates and food ingredients and percentages by weight.

- Hand-held integrated scanners can also select food for purchase in food stores such as supermarkets that should be avoided on health or personal choice grounds.

- The system can identify who buys which kind of food in the supermarket. The system enables meal recipes to be automatically configured to adapt to the ingredients in stock. The food in stock can be periodically monitored to alert users when food will becomes out of date and when the supply of main food items is low. The amount of food, at different levels of granularity in terms of the overall amount of food and in terms of weight in grams of fat, salt and sugar, etc, consumed per unit time and per person can be monitored.

- The system can incorporate policies about eating a balanced diet, e.g., to consume five pieces of fruit or vegetables a day.

System design includes the following components :

Scanners are used to identify the types and quantities of ingredients based upon the packaging. This may include a barcode but perhaps not all food has barcodes and can be identified in this way.

- The home food store can be designed to check when (selected) food items are running low. Food running low can be defined as there is a quantity of one item remaining but items can be large and partially full.

- The quantity of a foodstuff remaining needs to be measured using a weight transducer but the container weight overhead is needed in order to calculate the weight of the foodstuff. The home food store could be programmed to detect when food is out of date by reading the expiry date and signalling the food as inedible. Many exceptions or conditions may need to be specified for the system in order to manage the food store.

- For example : food may still be edible even if its expiry date has past. Food that is frozen and then thawed in the fridge may be past its sell-by date but is still edible. Selected system events could automatically trigger actions, e.g., low quantities of food could trigger actions to automatically purchase food and have it delivered. Operational policies must be linked to context or situation and to the authorisation to act on behalf of owner, e.g., food is not ordered when consumers are absent or consumers specify that they do not want infinite repeat orders of food that has expired or is low in quantity. There can be limitations to full system automation. Unless the system can act on behalf of the human owner to accept delivery, to allow physical access to the home food store and to the building where consumers live, and has robots to move physical objects and to open and close the home food store to maintain temperature controlled environments there, these scenarios will require some human intervention. An important issue in this scenario is balancing what the system can and should do versus what humans can and should do.

5. **Utility Regulation**

- A ubiquitous home environment is designed to regulate the consumption of a utility (such as water, energy or heating) and to improve usage efficiency. For example : currently utility management, e.g., energy management, products are manually configurable by human users, utilize stand-alone devices and are designed to detect local user context changes.

- User context aware energy devices can be designed to switch themselves on in a particular way, e.g., a light switches on, and heating switches on when it detects the presence of a user otherwise it switches off. These devices must also be aware of environmental conditions so that artificial lights and heating would not switch on if it determines that the natural lighting and heating levels will suffice.

- System design includes the following components and usage patterns. Devices that are configured manually may waste energy because users may forget to switch them off. Devices that are set to be active, according to pre-set user policies, e.g., to control a timer, may waste energy because users cannot always schedule their activities to adhere to the static schedule of the timer. Individually, context-aware devices such as lights, can waste energy because several overlapping devices may be activated and switch on, e.g., when a user's presence is detected.

- A ubiquitous system can be designed, using multi-agent system and autonomic system models, to operate as a Smart Grid. Multiple devices can self-manage themselves and cooperate to adhere to users' policies such as minimizing energy expenditure.

- For example : If several overlapping devices are deemed to be redundant, the system will decide which individual one to switch on. Energy usage costs will depend upon multiple factors, not just the time a device is switched on, but also upon the energy rating which varies across devices and the tariff, i.e., the cost of energy usage varies according to the time of day.

- Advanced utility consumption meters can be used to present the consumption per unit-time and per device and can empower customers to see how they are using energy and to manage its use more efficiently. Demand-response designs can adjust energy use in response to dynamic price signals and policies. For example, during peak periods, when prices are higher, energy-consuming devices could be operated more frugally to save money. A direct load control system, a form of demand-response system, can also be used, in which certain customer energy-consuming devices are controlled remotely by the electricity provider or a third party during peak demand periods.

6. Physical Components of a Smart Device

- There are several organisations that publish standards to which manufacturers must follow if their products are to function with the desired capabilities. One such organisation is the DMFT3, which created the specification called the Common Information Model (CIM) . This is an object oriented information model, which defines a conceptual framework for describing management data.

- In this model the DMTF describe a schema to represent the physical and logical representation of various devices. The concept of this schema is a good candidate to follow with respect to describing a smart device with two models, one being physical requirements and the other logical requirements.

An intelligent device is any type of equipment, instrument, or machine that has its own computing capability. On top of this definition is a smart device, capable of communicating with other devices within the environment. It can perform intelligent operations on its own behave with respect to its functionality and its relevant surrounding environment. Embedded systems are being places in a wide range of products from microwaves to car keys. These devices must have a minimum set of physical components to be categorised as smart devices. These components are as follows.

6.2 POWER COMPONENT

- A power component is any source of power being provided to a device. This may be provided in a variety of ways, such as a mains power supply, battery, solar etc. It may be a one-time battery charge or a replenishable supply of power scavenged from the environment. A power component has the responsibility of providing all electrical

  (or otherwise) components of a device with sufficient power to operate within reasonable parameters.

- In the DMFT – CIM model of a device, a power component may include sub components in addition to aid its function such as a controller for an uninterrupted power supply or power saving components. A power component must be aware of the energy demands of the device and be able to operate the device within normal working parameters.

6.3 MEMORY COMPONENT

- A smart device is able to made intelligent decisions on its own behave with respect to its environment. Almost all embedded systems contain internal memory to store operations. The reason this is such an important component with regards to the smart device is that the requirement of memory will increase with the complexity of the operations being performed by the smart device.

- With the ever- increasing miniaturisation of computer components, there is no doubt that this will not be a major factor in the evolution of smart device production. In the DMTF – CIM model, the memory component is split up into processor memory, cache, volatile and non-volatile memory. It takes a logical view of the physical components being independent from any implementation.

6.4 PROCESSING COMPONENT

- The need for an adequate processing component is evident. As intelligence in devices increases so does the requirement for their operations to execute faster and more efficiently. It can be seen for example in the mobile phone industry the increasing demand on manufacturers to supply mobile phones with the capability of running operating systems such as Symbian OS, 2003 or Java virtual machines for running J2ME, 2003.

6.5 COMMUNICATIONS INTERFACE

- This component lets a device to (at the least) communicate with other devices and service within its smart space. This is an important component because if a device is to be able to interact with other devices within its smart space and let other devices and services interact with it; it must provide a means of communication to these other devices.

- There are a variety of physical communications that may be used ranging from wired digital and analog connections such as Ethernet, IEEE 1394, USB (Universal Serial Bus), ProfiBus, serial and parallel cables, etc. to wireless connections including IEEE 802.11, Bluetooth, IrDA, GSM, GPRS, transceivers, etc. In the DMFT – CIM model, there is no standard communications interface component, but the bases of the smart device model is that any communications interface is possible. This model is independent of how devices communicate (physical links), but does reinforce the fact that there must be a means of device access by the environment if a device is to interact with the smart space environment.

6.5.1 Present Device Service and Interaction Methods

- Apart from a physical model of a smart device, there is also a need for a logical model for a smart device. Such a model must outline what a smart device offers to a smart space with regards to the services it can provide to the environment. The model must also outline interactions between smart devices, changes in the state of smart device operation, and smart services within a smart space.

- There are various models present today that have similar approaches to modelling device. Two such models would include Home Plug and Play (HPnP), which is slightly out of date but still applicable, and the newer Universal Plug and Play (UPnP), which is an open standards body. These two standards bodies have modelled devices by the services that they offer and have also developed interaction models for device communication.

- Another emerging standard for defining services in an abstract way is with the use of the Web Services Definition Language (WSDL). Along with describing services a smart device can provide, there must also be a way of representing changes in states of smart devices and how devices react to these changes within a smart environment.

6.6 HOME PLUG 'N' PLAY DEVICE INTERACTIONS

The Home Plug'n'Play architecture describes devices being composed of three hierarchical layers, namely objects, contexts and devices.

- **Object :** A term used to define a single control function within a context. For example, an Audiocontext contains a Gain Object.

- **Context :** A group of one or more objects representing a common device function. Several ofthese contexts may be present in a single device.

- **Device :** A mechanism that exposes state and control variables through a home networkusing the Common Application Language (CAL) protocol. Devices might be stand-alone hardware devices or might be implemented in software on a PC. A device is a container for a set of contexts that collectively receive messages addressed to the same transport layer address. This address may be a unique system or unit address, one of many group addresses, or a broadcast address. Contexts receive messages from other devices to invoke actions on objects, which are contained within a context.

- This hierarchical model describes a good logical layout for how smart devices may offer services and interact with each other. Another method of devices description and interaction can be seen in a newer model developed by the Universal Plug and Play Group.

6.7 UNIVERSAL PLUG 'N' PLAY DEVICE INTERACTION

- Another more generic model that is aimed at total device interoperability is the UPnP model. UPnP is a lot newer than HPnP, first being developed by Microsoft to be an extension to the concept of Plug'n'Play technology in desktop computer systems. UPnP describes three components within its model, the device, the service and the controlpoint.

- A device is a container of services and embedded devices, similar to that of the HPnP model. Each device contains an XML document describing it and what services it has to offer. Information would include device name, model, serial number, etc, and a list of available services.

- A service exposes actions and models its state with state variables. For instance, a clock service could be modelled as having a state variable, current_time, which defines the state of the clock, and two actions, set_time and get_time, which allow you to control the service. Similar to the device description, this information is part of an XML service description standardized by the UPnP forum. A pointer (URL) to these service descriptions is contained within the device description document.

- Devices may contain multiple services. A service in a UPnP device consists of a state table, a control server and an event server. The state table models the state of the service through state variables and updates them when the state changes. The control server receives action requests (such as set_ time), executes them, and updates the state table and returns responses.

- The event server publishes events to interested subscribers anytime the state of the service changes. For instance, the fire alarm service would send an event to interested subscribers when its state changes to "ringing."

A control point in the UPnP network is a controller capable of discovering and controlling other devices. After discovery, a control point could:

- Retrieve the device description and get a list of associated services.
- Retrieve service descriptions for interesting services.
- Invoke actions to control the service.
- Subscribe to the service's event source. Anytime the state of the service changes, the event server will send an event to the control point.
- It is expected that devices will incorporate control point functionality (and vice-versa) to enable true peer-to-peer networking.

6.8 WEB SERVICES DESCRIPTION LANGUAGE (WSDL)

WSDL is a rapidly emerging technology for describing services in an abstract way. It provides a way of offering a service, regardless of its implementation to other heterogeneous systems over the Internet. WSDL lets a client talk to a service through a common protocol known as Simple Object Access Protocol (SOAP). WSDL and SOAP are XML based, so as long as the client and server can parse and understand the XML documents, the implementation of the client and server can be completely independent.

A WSDL document is made up of six major elements

- **Type :** Which provides data type definitions used to describe the messagesexchanges between endpoints.
- **Message :** Which represents an abstract definition of the data being transmitted. Amessage consists of logical parts, each of which is associated with a definition within some type system.
- **Port Type :** Which is a set of abstract operations. Each operation refers to an inputmessage and output messages.
- **Binding :** Which specifies concrete protocol and data format specifications for theoperations and messages defined by a particular port Type.
- **Port :** Which specifies an address for a binding, thus defining a singlecommunication endpoint.
- **Service :** Which is used to aggregate a set of related ports.

Using these six major elements it is possible to describe homogeneous interactions between heterogeneous services. As manufacturers of devices develop the services of these devices (at most) in house, offering these heterogeneous services to an environment in a homogeneous way would not be possible without a level of service abstraction. The concept of using WSDL to hide heterogeneity of service implementations is very applicable to smart spaces and the interoperability of smart devices.

6.9 REFLECTION

- A Smart Space is a physical space rich in devices and software services that is capable of interacting with people, the physical environment and external networked services. In line with this paradigm smart devices are pieces of physical equipment that offer services and are capable of interacting with the user and each other. Smart devices must be able to react to changes within the environment with respect to the user and other devices and services within the smart space. As this is a major feature of the smart space, it is important that a smart device can reflect its present state of operation within the smart space.

- A smart device with reflective capabilities provides a representation of its own behaviour, which is amenable to inspection and adaptation, and is causally connected to the underlying behaviour it describes. "Causally-connected" means that changes made to the self-representation are immediately mirrored in the underlying system's actual state and behaviour, and vice-versa. This Meta representation of a device's state of operation must also be visible to all other devices and services within the smart space, if they are to be able to react to changes in this Meta representation.

- A simple example where a reflective state of a smart device may be required would be in the case of an alarm clock. When the alarm clock reaches a certain time it will start ringing. Other devices within the smart space may wish to perform some operation when the state of operation of the alarm clock changes, such as a kettle switching itself on.

- There are other important considerations that must be reflected by devices, such as power levels, and bandwidth consumption. Licia Capra put forward the idea of having an application profile for each application on a mobile device, defining a specific reaction to chances in the reflective state of the resources of a device. This application profile is an XML document defining a condition and reaction to resource states of devices.

```
<RESOURCE name="battery">
    <STATUS operator="lessEqual" value=x/>  % context configuration
    <BEHAVIOUR policy="disconnect"/>        % policy
</RESOURCE>
```
The above describes the reaction of an application when battery power is low.

- **Smart Device Services and Interactions**

The above section has outlined present methods of modelling the description and services a device can offer to a network, and how reflection can be used to allow inspection and adaptation of the state of operation of a device on a network. The following section will discuss how such methods can apply to a smart device and produce a logical smart device model for representing smart device services and interactions.

6.10 SERVICES COMPONENT

- The service component of a smart device is made up of various internal components. Together these components allow a smart device to publish its services to a smart space on entering, allow other smart devices and services to understand and invoke these services in an abstract way. The services component allows other smart devices and services within the smart space to access the internal operations of a device without the requirement of manufacture specific controls or drivers. This is done by using an abstract services definition to describe to other smart devices and services within the smart space, how to invoke the smart devices operations. Through this abstract interface a smart device's internal operations can be invoked.

6.11 REFLECTIVE STATE COMPONENT

- A reflective state component of a smart device can be taught of a Meta representation of the devices own internal states. The reflective state component contains various internal components that allow the smart device to publish a Reflective Meta Representation (RMR) of itself so other smart devices and services may be able to see the present state of the smart device and react to changes. The main internal component of the reflective state component is the internal states component. This component will hold values on various states the smart device can take on, e.g. POWER ON/OFF/LOW, ALARM RINGING, PRESENT_TIME, TEMPERATURE, etc. The internal states may be manipulates by the invocation of an internal operation of the smart device, or may be reflecting the status of a physical component such as power supply or bandwidth.

- Smart devices and services can subscribe the RMR of a smart device and manipulate it, through what is called the control component. Manipulation of the RMR will change the internal operation of a smart device.

- For example : An alarm clock may have a RMR showing that the alarm functionality is turned off. If a Control Component of a smart device or service were to set this attribute to on, the necessary internal operations of the smart device would be invoked to reflect this change.

6.12 CONTROL COMPONENT

If a smart device wishes to participate in invoking a smart device service, or subscribe to state change notifications, it must contain a control component. The control component effectively acts as a client of the services smart devices offer to the smart space. The control component contains various internal components, which allow it to interact with smart devices.

6.12.1 Service Publication Listener

This component listens out for any new services being introduced by a smart device entering a smart space. This component also would handle such things as leasing and deregistering of smart device services.

6.12.2 Query Services

This component can query its registry of available services for a service of a particular type. It can also query the registry of other control points or broadcast a search query to available smart devices within the smart space.

6.12.3 Invoke Services

The control component can invoke services belonging to other smart devices within the smart space by binding with them through this component. An example of how this component may work can be seen in WSDL web service binding through the use of SOAP and URLs.

6.12.4 Subscribe RMR (Reflective Meta Representation)

When a device enters the smart space, it can publish its reflective meta representation to any interested smart devices and services containing a control component. The control component uses this internal component to listen and subscribe to the smart devices RMR publications. This component can also request an RMR of a smart device. The control component will then store a list of the RMRs it's subscribed to in the **Available RMR Subscriptions** component.

6.12.5 Manipulate RMR

A control component can manipulate the RMR, it is subscribed too. Through this process the change in an RMR value will be sent to the corresponding smart device, which will then reflect this change through the use of internal operations. This operation also requires a binding between the smart device and the Control Component.

6.12.6 Available Services List

The control component must hold a list of all smart device services available to it within the smart space. This list can be queried for services of a certain category, returning information on how these services are to be invoked, i.e. parameters, location, device etc.

6.12.7 Available RMR Subscriptions

The control point must hold a list of smart device RMRs it is currently subscribed to. This component holds information on how to update any given RMR of a smart device.

6.13 HUMAN COMPUTER INTERACTIONS (HCI) REQUIREMENTS FOR UBIQUITOUS COMPUTING

HCI should not only consider ease of use but also focus on assisting user tasks, proving access to information in best way and concentrate on more powerful form of interactions. After considering its perspective HCI has taken new dimension especially in Ubiquitous computing. All the fantasy and novelty of ubiquitous systems based on the novel way of user interaction with the systems. Some core characteristics of Human Computer Interaction (HCI) in Ubiquitous system are given below;

- HCI in ubiquitous system would be hidden and implicit rather than traditional explicit interactions of user with the system.
- Ubiquitous system environment shouldallowthe user to focus on the tasks rather than on the technology.
- HCI in ubiquitous computing involves adaptive to situation and support for multimodal of interaction with the user. This requires some sortof intelligence work integrated with interaction paradigm.
- Human interaction pattern in Ubiquitous environment would multimodal of interaction support.
- With advance in technology the interaction in ubiquitous computing tends to be supported with natural interactions like interaction of human to human.

HUMAN COMPUTER INTERACTION FRAMEWORK FOR UBIQUITOUS COMPUTING

All these requirements of HCI in ubiquitous computing require an enhanced model of interaction with clear defined goals. The agenda of ubiquitous computing require implicit Human Computer Interactions (iHCI) with the help of context aware interactions and natural, intelligent multimodal interfaces. Traditional interactions theme can also be utilized when they can prove to be useful in ubiquitous computing environment.

6.14 IMPLICIT HUMAN COMPUTER INTERACTIONS

- The ubiquitous computing had the agenda of implicit Human Computer Interactions (iHCI) with minimum distraction of user from their core activities. The main goal is to focus on the user task rather than user focus on technology. Weiser vision of calm, disappearing computers is manifold and multidimensional. Important context of calm and disappearing computers is their working without much interaction with the user.

- The system should support the user tasks without much intervention and with minimal distraction of user from their core activities. The system tends to disappear and become calm because human interactions with this system tend to implicit rather than explicit.

- Due to effective use of implicit mode of interaction the calm or disappearing computers would be reality in very near future. The basic purpose of calm and disappearing computer is that system should proactive rather than user involve in explicit interaction with the system. Clam computing removes user from the system and hope that system work proactive rather than reactive to the user.

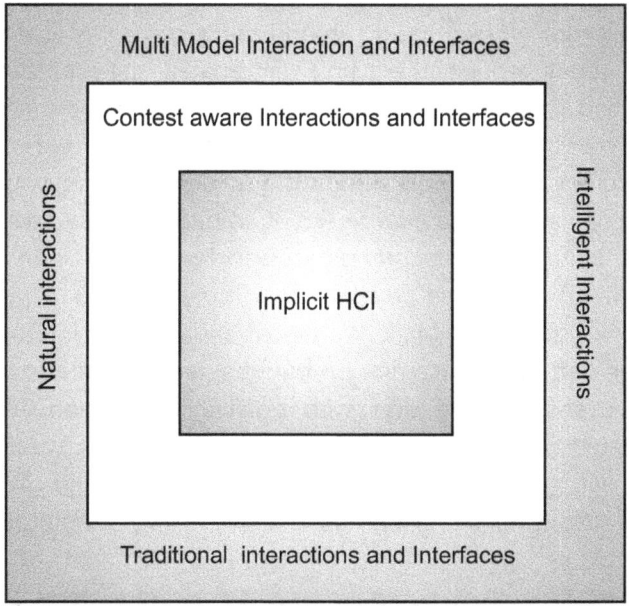

Fig. 6.2 : Human Computer Interaction in Ubiquitous Computing

6.15 CONTEXT AWARE INTERACTIONS   (Nov. 16, May 17)

- Ubiquitous application has to be context ware system. Previous research on the issue of HCI in Ubiquitous computing has posed the agenda of context ware applications in order to be proactive. The context would play an integral part in ubiquitous application that help to achieve the implicit interaction but there are still unresolved issues relating to representation of context, acquisition of context and its distribution.

- Context aware systems are system that are aware of their situation and adopt accordingly. Context aware systems are aware of their environment, situation or context so that system can adapt to the situation and provide services according to the changed situation or context. According to Dey, "a system is said to be context aware if it exploit relevant context to provide services". Dey and Abowd define context as information that used to characterize the situation of an entity that is relevant to the interaction between the user and application.

- Context information's depends upon the type of services and application like location, temperature, light etc.

For example : many smart phones turned automatically to silent mode for some location without explicit interaction with the user. Context information can be very helpful in proactively of the interactions but it may cause problem if desired level of accuracy not achieved. In order to be successful in ubiquitous environment interactions, different context information and accuracy of this context information is very crucial. Context of use and adaption of application and user interfaces according to the context of use help to create applications that are easy to use especially in ubiquitous computing environment. For application in ubiquitous computing we have to consider context of use not only in design process but also for different usage scenarios of application and its services in order to adapt according to the situation and environment.

- For traditional application HCI we design around single context of use and user. Most of our efforts in design spent around the single anticipated use context. For application in ubiquitous computing environment that have to change and provide services according to the situation and environment the traditional approach of HCI may fail. If we attempt to support multiple contexts with single design it also turn to complex one as the number of context and users may increase to a large extent. In order to provide support for a range of context support of Context aware system is necessary for HCI in ubiquitous applications.

- Context aware system has strong relationship with ubiquitous computing and can play important role in realization of Mark Weiser vision about Ubiquitous computing. When computer would be part of everyday life it would be necessary that such system are easy to use and do not overwhelm the user with explicitly interaction with the system. User environment saturated with thousands of computers may distract user from their tasks and involve user in explicit interaction with the system rather than allow them to focus on their tasks and activities. This is against the vision and spirit of the Ubiquitous computing or clam computing.

- For the realization of Ubiquitous computing context aware systems are very important for optimal use and performance of different system in ubiquitous computing environment. Computers with different shapes and sized had already integrated into our life and activities. Different home usage devices and appliances had acquired the smart capabilities due to installations of microprocessors and memories capabilities. These smart integrated devices also have the capabilities for interconnections with available network high capacity bandwidth. What remain is to judge the user situations and environment and provide services according to the environment. In order to provide services by adapting to the user environment it is necessary for the system to have the capabilities of context aware system. Context aware system enables to sense the environment and help the ubiquitous system to adopt and provide services according to changing situation.

6.16 INTELLIGENT, NATURAL AND MULTIMODAL INTERFACES

- Intelligent user interfaces aim to enhance the efficiency, naturalness, and effectiveness of HCI by using artificial intelligence techniques. If we look into history, user note taking capabilities evaluation starts with typewriter. From typewriter it shifted to keyboard and from keyboard to touch and voice input capabilities suggest that interactions pattern in modern days shifting towards natural paradigm. Intelligent user interfaces enhance user experience by content support for input and output of data and navigational support for navigation between applications. One type of such support is that highlight important information and reduces the user effort to find desired information. Intelligent interfaces can also adapt to provide access to most relevant functionality and information.

- Single independent channel of interaction is called modality. This is the channel through which information transferred between system and user. A system that is based on single channel is called uni-model whereas system with multiple channels is called multi-model. The most common system based on different modalities is visual, audio and sensors based. With the help of context aware system different input and output modalities can be included in order to increase user experience according to specific context. With help of context user interface can be tailored to specific context and adapt behavior according to context, situation or user requirement. But it is not as simple as it seems to be. User has to learn how to use the system and how to cope with change behavior with change of context. When the user interfaces are adaptive and change their behavior dynamically it becomes very difficult for the user to learn and adjust with the system. It is necessary that user also aware of cause of change of interface. Otherwise user feels very difficult in remember of navigations and interaction with a dynamic changing context of the system. User interface adaptation to context should be designed in careful way so that user can understand it easily. Good design should focus in stability and help the user in memorizing and causes of adaptation of user interface with each change of context. A carful design should avoid user from complexity.

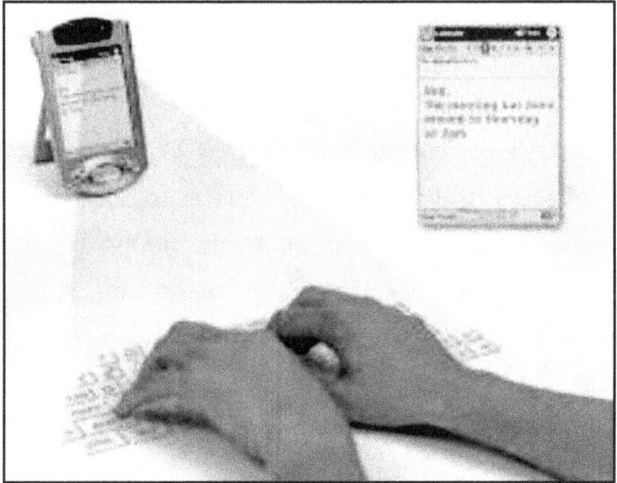

Fig. 6.3 : Canasta Key board

- Due to multiple focus of HCI research there is also trend in multimodality interfaces from traditional interfaces. Along with shift from traditional to multimodality there is also trend of intelligent, context aware, adaptive interface with implicit human computer interactions rather than explicit interaction pattern through command line and GUI interfaces. Multimodal interaction should be focus of HCI in future. Multimodal interfaces offer additional models like dialogue, gesture and context of use. Challenge is to identify what task fit to what modality. Human to human communication is an ideal standard for future multimodal interactions in Ubiquitous computing.

- The ubiquitous applications would be different from the desktop model of computing therefore it is known as off the desktop or post desktop interaction paradigm. The interaction pattern in this paradigm would be quite different from desktop computing environment and should be in natural style. It would much like the way human interact with their physical environment. Human exploit speech, gesture and pen based interactions to communicate with the physical artifacts and human being. These natural actions of the human would be source of implicit or explicit interaction with the system. This theme poses an agenda of implicit interaction from the user environment, from user activities and even from user expression. Ideally it should be like man to man communication. Though a lot of research along the lines of pen and gesture input introduced but the inherent error rate still very high and need to be lowered in future. These natural interfaces would be easy to use and have the capability to learn from their environment. They also have the ability to support user task rather than distracting the user from their task to focus on technological issues.

- **Context-Awareness**

The aim of UbiCom systems is not to support global ubiquity, to interlink all systems to form one omnipresent service domain, but rather to support context-based ubiquity, e.g., situated access versus mass access. The benefits of context-based ubiquity include :

(1) Limiting the resources needed to deliver ubiquitous services because delivering omnipresent services would be cost-prohibitive.

(2) Limiting the choice of access from all possible services to only the useful services;

(3) Avoiding overburdening the user with too much information and decision-making; and

(4) Supporting a natural locus of attention and calm decision-making by users.

There are three main types of external environment context-awareness supported in UbiCom:

Physical environment context: pertaining to some physical world dimension or phenomena such as location, time, temperature, rainfall, light level, etc.

- Human context (or user context or person context): interaction is usefully constrained by users: in

- terms of identity; preferences; task requirements; social context and other activities; user experi-ence and prior knowledge and types of user.
- ICT context or virtual environment context: a particular component in a distributed system is aware of the services that are available internally and externally, locally and remotely, in the distributed system.

Generally, the context-aware focus of UbiCom systems is on physical world awareness, often in relation to user models and tasks. Ubiquitous computers can utilise where they are and their physical situation or context in order to optimise their services on behalf of users. This is sometimes referred to as context-awareness in general but more accurately refers to physical context-awareness. A greater awareness of the immediate physical environ-ment could reduce the energy and other costs of physical resource access – making systems more eco-friendly.

Consider the use of the digital camera in the personal visual memories application. It can be aware of its location and time so that it can record where and when a recording is made. Rather than just expressing the location in terms of a set of co-ordinates, it can also use a Geographical Information System to map these to meaningful physical objects at that location. It can also be aware of its locality so that it can print on the nearest accessible computer.

- **User-Awareness**

A camera can be person-aware in a number of ways in order to detect and make sure people are being recorded in focus, so that it configures itself to a person's preferences and interests. These are all specific examples of physical context-awareness.

User context-awareness, also known as person-awareness, refers to ubiquitous services, resources and devices being used to support user-centred tasks and goals. For example, a photo-grapher may be primarily interested in capturing digital memories of people (the user activity goal) rather than capturing memories of places or of people situated in places. For this reason, aUbiCom camera can be automatically configured to detect faces and to put people in focus when taking pictures. In addition, in such a scenario, people in images may be automatically recognised and annotated with names and named human relationships.

world context, e.g., the location within and the temperature of the environment, and aware of the virtual world or ICT context, e.g., the network bandwidth being consumed for communication.

In practice, many current devices have little idea of their physical context such as their location and surroundings. The physical context may not be able to be accurately deter-mined or even determined at all, e.g., the camera uses a particular location determination system that does not work indoors. The user context is even harder to determine because the users' goals may not be published and are often weakly defined. For this reason, the user context is often derived from users' actions but these in turn may also be ambiguous and non-deterministic.

- **Active Versus Passive Context-Awareness**

A key design issue for context-aware systems is to balance the degree of user control and awareness of their environment. At one extreme, in a (pure) active context-aware system, the UbiCom system is aware of the environment context on behalf of the user, automatically adjusting the system to the context without the user being aware of it. This may be useful in applications where there are strict time constraints and the user would not otherwise be able to adapt to the context quickly enough. An example of this is a collision avoidance system built into a vehicle to automatically brake when it detects an obstacle in front of it. In contrast, in a (pure) passive context-aware system, the UbiCom system is aware of the environment context on behalf of the user. It just reports the current context to the user without any adaptation, e.g., a positioning system reports the location of a moving object on a map. A passive context-aware system can also be configured to report deviations from a pre-planned context path, e.g., deviations from a pre-planned transport route to a destination. Design issues include how much control or privacy a human subject has over his or her context in terms of whether the subject knows: if his or her context is being acquired, where the context is being kept and to who and what the context is distributed to.

6.16.1 Tagging, Sensing and Controlling Environments

Smart environment devices support several types of interaction with environments such as the physical environment as follows :

- **Tagging and annotating the physical environment :** Tags, e.g., RFID32 tags, can be attached to physical objects. Tag readers can be used to find the location of tags and to track them. Virtual tags can be attached to virtual views of the environment, e.g., a tag can be attached to a location in a virtual map.

- **Sensing or monitoring the physical environment :** Transducers take inputs from the physical environment to convert some phenomena in the physical world into electrical signals that can be digitised, e.g., how much ink is in a printer's cartridges. Sensors provide the raw information about the state of the physical environment as input to help determine the context in a context-aware system. Sensing is often a pre-stage to filtering and adapting.

- **Filtering :** A system forms an abstract or virtual view of part of its environment such as the physical world. This reduces the number of features in the view and enables viewers to focus on the features of interest.

- **Adapting :** System behaviour can adapt to the features of interest in the environment of adapt to changes in the environment, e.g., a physical environment route is based upon the relation of the current location to a destination location.

- **Controlling the physical world.** Controllers normally require sensors to determine the state of the physical phenomena e.g., heating or cooling systems that sense the temperature in an environment. Controlling can involve actions to modify the state of environment, to cause it to transition to another state. Control may involve changing the order (assembly) of artefacts in the environment or may involve regulation of the physical environment.

- **Assembling :** Robots are used to act on a part of the physical world. There is a variety of robots. They may be pre-programmed to schedule a series of actions in the world to achieve some goal, e.g., a robot can incorporate sensors to detect objects in a source location, move them and stack them in a destination location (palletisation). Robots may be stationary, e.g., a robot arm, or be mobile.

- **Regulating :** Regulators tend to work in a fixed location, e.g., a heating system uses feedback control to regulate the temperature in an environment within a selected range.

6.16.2 Interaction in Ubiquitous Computing

- The terms calm computing, invisible computingand disappearing computer describe the user interface perspective on Ubiquitous Computing. As the interaction is interwoven with the user's actions the concept goes beyond the traditional understanding of a human computer interface towards describing the relationship between the user and their augmented environment. Making the computer invisible is not a matter of size or a challenge of seamless integration of hardware, it's about how the human perceives the computer. To make the computer disappear (at least in the user's perception), the interaction has to be seamlessly integrated with the primary task of the user. The user still interacts with the tools that help them to do a certain job, buttheir focus is on the task itself. This is in contrast to typical usage of a computeras a tool, where the focus usually ends on the computer not on the task. Ina Ubiquitous Computing paradigm tools are enhanced with processing and communication capabilities to help with achieving the task not drawing focus away from it.

- Embedding interaction into tasks seems to be the obvious approach to take. However, when it comes to modelling and implementing this vision many unresolved issues appear. Using explicit interaction, as in conversational computer systems, there is provision for a choice of varying modalities. The interaction designer can chose from command line user interfaces, graphical user interfaces, and speech and gesture interfaces. Independent of the modality the user still is required to interact with a computer. Another issue that makes conversional interaction methods difficult is that interface components can be physically distributed and dependent on each other. On the other hand as there is also the potential for many applications to run at the same time, inputs have to be directed to a particular one. Using solely this approach would inevitably result in a complex interface and require a great deal of the user's attention, which is regarded as one of the most precious resources because it is limited. When interaction is embedded it happens in context.

- The physical environment, the situation, the role of the user, their relation to other users and to the environment, and their goals and preferences can all be rich source of information. Using this information when making a system context-aware can make the explicit interaction process much easier or even eliminate the need for explicit interaction. A reduction in explicit interaction will also reduce the demands on the user's attention, assuming that the system gets it right. This raises a further issue: how to acquire and provide context?

6.16.3 Context-Awareness is an Enabling Technology

- In Ubiquitous Computing, interaction with computers is inevitably in context and in most cases context matters for not only the users directly, but it also matters indirectly for the system. The user's expectations about a system and their anticipation of the reaction of a system that they are interacting with, is highly dependent on the situation and environment, as well as on prior experience.

- Interaction in the physical world is experienced from a very early age and the knowledge about the reaction of the environment accumulated over a lifetime. This knowledge allows intelligent behaviour; in particular the ability to predict the reaction that a certain action will provoke is a major advantage, and at large essential for survival. Many expectations are just extrapolated from previous experience, e.g. when operating a light switch on a bedside lamp in a hotel we expect that this particular light will switch on. We would be rather surprised if instead of the bedside light coming on the fan in the shower started or the radio in our car outside the hotel starts playing. Our expectations are based on experience and are essential to the way we live.

- In Ubiquitous Computing environments, where the real world becomes a part of the computer and of the user interface, users expectations towards the system are also widely based on the experience of interaction in the real world. The designer however has a great freedom of how to design interaction processes in such systems. Many limitations inherent in conventional engineering are no longer an issue in Ubiquitous Computing, in fact a networked switch could operate anything else that is networked.

- To make a system useful and give the user the feeling of being in charge of the system a switch should operate what the user anticipates in a particular situation. This simple example of a switch shows that context is essential for building usable Ubiquitous Computing systems that respond ina way that is anticipated by the user. Context-awareness becomes a fundamentalenabling technology for Ubiquitous Computing and is a key issue when creating computers that are invisible and disappear in terms of the user's perception. In these terms context-awareness goes beyond providing context information, it also requires understanding context and ultimately understanding situations.

6.16.4 Challenges in Context-Aware Computing

Examples, demonstrators, and prototypes havebeen used to demonstrate that context-awareness can enhance applications and systems. Typically location is sensed and then based on the location further assumptions about the more general context are made. As the concept of position and location is well understood, it also provides a powerful and easy to apply model for context-aware applications. In many cases however awareness based solely on location lacks information that can be of interest to a system for making it context-aware. Ifinformation beyond location information is required, further complexity is introduced.

6.16.5 The Following Issues are Central Research Challenges in Context-Awareness

- **Understanding the concept of context**

What does context mean and how is it connected to situations in the real world? There is still a fundamental lack of understanding in terms how contexts relate to situations and how general context information can be used to help enhance applications. This is also associated with the question of how to represent context in a universal way.

- **How to make use of context?**

Assuming that context is available in a system the question what is context useful for becomes imminent: especially if contexts beyond location and available resources are considered. In this instance a central question is what type of applications can be enhanced? When considering context as additional input, issues of reliability and ambiguity are important. Furthermore the relation between context and other inputs into the system and how they influence each other, have to be addressed. Ultimately this requires the smartness of the system to understand the context it is dealing with.

- **How to acquire context information?**

Acquiring context is a prerequisite for any context-aware system.

Generally context acquisition can be seen as the process where the real situation in the world is captured, the significant features are assessed, and an abstract representation is created, which is then provided to components in the system for further use. Approaches to acquire context are manifold and include computer vision, location tracking, sensor systems, and also more predictive approaches such as modelling users and their behaviour.

- **Connecting context acquisition to context use**

In a location-aware system there is a close relationship between context acquisition and context use, most often the location sensor is attached to the device using position as context. In this case the context representation is also agreed between these components. In more general environments context use and context acquisition is distributed. It can be assumed that context is provided for various applications, potentially in dynamic configurations. This makes it obvious that mechanisms to connect context acquisition and context use become essential. Here the challenge is twofold: overcoming the distribution issue by networking components and agreeing on representations that are useful for a multitude of components.

- **Understanding the influence on human computer interaction**

When systems are context-aware their behaviour is dependent on the context of use or the general situation of use. The ultimate goal is to make systems in such a way that they react as anticipated by the user. In real life however this creates complex problems, in particular if the system reacts differently from the users expectations. Two critical issues are how can the user understand the system and its behaviour? And how to give the user control over the system?

- **Support for building context-aware Ubiquitous Computing systems**

Context-awareness is an enabling technology for Ubiquitous Computing systems and therefore commonly required when realising such systems. To build Ubiquitous Computing environments efficiently, it is inevitable that we need to provide support for building context-aware applications. Up to now, there are many cases where the wheel is re-invented; where all the problems have to be solved over and over again in each system. Providing support for context acquisition, context provision, and contextuse will make the process of implementing context-aware applications much simpler.

- **Evaluation of context-aware system**

As context-aware systems are used in context, evaluationit self is also required to be done in context. In cases where functionality is only available and useful in a certain context it is required to create or simulate a particular situation that results in the wanted context in order to assess the system. Inducing a particular situation and context however may have also a significant effect on measures in the evaluation

6.16.6 Ubiquitous Communication

Mobile devices usually refer to communicators, multimedia entertainment and business processing devices designed to be transported by their human owners, e.g., mobile phone, games consoles, etc. There is a range of different types of mobiles as follows:

- **Accompanied :** These are devices that are not worn or implanted. They can either be portable or hand-held, separate from, but carried in clothes or fashion accessories.
- **Portable :** Such as laptop computers which are oriented to two-handed operation while seated. These are generally the highest resource devices.
- **Hand-held :** Devices are usually operated one handed and on occasion hands-free, combining multiple applications such as communication, audio-video recording and playback and mobile office. These are low resource devices.
- **Wearable :** Devices such as accessories and jewellery are usually operated hands-free and operate autonomously, e.g., watches that act as personal information managers, earpieces that act as audio transceivers, glasses that act as visual transceivers and contact lenses. These are low resource devices.
- **Implanted or embedded :** These are often used for medical reasons to augment human functions, e.g., a heart pacemaker. They may also be used to enhance the abilities of physically and mentally able humans. Implants may be silicon-based macro- or micro-sized integrated circuits or they may be carbon-based, e.g., nanotechnology.

Static can be regarded as an antonym for mobile. Static devices tend to be moved before installation to a fixed location and then reside there for their full operational life-cycle. They tend to use a continuous network connection (wired or wireless) and fixed energy source. They can incorporate high levels of local computation resources, e.g., personal computer, AV recorders and players, various home and office appliances, etc. The division between statics and mobiles can be more finely grained.

For example, statics could move between sessions of usage, e.g., a mobile circus containing different leisure rides in contrast to the rides in a fixed leisure park

6.16.7 Smart Interaction

- In order for smart devices and smart environments to support the core properties of UbiCom, an additional type of design is needed to knit together their many individual activity interactions. Smart interaction is needed to promote a unified and continuous interaction model between UbiCom applications and their UbiCom infrastructure, physical world and human environments.

- In the smart interaction design model, system components dynamically organise and interact to achieve shared goals. This organisation may occur internally without any external influence, a self-organising system, or this may be driven in part by external events. Components interact to achieve goals jointly because they are deliberately not designed to execute and complete sets of tasks to achieve goals all by themselves they are not monolithic system components. There are several benefits to designs based upon sets of interacting components.

- A range of levels of interaction between UbiCom system components exists from basic to smart. A distinction is made between (basic) interaction that uses fixed interaction protocols between two statically linked dependent parties versus (smart) interaction that uses richer interaction protocols between multiple dynamic independent parties or entities.

6.16.8 Basic Interaction

- Basic interaction typically involves two dependent parties: a sender and a receiver. The sender knows the address of the receiver in advance; the structure and meaning of the messages exchanged are agreed in advance, the control of flow, i.e., the sequencing of the individual messages, is known in advance. However, the content, the instances of the message that adhere to the accepted structure and meaning, can vary. There are two main types of basic interaction, synchronous versus asynchronous :

  - **Synchronous Interaction :** The interaction protocol consists of a flow of control of two messages, a request then a reply or response. The sender sends a request message to the specified receiver and waits for a reply to be received,e.g., a client component makes a request to a server component and gets a response.

  - **Asynchronous Interaction :** The interaction protocol consists of single messages that have no control of flow, a sender sends a message to a receiver without knowing necessarily if the receivers will receive the message or if there will be a subsequent reply, e.g., an error message is generated but it is not clear if the error will be handled leading to a response message.

Smart Interaction

- **Asynchronous and Synchronous interaction** is considered part of the distributed system communication functions In contrast, interactions that are co-ordinated, conventions-based, semantics and linguistic-based and whose interactions are driven by dynamic organisations are considered to be smart interaction.

- Hence, smart interaction extends basic interactions as follows:

- **Co-ordinated Interactions :** Different components act together to achieve a common goal using explicit communication, e.g., a sender requests a receiver to handle a request to complete a sub-task on the sender's behalf and the interaction is synchronised to achieve this. There are different types of co-ordination such as orchestration (use of a central co-ordinator) versus choreography (use of a distributed co-ordinator).

- **Policy and Convention-based Interaction :** Different components act together to achieve a common organisational goal but it is based upon agreed rules or contractual policies without necessarily requiring significant explicit communication protocols between them. This is based upon previously understood rules to define norms and abnormal behaviour and the use of commitments by members of organisations to adhere to policies or norms, e.g., movement of herds or flocks of animals are co-ordinated based upon rules such as keeping a minimum distance away from each other and moving with the centre of gravity, etc.

- **Dynamic Organisational Interaction :** Organisations are systems which are an arrangement of relationships (interactions) between individuals so that they produce a system with qualities not present at the level of individuals. Rich types of mediations can be used to engage others in organisations to complete tasks. There are many types of organisational interactional protocol such as auctions, brokers, contract-nets, subscriptions, etc.

- **Semantic and Linguistic Interactions :** Communication, interoperability (shared definitions about the use of the communication) and co-ordination are enhanced if the components concerned share common meanings of the terms exchanged and share a common language to express basic structures for the semantic terms exchanged.

Consider a scenario in which light resources are designed to be context-aware in order to save energy. They are designed to be actuated by human presence. If they detect a human is present, they automatically switch on. If they detect no one is present, they switch themselves off to save energy. However, if there were several lights in a semi-dark room and they were merely context-sensitive, they would all switch on when someone enters, but this wastes energy unnecessarily. If instead they were designed to support smart interaction, they could decide among themselves which lights to switch on in order to best support particular human activities and goals. Smart interaction requires devices to interact to share resource descrip-tions (e.g., desk-light, wall light, main ceiling light) and goals (e.g., reading, watching a video, retrieving something). This example is more complex in practice as it may need to support several users and possibly conflicting user-goals. Smart interaction also requires some smart orchestrator (central planner) entity or choreographer (distributed planning) entities to establish goals and be able to plan tasks with the participation of others, directed towards achieving those goals.

Resources and users could compete against each other and participate in market-places in which the use of a resource is assigned a utility value and users are required to make the best bid to acquire the use of a resource (auction interaction). Resources may interact and self-organise themselves to offer a combined service

6.17 UBIQUITOUS SYSTEM CHALLENGES AND OUTLOOK
(Nov. 16, MAY 17)

6.17.1 Autonomy

- Autonomy refers to the property of a system that enables a system to control its own actions independently. An autonomous system may still be interfaced with other systems and environ-ments. However, it controls its own actions. Autonomous systems are defined as systems that are self-governing and are capable of their own independent decisions and actions. Autonomous systems may be goal- or policy-oriented: they operate primarily to adhere to a policy or to achieve a goal.

- There are several different types of autonomous system. On the Internet, an autonomous system is a system which is governed by a router policy for one or more networks, controlled by a common network administrator on behalf of a single administrative entity. A software agent system is often characterised as an autonomous system. Autonomous systems can be designed so that these goals can be assigned to them dynamically, perhaps by users. Thus, rather than users needing to interact and control each low-level task interaction, users only need to interact to specify high-level tasks or goals. The system itself will then automatically plan the set of low-level tasks needed and schedule them automatically, reducing the complexity for the user. The system can also replan in case a particular plan or schedule of tasks to achieve goals cannot be reached. Note the planning problem is often solved using Artificial Intelligence (AI).

6.17.2 Reducing Human Interaction

Much of the ubiquitous system interaction cannot be entirely human-centred even if computers become less obtrusive to interact with, because:

- Human interaction can quickly become a bottleneck to operate a complex system. Systems can be designed to rely on humans being in the control loop. The bottleneck can happen at each step, if the user is required to validate or understand that task step.

- It may not be feasible to make some or much machine interaction intelligible to some humans in specific situations.

- This may overload the cognitive and haptic (touch) capabilities of humans, in part because of the sheer number of decisions and amount of information that occur.

- This original vision needs to be revisited and extended to cover networks of devices that can interact intelligently, for the benefit of people, but without human intervention. These types of systems are called automated systems.

6.17.3 Easing System Maintenance Versus Self-Maintaining Systems

- Building, maintaining and interlinking individual systems to be larger, more open, more hetero-geneous and complex systems is more challenging. Some systems can be relatively simply interlinked at the network layer. However, this does not mean that these can be so easily interlinked at the service layer, e.g., interlinking two independent heterogeneous data sources, defined using different data schemas, so that data from both can be aggregated. Such main-tenance requires a lot of additional design in order to develop mapping and mediating data models. Complex system interaction, even for automated systems, reintroduces humans in order to manage and maintain the system.

- Rather than design systems to focus on pure automation but which end up requiring manual intervention, systems need to be designed to operate more autonomously, to operate in a self-governed way to achieve operational goals.

Autonomous systems are related to both context aware systems and intelligence as follows.

- System autonomy can improve when a system can determine the state of its environment, when it can create and maintain an intelligent behavioural model of its environment and itself, and when it can adapt its actions to this model and to the context.

  For example : a printer can estimate the expected time before the printer toner runs out based upon current usage patterns and notify someone to replace the toner.

- Note that autonomous behaviour may not necessarily always act in ways that human users expect and understand, e.g., self-upgrading may make some services unresponsive while these management processes are occurring. Users may require further explanation and mediated support because of perceived differences between the system image (how the system actually works) and users' mental model of the system (how users understand the system to work).

- From a software engineering system perspective, autonomous systems are similar to functionally independent systems in which systems are designed to be self-contained, single-minded, functional, systems with high cohesion19 and that are relatively independent of other systems (low-coupling)

Such systems are easier to design to support composition, defined as atomic modules that can be combined into larger, more complex, composite modules.

6.17.4 Intelligence

- It is possible for UbiCom systems to be context-aware, to be autonomous and for systems to adapt their behaviour in dynamic environments in significant ways, without using any artificial intelli-gence in the system. Systems could simply use a directory service and simple event condition action rules to identify available resources and to select from them, e.g., to discover local resources such as the nearest printer. There are several ways to characterise intelligent systems. Intelligence can enable systems to act more proactively and dynamically in order to support the following behaviours in UbiCom systems:

- **Modelling of its physical environment :** An Intelligent System (IS) can attune its behaviour to act more effectively by taking into account a model of how its environment changes when deciding how it should act.

- **Modelling and mimicking its human environment :** It is useful for a IS to have a model of a human in order to better support iHCI. IS could enable humans to be able to delegate high-level goals to the system rather than interact with it through specifying the low-level tasks needed to complete the goal.

- **Handling incompleteness :** Systems may also be incomplete because environments are open to change and because system components may fail. AI planning can support re-planning to present alternative plans. Part of the system may only be partially observable. Incomplete knowledge of a system's environment can be supplemented by AI type reasoning about the model of its environment in order to deduce what it cannot see is happening.

- **Handling non-deterministic behaviour :** UbiCom systems can operate in open, service dynamic environments. Actions and goals of users may not be completely determined. System design may need to assume that their environment is a semi-deterministic environment (also referred to as a volatile system environment) and be designed to handle this. Intelligent systems use explicit models to handle uncertainty.

- **Semantic and knowledge-based behaviour :** UbiCom systems are also likely to operate in open and heterogeneous environments. Types of intelligent systems define powerful models to support inter-operability between heterogeneous systems and their components, e.g., semantic-based interaction.

6.17.5 Implicit Human-Computer Interaction (iHCI)

Much human device interaction is designed to support explicit human–computer interaction which is expressed at a syntactical low level, e.g., to activate particular controls in this particular order. In addition, as more tasks are automated, the variety of devices increases and more devices need to interoperate to achieve tasks. The sheer amount of explicit interaction can easily disrupt, distract and overwhelm users. Interactive systems need to be designed to support greater degrees of implicit human–computer interaction or iHCI.

- **The Calm Computer**

The concept of the calm or disappearing computer model has several dimensions. It can mean that programmable computers as we know them today are replaced by something else, e.g., human brain implants, that they are no longer physically visible. It can mean that computers are present but they are hidden, e.g., they are implants or miniature systems.

Alternatively, the focus of the disappearing computer can mean that computers are not really hidden; they are visible but are not noticeable as they form part of the peripheral senses. They are not noticeable because of the effective use of implicit human–computer interaction. The forms and modes of interaction to enable computers to disappear will depend in part on the target audience because social and cultural boundaries in relation to technology drivers may have different profile-clustering attri-butes. For some groups of people, ubiquitous computing is already here. Applications and technologies, such as mobile phones, email and chat messaging systems, are considered as a necessity by some people in order to function on a daily basis.

The promise of ubiquitous computing as technology dissolving into behaviour, invisibly per-meating the natural world, is regarded as being unattainable by some researchers, e.g., Rogers (2006). Several reasons are given to support this view. The general use of calm computing removes humans from being proactive – systems are proactive instead of humans. Calm computing is a computationally intractable problem if used generally and ubiquitously. Because technology by its very nature is artificial, it separates the artificial from the natural. What is considered natural is subjective and cultural and to an extent technological. This is blurring the distinction between the means to directly re-engineer nature at the molecular level and the means to influence nature at the macro-level, e.g., pollution and global warming.

The obtrusiveness of technology depends in part on the user's familiarity and experience with it. Alan Kay is attributed as saying that 'Technology is anything that was invented after you were born.' Everyone considers the technology to be something invented before they were born. If calm computing is used in a more bounded sense in deterministic environments, in limited applications environments and is supported at multiple levels depending on the application requirements, it becomes second nature calm computing models can then succeed.

QUESTIONS

1. Explain the term Ubiquitous Computing with suitable example.
2. Explain the various components involved in Ubiquitous Computing.
3. Explain the following device interactions
   (a) Home plug 'n' play
   (b) Universal plug 'n' play
4. Write short note on Human Computer Interaction.
5. What do you mean by Context Aware Interactions.
6. Write short note on Intelligent and Multimodal interfaces.
7. Write short note on tagging, sensing and controlling environment in the context of Ubiquitous Computing.
8. What are the challenges and difficulties involved in Ubiquitous Computing.

Sample Question Paper for
In-Semester Examination (30 Marks)

Time: 1 Hour   **Marks : 30**

1. (a) Define cloud computing. Explain the characteristics of cloud computing. **[6 M]**

   (b) Write short note on cloud types and service scalability over cloud. **[4 M]**

2. (a) Write short note on the following :

   (i) Virtual machines

   (ii) Hypervisor

   (iii) Virtual machine monitor **[6 M]**

   (b) State the types of virtualization and explain them in detail. **[4 M]**

3. (a) Explain the architecture for federated cloud computing. **[4 M]**

   (b) Explain SLA management in cloud computing. **[4 M]**

   (c) Name the monitoring tools in the context of cloud computing. **[2 M]**

Sample Question Paper for
End-Semester Examination (70 Marks)

Time : 2:30 Hours   **Marks : 70**

1. (a) Define cloud computing. Explain the characteristics of cloud computing.   **[6 M]**

(b) What are the advantages of cloud computing ?   **[2 M]**

2. (a) What is XEN ? What are the components of XEN environment ?   **[6 M]**

(b) Explain the SLA management in cloud computing.   **[6 M]**

3. (a) What are the security risks involved in cloud computing ?   **[6 M]**

(b) Draw and explain an architecture for federated cloud computing.   **[6 M]**

(c) Explain the monitoring tools in the context of cloud computing.   **[4 M]**

4. (a) What are the advantages of Amazon EC2 and S3 ?   **[6 M]**

(b) Explain the following terms in detail :

   (i) Cloudstack

   (ii) Intercloud

   (iii) Google App Engine   **[6 M]**

(c) Explain the following terms in detail

   (i) Open source cloud Eucalyptus

   (ii) Open stack

   (iii) Open Nebulla   **[6 M]**

5. (a) Explain the term ubiquitous computing with suitable example.   **[6 M]**

(b) Write short note on tagging, sensing and controlling for controlling the ubiquitous environment.   **[6 M]**

(c) What are the challenges and difficulties in ubiquitous computing ?   **[4 M]**

Time : 1 Hour   **Max. Marks : 30**

Instructions to the candidates :

(1) Answer Q. 1 or Q. 2, Q. 3 or Q. 4, Q. 5 or Q. 6.

(2) Neat diagrams must be drawn wherever necessary.

(3) Figures to the right carries full marks.

(4) Assume suitable data, if necessary.

1. **(a)** Define cloud computing. Discuss different cloud computing service models. **[6]**

   (b) Explain the characteristics of cloud. **[4]**

   OR

2. **(a)** Define could computing. Explain deployment models of CC. **[6]**

   (b) Explain the benefits of IaaS. **[4]**

3. **(a)** Explain the need of virtualization. **[4]**

   (b) Describe different types of virtualization. **[6]**

   OR

4. What is hypervisor? Explain different hypervisors and their features. **[10]**

5. **(a)** What is SLA? Explain type of SLA. **[5]**

   (b) Enlist features of federation types. **[5]**

   OR

6. Explain RESERVOIR architecture with major components and interfaces. **[10]**

Time : $2\frac{1}{2}$ Hours   **Max. Marks : 70**

Instructions to the candidates :

(1) Answer Q. 1 or Q. 2, Q. 3 or Q. 4, Q. 5 or Q. 6, Q. 7 or Q. 8, Q. 9 or Q. 10.

(2) Figures to the right indicate full marks.

1. **(a)** Discuss pros and cons of CC. **[5]**

   (b) Explain applications of virtualization. **[5]**

   OR

2. **(a)** Explain the cloud cube model. **[5]**

   (b) Explain different levels of virtualization. **[5]**

3. **(a)** State and describe life cycle of SLA.   **[6]**

   (b) Define following terms:

   (i)   Community cloud

   (ii) Hypervisor.   **[4]**

OR

4. **(a)** Explain the model for federated cloud computing.   **[6]**

   (b) Explain in brief following terms :   **[4]**

   (i)   Public cloud economics

   (ii) Vmware.

5. **(a)** Discuss with diagram surfaces of attacks in cloud computing.   **[8]**

   (b) What are the several useful implications of the fact that 'OS state is saved in file and copied and shared' ?   **[8]**

OR

6. **(a)** Enlist and describe security risks posed by shared images.   **[8]**

   (b) Define steps to build DomU managed by Dom0.   **[4]**

   (c) Discuss the nasty tricks played by malicious Dom0.   **[4]**

7. **(a)** Describe Amazon EC2 cloud in brief considering following points: **[8]**

   (i)   AMI and Instances

   (ii)   Amazon S3

   (iii) Databases

   (iv)   Amazon cloud watch.

   (b) Explain with diagram the term 'Cloud Stack'.   **[8]**

OR

8. **(a)** Explain Google App Engine with diagram.   **[8]**

   (b) Explain the open source cloud 'Eucalyptus'.   **[8]**

9. **(a)** Explain in brief any two ubiquitous computing applications.   **[8]**

   (b) State and explain with diagram Human Centered Design Life Cycle.   **[10]**

OR

10. **(a)** Write short note RFID tag.   **[8]**

    (b) Describe in brief any five network design issues.   **[10]**

END SEM EXAM. MAY 2016

Time : $2\frac{1}{2}$ Hours   Max. Marks : 70

Instructions to the candidates :

 (1) Answer Q. 1 or Q. 2, Q. 3 or Q. 4, Q. 5 or Q. 6, Q. 7 or Q. 8, Q. 9 or Q. 10.

 (2) Neat diagrams must be drawn wherever necessary.

 (3) Figures to the right indicate full marks.

 (4) Use of calculator is allowed.

 (5) Assume suitable data, if necessary.

1. **(a)** Define cloud computing. Explain essential characteristics of cloud computing. **[4]**

 (b) Explain benefits of IaaS. **[4]OR**

2. **(a)** Explain the cloud deployment model. **[4]**

 (b) Write short note on SaaS. **[4]**

3. **(a)** State and describe life cycle of SLA. **[6]**

 (b) What is virtualization? Explain different types of virtualization. **[6]OR**

4. **(a)** State and explain different phases of SLA management of applications hosted on cloud platform. **[6]**

 (b) Write short note on KVM. **[6]**

5. **(a)** Discuss two ways of determining Trust. **[8]**

 (b) Describe issues related to the run time interaction between DomO and DomU. **[8]OR**

6. **(a)** Discuss the undesirable effects of virtualization. **[8]**

 (b) Discuss mandatory OS security elements. **[8]**

7. **(a)** Explain Google App Engine with diagram. **[10]**

 (b) Write short note on cloud implementation and application. **[8]OR**

8. **(a)** Explain the services offered by Amazon S3. **[10]**

 (b) Explain the open source cloud 'open Nebulla'. **[8]**

9. **(a)** Describe methods to acquire user input related to Human Centered Design (HCD). **[8]**

 (b) Enlist and explain benefits of using wireless networks for UbiCom. **[8]OR**

10. **(a)** Describe challenges in modeling context. **[8]**

 (b) Write short note on Ubiquitous System Challenge and outlook. **[8]**

✾ ✾ ✾

IN SEM. EXAM. AUGUST 2016

Time : 1 Hour   **Max. Marks : 30**

Instructions to the candidates :

    (1) Answer Q. 1 or Q. 2, Q. 3 or Q. 4, Q. 5 or Q. 6.

    (2) Neat diagrams must be drawn wherever necessary.

    (3) Figures to the right carries full marks.

    (4) Assume suitable data, if necessary.

1. **(a)** Discuss pros and cons of CC.   **[5]**

    (b) Explain any 2 major companies which offer pass service.   **[5]**

OR

2. **(a)** Explain the cloud cube model.   **[6]**

    (b) Explain in brief how cloud helps in reducing capital expenditure.   **[4]**

3. **(a)** What is virtual machine? Discuss VMM in detail.   **[6]**

    (b) Explain applications of virtualization.   **[4]**

OR

4. **(a)** Explain different levels of virtualization.   **[6]**

    (b) Explain the need of virtualization.   **[4]**

5. **(a)** Draw and explain model for federated cloud computing.   **[8]**

    (b) Explain Grid verses Cloud.   **[2]**

OR

6. **(a)** State and describe life cycle of SLA.   **[5]**

    (b) Explain the different phases involved in SLA management while hosting application on cloud.   **[5]**

END SEM. EXAM. NOVEMBER 2016

Time : $2\frac{1}{2}$ Hours   **Max. Marks : 70**

Instructions to the candidates :

    (1) Answer Q. 1 or Q. 2, Q. 3 or Q. 4, Q. 5 or Q. 6, Q. 7 or Q. 8, Q. 9 or Q. 10.

    (2) Neat diagrams must be drawn wherever necessary.

    (3) Figures to the right indicate full marks.

    (4) Use of calculator is allowed.

    (5) Assume suitable data, if necessary.

1. **(a)** Explain in brief the services offered by cloud computing?   **[6]**

    (b) Enlist the essential characteristics of cloud computing.   **[2]**

OR

2. **(a)** Explain in brief advantages and limitations of cloud computing.   **[6]**
   (b) Compare Public cloud and Private cloud.   **[2]**
3. **(a)** Explain the virtualization techniques in cloud computing.   **[6]**
   (b) Enlist features of federation types. Explain any one in brief.   **[6]**

OR

4. **(a)** Discuss in brief following basic principles of cloud computing.   **[6]**
       (i) Federation   (ii) Independence   (iii) elasticity
   (b) Compare KVM, Xen and HyperV.   **[6]**
5. **(a)** Describe in brief 'Operating System Security'.   **[8]**
   (b) Enlist & describe security risks posed by shared images.   **[8]**

OR

6. **(a)** Discuss the top security concerns for cloud users.   **[8]**
   (b) Discuss two ways of determining trust.   **[8]**
7. **(a)** Explain Google App Engine with diagram.   **[8]**
   (b) Write short note on 'Open Nebulla'.   **[8]**

OR

8. **(a)** Explain the storage services offered by Amazon EC2 cloud.   **[8]**
   (b) State and explain any two cloud computing applications.   **[8]**
9. **(a)** Describe Context Aware operational life cycle.   **[10]**
   (b) Discuss any four common myths about ubiquitous computing.   **[8]**

OR

10. **(a)** Describe methods to acquire user Inputs related to human centered design.   **[8]**
    (b) Explain the following service architectural models :   **[10]**
        (i) Multi tier client service model
        (i) Service oriented computing model

END SEM. EXAM. MAY 2017

Time : 2$\frac{1}{2}$ Hours   **Total Marks : 70**

Instructions to the candidates :

    (1) Answer Q. 1 or Q. 2, Q. 3 or Q. 4, Q. 5 or Q. 6, Q. 7 or Q. 8, Q. 9 or Q. 10.
    (2) Neat diagrams must be drawn wherever necessary.
    (3) Figures to the right side indicate full marks.
    (4) Use of Calculator is allowed.
    (5) Assume suitable data, if necessary.

1. **(a)** Describe in brief the services offered by cloud computing.   **[6]**
   (b) Explain in brief following terms with reference to cloud computing.   **[2]**
      (i)   On demand self provisioning.
      (ii)   Elasticity
      (iii) Cost reduction
      (iv)   Application program interfaces.

OR

2. **(a)** Which type of Cloud service is provided by 'gmail' ? Justify.   **[6]**
   (b) Define cloud computing as per NIST.   **[2]**

3. **(a)** Explain the virtualization techniques in cloud computing.   **[6]**
   (b) Enlist features of federation types. Explain any one in brief.   **[6]**

OR

4. **(a)** Discuss in brief following basic principles of cloud computing.   **[6]**
      (i)   Federation
      (ii)   Independence
      (iii) elasticity
   (b) Compare KVM, Xen and HyperV.   **[6]**

5. **(a)** Discuss the top security concerns for cloud users.   **[8]**
   (b) Enlist and describe security risks posed by shared images.   **[8]**

OR

6. **(a)** Describe in brief 'Operating System Security'.   **[8]**
   (b) Enlist and explain different forms of Trust.   **[4]**
   (c) Discuss different aspects related to contract between the user and the cloud Service Provider to minimize security risks.   **[4]**

7. **(a)** Explain Google App Engine with the help of diagram.   **[8]**
   (b) State and explain any two cloud computing applications.   **[8]**

OR

8. **(a)** Explain the storage services offered by Amazon EC2 cloud.   **[8]**
   (b) Write short notes on 'Open Nebulla'   **[8]**

9. **(a)** Describe Context. Aware operational life cycle.   **[10]**
   (b) Discuss any four common myths about ubiquitous computing.   **[8]**

OR

10. **(a)** Describe methods to acquire user Inputs related to human centred design.**[8]**
   (b) Explain the following service architectural models: **[10]**
      (i)   Multi tier client service model
      (ii)   Service oriented computing model.

❉ ❉ ❉

www.ingramcontent.com/pod-product-compliance
Lightning Source LLC
Chambersburg PA
CBHW080956020726
47505CB00009B/2222